JANET TRONSTAD

A Rich Man for Dry Creek

A Hero for Dry Creek

Love Inspired

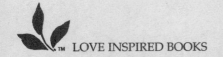

LOVE INSPIRED BOOKS

ISBN-13: 978-0-373-68883-8

A RICH MAN FOR DRY CREEK AND A HERO FOR DRY CREEK

A RICH MAN FOR DRY CREEK
Copyright © 2002 by Janet Tronstad

A HERO FOR DRY CREEK
Copyright © 2003 by Janet Tronstad

www.LoveInspiredBooks.com

Printed in U.S.A.

CONTENTS

Books by Janet Tronstad

Steeple Hill Love Inspired

An Angel for Dry Creek #81
A Gentleman for Dry Creek #110
A Bride for Dry Creek #138
A Rich Man for Dry Creek #176
A Hero for Dry Creek #228
A Baby for Dry Creek #240
A Dry Creek Christmas #276
Sugar Plums for Dry Creek #329
At Home in Dry Creek #371
The Sisterhood of the Dropped Stitches #385
A Match Made in Dry Creek #391

*Dry Creek

JANET TRONSTAD

grew up on a small farm in central Montana. One of
her favorite things to do was to visit her grandfather's
bookshelves, where he had a large collection of
Zane Grey novels. She's always loved a good story.

Today, Janet lives in Pasadena, California, where she
is a full-time writer. In addition to writing novels, she
researches and writes nonfiction magazine articles.

A RICH MAN
FOR DRY CREEK

It is easier for a camel
to go through the eye of a needle
than for a rich man to enter into the kingdom of God.
—*Mark* 10:25

This book is dedicated with love to my nieces

Julie Miller
Sara Enger
Marcy Enger MacDonald
LaRae Tronstad
Starla Tronstad

Chapter One

"Just because he's rich doesn't mean he's crazy." Jenny Black pressed the cell phone to one ear and stood on her tiptoes to look at another dusty shelf in the old pantry. Her sister should stop worrying about Robert Buckwalter's sanity.

She should worry about Jenny's instead.

Jenny was the one who was crazy.

What was she thinking? Trying to cater a black-tie dinner in a place like Dry Creek, Montana. Right now Jenny was in the pantry of the town's small café and she was desperately looking for paprika.

Jenny had made a big mistake. She should never have promised hors d'oeuvres to go with the lobsters she was serving tonight.

The ranching community of Dry Creek, tucked

up close to the Big Sheep Mountains in southern Montana, was absolutely delightful. But any sane chef would have insisted the menu be switched to chili dogs and corn chips the minute she discovered the only store in town sold ten kinds of cattle feed and not one single thing for a human to eat.

Jenny had not been able to buy any of her last-minute supplies.

She'd turned for help to the couple who ran the café but they were only set up to serve hamburgers, biscuits and spaghetti. They had sugar packets, squeeze bottles of honey and those plastic packets filled with ketchup. There was not one obvious hors d'oeuvre in sight.

She was doomed.

Jenny heard an impatient grunt on the other end of the phone.

"Sorry, but if you ask me, Mr. Buckwalter is so sane he's almost comatose." Jenny had tried earlier to make conversation with the man. No luck. "Stuffed-shirt kind of sane. Think Dad."

"But Dad's fifty years old!"

"Well, Robert Buckwalter acts like he's a hundred." Jenny still felt a twinge of pique. The whole world knew that her employer's son, Robert Buckwalter, was a ladies' man. He was supposed to flirt with all women.

Jenny had expected to dodge a compliment or two

Janet Tronstad 13

on the flight over. But the man had sat in the pilot's seat next to her the whole flight and not said anything at all once he'd made sure she'd fastened her seat belt. For which, she told herself firmly, she should be grateful. And she should be fair to the man. "Of course he's most helpful—especially when he's got an apron around his waist."

"He's got an apron on!"

"Well, he's helping me with the hors d'oeuvres. We've got a hundred people coming for dinner— Maine lobsters—and I've had to improvise with the hors d'oeuvres."

Improvise was putting it lightly, Jenny thought. Try egg salad on toast—which wouldn't be so bad if she could at least find something to sprinkle on top of it.

"Robert Buckwalter the Third is cooking for you— and he has an apron on!" Jenny's sister couldn't let go of that thought.

"Well, it's only some carrot stubs. It's not like he's whipping up a soufflé or anything complicated."

"But he doesn't even grill. It says that in his bio. My word, do you know how much money the man has?"

The question was obviously rhetorical and Jenny didn't answer.

She had enough to do pushing aside spice tins hoping for some paprika.

The Dry Creek café had been abandoned years ago and left empty until a couple of teenagers had reopened it this past December on the night of the town's first annual Christmas pageant. The original owners must have decided some supplies weren't worth hauling out of Dry Creek because stray cans and tins had been left behind to sit quietly, collecting dust, for all those years.

"A little kitchen work never hurt anyone," Jenny said. You'd think she was exploiting children or something. The idle rich were not a protected species.

"You're not bossing him around, are you? Please tell me you're not bossing him around."

"He volunteered!"

"Good, because he *is* Robert Buckwalter the Third."

"Give me some credit. I know how it is with the rich."

Jenny didn't have to remind her sister that, when they were kids, it was the fancy cars of the rich people who had always come to the suburban area near them to drop off their unwanted pets.

Apparently her sister not only remembered the cars, she also remembered that Jenny had been the one to shake her fist at the drivers as they sped away. "Look, Jenny, it's important that you're nice—you know, give him a chance to like you."

"Me? Why?"

"Well, maybe he'll talk to you. Tell you things. I

could use some help here. I think the only reason I got my job is because you are working for the Buckwalters and my boss thought you'd be able to tell me stuff for the paper. Like this list of one hundred bachelors we're working on. Buckwalter's at the top, so far, and I'm counting on you to tell me about him."

Jenny sighed. "You shouldn't have taken the job then. It's not right. Besides, I don't have anything to tell. I hardly know the man."

"He answered your phone."

"This isn't my phone. It's the Buckwalter business phone. It's supposed to be for business calls only. I'm surprised the main office gave you the number."

A dim lightbulb hung down from the ceiling and Jenny had to squint to see the top shelf where restaurant-size spice containers were shoved behind several cans of what must be lard even though the labels were so faded they were hard to identify.

"Well, I may have said something about business—"

"What business?"

"Well, this *is* a business question. Something's wrong. I've been working it out. The man is either crazy or secretly married. He's always been in the tabloids. I know—I almost crashed my computer doing a word search on him. Dozens of pieces. This party. That woman. The next party. The next woman.

And then—bingo—it all stops. Our top sources couldn't even get the man to return a phone call! And they're his friends."

"His friends spy on him?"

"Well, you know how it is with the rich. They all do that. But that's not the point. The point is that no one's seen him. There's been nothing for the last five months." Jenny's sister paused and then continued. "I'm hoping you know why. My editor is getting nervous. We need to decide if we're going to make Robert Buckwalter number one on our bachelor list. Do you know what that means to be number one? Men would kill for that spot. You can make a million just endorsing stuff—shaving cream, shoes, clothes. It's a gold mine. But we certainly don't want to give the title to Buckwalter if he's wacko or married. We'd look like fools who didn't even know what was going on in the world." She sighed. "Do you really think he could be married?"

"I doubt it—surely, he'd tell his friends if he got married."

"Not if she was unsuitable."

Jenny paused. She remembered she wasn't the only one to protest those rich cars when they were kids. Her sister was there, too. "You don't need to worry. It's not like he married a kitten who grew up to be too much

trouble. Even the rich don't treat their wives that way."
Well, usually not, she added silently. "Besides, I
thought that anything goes with the rich these days—
look at that blond singer. Underwear in public. Pierced
tongues. There's not much left to be unsuitable."

"She could be poor."

Jenny's lips tightened. "If that bothers him, then he
shouldn't have married her in the first place."

"Is he wearing a wedding ring?" her sister asked.

"I don't think so."

"Don't you know? Goodness, Jenny, don't you even
look anymore? Talk about him being comatose. You're
turning positively ancient yourself."

"I am not! Twenty-nine is young."

"If you don't look at the ring finger, believe me,
you're old."

"Well, I'm pretty sure he didn't have a ring. I
remember giving him the knife, and I always check
for rings—some people like to take them off so they
don't get wet."

"You're getting him wet! Robert Buckwalter the
Third."

"Even rich people need their vegetables washed."

Her sister was silent for a minute before continuing.
"Wait a minute. Are you sure this is Robert Buckwalter the Third? Maybe there's been some kind of a mix-

up. A kidnapping or something. This just doesn't sound right—vegetables and aprons. He doesn't even know how to make coffee. It says that, right in his bio."

Jenny smiled. "So far, he hasn't made coffee, and his mother seems to believe it's him."

"Well, what does she say about him being gone all that time? Is she worried he's married?"

"She hasn't said a thing. And I don't know why you think he's married. Just because he kept to himself for a while, doesn't necessarily mean he's been to the altar. Maybe he's just tired," Jenny said as she spied the can of paprika and reached for it. "Five months isn't so long to rest if he keeps a social schedule like the one you've talked about—it sounds grueling."

"I never thought of that." Her sister was horrified. "Maybe he's worse than tired—maybe he's sick."

"Oh, I doubt he's sick," Jenny said as her hand wrapped around the can of paprika. She'd have to taste it to see if it was still good. "But I wouldn't know for sure. I just work for him—well, really for his mother. I'm the chef—I'm in charge of parties like this one tonight. That's it. It's not like I know the man personally."

"You must know something about him."

"I know what he eats." Jenny looked through the pantry door into the kitchen at the man in question. "Heavy into vegetables and meats—beef, lamb, duck—he likes them all." That certainly didn't sound like a man who was sick.

She suddenly remembered that she did know more about Robert Buckwalter than what he ate. But her sister wasn't interested in the fact that some man had an odd aversion to her hairnet, which was a perfectly fine hairnet and required for food handling—even if it did make her look like a monk.

"There's got to be more. Think. This is important."

Jenny wiped the dust off the can of paprika. She'd been more mother than older sister to her three siblings and it seemed like one or the other of them always had something important that needed her help even though they were all over eighteen by now and should be adults.

She stood in the open doorway and studied the tall man that was causing her sister so much worry.

The light in the kitchen came from two bare bulbs hanging directly over the long counter that divided the square room. The kitchen walls were white. The sink and refrigerator were both forty years old and chipped. It was a humble kitchen.

Now that her sister mentioned it, Jenny wondered why the man had volunteered to help. She certainly hadn't expected it of him. No one else had, either. Even his mother had looked up in pleased surprise when he'd demanded a knife and a bunch of carrots.

Jenny studied his profile, looking for answers.

At first glance, the man was the classic movie star ideal. The kind of actor that always wore the white hat. The aristocratic nose was perfectly balanced. The glossy black hair was combed stylishly in place. The cheekbones closely barbered. He looked like a luxury car ad. Definitely your playboy kind of a guy.

But as she looked closer, Jenny noticed some fraying. He had a bruise on the side of his forehead. It was faint, but it was there. His hair was nicely combed, but there was something off center and a little ragged about the cut. And his tan was uneven, like he might have been wearing a cap—not a designer cap with the bill turned to the back like a baseball player, but an old-fashioned cap like a farmer would wear.

My word, Jenny thought, my sister might be on to something.

Jenny didn't think the man was sick—his cheeks looked too healthy—but Robert Buckwalter certainly had the neglected air of someone who was letting himself go to seed.

He might just be married at that.

That would certainly explain the plane trip over here. The man had insisted—not offered, but flat-out insisted—on personally flying Jenny and the lobsters from Seattle to Dry Creek in his fancy plane.

Jenny had been surprised he was going to Montana. He had just arrived at his mother's house in Seattle from some trip that he wouldn't explain. He looked tired and was limping. The housekeeper had his suite of rooms made up and ordered the customary orchids for his bedside table. Then the housekeeper put in the standing order for extra staff to handle the usual parties.

Robert Buckwalter hadn't been home for twenty minutes before he canceled the orders. The house-keeper said he walked into his rooms and looked around as though he didn't know where he was or why he was there.

Then he announced he was going to fly to Dry Creek to talk to his mother. He must have had some-thing urgent to tell her—like maybe that he had a wife. Jenny wondered how the older woman would take the news of a strange daughter-in-law.

Mrs. Buckwalter was financing a winter camp for some teenagers from Seattle and the woman was staying in Dry Creek to be sure that all went well. It was a fine, giving gesture and Jenny respected the older woman for it.

But Jenny knew her sister wasn't interested in Mrs. Buckwalter. There must be something useful about the man in question that she could share with her sister.

"Even if he's not sick, I think he might have corns."

"What?"

"You know—corns on his feet. And bad. I remember his mother commenting on some bill he'd run up for corn pads. Hundreds of dollars."

Her sister grunted. "The man's an Adonis. He can have a gazillion corns on his feet and who cares? No one's looking at his feet. Have you even stopped your cooking long enough to look at the man?"

"Well, of course, I have."

"And?"

"He's neat, well dressed, clean—"

"Clean!"

"Well, he is—more than most."

"I've got a news flash for you! He's a whole lot more than clean. He's hot. Drop-dead gorgeous. And if you haven't noticed that I'm really worried about you. Might even talk to Mom about it. She always says you're too picky—wait until she finds out you're even picky with him. Robert Buckwalter—"

"I know."

"—the Third."

A timer went off in the kitchen.

"Look, I've got to go," Jenny said in relief. "I've got egg puffs that need to come out of the oven."

The café kitchen was noisy. A group of teenage girls, wearing prom dresses from the fifties, stood at a table in the corner laughing and folding pink paper napkins into the shape of swans. A dozen of the boys stood beside Robert Buckwalter, following his moves as they cut chunks of carrot into the closest thing they could get to a flower. The carrot nubs were more tulips than roses, but they had a charm all their own.

Jenny had forgotten the boys were from a Seattle street gang until she saw their ease with knives. Some of those boys could have done credible surgery on something larger and more alive than a hunk of carrot.

Jenny was thankful for people like Sylvia Bannister who ran a center for gang kids in Seattle, and for Garth Elkton who had welcomed the kids to his ranch for a winter camp program. Jenny had seen how peaceful the Big Sheep Mountains looked in the snow. Low mountains skirted by gentle foothills. This little ranching community was a perfect haven for gang kids.

Sylvia and Garth were giving those kids a second chance. Mrs. Buckwalter was funding the winter camp and providing the lobsters tonight, both as a thanks to the community of Dry Creek, especially to the minister who had recently gotten married, and as a reward to the teenagers from Seattle for putting down their knives and learning to dance.

Sylvia and Garth were the kind of people that deserved to be number one on some New York tabloid list, not some hotshot rich man like Robert Buckwalter who spent half his life in Europe attending art shows, Jenny told herself. He didn't even organize the shows; he just sat there and gave away money.

Jenny felt a twinge of annoyance. An able-bodied man like Robert Buckwalter should be more useful in life. Giving away money hardly qualified as a job— not when he had so much of it. She doubted he even wrote the checks himself.

"I ruined one of the mushrooms," a girl wailed from the sink. "Totally ruined it. The stem didn't come out right and—"

"Not a problem. We just cut it up and put it with the stuffing." Jenny walked to the refrigerator to get out the herbed bread mixture that went in the few mushroom caps they'd found in the café's refrigerator bin. "Nothing goes to waste in a good kitchen. There's always some other place for it. If nothing else, there's soup. 'Waste not, want not' my mother always used to say. And remember, aprons everyone."

The kids groaned.

Robert Buckwalter grunted. He wondered if he was crazy. He shouldn't be annoyed with the ever-resourceful Jenny. He should be grateful to her. After all, he'd hired her because of her apparent good cheer and her complete indifference to him.

During her job interview, she'd asked no personal questions about him—no sly inquiries about how often he'd be present for dinner at his mother's home in Seattle, or whether as the family chef, she'd be required to fly to the flat he must have in London or maybe the villa he had in Venice or the chalet he had in the Alps...and surely he must have at least one of those, didn't he? Or maybe he just traveled around in the plane he had, the one especially designed with all the gadgets, the one she'd read about in the papers, the one they called the ultimate "rich man's" toy?

The questions would come. They always did.

Except with Jenny.

But then, maybe she'd just been more clever than most.

"Finished with the phone?" Robert asked politely. He hadn't been fooled for a minute by the woman who had called claiming she needed to speak to Jenny urgently about some pudding order. Pudding, my foot. The woman was no salesperson.

Why else would Jenny take the call and disappear into that hole of a pantry where no one could hear her conversation?

Not even bats would go into that pantry if they

didn't have to. Jenny had literally needed to pry the door open earlier with a crowbar. The wood was half-rotted and the wind blew in through the knotholes.

No, it wasn't a place where anyone would go for a cozy phone conversation with a pudding salesperson.

Robert Buckwalter swore he could spot a reporter a mile off and he had a bad feeling about that call.

Maybe his time was up.

Robert knew how to keep a low profile with the press but he was off his game. He'd gone completely rustic. On the flight over here, he'd looked at all the extra knobs on his plane's instrument panel and wondered what he'd ever need with all the unnecessary attachments he'd asked the manufacturer to add. He couldn't even remember why he'd wanted a cup-size blender added on the passenger side.

He hardly knew himself anymore. It came from spending a whole five months as someone else.

Jenny carefully laid the phone back down on the counter where it had been when the last call arrived and then picked it up again to wipe off the dust that had followed her out of the pantry.

Robert watched her as he untied the apron strings from around himself and put the damp apron on the nearby counter. "Hope there was no problem."

She looked up at him in alarm. "What?"

"About the pudding," Robert elaborated grimly. She looked confused and guilty as sin. "I hope there was no problem with the order."

"No, no, everything's fine." Jenny blushed.

Robert wondered what the tabloids were paying these days. "Good. I'm glad to hear that. Wouldn't want anything to go wrong with…things."

Jenny stiffened. "I run an efficient kitchen. Everything will be fine."

"Of course."

"I'll admit we are a little behind schedule, but your mother assured me that people will be late arriving because of the cold weather. And everything's set up in the barn. Tables, chairs—the works. The kids even decorated."

Jenny hadn't worried when she was in Seattle and Mrs. Buckwalter had called to ask her to come cater this event. The older woman had said the party was to be held in The Barn. She'd announced the fact with such flourish that Jenny assumed it was some bohemian restaurant with theme.

Jenny was startled when they drove into Dry Creek and she saw that The Barn really was a barn, complete with hayloft and straw. Then she looked around at the few buildings in town and realized there probably wasn't an industrial oven in any one of them.

That's when she first knew she was in trouble. Not that it would do to admit it to her employer's son.

"We'll have the platters ready just as soon as those puffs cool. And the water's heating for the lobsters. A half hour and dinner will be served."

Robert nodded as he picked up the cell phone she had laid back on the kitchen counter. He slipped it into his pocket. His phone had a redial feature built into it. Maybe he could call the reporter and stop the story.

Robert put on his wool overcoat and stepped outside. Snow covered patches on the ground and the frigid air made his breath catch. He'd been in cold weather before at ski resorts, but the cold in rural Montana bit harder.

The back door to the kitchen led to a dirt path that was lined with garbage cans. Fortunately, the temperature was so cold the garbage wasn't rotting. Not that Robert minded the smells of garbage anymore.

Robert wondered if he'd ever be the same again. He hadn't intended to spend five months as someone else. It had started as the adventure of a bored rich man. He knew that. There was something supremely arrogant about shedding his identity like it was last year's fashion.

But he had done it and wasn't the least bit sorry.

He'd flown down to the Tucson airport last October. From there he'd headed on foot toward a little town on the Arizona/New Mexico border. He'd left his suit with his plane in a locked area of the airport. He also left his black diamond watch and his laptop computer.

He walked away wearing an old pair of denim jeans and a flannel shirt. The only thing expensive about his clothes had been his tennis shoes. He had no car. No cell phone. A dozen twenty-dollar bills, but no credit cards.

He still remembered how good it felt.

That day he left behind Robert Buckwalter III and became simply Bob. He rolled the name around on his lips again. Bob. He liked the sound of it. It was friendly in a way Robert could never be.

Robert had intended to spend a week alone in the desert at some flea-bitten motel along the highway so that he could return to his parties with more enthusiasm. He certainly didn't intend to be stuck as Bob. He was merely cleansing his palate, not giving up the rich life he enjoyed.

But that first day he discovered Bob was the kind of guy people talked to. Robert was amazed. He'd never realized until then that people didn't talk to him; they mostly just told amusing stories and agreed with everything he said.

They were, he concluded in astonishment, handling him. How could he have not noticed?

He didn't have friends, he realized. He had groupies.

An old man in a beat-up truck had given Robert a ride south out of Tucson and invited him to share supper. Supper had been spicy beans and warm rice with a toaster pastry for dessert. The plate he used had been an old pie tin and the glass had been a jelly jar. The fork he ate with had a tine missing.

But the whole meal had been given in kindness and it tasted very good. When it was finished, the old man offered him a job earning twenty-five dollars a day chopping wood for his winter's supply.

Robert had been about to refuse. He had enough money in his pocket for meals and a cheap hotel. He didn't need a charity job. But something in the man's eyes tipped him off and instead he looked at the woodpile and saw it was empty except for a few scrub branches.

The old man couldn't chop anymore. He needed help. Robert offered to chop some wood to repay the man for supper.

One meal led to the next and the woodpile grew. Robert's days found a rhythm. He slept in a camper shell by one of the old sheds on the man's property. The nights were a deep quiet and he slept more peacefully than he ever remembered.

Each morning he woke up to the disgruntled crowing of a red rooster he'd nicknamed Charlie. Charlie had no trouble making his opinions known;

he had never learned to bow down to the opinions of the rich. He didn't even respect the opinions of nature. He seemed to be particularly unhappy with the sun each morning.

Robert didn't want to chop wood in the chill of the early morning—and especially not with Charlie strutting around. Robert had never seen anything as cranky as that red bird in the morning. You'd think the morning had come up as a personal insult to the rooster. At least Charlie took it that way.

So, instead of listening to Charlie, Robert would jog down the hard-packed dirt road for several miles. He aimed himself in the general direction of the mountains even though they were so far away he'd never get there by running. But he liked to look at them anyway.

His morning run took him past two run-down houses with an astonishing assortment of children spilling out of each. Toddlers. Teens. Boys. Girls. One morning some of the children started to follow him on his run. Before the end of the week, a dozen kids were trailing after him and he was carrying the smallest in a backpack he made from a blanket.

It took a full week for them all to tell him their names.

It was the second week before Robert noticed most of them were running in thin sandals and slippers.

Robert almost scolded them for not dressing right

for running, when he realized they were wearing the only shoes they had. The next morning he brought some old newspaper with him and had the kids each make a drawing of their right foot for him.

Later that day he hitchhiked to the nearest post office and sent an overnight package to his secretary ordering fourteen pairs of designer tennis shoes just like his.

The shoes arrived on a Monday.

It was Thursday before Robert saw the children were all limping and he realized he had forgotten socks. How blind could he be? He'd realized then just how removed he'd always been from the needs of others.

He gave money, but it was other people on his staff who actually worried about the arrangements. He, himself, paid very little attention to the needs of others. His contribution was reduced to a dollar sign. It was a picture of himself that he didn't particularly like.

Unfortunately, others still had a fascination with his wealth and the tabloids fed their interest.

Too bad he wasn't still living in the camper shell with Charlie, Robert thought. Charlie might like being in the tabloids.

Robert had discovered he didn't like being in tabloids. In fact, he could honestly say he hated it more than Charlie hated the morning.

Robert removed the phone from his pocket and

pushed the redial button. He wondered how much it would cost to kill the story.

Not that it mattered. Whatever it was, he already knew he'd pay it.

Chapter Two

Robert Buckwalter didn't ordinarily notice the stars in the sky. But, standing still, holding the cell phone in his right hand, he looked up and blinked. Montana had a blackness to the nights that calmed him. He'd spent too much time in cities with all their noise and lights.

All of the commotion stopped a man from thinking.

And he needed to think his way out of this situation. Money wasn't enough this time.

Jenny's sister had crumbled when she realized who was on the other end of the phone. Robert had not even needed to be stern. The young woman confessed why she'd called her sister and apologized for asking questions.

She was contrite. She was abashed.

She was useless.

Robert had groaned inside when he found out why the young woman had called. He had dreaded the bachelor list even before his five months in Arizona. What sane man wouldn't?

The bachelor list winners might as well enroll in a circus freak show. No one left them an ounce of privacy. Or dignity. Last year he'd been number seventeen. Some tabloid had printed the sizes of all one hundred men's underwear. Ten different women had actually sent him silk boxers with their names screened on them.

And the letters! He had over a hundred letters from strange women asking him to marry them.

Just imagine if he was in the number one spot. They might as well shoot him now before his mailman filed for workmen's compensation because of the backache from delivering those letters—a fair number of which would come with a string-tied package. Somehow the packages with string on them always included baked goods. Chocolate-chip cookies. Plum bread. One enterprising woman had shipped a pot roast in a gallon-size zipper bag because some tabloid story had mentioned he liked beef.

And the underwear givers and the cookie bakers were not even the worst of the lot. The more aggressive called on the telephone and demanded to talk to him. They wouldn't take no for an answer. They knew how to dodge every polite refusal. His secretary was likely to quit this time around.

Maybe he should hire Charlie to take those calls.

Robert, himself, wasn't interested in a wife that came from a list.

It was old-fashioned, but Robert knew if he ever did marry it would be a real marriage. One that lasted a lifetime. Not one based on lists or money. Odd as it sounded, he'd realized in his five months away that he wanted a wife who would want a simple home with him. Without servants and expensive antiques. Someone who would want him to mow the lawn and take out the trash. Someone who would talk to him and not just quietly pretend to find whatever he was talking about fascinating enough for both of them.

A woman like that probably didn't even read the tabloids. She certainly wouldn't mail him a pot roast or a pair of boxers if she didn't know him.

No, if Robert ever wanted to live a normal Bob-like life, he needed to start it now. He needed to get off the list.

The trouble was he didn't trust the young woman he'd spoken with to simply tell her editors that Robert Buckwalter thanked them very much for thinking of him, but could they please think of someone else for their bachelor list.

Fortunately, Robert knew one thing and that was the celebrity world. He'd been forced to learn how it worked. He knew stories were killed every day and that lists could go up in smoke with the wrong move.

As Robert saw it, he had one chance to change things and that was to make himself very unpopular. He needed to do something that would alienate women everywhere. He'd asked the woman and she'd confessed that the list was to be released on February 29. Leap Year's Day. Women's choice. It was already February 20. He needed to act fast.

First, a victim must be found. He found that nothing set off women better than mistreatment of one of their own. And Jenny, the chef, must know about the action so she could tell her sister who would then tell her employers. That should get his name thrown off the list and into the trash.

Robert felt better already. All he had to do was be obnoxious. His feet were still sore, but he was sure he could be sufficiently unpleasant to raise some eyebrows.

Confident that his troubles would soon be over, Robert slipped the cell phone back into the pocket of his overcoat and started to whistle.

He was almost cheerful when he stepped back into

the kitchen. It wouldn't be too hard. Before long his reputation would be back where it belonged—in tatters.

All he needed to do was find a woman to persecute.

Robert stepped into the kitchen to find it empty of everything except steam. He walked over to the stove and looked into one of the big lobster pots. It was empty, as well.

Good, he thought to himself in satisfaction, the party was starting. An audience would be helpful for what he needed to do.

The dining room of the café had been turned into a girl's dressing room and Robert walked quickly through the haze of perfume. Makeup was scattered over the table closest to the door and several pairs of high heels were lined up along the right wall.

Robert stopped in front of the mirror taped to the inside of the door and ran a comb through his own hair. He brushed a few snowflakes off the shoulders of his overcoat. The overcoat was black. His suit underneath was black. Each cost more than most men made in a month.

Robert nodded at his reflection with satisfaction; he looked good. Every man should look good on his way to his own public scandal.

The first bite of the cold when he stepped out the front door made him step even faster. The café was just down the gravel road from the barn where the party was to be held and the space between was full of old cars and trucks. This part of Montana certainly wasn't prosperous, he thought as he spied the old cattle truck that was parked next to the bus his mother had rented to haul all the teenagers around.

He nodded to an old man who was weaving between the cars with a bottle of beer in his hand.

"Coming to the party?" Robert looked closer at the man.

"Ain't been invited." The man's beaten face looked anxious in the moonlight.

"Everyone's invited," Robert said firmly. The old man looked like he could use a good meal that didn't slide down from the neck of a brown bottle. "What's your name?"

The old man looked startled. Robert didn't blame him. He was startled himself. Since when had he cared about the names of poor old men?

"Gossett."

"Well, Mr. Gossett, I hope you'll come have some dinner with us."

"I ain't dressed for it."

The man was wearing a beige cardigan sweater covered with what looked like cat hair and a thermal undershirt that had a yellow ring around the band. His neck was scrawny and his eyes were bloodshot. His denim jeans had grease stains on the knees. Only the man's boots looked new.

"This will set you up," Robert said as he took off his overcoat and offered it to the old man. "Put that on and you'll be right in fashion."

Warm, too, Robert thought to himself.

The man's startled look turned to alarm. "You with the Feds?"

"The who?"

"The FBI. They don't think I seen them. But they're here. Sneaking around in the dark. Watching me."

"They're not watching you," Robert said gently as he offered the coat again. "I've heard there's been some cattle rustling reported. Interstate stuff. It's been going on for some time and they can't get a handle on it. That's why they're here. It's just the cattle. It's nothing for you to worry about."

Robert knew the FBI was in Dry Creek. One of their agents had questioned Jenny and himself when they'd landed with the lobsters out near Garth Elkton's ranch the other night.

"You know who they think done it?" the man asked, leaning so close that Robert got a strong whiff of alcohol. "The rustling?"

"No, I don't think they know yet." Robert wondered

if he should insist the man come into the warmth of the barn. With the amount of alcohol the man was drinking, it was dangerous for him to be out in the freezing temperatures. "You're sure you don't want to borrow the coat? You'd be welcome to eat with us."

The man carefully set his bottle of beer on the hood of an old car before reaching out toward the coat. "I might just get me a little bit of something. It sure smells good."

The two men walked inside the barn together.

The old man headed toward the table set up with appetizers. Robert resisted the urge to go over and visit his carrot flowers. Instead he looked around for the woman he needed.

There was a sea of taffeta and silk. Young teenage girls with heavy lipstick and strappy high heels. Farm wives with sweaters over their simple long dresses. A couple of women who looked unattached.

And, of course, the chef.

If he had his choice, Robert would persecute the chef. If for no other reason than to rattle her calm and make her take off that hairnet of hers. It was a party. She could loosen up. But the only thing he could think to do was to kiss her, and that certainly wasn't outrageous. The media would just think he'd taken another in a long line of girlfriends. They'd yawn in his face.

No, he needed something shocking.

He looked over the teenagers and settled on the youngest one. His kissing her would raise the hackles of the tabloid world. She looked to be little more than a child, no more than twelve. Women all across the country would raise their handbags in unison to clip him a good one and he'd deserve it.

Robert went over to the buffet table. He'd look less threatening if he had one of those plastic cups in his hand. After all, he wanted to kiss the girl, not have her pass out in terror. She might be wearing lipstick, but twelve was still awfully young.

He nodded to the older woman behind the table. "I'll have some champagne."

The woman looked at him blankly. "I think there's punch in the bowl."

Robert looked over and saw the punch. It was pink. "I don't suppose there's any bottled water?"

The woman shook her head no. "There might be coffee later."

Robert nodded. He'd have to do this empty-handed. He walked over to the girl. She was leaning against the side of the barn and watching the other kids sort through some old records. Now who had those relics? He couldn't remember ever seeing records played. Not with cassettes and CDs available.

"Know any musicians?"

The girl looked up and shook her head shyly. "Do you?"

Robert nodded. He'd be able to score a few points with this one. "Name a group and I probably know them."

He realized when he said it that it was true. The world of the truly famous was pathetically small.

"Elvis," the girl named softly.

"Elvis is dead."

"I thought maybe you had known him. When you were young."

Robert wondered if he'd fallen down a time warp. "How old do you think I am?"

The girl shrugged. "He's my favorite is all."

"He'll always be the King," Robert agreed gently. Maybe this girl wasn't the one, after all. Her eyes reminded him of Bambi. He didn't want to see the confusion in them that would surely come if a man as old as Elvis kissed her.

"You got a camera?" he asked instead.

"A disposable one."

"Do me a favor and take a few pictures of me tonight. I'll tell you when."

"Sure."

Robert nodded his thanks. Tabloids loved pictures like that and even sweet-eyed Bambis needed a college fund. Somebody might as well get some good out of tonight.

The lights in the barn were subdued and the whole place seemed to smell of butter and steam. Long tables were set up in the back of the barn and covered with white cotton tablecloths. Stacks of heavy plates, the kind found in truck stops, stood at the end of each table.

Several teams of ranch hands were holding big trays with a towel draped over steaming lobsters. Robert frowned at the men. Why hadn't Jenny asked him to help? He'd had to practically demand a knife and some carrots earlier.

Jenny put a dozen silver tongs down on the head table and blessed Mrs. Buckwalter for requesting that they be brought to Dry Creek along with dozens of tiny silver lobster picks. Even Jenny wasn't sure she'd tackle the lobster dinner with plastic forks and no tongs. "Can someone go back and get the last pan of butter?"

"I'll do it."

Jenny stopped arranging the tongs and looked up in panic. It was Robert Buckwalter. "But you can't—I mean you don't need to—"

"Well, someone needs to."

"I can do it myself," Jenny said. She could at least

try to remember the difference in their social standing. He was, after all, her employer's son. "You don't want to spill butter on that suit. It looks expensive." Jenny took a deep breath and smiled. Her sister owed her for this one. "I mean, it's a tuxedo, isn't it? Good enough to wear to a wedding."

"Tonight's a special occasion."

"Aren't they all?" She struggled upstream. "These receptions—nothing brings out the good suits like a reception or a wedding."

Robert nodded. "Or a funeral."

Jenny started to sweat. Being a news source was more difficult than one would think. "Funerals and weddings. Sometimes it's hard to tell the difference."

Robert looked at her like she'd lost her mind.

"I mean sometimes weddings get off to a rocky start." Boy, did her sister owe her.

Robert nodded. "I suppose so."

"Been to any weddings lately?"

Robert shrugged. "Not for a while. I've been away from the social scene."

"Oh?" Jenny looked up brightly. Now they were getting somewhere.

"Haven't missed it." Robert looked toward the barn door. "It won't take me a minute to run back to the café and get that butter."

Jenny nodded in defeat. "It's on the back of the stove. Be sure and use a pot holder." She suddenly remembered to whom she was talking. "That's a padded square of cloth. It'll be on the counter."

"I know what a pot holder is." Robert didn't add that he hadn't known until five months ago.

Jenny stood with her back to the tables and watched Robert walk out of the barn. He was limping. Now she wondered why a man who had spent five months resting would be limping.

"Handsome, isn't he?"

Jenny turned to look at the woman standing next to her. Mrs. Hargrove was one of the people in Dry Creek that Jenny liked the best. She'd organized the apron brigade for Jenny, using aprons from the church. Towel aprons. Frilly aprons. Patched aprons. They'd used them all.

"You're pretty good-looking yourself," Jenny said.

The older woman had worn a gingham cotton dress every other time Jenny had seen her. Tonight she was in a silk mauve dress with a strand of pearls around her neck. A lemon scent floated around her.

"Maybe he'll ask you to dance," Jenny continued. Mrs. Hargrove had said earlier that this was the first dance she'd attended since her husband died two years ago.

"Me?" Mrs. Hargrove laughed. "I was thinking he'd ask you to dance."

"No time. I'll be busy with the food."

"Not when the dancing starts."

"No, by then I'll be busy with the pots and pans— washing dishes."

"Goodness, no! The dishes can wait. Tomorrow's soon enough for that. We'll all pitch in then. That's the way it's done here. I might even ask old man Gossett to help us. Be good for him to get out. You'd be doing him a favor."

Jenny had a sudden wish that she could dance. "But I'm not dressed for a party."

Mrs. Hargrove shrugged. "I'll bet there's a few more dresses at the café."

The women of Dry Creek had loaned their old prom dresses and bridesmaids dresses to the teenage girls from Seattle. For most of the girls, this was the first time in their lives they had worn a formal dress.

"He's back," the older woman announced.

Robert Buckwalter entered the barn doorway and stood for a moment. Jenny could see the blackness of the outside air. Snowflakes were scattered on his head and shoulders. His hands were carefully wrapped around the handle of the saucepan he was holding. He hesitated in the doorway as though he was shy, unsure of his place among the guests. His shyness, combined with the perfect balance of his face almost took her breath away. Maybe he did deserve to be the number one bachelor.

He certainly didn't deserve to carry the butter.

"Here, let me get that." Jenny wiped her hands on her apron and started toward him. The steam from the lobsters had made her hands clammy. "You shouldn't have to—"

"I can carry a pan of butter."

"Of course." Jenny stopped. Of course he could. Why in the world was she so nervous around the man? It must be her sister. Making him sound so mysterious. Just because he was rich, it didn't mean he wasn't just a regular kind of a guy, too. He just had more change in his pockets than most.

"Dinner's almost ready." Jenny turned to talk again with Mrs. Hargrove.

The regular guy walked around her toward the table.

"Then your troubles for the evening will be over," Mrs. Hargrove said kindly as she put a hand on Jenny's arm. "We're so grateful for all the work you've done, dear."

Robert frowned as he set the saucepan on the table. If dinner was coming soon, he had work to do fast. He suspected people were always more easily shocked on an empty stomach. Plus, after dinner, the sounds of those records playing would mask his attempts at being outrageous.

He'd given some thought to his dilemma while outside and he'd decided age could go two ways. Instead of focusing on someone young like Bambi, he could try someone old enough to be his grandmother.

"Ah, there you are." Robert turned back to Mrs. Hargrove. He understood she was the Sunday school teacher for most of the little people in Dry Creek. She should be thoroughly offended by a kiss from a strange man. Everyone else should be shocked, too.

He looked around for Bambi and called her over. There'd be no point in rattling the people of Dry Creek if he couldn't shake up the rest of the country, too.

"Yes?" Mrs. Hargrove looked up at him. Her eyes were bright with curiosity. Her cheeks were pink. She must be seventy years old. She looked like every cookie-lover's picture of Grandma.

Robert dove right in. "I love you."

"Why, I love you, too." She beamed back.

"What?" Robert stalled. This wasn't the way it was supposed to go.

"I love all of God's children," Mrs. Hargrove continued. "They say that's how Christians will know each other. By the love they have for others. I John 4:7. Does this mean you're a Christian?"

"Well, no, I—I mean I'm not opposed to Christianity." Robert started to sweat in earnest. How had God gotten into this? "Don't really even know much about it—"

"Well, I'd be happy to tell you."

"Great, maybe later. It's just that's not what I meant when I said I love you."

"Well, then, what did you mean?"

Robert was desperate. He looked over and nodded at Bambi. She was in position. Then he started to bend down.

Unfortunately, Mrs. Hargrove bent, too. "My beads."

Robert heard the scattered dropping of pearls as his kiss landed smack on the top of Mrs. Hargrove's gray head. His lips met the scalp where her hair was parted.

"Oh, dear," Mrs. Hargrove said as she bent down farther.

Now Robert couldn't even kiss the top of her head unless he squatted down to where his kneecaps should be.

"Here, let me help you," Jenny said as she stepped closer to both of them.

Robert wasn't about to give up. It wasn't ideal. But the camera was in place and he was determined to kiss someone. Even if it was Jenny.

He heard her first soft shocked breath as he drew Jenny to him. He was close enough to feel her second indignant breath as he bent his head.

The camera flashed. The talking stopped. A bead rolled.

Robert was triumphant. His big moment was recorded. He could end the kiss. But he didn't. Something was happening.

The kiss blossomed. Jenny tasted of home. The minute Robert felt her lips tremble beneath his, he was lost. He didn't want the kiss to end. He felt like he had caught a fragile thread of something precious he didn't even understand.

"Mmmm, sweet. I like that—I mean you—I like you," he whispered when he finally drew away.

"Not love?" Bright red dots stood out on both of Jenny's cheeks. "I thought 'I love you' came easy enough to your type."

Robert felt like he was coming out of a cozy cave and facing the frost of winter.

"My type?" he asked cautiously.

Jenny's brown eyes had deepened to a snapping black. She bristled.

"The type of man who kisses his employees—whom he *likes*—even when he says he loves Mrs. Hargrove."

"I don't kiss my employ—" Robert stopped. That was no longer true. "I mean, I don't. Well, I didn't—"

There was an incessant ringing somewhere and a gnarled old hand reached from behind Robert. Mr. Gossett had pulled the ringing phone out of the coat pocket. "This yours?"

"You want it?" Robert asked Jenny.

Jenny's cheeks were red still and her breathing quick. She was adorable.

Robert suspected she reached for the phone more for something to do than because she wanted to talk.

"Yes." Jenny turned her back to him and walked a few feet away.

"You talked to him!" She looked over her shoulder in a betraying move. It was the sister. "So he knows."

Robert knew he should pick up on the accusation Jenny had left dangling and make some strong sexual harassment statements. Publicly threaten to fire her unless she kissed him again. That would certainly knock him off the bachelor list. Women didn't tolerate sexual harassment anymore and they shouldn't.

But Robert didn't open his mouth. Suddenly the list was not all that important.

He had met the woman the Bob inside him wanted to marry and she was looking at him this very minute like he was some hair ball a very unwelcome stray cat had coughed up.

Considering the set of her jaw as she talked to her sister, Robert figured he had as much chance of ever kissing her again as he had of teaching that stray cat to dance a tango.

Chapter Three

"He kissed you! You're telling me he kissed you! Robert Buckwalter the Third kissed you!"

Jenny's sister was screeching so loudly Jenny had to hold the cell phone away from her ear. She'd slipped outside so that she could finish the phone conversation in private. She shivered from the cold.

"After he kissed Mrs. Hargrove," Jenny said as she wiped one hand on her chef's apron. The coarse bleached muslin steadied her. She was a chef. An employee. "He's my boss. He can't kiss me. He didn't even say he loved me."

"Love! He loves you!" her sister screeched even louder.

"No, he didn't say that—that's what I'm saying. He didn't even attempt to be sincere."

"But he kissed you."

The Montana night was lit by some stars and a perfectly round moon. Silver shadows fell on the snow where the reflection of the barn light showed through the barn door and two square side windows. A jumble of cars and trucks were parked in the road leading up to the barn.

"Maybe he did it because I talked to you about him. Maybe there's some servant's code I breached when I told secrets about the master. You know, maybe it's a revenge thing."

Jenny could hear the pause on the other end of the phone. The silence lasted for a full minute.

Finally her sister spoke. "Have you been taking those vitamins Mom sent you?"

"Well, yes, but what does that have to do with anything?"

"You're getting old. First you don't even wonder about whether or not the man is married and now he kisses you—Robert Buckwalter the Third actually kisses you—and you think it's for revenge!"

"Well, it could be."

"Men like him don't kiss for revenge! They use lawsuits. Or buyouts. Corporate takeovers. They use termination. He could fire you. But not kisses! Kisses are for romance."

Jenny snorted. "I smell like fish and my hair is flat. No man's kissing me for romance."

"You're in your chef's apron?" Some of the bubble drained out of her sister's voice. "With that funny hairnet on?"

"And orthopedic white shoes because I'm standing so much. And no makeup because the steam from the lobster pots would make my mascara run. And I even have a butter stain on my apron—not a big one, but it's there in the left corner."

"Then why is he kissing you?" her sister wailed and then caught herself. "Not that—I mean you're real attractive when you're…well, you know—"

"Those are my thoughts exactly. I might pass for someone in his social circle when I'm dressed up— heels, makeup, the works."

"You looked real good in that black dress you wore last New Year's."

"But in my working clothes, I'm more likely to attract a raving lunatic than a rich man."

"Are you sure you don't have some exotic perfume on? One of those musk oil scents?"

"Not a drop."

"Well, this isn't fair, then. A man like this Buckwalter fellow shouldn't go around kissing women just for kicks. He could hurt their feelings."

"That's what I'm trying to tell you. He's so rich he doesn't need to worry about anyone's feelings. Especially the feelings of his employees."

It was the dumped pet thing all over again. The rich were rich enough to be selfish. They didn't care about their pets. They didn't care about other people. That was all there was to it. The normal courtesies of life didn't apply to people like Robert Buckwalter.

Jenny looked over toward the barn. Mrs. Hargrove stood in the open doorway watching her anxiously. She was motioning for her to come back inside.

"I think they need me." Jenny waved Mrs. Hargrove back into the warm barn. "It must be lobster time. Talk to you later."

"Call me."

"I will—wait." She'd just thought of something. "When you talked to Robert Buckwalter earlier, did you tell him he was number one on the list or did you just say you were thinking of making him number one?"

"Oh, I couldn't tell him he was number one. I said maybe, but I didn't say it had been settled. That's not decided. Besides, it's confidential."

"I see. Thanks. I'll call you later."

Jenny slipped the cell phone into the front pocket of her chef's apron. Well, that explained everything. Robert Buckwalter thought a kiss might nudge him into that first-place position. Cozy up to the sister of someone with influence on the list and—presto—he's at the top. It was a game as old as mankind.

The heat inside the barn enfolded Jenny when she stepped across the threshold. She rubbed her arms. She'd been so angry she hadn't noticed the goose bumps that had crept up her arms. It was freezing outside.

"There you are, dear," Mrs. Hargrove said. The older woman stepped toward her. "I was worried. I forgot to tell you that there's been a threat of kidnapping tonight. Garth Elkton has cautioned all the women to stay inside."

"A kidnapping? Here?"

Jenny looked around in astonishment. She couldn't imagine a less likely place for a kidnapping. The teenagers had strung pink and white crepe paper from the rafters, making Jenny feel as if she were trapped in Candy Land. Dozens of ranchers and their wives sat at the long white tables at the back of the barn. Some of the ranchers had arms as big as wrestlers. What kind of army would it take to kidnap someone from here tonight?

"But who—?" Jenny asked.

"Garth Elkton got a strange call warning him that someone was out to get his sister."

"Francis!" Jenny had met the woman earlier and liked her instantly. "But who would want to kidnap her?"

Mrs. Hargrove leaned close. "Some folks say it's an old boyfriend of hers. But I don't believe them. Flint Harris is a good boy. I always thought Dry Creek would be proud of him one day."

Jenny looked over at the string of men standing along the far side of the barn. Most of them wore dark cowboy work boots and had the raw look of a new shave on their faces. "Which one is he?"

"Why, none of them, dear. Flint Harris hasn't been in Dry Creek for almost twenty years now."

"Well, then, surely he's not a threat."

Mrs. Hargrove shrugged. "I've never believed he was. Everyone's so wound up about this cattle rustling that's going on that we're making fools of ourselves, I'm afraid. Folks are saying now that the FBI thinks that someone from Dry Creek is tipping off the cattle rustlers. Imagine that! It's rattled a lot of folks, but I don't set much store by it. It'll all blow over. But it's best that you be careful. If you need to go over to the café, let me know and I'll get one of the ranch hands to go with you."

Jenny nodded. "I think we have everything we need to get started."

Steam from the lobsters kept the air inside the barn moist and Jenny could smell the coffee someone had set to brew.

Mrs. Buckwalter took charge, thanking everyone for coming and asking Matthew Curtis, the newly married minister, to say a blessing on the celebration meal. He agreed and asked everyone to join hands.

Jenny offered one hand to Mrs. Hargrove and the other to a young girl with rosy cheeks standing next to her.

The whole town of Dry Creek held hands and then closed their eyes.

"For the blessings You have given, we thank You, Lord," the minister prayed. He held the hand of his new bride, a fresh-faced redhead that people had been calling Angel all night long. "For this food eaten with friends, we are most grateful. Keep us in Your love. Amen."

"And thanks for my money, too," the young girl at Jenny's side whispered quietly, her eyes still squeezed shut.

Jenny hadn't noticed that the girl wasn't holding someone's hand on the other side of her. Instead she was clutching a green piece of paper that looked like a check.

"Maybe you should put that with your coat." Jenny nodded her head in the general direction of a few chairs near the door that were haphazardly piled with coats. "You wouldn't want to lose your allowance."

"I don't get an allowance," the girl whispered. "But I don't need one now, because I'm rich."

"We've got a lot to be grateful for." Jenny smiled

down at the girl. What did it matter if the girl kept her few dollars in her hand if it made her feel better?

"I'm especially grateful for him," the girl whispered again.

Jenny followed the girl's gaze and it led her straight to the tuxedoed back of—"Robert Buckwalter!" Jenny looked down at the girl in alarm. The sweet young thing's face glowed in adoration. "What's he done to you?"

Jenny looked at the broad shoulders of the man who was causing trouble. It wasn't enough that he'd kissed Jenny and Mrs. Hargrove, he'd obviously kissed others, too.

Robert looked perfectly at ease, talking with a couple of teenage boys who were fidgeting with their ties. It almost looked like he was giving them a lesson in how to make a tie bearable.

Jenny wished he would turn around and face her. It wasn't nearly as satisfying to scowl at a man's back as it would be to scowl at his face.

Folding chairs had been pulled close to the long table. People everywhere were walking toward the chairs and sitting down.

Jenny looked over and caught the eye of one of the ranch hands. She nodded for him to begin serving the lobsters like they had arranged earlier.

"I'll be right with you." Jenny was in charge of bringing the melted butter to the table, but it would take a minute for the lobsters to make the rounds and she had something to do before she served it.

"Excuse me," Jenny said. Her eyes were level with the back shoulder of Robert Buckwalter and she could feel the stiffness in her own spine. That poor innocent girl was no match for a man like this and Jenny felt she must protest his flirtation with her.

The man turned around. "Jenny!"

Jenny almost stumbled. The man said her name with joy.

"I know this is a party—" Jenny kept her eyes focused on Robert Buckwalter's chin. She didn't want to lose her nerve. She had stuck up for her younger siblings for years. She'd stick up for that young girl. "—and a dance at that. But you're an adult and you have to know that a child—well, you're old enough to be her father and I think you should remember that."

"I'm old enough to be whose father?"

Jenny lifted her gaze from his chin to his eyes. If she didn't know better, she would say he was puzzled. And his eyes were distracting. A clear sky blue. They made her dizzy and annoyed at the same time.

"All of them," she snapped. "You're old enough to be father to all of the kids here."

"Well, that's stretching it, but if it makes you feel better, I assure you I'm not father to anyone—especially no one in this room."

"You shouldn't kiss them then."

Jenny kept her voice low. She hadn't forgotten about the teenage boys who were standing close enough to hear what she was saying if she wasn't careful.

Robert had no such need for privacy. "Kissing? When?"

Suddenly the air became supercharged.

"Kissing!" A teenage boy yelled out and then gave a piercing basketball whistle. "Hey everybody—he's gonna kiss her again!"

Jenny paled and she looked back at Robert. His eyes had deepened from sky blue to a midnight blue. And he was starting to grin.

"You shouldn't have mentioned kisses," he said.

"What's going on?" Jenny felt as if she'd landed in a science-fiction movie. She turned around. She was suddenly surrounded by twenty, maybe thirty teenagers and they were all noisily aiming cheap disposable cameras at her.

"I suppose we should blame my mother. She bought them the cameras so they could take pictures of the wildlife in Montana."

"But what do they want with us? We don't even live

in Montana. I grew up in Seattle. I don't even know what the wildlife here looks like. I've never seen an elk, or a mountain sheep, or—"

"I think," Robert said, as he touched her shoulders and turned her around until she was facing him again, "they want to see this."

Robert dipped his head toward her and Jenny's heart stopped. She knew he meant to kiss her. It was obvious. But she couldn't move. She meant to move. Her mind assured her of that. It was her feet. Her feet had betrayed her and turned to stone.

Robert's lips met hers and Jenny's feet melted. She could hardly stand. She put her arms on his shoulders more for support than anything.

Ahhh. It was sweet. Very sweet.

Jenny felt like she went to a distant place where there was nothing but this man kissing her. Everything else was fuzzy. Then she saw a bright light. And heard a faint click. Then another click. This is it, she thought. Her heart was giving out. The end was always described as coming with a bright light. She wasn't sure about the clicking. She should have paid more attention in Sunday school. She bet Mrs. Hargrove knew about the clicking. Jenny only hoped it didn't have anything to do with that other place. Could it be fire crackling? She really should have paid more attention.

Then the light wavered and Jenny blinked.

The kiss stopped.

She glanced up and saw his face. Robert Buckwalter looked as stunned as she felt.

"It's the cameras," Jenny finally whispered. She wasn't dying, after all.

"I heard bells."

"No, it was just the clicking." Jenny pulled away from him slightly so she could check her feet.

Her feet would work, Jenny assured herself as she pulled away farther. She suddenly needed more room. "I've got to see to the butter."

"Are you going for it again?" one of the teenage boys yelled out. "I've still got five shots left on my camera. Might as well fill it up."

"Yeah, me, too," another boy added.

"I heard bells," Robert Buckwalter repeated slowly.

"You heard clicking," Jenny said forcefully. She took a deep breath. "To you it sounded like bells. To me it sounded like the fires of…" She took another quick breath. "Just how gullible do you think I am? I'm not doing anything about that list, so you can just forget this—this—" Jenny waved her hand, but could not finish the sentence. This what? This earthquake? This landslide? Everything seemed more something than simply this kiss.

"Besides, I have the butter to serve," Jenny said with dignity as she pulled herself away. She congratulated herself. Her feet worked perfectly well.

The lobsters were all eaten and the butter dishes empty before Robert felt free to escape from the party and sit on the steps leading out of the barn door.

He was a mess. Some love song was filling the barn with swaying rhythm and dozens of couples were dancing together. He should be dancing. He should be in there dancing with the woman who had turned him inside out, but he wasn't. Jenny was bustling around making sure everyone had coffee. Everyone, that is, except him. He was sure she wouldn't offer him any even if he stood in front of her like a beggar with an empty cup.

One thing was clear—Jenny had little use for Robert Buckwalter. What wasn't clear was if she could love Bob instead.

"Mind if I join you?"

Robert looked up to see Matthew Curtis, the minister, coming out of the barn.

"Help yourself." Robert moved over on the steps. The steps were wooden and had been swept clean of snow even though they were still cold enough to make a man notice when he was changing spots. "There's room for both of us on these steps."

"I could get us chairs from inside," Matthew offered as he turned to go back in the barn. "That's what I should do—get us some nice folding chairs."

"I haven't seen anyone else use folding chairs."

"Well, we don't, but you're—"

"I'm what?"

Robert wondered how much trouble he could get in if he took a swing at a minister. "Go ahead, tell me. I'm what?"

The night air was damp. Snow wasn't falling, but the air was heavy with the promise of a blizzard later. Clouds covered most of the stars and half of the moon.

Matthew turned and stepped down next to Robert. "I'd guess right now you're a man who's just feeling bad. Want to talk about it?"

Robert realized he did. "You might not understand how it is with me."

"No, probably not," Matthew agreed as he settled onto the steps. "Can't say I've ever had the problems of a rich man."

"What makes you think it's got to do with money?"

Matthew shrugged. "Just a guess. You're rich. That's got to be a burden—although I'd guess it's a little less of a burden after tonight."

Robert looked at him.

"All those rolls of film you bought from the kids

must have set you back a pretty penny. I heard them saying you were paying one thousand dollars for each picture they got of you kissing Jenny. I heard them cameras each take twenty-four shots. One of the kids is still kicking himself for taking three shots of the decorations before you started your kissing. Can't blame him. I almost got a camera myself and started taking pictures. That's going to be a half-million-dollar kiss when you've paid off all the kids."

"Does Jenny know about this?" Robert wasn't so sure he wanted her to find out about this when she was carrying around a pot of hot coffee. She might be inclined to throw some of it his way without benefit of a cup.

"No. The kids are keeping quiet like you asked. They're tiptoeing around her. But they're so excited, they're going to burst if they don't tell someone. I'd guess a few of the adults know. And they're all wondering why—"

"It seemed like a good idea." Robert paused. The air was cold enough to make puff clouds of his breath. "It started with Bambi. I thought she should go to college someday."

Matthew nodded. "You're a generous man. That should make you feel good."

"It should."

"But it doesn't?"

"It's not enough. The way I see it, I'm missing something."

Matthew nodded. "Go on."

"I have too many friends. No, that's not right. They're not really friends. They're only people who like me because I'm rich. Because I have all the toys. Each one of those kids in there has a better friend and is a better friend to someone than I am. That's a hard realization to come to. If I died, it's not me people would miss, it's my toys."

"You planning on dying?"

"Well, no, not anytime soon." Robert realized it was hard to pin down the hollow feeling he had. "But if I did—"

Matthew nodded again "What's troubling you is that you need to be part of the kingdom and you're not."

Robert stopped. He'd heard there were militia groups in Montana. He wondered if he'd stumbled across one. They'd sure love to recruit a rich man like him who could buy them enough ammunition to start a small war.

"The kingdom?" Robert asked cautiously.

"Sure, the kingdom of God," Matthew said calmly. "It's all that will fill up that empty feeling. When you're ready, we'll talk about it."

"I don't think it has to do with God."

Matthew grinned as he stood. "I know. You think it all has to do with that cute chef inside who's in need of a dance. If you don't ask her, somebody else is going to beat you to it."

"She won't dance with me."

Matthew grinned even wider. "Well, maybe not the first time you ask her. But you're Robert Buckwalter the Third. Way I hear it, you know about all there is about charming women."

The minister stepped inside the barn and Robert stood up and brushed himself off before following him.

The minister was right. He did know how to charm women. He just wasn't sure charm would work with someone like Jenny.

The music was softer now. Even the kids were slowing down.

Robert went over to the refreshment table and got a glass of punch to work up his nerve. Jenny was still flitting about filling up coffee cups for those people who were sitting around the edge of the dance space and talking. He'd studied her pattern. She needed to return to the refreshment table to refill her thermal pot after every tenth cup. She was due back any minute now.

When she came back, he would ask her to dance with him.

Chapter Four

"Well, I hope you're happy now," Jenny said as she set the thermal coffeepot down on the refreshment table and glared at Robert Buckwalter. "Throwing your money around like it's confetti."

Robert stiffened. He looked around at the teenagers dancing. He hoped no one had told her what he was buying with the money. None of the dancers were looking at him in apology. "No one else is complaining."

"Of course they're not complaining." Jenny turned to the big coffeepot and twisted the knob on its spigot so it would slowly fill the smaller thermal coffeepot. The mellow smell of brewed coffee drifted up from the pot. She looked up and continued her conversation. "What do you expect? They're teenagers. They love money."

"Money has its uses."

Jenny switched off the knob. The small pot was full. And she was tired to the bone. She'd been a fool. There for a blinding moment she'd thought Robert Buckwalter was a regular kind of a guy who just happened to be rich. What kind of rabbit hole had she fallen down? She should know better. No one just happened to be rich. Money changed everyone. "Not everything in the world revolves around money."

"I know."

"You can't buy friends with money—not even the friendship of teenagers." After Jenny said the words, she corrected herself. Those teenagers certainly spoke of Robert with enough enthusiasm to count him a friend. And the checks were awfully big. She'd seen one of them.

Robert grinned. The kids had managed to keep his secret. Jenny didn't know why he'd been throwing checks around. "I didn't give them the money so they'd be my friends."

"Well, with the size of those checks—they should be something."

"I'm hoping they will be something someday."

Jenny looked at him suspiciously.

"Something for themselves. I'm hoping they'll go to college—maybe learn a trade—be good citizens,"

Robert explained. "Grow up to be their own something. What's wrong with that?"

Jenny was silent for a moment. "Nothing."

Her sister was right, Jenny thought in defeat. She,
Jenny M. Black, was turning into one of those fussy
old women. Picking a fight with a perfectly innocent
man just because he'd given away some of his money.
And that wasn't even the real reason. The real reason
was the kiss. And that was just as foolish. In his social
circles, a kiss was nothing more than a handshake.

"Who you give money to is none of my business,"
Jenny said stiffly as she put the lid back on the small
coffeepot. "I owe you an apology."

"I'll take a dance instead." Robert held his breath.
He'd seen the loophole and dived through it, but it wasn't
a smooth move. He'd done better courting when he was
sixteen. He had no polish left. He was reduced to the bare
truth. "I've been hoping you'd save a dance for me."

Jenny looked at him like he was crazy. "Save a
dance? Me? I'm not dancing."

"And why not?"

Jenny held up the coffeepot. She hated to point out
the obvious. "I'm here to see that others have a good
time. That's what your mother pays me to do and I
intend to do it. I, for one, believe in earning my money."

"I could pa—" Robert started to tease and then

stopped. He didn't know how she'd twist his offer to pay for a dance, but he could see trouble snapping in her eyes already. "My mother doesn't expect you to wait on people all night."

Robert looked over to where his mother was talking with Mrs. Hargrove. They were sitting on two folding chairs by the door to the barn. If his mother wasn't so intent on the conversation, he knew she would have already come over and told Jenny to take it easy.

"You're not going to ask her, are you?" Jenny looked horrified.

"Not if you don't want me to. But if you're so determined to give people coffee. I could pass some around for you. With two of us working, it'd take half the time. How much coffee can everyone drink?"

"I can manage."

"No one should be drinking coffee at this time of night anyway." Robert wondered if he'd completely lost his touch. She shouldn't still be frowning at him. Any other woman would be untying those apron strings and smiling at him by now.

"It's decaf."

"Still. There's all this punch." Robert gestured to the half-full bowl of pink punch. The color of the punch had faded as the evening wore on, and the ice had melted. The plastic dipper was half floating in the liquid. "Pity to see it go to waste."

"The punch drinkers are all dancing." Jenny looked out at the dance floor wistfully. The only people left drinking coffee were the single men, mostly the ranch hands from Garth Elkton's place. The teenagers had downed many a cup of punch after dinner, but they were all dancing now.

Robert followed her gaze. "The kids are doing their best, aren't they?"

The swish of taffeta skirts rustled all along the dance floor. A long, slow sixties love song whispered low and throaty from the record player. Most of the teenagers were paired up and dancing with a determined concentration that Robert applauded. He even saw one or two of the boys try a dip with their partners. Now that was courage.

"They remind me of an old Fred Astaire and Ginger Rogers movie—all those colors swirling around."

The old prom dresses were lavender, slate gray, buttercup yellow, forest green, primrose pink—and they all seemed to have full skirts that trailed on the plank flooring of the barn. Their skirts reminded Jenny of a bed of pansies.

"We could be swirling, too—" Robert held out one hand for the coffeepot and the other for Jenny's hand.

The light in the old barn had been softened when the music started. Someone had turned off a few of the side lights and shadows crowded the tall corners of the structure. The air was cool and, by the sounds of it, a winter wind was blowing outside.

When Jenny had looked outside earlier, she'd thought that the snow falling in the black night looked like a snow globe turned upside down—with the barn at the center and an old-fashioned waltz playing while the snow fell around the globe.

"I can't dance in this." Jenny brought her mind back to reality. She gestured to her chef's apron. Her broad white apron was serviceable for working with food, but it had nothing of taffeta or silk about it. Even Ginger didn't dance in coarse cotton. "And there's my hair—"

"Your hair is beautiful. You just need to get rid of this." Robert reached over and lifted Jenny's hairnet off her head.

Jenny's hands flew up. "But that's my hairnet—the health code."

"No one needs a hairnet for dancing."

No, Jenny thought, but they did need air in their lungs. She felt dizzy. She could almost hear her sister's squeal of delight if she knew Robert Buckwalter had plucked the net off her hair and asked her to dance.

But Jenny had always been more practical than her sister.

Jenny knew that Prince Charming didn't even notice Cinderella until after the Fairy Godmother had given her a whole new look. Men, especially handsome men like the one in front of her, just didn't dance with women with working shoes and flat hair. Not even the coachmen would have danced with Cinderella if she'd arrived at the ball with a net over her hair and an apron around her waist.

"I should change."

Jenny's hand had already found its way into his and now she was twisting away from him to go do something as foolish as change her clothes.

"You're fine." Fine didn't begin to cover it, Robert thought to himself. Jenny's eyes, usually a dark brown, had lightened to a caramel. She had a dazed look about her that made him want to dance with her in a quiet corner instead of in the middle of a throng of teenagers.

It wasn't that she was beautiful, he decided after a moment. He'd seen dozens of women whose features were more perfect. But he'd never seen anyone who looked like Jenny. He could almost trace her thoughts in her eyes. She wasn't trying to hide who she was or what she thought. He wondered if she even knew how rare that was. Or how compelling.

"But my hair…" Jenny frantically tried to fluff her hair up a little. It was all about bone structure. With flat hair, the small features on her face made her look like a Christmas elf. With just a little bit of fluff, she managed to look merely petite instead of childish.

Robert captured her hand and calmed her.

"Your hair is—" He'd been going to say "fine." But then he felt the cloud of her hair fall against the back of his hand. "—incredible."

"It's brown." Jenny shook her hair away from his hand. No wonder he was in the running for the number one bachelor. He was a charmer, all right. "Plain brown and flyaway on top of that."

Robert shook his head. "I'd say more chestnut than anything, golden highlights. The kind of hair the masters used to paint in all those old European pictures. Mona Lisa colors."

"Next you'll be saying my apron is the latest fashion from Paris."

Robert could see the amusement begin in her eyes and he could feel her relaxing.

"Just see if it doesn't catch on." Robert guided her closer so they could waltz. He felt her momentary resistance before she moved toward him.

"I used to love to dance." Maybe the shadows will

hide my apron, Jenny thought to herself as Robert started them on their way.

"Ever dip?"

Jenny shook her head. "And don't you dare. I'd feel foolish with everyone looking."

"Everybody's too busy to care."

Jenny looked around at the other couples. It was true. Almost. "The ranch hands are watching."

Robert looked at the cluster of men standing by one of the side heaters. Half of them held coffee cups in their hands. A few of them did seem to be looking at him and Jenny, although he'd wager they weren't interested in her apron. The dismay he saw in the eyes of a couple of them told him they'd been waiting for the coffee passing to stop so they'd have their own chance at a dance with Jenny.

"They'll just have to get their own dates," Robert stated firmly as he gathered Jenny a little closer and inhaled. She smelled of some very pleasing scent. He'd guess cinnamon.

Jenny almost stumbled. "Date?"

Robert looked down at her face and smiled. "You. Me. Dancing. That's a date, isn't it?"

"But we can't be on a date." Jenny stopped dancing.

"Why not?"

"You're my boss."

"I've never paid you a dime. You work for my mother."

"It's the same difference," Jenny sputtered. "Besides—" she hated to sound like her sister, but there it was "—I'm Jenny, the chef, and you're Robert Buckwalter the Third."

"You can call me Bob."

"What?" Jenny hadn't realized how close Robert had pulled her until she'd stopped dancing.

"Bob. Call me Bob."

Jenny looked up at him skeptically. He smelled faintly of some expensive aftershave. The tie around his neck was pure silk and probably Italian. His suit had to be hand tailored. "You don't look like a Bob."

Robert gently started Jenny dancing again. He liked the way she felt in his arms. Her head reached his chin. Not too tall. Not too short. Just right. "What does a Bob look like anyway?"

Jenny was silent a moment. "Plaid shirt. Sneakers."

Robert started to chuckle. "I can't do much about the shirt right now, but I left my sneakers in the bus when we drove over. I could go get them if it'd make you happy. We could both go."

"It's dark out there."

"The stars are out."

"Mrs. Hargrove said we're supposed to stay close to the barn." Jenny tried to hold on to her propriety.

Jenny remembered how soft the black sky was

outside. Shadows layered over shadows amid the cars and trucks parked in the middle of Dry Creek. The bite of the air would be cold and sharp enough to make the inside of the bus a cozy place to talk. A much too cozy place when all was said and done.

"She's just worried about that kidnapping rumor." Robert watched the temptation play across Jenny's face. He could watch her for hours. "But only a fool would kidnap anyone in a cold spell like the one tonight. There's three feet of snow out there in some places."

"I suppose."

Robert noticed the frown didn't go away. "If you're worried about me, don't be. I'm a gentleman. You can trust me."

Jenny snapped back to reality. "You're not a gentleman. You're the bachelor of the year."

Robert came back to reality with her. "I am? Have you talked to your sister? Have they decided?"

"No."

"The whole thing is cruel and unusual punishment."

Jenny nodded. She supposed the waiting and suspense did seem like that to him. He must really want the slot. "My sister says the winner will be able to write his own ticket with the advertising companies."

Robert groaned. "I'd forgotten about that part of it. I may need to fly Charlie in to take those calls after all."

"Who's Charlie? Your attorney?"

Robert started to chuckle. "No, Charlie is an acquaintance of another kind."

"Oh." Don't tell me he has an agent, Jenny thought in dismay. He certainly had the looks to go into modeling. But somehow, she was disappointed. "I hope you draw the line at underwear."

Robert blinked. "Underwear?"

"You know, in the endorsements. I wouldn't want to see you in a magazine in your underwear."

Jenny felt the blush creep up her neck. He didn't have to look at her that way—like she was picturing him right now in his underwear. "I just think it wouldn't be a good example for the kids around here."

"You're worried they'll grow up to be underwear salesmen?" Robert was entranced. He'd seen precious few blushes in his day. That must say something about the kind of women that usually flocked around him.

"Well, it's not very steady work."

"I don't know about that. People always need underwear."

If they hadn't been talking, Jenny was sure she would have noticed that the music had stopped.

She did notice the loud voices from the front of the barn near the door.

A woman's voice called, "Francis? Anyone seen Francis?"

There was a loud shuffling as the boots of the ranch hands who were sitting by the heater hit the floor with a united thud.

A man's rough voice demanded, "Garth? Where's Garth?"

Finally one of the teenage girls opened the barn door from the outside and shrieked, "Kidnapping! They were right! There's a kidnapping! We saw the truck—we saw them!" The girl's face was white, but Jenny couldn't tell if it was from the outside cold or from shock.

"Come in, dear. Tell us what you saw." Mrs. Hargrove was drawing the girl inside as Jenny and Robert arrived at her side.

"Bryan and I were outside looking at the stars when we heard a gunshot."

"I told you that was a gunshot," one of the ranch hands muttered to another.

"Are you sure it was a gunshot?" Mrs. Hargrove put a jacket around the shivering girl. "It might have been a car misfiring."

"But there weren't any cars running. Not even that big truck was going when we heard the shot," the girl insisted. "Besides, I know the difference between a gunshot and a car backfiring."

Mrs. Hargrove took a quick, assessing look at the girl. The girl was tall and skinny with a light brown skin that could signal almost any race. Finally, the older woman nodded. "We'd best call out the sheriff."

"The sheriff? Where's he off to anyway?" one ranch hand said.

"Some guy called in an emergency from the Billings airport," another answered. "Something to do with some VIP."

"I think the guys with the guns are in that big truck that just left," the girl continued. "Bryan saw something shiny that looked like a gun."

"Where's Bryan now?" Robert asked the girl quietly. Something about the whole story didn't seem right to him. Any teenage boy he knew would be in here claiming the glory of the moment. But there was no Bryan.

The girl bit her lip.

Robert looked around. There were a lot more dresses than tuxedoes in the crowd.

"Where's Bryan?" he asked again.

"He wanted to be sure. I told him it was a gunshot, but he wanted to be sure before he told everyone." The girl's brown complexion went a little yellow and she swallowed hard.

"Where is he?"

"He took the bus to follow them."

"Mercy!" Mrs. Hargrove put her hands to her mouth. "When they have guns! And the boy all alone."

"I don't think he's quite all alone," Robert said grimly as he looked over the teenagers again. Then he looked at the girl. "How many other guys are with him?"

The girl looked miserable. "Ten."

"Lord have mercy," Mrs. Hargrove said again.

"We'll have to catch them," Robert said, looking over at the ranch hands. He recognized the men's faces from the ride into Dry Creek on the bus that was now in hot pursuit of the cattle truck. None of them would have a vehicle here. "Who's got a pickup we can borrow?"

"You can take ours," one of the farm wives offered as she bent to fumble in her purse for the keys.

"Anyone call the sheriff yet?" Robert asked as he eyed half a dozen of the ranch hands. "I don't suppose anyone here has a hunting gun in their truck?"

"We called the sheriff," Jenny said with a nod to another one of the ranch women. She held up the cell phone that had been resting in her apron pocket. "But he's tied up at the Billings airport with some woman who came in, named Laurel Carlton or something like that."

"Laurel?" Robert paled. "Here?"

Well, this is it, Jenny thought. Robert certainly looked uncomfortable with the thought of this woman, whoever she was. Maybe her sister was right and he was married after all.

"Fred has a gun," one of the ranch hands yelled from the other side of the barn. "Uses it to scare off coyotes on his place."

"It's an old rifle—draws a little to the left," the man explained as he walked fast toward the door. "But I'll get it. It's better than nothing."

"I think everyone should just wait for the authorities," Mrs. Buckwalter said. "Let them handle it. A gun can be a dangerous thing."

One of the ranch hands snorted. "Tell that to whoever's in the truck. We can't wait for the sheriff. They'll be long gone by the time he gets here."

"He's right," Robert said.

The farm woman with the pickup pressed a set of keys into the palm of Robert's hand. "The tank's half-full."

The other men looked at Robert. He nodded his head at five or six of the sturdiest-looking ones and they, almost in unison, dipped their heads to drop a kiss on their wives' cheeks before starting toward the door.

Now that's what marriage is about, Robert thought to himself. The automatic, comfortable affection of settled love. Having someone to kiss goodbye when you're going off to war or even just heading to the store.

Seeing all those kisses made him feel lonely enough to be brave. What could it hurt?

Jenny was talking to Robert's mother, her head bent slightly to hear his shorter mother. The dark wave of Jenny's hair lay on her neck. Wisps of hair moved with his hand as Robert brushed the hair aside. He hoped to get Jenny's full attention. He'd kissed Mrs. Hargrove on her hair part earlier and had no more appetite for hair kisses.

Jenny looked up. His mother looked up. Satisfied, Robert bent his head to kiss Jenny on her cheek. Her skin was soft as a petal. He could hear her surprised gasp even though it was little more than an indrawn breath.

"I'll be fine," Robert assured Jenny quickly, overlooking the fact that she hadn't asked.

"You're not going with them," Robert's mother said. Jenny still seemed a little dazed. The older woman repeated, "You can't possibly be thinking of going with them."

"I'll be fine." Robert moved to kiss his mother, as well. "Don't worry."

"But they have guns!" Mrs. Buckwalter said, as though that settled everything.

"I'll be back," Robert said as he started to walk toward the door. "Just tell that sheriff to get back here."

"But he can't go." Mrs. Buckwalter repeated the

words to Jenny as they watched Robert go through the barn door. A gust of cold wind blew in as the men stepped outside.

"I'm sure he'll be fine." Jenny echoed her son's words for the older woman's benefit.

"But this isn't like him." Mrs. Buckwalter looked at Jenny. "He'd told me he was a changed man, but…" Her voice trailed off. "I thought he meant he was going to move back to Seattle or take up watercolors or get engaged or something sensible—not take off looking for men with guns."

Jenny tried to smile reassuringly. "I'm sure he'll be fine."

Chapter Five

Jenny left the cell phone with Mrs. Buckwalter and walked over to the refreshment table to see how much coffee was left in the big pot. She had a feeling punch wouldn't be enough for the men when they came back.

"The sheriff's coming back as soon as he can," Mrs. Buckwalter reported as she joined Jenny over by the table. "Which probably won't be soon enough to do any good so I called in some of the other authorities around."

Jenny looked up. "I didn't know there was anyone else around here but the county sheriffs."

Mrs. Buckwalter grunted. "There's some fool FBI agent riding around on a horse."

"On a horse!"

"And his boss is here in some kind of a Jeep. They both travel a bit unconventionally I'm afraid but—"

"I don't care if they get here in a flying saucer," Jenny said as she lifted the smaller pot of coffee to start making the rounds. "Just as long as they get here fast."

"You're really worried, aren't you?" Mrs. Buckwalter looked at Jenny as though she were seeing her for the first time.

"Of course." Jenny blushed. "Anyone would be."

"But you're particularly worried about my son."

"Only because I know him a little better than the others."

"I see." Mrs. Buckwalter started to smile. "You know, I've never known my son to kiss a woman on the cheek before."

Jenny grimaced. She didn't need a reminder. If she ever had any illusions of being irresistible, that kiss certainly dampened them. It wasn't a passionate kiss. A Boy Scout could have done better kissing his grandmother. "I think he's just trying to be democratic. Being a regular Joe."

Mrs. Buckwalter looked up questioningly.

"I mean Bob. He wanted me to call him Bob. I think he's trying to be one with the people or something. And he focused on me because I'm—" she straightened her shoulders "—because I'm of the class that works for a living."

"Well, there's nothing wrong with working, dear. I haven't raised Robert to be a snob."

"No, but I can't imagine he has many friends who scrub vegetables for a living. I mean, sure he knows people who work, but they're probably stockbrokers or lawyers or something classy."

"My dear, you're a very classy chef. I dare anyone to make a crème brûlée that surpasses yours," Mrs. Buckwalter said indignantly. "But I don't think it's that at all. I'm beginning to think it's something quite different. He did ask me if I'd brought the family album with me. I was thinking it was because my anniversary would have been next week if my husband had lived. Robert knew I'd have it with me for that day."

"Oh, I'm sorry."

Mrs. Buckwalter smiled wistfully. "My husband's been gone a long time now but the album brings it all back to me. All three generations of Buckwalters are in the album—my husband and I especially. There are pictures right up to the final anniversary we celebrated seven years ago. My husband just kept adding pages to the thing. The Buckwalter men have a knack for knowing right away the women they want to marry. My husband has a picture of the first time we met—at a charity auction back in 1955. We were both there with other people, but he managed a picture anyway. We were saving something at the time. A local park, I think. Long before it was fashionable to save anything. There we were. It's a picture I treasure."

"What a lovely way to remember the past." Jenny saw the soft light in Mrs. Buckwalter's eyes and envied the woman. The older woman didn't talk often about her late husband, but Jenny had wondered before if she thought of him. She frequently had that same half smile on her face when she seemed lost in thought.

"They're coming back!" one of the teenage girls yelled from the hayloft. Several of the girls had climbed the steps up to the loft so they could watch the road from the small window there. "I see lights coming this way! And a horse!"

"Thank God," Mrs. Buckwalter said, all memories gone from her face. She turned to Jenny. "Can I help with the coffee, dear? Or anything else? My experience with crises is that they always make people hungry and thirsty."

Jenny laughed. "I've got plenty of coffee. And there's enough of that cake left for another round."

Mrs. Buckwalter was right. The ranch hands were the first ones through the door, their boisterous good humor relieving the last of the fears of the women inside.

"We got them. Everyone's back safe," one stocky

man stopped to announce on his way to the refreshment table. "But it's colder than blazes out there. Hope there's some coffee left."

Jenny started pouring coffee into the thick porcelain mugs that had been brought over from the restaurant. Thankfully the restaurant had been well stocked with dishes when the young engaged couple decided to reopen it this past Christmas. Linda and Duane, the couple, had volunteered the use of all the dishes for tonight's party and Jenny believed they would use every single one of them. There would be an enormous number of dishes to wash at some point and, as far as she could tell, there wasn't an automatic dishwasher anywhere around.

The barn door was opened and a damp cold filled the dance floor. Not that anyone was thinking about dancing. The music had stopped when the men left earlier and only the sound of muffled talking was heard now.

"The guy on the horse is bringing in the kidnappers," one short rancher offered to Jenny as he held his cup out to be filled. "He had some fancy moves, I don't mind telling you."

"The FBI agent?" Jenny was trying not to watch the door as it kept opening, but she couldn't help but notice that Robert wasn't back yet.

"Don't know what he is." The rancher picked up a

stuffed mushroom as he held his cup in the other hand. "Didn't say nothing about who he was. Buckwalter seemed to know him, though. They made a fine team."

The rancher put the mushroom in his mouth.

"Glad it all worked out." Jenny wondered if they'd need more paper napkins.

The rancher didn't seem inclined to leave the refreshment table. He picked up a carved carrot piece and eyed Jenny shyly. "That fella Buckwalter—noticed you dancing with him. Are you—you know—"

Jenny looked up from the napkins.

"—you know, involved?"

"Mr. Buckwalter and me?"

The rancher beamed. "Guess not if you still call him Mister. I figured you weren't—what with all his money and everything. But wanted to be sure. Never held with moving in on another man's territory, not even when anyone could see the two of you are from different worlds. Guess you're free then."

Jenny started to protest, but the man didn't stop to draw a breath.

"My name's Chester, by the way. The boys call me Harry on account of Chest. You know, Chest, Hairy—"

"I'm sorry, but—"

"Not that there's any problem. With my chest, I mean. I got just the right amount of hair. You got nothing to worry about with me. I got me n-o-o defects. Just a regular kind of guy. That's me."

"I'm sure you're a fine man," Jenny moved a platter of toast squares to the back of the table. She'd take those over to the kitchen and make some new ones. She looked up at Chester. "But I'm too busy right now to visit."

"Maybe later?"

"There'll be cleanup later. Dishes."

The rancher looked dismayed. "I suppose I could help, even though with the touch of arthritis I get in my joints—well, I'm likely to be more trouble than good to you."

Jenny looked up and smiled. "I'll do fine with the dishes. Thanks anyway."

The barn door opened this time to a loud grumbling noise. A steady stream of frigid air blew into the barn making the pink streamers hanging from the beams start to sway.

The temperature in the room dropped ten degrees, but no one complained about the cold. Everyone was looking at the three unkempt men who reluctantly stomped into the barn, swearing as they were forced by their captors to come inside.

Jenny recognized two of the three men who were holding the shoulders of the prisoners. Garth Elkton was one. His top ranch hand was another. The third man, a stranger who obviously hadn't been to the dance because he wasn't in a suit, seemed to be in charge.

Jenny looked past all those men and saw nothing but the snow falling in the black night outside. The teenage boys had come inside minutes ago. The ranch hands all seemed to be back. Men and women were giving each other quick hugs of relief. A dusting of snow had settled on the walkway outside the barn and it was covered with a score or more of large boot prints. There were no other figures standing in the doorway waiting to come inside.

"That Buckwalter fella must be still parking the bus—if that's who you're looking for," the rancher who had stood at the table offered quietly. "He was the only one who knew how to drive the bus after the kids stripped the gears. Guess it's on account of him flying planes. We would have had to walk back if it weren't for him. He nursed the bus all the way back. He's not a bad guy for a rich man."

Then a final man appeared in the doorway and Jenny relaxed. Robert. I mean, she corrected herself, Mr. Buckwalter, was back safe. "No, he's not a bad guy."

"I wish you luck with him," the rancher offered quietly.

"Oh, no, I'm not—I mean there's no need—"

Just then Jenny heard the cell phone ring. The ring

was faint and hard to hear over the talking of the ranchers and teenagers. She remembered Mrs. Buckwalter making a call so she assumed the older woman still had the phone and she was right.

"This is for you," Mrs. Buckwalter shouted to Jenny as she moved through the couples who were now brushing snow off of each other. The older woman was weaving between couples and getting closer to the refreshment table but she continued to yell, "Something about a pudding order that's late—"

Jenny winced. She was a full ten yards away from Robert. But she could hear his low chuckle over the murmured conversation of everyone else.

"Tell your sister hi," Robert called over to her. "And tell her I want a case of chocolate pudding with sprinkles if they have such a thing."

"Your sister sells pudding, dear?" Mrs. Buckwalter asked as she handed the phone to Jenny.

"She will be if she's not careful," Jenny said as she took the phone and stepped behind the refreshment table where it was quieter.

"I heard that," Jenny's sister said when Jenny put the phone to her ear. "And rest assured, I won't need to be looking for a new job. My boss is very happy with what I've discovered."

"And what would that be?" Jenny kept her voice low

so that no one else could hear. Six or seven of the teen-agers had drifted over to the refreshment table and were staring down at the punch bowl trying to decide whether or not to scoop some of the watered-down beverage into their plastic cups.

"Well, for starters, I know where Robert Buckwalter the Third is."

"Any number of people know that. It's not a secret."

"Well, none of the other tabloids know where he is these days. And I know something's up. I told my boss that the man was very touchy about talking to the press."

"He thought you were a pudding salesman, for Pete's sake. It had nothing to do with the press."

"Still, I think he's hiding something. Some secret."

"Well, if he is, it's his to keep. I, for one, am not going to ask him another thing about his life."

"Oh, you've been talking to him?"

"No, I haven't been talking to him."

"Oh." The disappointment in the voice of Jenny's sister was more personal than professional. She was suddenly Jenny's little sister again. "I'm sorry. I thought maybe after that kiss…"

Jenny couldn't help herself. She darted a quick look over her shoulder to be sure that no one was close enough to hear. "Well, he did ask me to dance."

"You danced with him!" Jenny's sister shrieked.

"You danced with Robert Buckwalter the Third! Wait until I tell Mom! You really danced with him."

"It was a short dance," Jenny was forced to admit. "The kidnapping sort of got everyone distracted."

"Kidnapping! Somebody kidnapped him! Why didn't you say so! Now that's a newsbreak."

"No, no, not Robert. It was someone else. He didn't have anything to do with it. It's all tied up with some rustling that's going on."

"Oh." Jenny's sister paused. "Rustling? You mean for cows? You're sure the kidnappers weren't really out for him and they just grabbed the wrong person or something. I mean if you were going to kidnap anyone, he'd be the one to pick. He's got more money than the president of the United States. He certainly has more money than some cow."

"Yes, I'm sure. He wasn't the target."

Jenny sensed someone standing slightly behind her before she heard the man clear his throat. She looked up.

"Make sure she knows I didn't even know the kidnap victims," Robert said firmly. Snowflakes were melting on his hair and he still looked as if he'd stepped out of the pages of a catalog. "Make sure she knows the kidnapping had nothing to do with me. It would have happened if I hadn't been here."

"That's what I told her I said you wouldn't have

even gone with the men if it hadn't been for the bus. I mean your mother rented it and all."

"Well, I don't know about that." Robert frowned. How is it that he had never noticed Jenny's eyes turned a snapping black when she was annoyed? Fascinating. He wondered if she was annoyed with her sister or with him. Maybe she thought he should have ridden to the rescue on a horse like the FBI agent instead of worrying about a big old bus. He guessed a bus wasn't very dashing. If that was it, he needed to explain. "I would like to think I would go to anyone's aid if they were being kidnapped. It wasn't just the bus."

"What's this about some bus?" Jenny's sister asked on the phone. "Was it a school bus? Were there kids in danger? That would make a good angle."

"There is no angle. Robert—I mean, Mr. Buckwalter—was just driving."

Robert frowned deeper. He wasn't sure he liked the turn this conversation was taking. Granted, he didn't want his life splattered all over some tabloid in the morning, but he didn't know that he cared to have Jenny dismiss his efforts so lightly.

"It wasn't just easy driving," Robert finally said. "The gears had been stripped. I had to get everyone back here. It was cold enough out there to freeze to death if we didn't get back."

There, that should let her know his actions were important, he thought.

"What's that?" Jenny's sister spoke forcefully in Jenny's ear. "Put the receiver out more. I need to hear. I got the part about the kids in the school bus almost freezing to death. This is great. My boss will love this story."

"There is no story," Jenny said firmly.

"But what about the children?"

"There are no children."

"Well, then, what was the school bus doing? Work with me here, Jenny. It's not like this won't hit the local papers anyway. School bus kind of stuff always does. This is practically real news."

"Listen, to me—there are no children. There was no school bus."

"Well, then, give me a little something. Right this minute—what is Robert Buckwalter the Third doing?"

"He's just—" Jenny looked up at Robert. The snow had melted and his hair was wet now. His cheeks were still red and his nose was white. His hands shivered slightly as he held a cup of coffee in them. "He's just warming up."

"Ohhh, that's a good quote. Can I use that? Sources close to the man said that he is warming up and looking to be hot again."

"Absolutely not!"

"Well, then, can I talk to him? Ask him if I can do an interview."

"I'm sure he doesn't—"

"Just ask him. Please."

"Oh, all right." Jenny began as she put her hand over the receiver so her sister could not hear the conversation. "I know you won't want to—that's why I only said I'd ask. Not that you'd agree."

Robert watched the blush creep up Jenny's face again. Her eyes had lightened again until he could see the caramel highlights in them.

"I'll do it," Robert said.

"But I haven't asked—"

"Oh."

"Not that you might not want to anyway. You might be able to sway the decision on the bachelor list and if that's what you want—"

"Did she give any hint of that?" Robert's face came to attention. "That she'd be willing to speak to the editors and plead my case?"

Robert wasn't sure that Jenny's sister could do anything to get him off that list, but if she was anything like Jenny he didn't want to underestimate her.

"I'll let you ask." Jenny held out the phone. She was defeated. Why try and protect the privacy of Robert

Buckwalter when he obviously wanted people all across the country to read about him as they stood in line to buy groceries? She suddenly wished she had told her sister he was hot.

Robert took the phone from Jenny's hand.

A faint siren filtered into the barn and could be heard even over the commotion caused by the three kidnappers being tied up on the barn floor against their wishes.

"I want to negotiate," Robert said into the phone. "Agree to my terms and we'll talk."

Jenny looked up. "You have terms?"

Robert nodded emphatically to Jenny as he continued speaking into the phone. "That's right. I'll cooperate if you cooperate. And I assure you you'll get your story somehow." He listened and then grinned. "Yes, something with pictures. It might take me a day or two to work it out first. Talk to the editors. See what they say."

Jenny felt stiffer than she could remember feeling for years. Terms. He had terms. He was planning to sell his soul and become an underwear model.

Jenny almost missed the barn door opening once again. If it wasn't for the siren growing louder and then stopping, she wouldn't have paid much attention. But then she heard the booming voice of Sheriff Carl Wall.

"Where are they?" the sheriff demanded as he stomped into the room carrying two large suitcases.

"Careful with those." A platinum blonde stepped daintily behind him. "Those are alligator skin cases."

Jenny had never seen such a woman. Now there was somebody who could get away with modeling underwear. She was tall, thin and reeked of style. She was just a touch haughty and Jenny knew without a doubt that the hair color she wore was not her own.

The FBI agent seemed to share Jenny's suspicions that the woman was not one of the locals and he walked over to the woman. "I'll need to see some identification."

"Identification?" The woman stopped. She managed to look very offended. "I don't need any identification. I'm with him."

The woman pointed at Robert Buckwalter.

Jenny saw Robert flinch. He'd quietly pressed the off button on the cell phone, hanging up on her sister. That meant that whatever was going to be said now was something that Robert wanted to be kept from the press.

This is it, Jenny braced herself. That woman spells a secret if anyone does.

"Now, Laurel, you know that's not—"

The FBI agent appeared to have no patience. He looked at Robert. "She's with you?"

"I wouldn't say 'with'—I know Laurel, of course. Our families are, well… My mother knows her better—so, no, I wouldn't say 'with.'"

"It was 'with' enough for you on Christmas!" Laurel staged a pout that would have done justice to a Hollywood starlet.

Jenny nodded to herself. Of course.

"I didn't see you on Christmas!" Robert protested. It was colder than an Arctic winter inside this barn and he was starting to sweat. "I haven't seen you for months!"

"Well, maybe not this Christmas," Laurel agreed prettily. "You were a naughty boy and didn't come to my party. And here I'd counted on you."

Jenny started to breathe again. He hadn't seen her for months.

"I never said I would come," Robert said wearily.

He'd never said he would come. Jenny started to sing inside.

"Don't worry, I forgive you. I figure we have lots and lots of Christmases to spend together." Laurel stepped close and smiled at Robert confidently. "Laurel knows these things."

Jenny dropped the teaspoon she held in her hand. She wondered if Laurel did know these things. If the other woman did, she was ten steps ahead of Jenny who couldn't seem to figure out much about anything.

Chapter Six

"Bring those bags over here." Laurel looked behind her and spoke sharply to Sheriff Wall who was standing staring at Laurel. The sheriff looked down at his arms as though he'd forgotten they were attached to his shoulders let alone that they held two expensive bags.

Jenny looked around. The sheriff was not alone in his fascination with Laurel. The ranch hands had forgotten all about the hot coffee they'd been lining up to get. By the looks on their faces they no longer needed the coffee to warm them.

"I need my lipstick." Laurel pouted for the benefit of the men standing around. "My lips aren't used to weather like this." She shivered delicately. "Why, it's terrible out there."

Silence greeted her pronouncement.

"It is cold at that, ma'am," one of the ranch hands finally ventured to say.

Laurel smiled up at him. "You really should pick better weather for doing these cow things." She turned her head so her smile hit Robert. "What is it they called it—the rustle or something?"

"Rustling," Robert said dryly. "You're talking about the cattle rustling that has been going on around here. A hundred thousand dollars worth of loss so far. Interstate stuff. Enough to put some of these ranchers under. The FBI is working on the case now. It's serious here."

"Well, they need to plan it for a warmer time of year, don't you think?" She appealed to the sheriff who was bringing her bags to her. "Maybe you could talk to the people in charge of the rustling. Ask them to do it in the summer instead. We could have a lawn picnic then with umbrellas and iced tea."

"Yes, ma'am," Sheriff Wall replied automatically. He looked worried. "Where do you want me to set these bags?"

Laurel looked around, her eyes finally settling on the refreshment table.

Jenny winced. The refreshment table had looked better when the evening began. The teenagers had wrapped the legs in swirls of pink crepe paper and had twisted streamers from the table edge to the floor all along the front of the table. But those streamers were gone now, leaving stubby pieces of tape behind. And the lace tablecloth borrowed from Mrs. Hargrove had a half-dozen brown circles where some coffee cup had spilled. The punch bowl still stood in the center, even though only an inch or two of liquid remained in its bottom.

"I can't put my bags there," Laurel appealed to Robert. "They're genuine alligator. They'll get wet with that stuff." She pointed to the punch bowl.

"If they're alligator, I expect they'll be fine if they get wet." Robert shook his head. He added in disgust, "The skin's been wet before when it was on the alligator. I can't believe you'd buy alligator skin luggage anyway. Aren't they some kind of endangered group or something?"

The other men were more forgiving and more eager to please. One of the ranch hands took off his vest and laid it over the tablecloth. "Here. I think your bags are beautiful. And don't worry. You can put your bags on this. Won't hurt my old vest any."

"Why, aren't you kind?" Laurel gushed at the man and then looked over at the sheriff. "You can put them there."

The sheriff set the bags on top of the vest and then ducked his head, mumbling something about getting back to the kidnappers.

"Kidnappers?" Laurel looked up with the first

genuine expression that Jenny had seen on the woman's face yet. Laurel's smile was gone and she looked twenty percent smarter. "I thought you said they were cattle rustlers."

"Well, they're also kidnappers," the sheriff said somewhat sourly.

"Oh, dear, I knew I shouldn't have come here to this end-of-the-world place where there aren't even police to protect me from the criminals that run loose."

"I'm the law around here." The sheriff stomped a little louder than he needed to on his way over to the tangle of kidnappers that were waiting for him on the floor. "I protect all the citizens of Dry Creek." He smiled up at Laurel. "And the visitors, too, of course. I take good care of visitors."

"But there's only one of you." Laurel looked aghast just thinking about it. "The Seattle police force must have thousands of people working. And they're trained. Police academy and all that."

"I've got my GED. I know it's not the same as a high school diploma, but I know the same information. And I read those police magazines every month. And not just the free ones they send. Sometimes I buy the ones off the shelves at that big drugstore in Billings. Just don't go listening to anyone spouting off about that hit man that came here after Miss Glory. There was no way I could have known he'd dress up like Santa Claus and come to the church pageant just like he belonged—"

"Hit man! You had a hit man, too. Right here in Dry Creek!" Laurel fanned her cheeks with one hand. "A girl like me just isn't safe."

"No one can get into Dry Creek that easily," Robert said, trying to stem her rising hysteria. When he said it, he looked at Laurel more closely. It was true. Dry Creek wasn't the easiest place to get to in the middle of a February blizzard. What had prompted Laurel to come?

"I'm sure we're all safe," Jenny added. She was standing behind the refreshment table still pouring coffee. The line of men wanting a cup was finally moving forward. The heat from the coffee urn had added a moist flush to Jenny's face and she was beginning to wish she had her hairnet back so that her hair would stay in place.

Laurel turned to Jenny and scrutinized her briefly before dismissing her. "Well, I'm sure you're perfectly safe, dear. But rich people have extra perils and anyone can see I have money."

"What anyone can see," Robert interrupted icily, "is that you don't have the manners you were born with. Look around you. Money isn't the measure of a person. Some of these people will never have an extra dime and they're still better people than you or I will ever be with our silver spoons and our trust funds."

One of two of the ranch hands looked at Robert in appreciation.

"Say what you want." Laurel stepped over and snapped open one of her small alligator suitcases. "But I've never heard of anyone pulling a gun on someone else because they wanted to steal from a better kind of person. They're after people with money and that's it."

Laurel lifted the lid on her suitcase and a wave of perfume hit the air.

The man holding his coffee cup out to Jenny strained to see over her shoulder so Jenny turned to see what the attraction was. There she saw it. Row after folded row of satin and silk lingerie. Some trimmed with lace. Some appliquéd. Slips. Nighties. In peach. Ivory. Lavender. White.

"And you're worried about the kids becoming underwear salesmen," Robert said quietly as he moved closer to Jenny. "I'd say she's set up for a sales tour of all fifty states."

The amused tone in Robert's voice cheered Jenny up considerably. He might be rich. But he surely could still see through a woman like Laurel.

"Didn't you pack any real clothes?" Robert finally asked. "You certainly can't survive a blizzard with that kind of stuff. You need long johns and sweaters with maybe some sweatpants and wool scarves."

"Oh, I had two other boxes of clothes, but they got lost in the airport baggage system somewhere. I expect they're at the Billings airport by now. Anyway, they're going to send them out when they can," Laurel answered cheerfully. "Not that they have any of those blizzard clothes in them. I brought some special-occasion clothes instead."

Laurel looked at Robert with a glance he could only call sweetly possessive. It made him nervous. He'd known Laurel for years. They'd actually gone to school together, so he was better prepared for her games than most. He knew the sweetness was an act. He just didn't know why she was playing up to him. "There are no special occasions planned here."

"We'll see." Laurel smiled smugly.

Laurel shut the lid on her suitcase and swung around a little designer purse. "You know, I think the lipstick is still in my purse. Silly me. I didn't need to rummage around in that suitcase after all."

Laurel pulled a long gold lipstick tube out of her purse along with a small mirror. She looked over at the men. "I don't suppose one of you would hold this mirror up for me, would you? I just don't feel right unless my lipstick is fresh."

The request almost caused a fight among the ranch hands until Laurel turned and asked. "Robert, would you help me?"

Robert grimaced. Yes, this was Laurel at her best. What could he do? If he didn't hold the mirror, a half dozen of those ranch hands would go home tonight with black eyes. And the punch bowl might get broken. He happened to know the bowl was a favorite of Mrs. Hargrove's.

"Why don't you prop the mirror up on that ledge over there?" Robert pointed. The barn, even though it was now a community center, had been built for working cattle and still showed the marks. "See, you can see where the stall used to be?"

Laurel gasped. "You expect me to use the remains of a cow stall!"

"Well, there hasn't been a cow along that wall in ten years. I don't see the harm."

Laurel tried to contain her annoyance, but it showed. Her normally pink cheeks got a little redder. Her baby blue eyes narrowed. Her chin jutted out in a stubborn angle. Then she took a deep breath and smiled sweetly back at Robert. "You're right, you know."

Laurel turned to walk over to the ledge and Robert watched her. She was definitely up to something.

"Anyone else want coffee?" Jenny asked the men

standing around the table. They were blocking the way for the other people who wanted something to drink by standing there and watching the blonde.

"I'll take another cup," one ranch hand said with a sigh. "She's way out of my league anyway."

"Well, of course she is, Kingman," another ranch hand responded as he got back in line, too. "She's way too pretty for any of us. But we can still look. She's like a picture in one of those fancy magazines."

"Yes, she is," Jenny agreed. She knew how the ranch hands felt. Sometimes you couldn't help being drawn to someone even though you knew you didn't have a chance in a million of anything happening.

"She shouldn't have come here," Robert said as he looked over the people of Dry Creek. Some ranch hands were still drooling over Laurel as she dramatically rubbed her lipstick on repeatedly. He'd lay odds there'd be some sharp words exchanged among those boys before the night was over. The teenage boys weren't far behind the ranch hands and the girls were looking like they were ready to mutiny. Even the married farm couples looked uneasy. "Laurel doesn't belong in a place like this."

Jenny lifted her chin. She'd emptied the coffeepot and the line had ended. "There's nothing wrong with this place."

"I didn't mean——" Robert was brought back sharply. "Of course, there's nothing wrong with this place. It's a great place full of great people."

"Just because it used to be a cow barn doesn't mean it's any less of a place," Jenny continued like he hadn't even spoken. "It's a place filled with friendship and good people—well except for them maybe." She nodded her chin at the kidnappers who were now neatly tied at one side of the barn. "And who knows—even they might not be so very bad when all is said and done."

"I agree." Robert moved closer to stand beside Jenny. He didn't know how to say what he was thinking. "I like the people here. I like that this used to be a cow barn."

"It's because you're slumming, isn't it?" Jenny said quietly. The punch bowl was now empty so she pulled the ladle out. "Getting a dose of real life before you settle down in some mansion somewhere with a perfect wife and perfect kids."

"That's not it at all."

Jenny had a sudden fierce wish to have her hairnet back. She knew now why she was always so insistent on wearing it even in food situations where the health code didn't require one. It reminded her of who she was in the situation. She was the chef. She knew her place. She wasn't a guest.

"Excuse me." Jenny forced a smile. "I better start cleaning up or I'll be here all night."

"Well, you're not going to clean up alone," Robert protested. "Tell me what to do and where to start."

"You can't help—not in that tuxedo. You'll ruin it."

"I don't care about the tuxedo."

"It's wasteful to ruin a ten-thousand dollar suit doing dishes." Jenny felt her jaw set. If she needed any reminding about the difference between herself and Robert Buckwalter, this was certainly it. He could ruin an Italian tuxedo just because he wanted to do something else at that point in time.

Robert looked down at the suit. It probably had cost over ten thousand dollars. But who needed a suit like this, for goodness' sake? He'd just never given any thought before to how much he spent on clothes.

"Even taking in the punch bowl won't work. It's sticky with sugar and almost impossible to carry without holding it against yourself," Jenny said as she reached for the bowl herself. "What you could do is gather up the coffee cups while I take the bowl to the café and rinse it out."

"You can't go outside alone."

"Why not? The kidnappers are caught."

"These guys are caught. There could be more out there."

Jenny looked up. Someone had put another slow song on the record player. But no one was dancing. She could tell that the party was winding down. "I think with all these people here they would have spotted a stranger."

"They didn't spot Santa Claus when he was the hit man and almost got that woman—the one they called Dry Creek's angel," he protested. "Besides, I'd prefer to come with you."

Jenny shrugged as she put on a jacket Mrs. Hargrove had lent her for the evening. "It's just across the parking lot."

"You need someone to open the doors anyway."

Robert followed Jenny to the barn door. The sheriff and some of the other men were squatted down on the floor in one corner talking to the kidnappers.

"Think they're the last of the lot?" Robert asked the men as he stood by the door.

The sheriff nodded. The man looked a lot more competent dealing with the kidnappers than when handling Laurel and her luggage. "I'm sure we're safe for now anyway. He—" the sheriff jerked his head at the FBI agent "—thinks someone in Dry Creek is an inside informant on this rustling business, but even if that's true we should be safe tonight."

Robert nodded his thanks as he opened the door for Jenny.

The stars were no longer showing in the night sky and flakes of snow steadily blew in from the north. The men had stomped down much of the snow earlier but the boot prints were filling with the latest batch of snow.

"I doubt half these cars will start," Robert said as he looked at the twenty-some odd vehicles parked around the barn.

Robert had never felt cold like this before. He'd given his coat to the old man earlier and had insisted the man keep it. Now he was glad one of the ranch hands had pressed a wool jacket into his hands as Robert was heading out. Even with the jacket, his heart pounded faster to keep warm. He'd swear his eyelids were freezing.

"They've got jumper cables," Jenny said through chattering teeth.

A dim light was on in the café's porch and Robert opened the porch door quickly. Even though the porch was boarded together and the wind blew in through some of the holes, it was several degrees warmer inside.

"Let me get the door," Robert said as he reached for the main door. "Do you have a key?"

"It's not locked. They left it open for us tonight."

"Then you better let me check it out first. Someone could have come inside."

In the yellow light of the porch, Jenny could see her

breath come out in white puffs. Her lips were stiff from the cold and she felt snowflakes melting in her hair.

"But what would you do anyway if someone was in there? You don't have a weapon."

"Well, neither one of us has a weapon."

"I have this bowl."

"You wouldn't dare break Mrs. Hargrove's bowl over someone's head. From what I hear, that bowl has served the punch for every wedding in this community for the past forty years. It's practically a tradition all by itself."

"It is a nice bowl. Heavier than it looks, too. Real cut glass."

Robert had bent low and was looking in the glass panes of the café door. It looked like the only upright shadows inside were from chairs although it was hard to tell because the girls had used the café as a changing room and there were T-shirts and jeans everywhere. "I'm going in. Give it a minute and then follow."

The doorknob was as cold as any metal Robert had ever gripped. But it turned easily and he stepped into the café. The air inside still smelled of cooking. He thought it was the stuffed mushrooms he smelled.

Robert flipped on the overhead light for the café and saw that the jumble looked undisturbed from the last time he had walked through. "Let me check out the kitchen first before you come in."

Without waiting for an answer, Robert walked toward the back of the room where the kitchen door was. The café was small so he reached the other side with a few strides. The light in the kitchen revealed all was safe there, as well.

Robert heard the cell phone ring on the porch. It must still be in Jenny's apron pocket. He'd bet a punch bowl full of pudding that it was Jenny's sister calling. Which reminded him, he owed her a story. Assuming, of course, that she was able to get him off that cursed list.

"For you," Jenny called as she walked across the café and into the kitchen. "It's my sister."

Jenny listened as Robert and her sister talked. Robert paced as he walked. Up and down the cold kitchen. His cheeks were red from the temperature and his dark hair was wet where snow had melted now that he was in the relative warmth of the kitchen. He looked excited though, wheeling and dealing with her sister. He said goodbye with laughter.

"Your sister is something," Robert reported as he hung up the phone. "Those editors will have their hands full with her."

"She is, isn't she?"

The outside door to the café opened and Jenny and Robert both stiffened until they heard Mrs. Hargrove. "I hope you're not doing dishes at this time of night."

The kitchen door opened and the older woman stood there with a wool scarf wrapped around her head and a blanket thrown over her shoulders like a shawl. "We've had so much excitement tonight, the dishes need to wait. Tomorrow's Saturday. Enough snow is predicted to close all the roads. We'll have nothing better to do than dishes. I've already asked Mr. Gossett to help us. It'll help settle him down. He's been anxious lately."

"But if the roads are closed, we won't be able to get to the café from Garth's ranch," Jenny said. "And I can't leave the two of you with all these dishes."

"I've got extra rooms at my house. You're both welcome to spend the night at my place."

"Robert doesn't need to," Jenny began in alarm. A man like him shouldn't be helping with cleanup.

"I'd be delighted." Robert accepted the older woman's invitation.

Robert grinned. Things were working out better than he could have hoped. He'd have some talking time with Jenny tonight and tomorrow.

"I already invited your friend—" Mrs. Hargrove smiled at Robert.

Robert's grin froze.

"—or fiancée, I guess I should say. Considering that she brought a wedding dress with her to Dry Creek."

"She brought a what!"

Chapter Seven

"Now, Laurel, you take the room at the top of the stairs and to your left. That's next to mine. Robert, you'll have the couch in the living room. And Jenny, the room down that hall has a bed in it already made up. That room is closest to the furnace and should be toasty." Mrs. Hargrove smiled at Jenny. "It's my sewing room and the bed in there is my best. You'll need a good night's sleep after all you've done today, dear. Such a wonderful dinner party."

"Thank you," Jenny whispered. She could have slept under a cardboard box in some old alley. A sewing room would be heaven. She was damp, cold and tired. She just wanted the day to end. She didn't know whether or not she believed Robert's vehement protests that he wasn't engaged to be married to anyone, but she did know she was ready to be alone. She'd been right not to trust a rich man with any tiny bit of her heart.

The walk across the snow to Mrs. Hargrove's house hadn't been long, but Jenny felt like it had taken an eternity. She didn't have snow boots so she had to follow in the footsteps Mrs. Hargrove made. But it wasn't just the snow that seeped into her shoes that made her cold and tired.

It was all of *this*. She glared at Robert. She just wasn't cut out for this—the kind of roller-coaster life that people like Robert and Laurel seemed to lead. Jenny was a simple person and liked to deal with people who were straightforward—people you could trust to be who they said they were. Not something like this.

Who really knew who was engaged to who? It was like the dating game with extra doors for people to pop in and out of whenever they took a fancy to do so.

The bottom line was that Laurel said she had a wedding dress sitting in a box at the Billings airport. That was part of the special-occasion clothes she'd talked about earlier. The sheriff hadn't had room to bring the box to Dry Creek in his patrol car. But there it was—waiting in Billings.

No woman traveled around with a wedding dress unless she had a reason. And if Robert Buckwalter III was getting a visit from a woman who was so sure of herself that she brought a wedding dress along, why was he kissing another woman? Especially when the kiss was a whopper of a kiss like the one Jenny had gotten from him.

Not that any kiss meant anything to a man like Robert, Jenny took a deep breath and reminded herself. She knew the rich kissed everyone, from their hairdressers to their dog trainers. A kiss from a rich man meant nothing. Absolutely nothing. A handshake was probably more sincere.

Robert watched Jenny walk down the hall. Her back was military straight. He knew she hadn't believed him about Laurel even though he'd said everything he could to convince her he wasn't secretly engaged to Laurel or anyone else. He certainly didn't know anything about a wedding dress!

To make it worse, Jenny wouldn't come right out and say she didn't believe him. She just kept repeating that it was none of her business and it didn't matter whom he married or what kind of a dress the woman wore.

Robert knew there was a world of difference between "I believe you" and "it doesn't matter." Especially when Jenny had pulled that hairnet of hers back on like it was armor.

"You run along, dear." Mrs. Hargrove smiled at

Laurel who had allowed herself to be coaxed into accepting Mrs. Hargrove's invitation when it was apparent there was no hotel around. "I want Robert to help me bring in some wood before we all bed down. We won't be long."

Laurel could have helped Robert out of his dilemma, but she wouldn't. She kept a bored smile on her face that revealed little.

Once Laurel made her bombshell announcement she apparently felt free to ignore him. Which would have been a dead giveaway about the true nature of their acquaintance if it wasn't for the pouty face that Laurel put on for the show. She looked enough like a woman who'd been wronged to turn others to her defense.

Robert sighed. His protests fell on skeptical ears. The truth was he hadn't even been around Laurel for months. They had moved in the same social circle for years, but he had long ago made it a policy to spend as little time alone with her as possible.

Even though the cold outside had iced every inch of tree and shrub, Robert was glad to be able to go out of the house and gather wood for the fire.

Mrs. Hargrove had a stack of logs neatly arranged in a small shed on the south side of her house. Robert had offered to get the logs by himself, but Mrs. Hargrove had politely insisted on coming with him.

He found out why when he had his arms half-full of frozen pine logs.

"I run a godly household," the older woman said. She had a plaid wool scarf wrapped around her chin, but her words still came out clear. "It's late so I'll come to the point—everyone sleeps in their own bed."

"Of course."

The woman nodded in satisfaction. "Just wanted to be sure we understood each other. I don't know who you're engaged to—"

"I'm not engaged to anyone."

Mrs. Hargrove pinned him with her eyes. "You've got one woman who says you are. Why would she be saying that if it's not true?"

"I don't know for sure." Robert added another log to the stack in his arms. "But my guess would be that she's trying to get her name in the paper."

Robert had been asking himself that same question for the past half hour and the only reason he could think of was that Laurel had somehow found out about the bachelor list.

He'd suspected before that Laurel funneled information about him to the tabloids. That was one of the reasons he'd started avoiding her. But she could still get information about him from other people in their social set and pass it along. If that was what she was doing, it would appear that the communication flowed in both directions.

Someone must have told Laurel he was a candidate for the big slot on the tabloid's list. Laurel loved the spotlight. She'd see it as quite a triumph to announce her engagement to the number one bachelor in the U.S. at the same time, or shortly after he was named the most eligible bachelor around. The fact that Robert would deny the engagement the next day wouldn't matter. Her picture would already be in every tabloid from here to Japan before Robert could get it all sorted out. Laurel would soak up the publicity. She might even get a book deal out of it.

Mrs. Hargrove looked perplexed. "She'd get engaged just to get her name in the paper? They put the names of the bridal couples in the *Billings Gazette*, too, but I've never heard of anyone getting married just to see their name there."

"It wouldn't be the *Billings Gazette*." Robert wished that that's all his marriage would ever mean to the media—just a nice paragraph in the Newly Married column of the local paper. "I'm trying to get out of it, but some New York paper has got me picked for number one in some one hundred best bachelor list they're doing. When the list hits the newsstands, it will be all across the country. There'll be pictures. My credit rating will rise. Companies will call me to be their spokesman. I'll be offered free cruises—free everything."

"Free cruises! My goodness! Well, congratulations!" Mrs. Hargrove beamed briefly until she looked at his face. She continued more carefully. "That's quite an honor to be number one. And a free cruise—I can't imagine—I've never even been to Seattle. And a cruise! I think that's exciting—to actually be on the ocean. But you don't look very happy about it. I can't imagine why you want out of the list if it has a free cruise with it."

"It's not just any free cruise. It's more like a free cruise on the *Titanic*."

"Well, still, being number one—that's got to be some kind of an accomplishment to take pride in."

Robert snorted. "Being number one is like being tagged Public Property Number One. You're nothing but an object for the curious. Men hate you. Women hunt you. Literally. They won't let you go. They want to know everything from your shoe size to the kind of grades you got in junior high school. It's like they want to be your best friend without even meeting you. And most of them don't want to meet you. The kind of crowd we're talking about here just wants to be seen with you."

Mrs. Hargrove was silent for a moment. "Let me

make you a cup of tea and we'll sit and talk if you'd like. Seems to me you've got yourself in quite a fix."

Robert looked up. "I'd like the tea, but I don't mean to worry anyone. I've been listed before. Not this big, but if I can't get out of it I'll still survive."

"Oh, it's not just the list. You can deal with that. It's the rest of your life I'm worried about. You need to know what kind of a life that will be. You haven't begun to understand the important questions in life." The older woman picked up a couple of logs of her own. "Even with the cruises and everything, I'm sure being a rich man can't be easy."

Robert snorted again. "Being rich is the least of my worries."

"That's good, because I don't know anything about being rich. I'm doing good just to understand the troubles of a poor person." Mrs. Hargrove stepped up the snow-packed stairs to her front door. She looked down at Robert who stood on the walk below her. "But I do know this—and I know it because I've got the best instruction book for life ever put down on paper—being rich can be dangerous to the soul. The rich need to be pitied sometimes. They used to say a rich man had a harder time getting into heaven than a camel had going through the eye of a needle."

Robert was startled. No one had ever pitied him. Ever. Especially not for having money.

Mrs. Hargrove turned the knob on her door and opened it. "Always did think it was strange to compare a rich man to a camel. I saw a camel on one of those nature shows on television once. It was an ugly beast."

"And they spit," Robert added as he stepped behind her into the house. He wasn't sure how he felt about being pitied. For starters, it made him cranky. And being compared to a camel? "Smelly, stubborn animals with the personality of a cardboard box. The only reason anyone tolerates them is because they store all the water inside those humps of theirs and people need them to get around."

Just like me, Robert realized with a start. *I store a great deal of money and people need me and my money to get around.*

Robert was back at the same place he had been earlier in the evening when he was talking to the minister. He knew people tolerated him—well, more than tolerated, they usually fawned all over him—because he could write big checks to support their favorite projects. Presto—be nice to Robert and he could make things happen. All kinds of things. Important things. Even silly things.

Right now, if he wanted, he could fly in a team of

real camels to meet Mrs. Hargrove. He could even pay the best Hollywood stylists to come and give them such glamorous makeovers that Mrs. Hargrove would change her mind about their camel looks.

All it took was money.

And he had money. A depressing amount of cold hard cash.

But, Robert admitted finally, in the end it was only money, And money was a poor lover of the heart.

The trouble with money was that it clouded the issue. Everyone loved him when he had money. But who would still love him if he were poor and ugly as a desert camel? There was his mother, of course. But his circle of friends dwindled dramatically at the thought of poverty. Robert had too many friends like Laurel. Lightweight friends at best.

He had made more true friends in his five months as Bob than he had made in a lifetime as Robert.

Maybe—the thought came in a whisper—maybe because Robert had always relied on his money to make him his friends.

Robert, he was afraid, was a lazy friend.

Oh, Robert was good at attracting women and he was good at writing checks to charity, but was he good at loving anyone?

Robert didn't want to admit it, but he was suddenly

unsure. He didn't even have a pet. No one depended on him and he let no one down. That rooster Charlie was the closest thing he'd ever had to a dependent—and Charlie didn't rely on Robert for anything more than the rooster's handful of morning grain.

"Of course, you might think you already know everything there is to know about life and love," Mrs. Hargrove said softly. "A lot of young people do, you know."

"I can't speak for other people," Robert said. "But when it comes to me, I don't know any more about love than a desert camel knows about swimming the English Channel. I'd be grateful if you'd help me learn a thing or two about it before I drown in my own misery."

Mrs. Hargrove started to unwind her wool scarf. "That's the spirit. Let's get ready. We've got work to do."

The morning crept up on Robert as he lay on the living room couch. Teacups sat in the kitchen sink. He had dozed throughout the night without going to sleep deeply. Mrs. Hargrove had given him one of the Bibles she gave to the kids in her Sunday school class. The book, just the New Testament and some of the Psalms, had a picture of Jesus on the cover, with his arm stretched out to children. Some blue sea was in the background and the children all had perfect teeth.

Robert had read snatches of the book throughout the

night. The words were simple enough so that a child could understand. By morning, Robert's mind was reeling from the freshness of his encounter.

Robert had gone to church services a few times in his life before, but this—this reading was intimate and disturbing. He knew in his bones that God was there with him. It was eerie and comforting all at the same time.

Still, he'd rather God had some flesh on Him. It would be easier to talk to Him face-to-face. And then maybe not, Robert thought. He wasn't ready for God to look him in the eye.

Robert's first thought was how unprepared he was. Mrs. Hargrove was right. He, Robert, didn't have a clue about how to love anyone, including God. However, if he learned one thing by reading the New Testament, it was that God helped those who came to Him and asked for help in learning to love both other people and Himself.

He also learned that there was no time like right now to begin.

Robert decided he'd practice by loving those around him. He'd start with Mrs. Hargrove.

"It's for a cruise," Robert announced when Mrs. Hargrove came downstairs and looked at the check he'd placed on the coffee table. "I'd thought about buying an ocean liner, but I knew you'd rather just go with other people. Maybe that man I saw you dancing with last night."

Mrs. Hargrove was in curlers and a fuzzy robe. The morning light was still thin but Robert was fully dressed in the tuxedo from last night. He felt good.

"That's Doris June's father! He's here visiting from Anchorage. Works for some television station there—KTCB or something. Last night, Doris June was dancing with some of the ranch hands. But she hated to leave her father sitting there alone so I helped out. I was only being friendly." Mrs. Hargrove looked at the check on the table like it was a coiled snake. "I couldn't just go off on a cruise with some television man from Alaska."

"There's enough money for separate cabins," Robert explained quickly. "I know you like everyone sleeping in their own bed."

"Still, I don't know him. I mean, of course, I know him. He's a very pleasant man and—in other circumstances—I mean, to dinner maybe. I'd even hoped—" Mrs. Hargrove blushed. "Maybe a movie. He'd mentioned driving into Miles City for a movie. But a cruise! Why, what would he think of me?"

"You don't have to go." Robert backtracked fast. "Or you can take a woman friend if you'd like. The only reason I thought of a man was the dancing."

Mrs. Hargrove had picked the check up and was

squinting at it with more interest now. "That's a check for twenty thousand dollars."

Robert nodded, satisfied. It wasn't even breakfast yet and he'd already got one down on the love situation. Pretty good, if he did say so himself.

Mrs. Hargrove grunted and then neatly tore the check in half.

"What are you doing? That's twenty thousand dollars!" He happened to know that Mrs. Hargrove was living on her Social Security check. She could use twenty thousand dollars.

"It's not about money." She tore the check into quarters.

"It is when it's twenty thousand dollars you just threw away! You could have taken a cruise around the world."

Mrs. Hargrove looked over at the sofa. The child's Bible was still lying facedown on the arm of the sofa. "I've dealt with children and their bribes before. Of course, theirs is usually some kind of candy or sometimes flowers. But for now, no presents for me. I'd rather have you recite me a verse of the Scriptures. What did you learn last night?"

"That check was solid, you know."

Mrs. Hargrove smiled. "I never doubted that. What I want to know is if you're as solid as your check— with God, I mean."

"I'm going to learn how to love Him."

"Good."

"I don't know how yet. I thought I'd start with people first."

"Keep reading that." She nodded to the Bible. "And you'll learn all about loving God and loving other people."

"Yes, ma'am. I was hoping you might give me some advice. I'm sort of in need of some quick fixes here." Robert nodded down the hall toward Jenny's door. He'd thought about her last night, too.

"Don't write a check. If you want to love someone, do it from your heart. Put yourself in their place and listen to what they want. That goes for other people and for God. Of course, God has always made it pretty clear what He wants from people."

"I know there's the ten percent thing," Robert said. He'd always been a generous person. He believed in giving his money away before the rust got to it. Of course, rust didn't grow that fast and no one had ever expected that big of a cut before. Robert took a deep breath. It was a lot, but he was willing to give it. He hadn't expected a new life to come cheap. "That's pretty steep, but I plan to speak to my accountant first thing Monday morning. It'll take some calculating, but we'll do it."

"It won't be enough."

"Ten percent's my limit."

"Not enough. It's worthless."

"Worthless!" Robert looked at the scraps of check that the older woman still held in her hands. Maybe her hair curlers were screwed on too tight. "You do know that check was good, don't you? I have a bank balance that would probably shock you."

"Your bank balance will never be enough."

Robert looked over at her. "It's pretty impressive."

Mrs. Hargrove smiled sweetly. "No, it isn't. God doesn't want your money. What God wants is you. You are all you've got to give to Him that matters."

Robert was speechless for a moment. He wasn't sure Mrs. Hargrove had conferred with the man upstairs on this one. "I think maybe I'll still talk to my accountant on Monday about that ten percent check."

"I wouldn't just yet, dear. Trust me. God wants much more than your money. He wants your heart."

Mrs. Hargrove's words stayed in Robert's mind until they sat at the kitchen table and the oatmeal was served. He'd talked a good game to himself earlier, but Robert never really expected anyone—not even the supreme ruler of the universe—to refuse a Buckwalter check. Robert's world was turned upside down and he didn't quite know how to walk yet.

It didn't help that both Laurel and Jenny sat at the table beside him.

Saturday breakfast was at eight o'clock, Mrs. Hargrove informed all three of them cheerfully as she passed a plate of wheat toast. She'd made an exception this morning and allowed everyone to sleep in until nine.

"With all the excitement last night, I knew you'd need some extra sleep," the older woman said. "It was quite the party."

Jenny nodded and accepted a piece of toast. "I'll always remember those kids dancing away. I haven't seen a group of kids enjoy themselves so much for a long time."

"You like dancing, then?" Robert asked. He hadn't thought Jenny was a fanatic about dancing, but if she was she'd be easy to please.

Give me a break on this one, Father, Robert said inside and then almost jumped. He'd never thought about doing that kind of praying before. His only other prayers had been spoken at public functions as a way of thanking some nonspecific deity for the overcooked chicken and peas. He could as well have been praying to the chicken for all the difference it made anywhere. But this inside praying was like handling electrical wires. He could feel the current ready to move.

"Not particularly," Jenny said suspiciously as she passed the plate of toast on to Laurel. "I dance some, but not often."

Robert smiled at Jenny. He tried to make it a reassuring smile. Grandfatherly. But he could tell from the blush that started climbing her neck that he only succeeded in looking like an old lech. His smile widened to a full grin. He loved Jenny in pink. She'd even worn that old hairnet of hers to breakfast, but he didn't care. He knew he was getting to her. She wouldn't blush up like this otherwise.

Jenny looked over at Laurel. "Toast?"

"I prefer rye," Laurel said as she made no attempt to reach for the plate.

Robert winced. He hoped he'd never been that dense.

"Mrs. Hargrove has wheat toast this morning," Robert said as pleasantly as he could. "Maybe you'd like a bowl of oatmeal instead."

Laurel looked at him like he'd suggested she suck on a raw egg. "I'm on a regime of food. It's the latest thing at Benji's." Robert recognized the famous Hollywood spa. "Everyone's doing it since Liz had such good success. But the items I must eat are very specific." Laurel looked over at Mrs. Hargrove and smiled slightly. "I'm sure you don't mind."

"Of course not," Mrs. Hargrove said as she accepted

the toast plate back and set it on the table. "But wheat bread is all I have."

"But surely, I can get…" Laurel's voice trailed off as her alarm grew. She drew herself together and gracefully conceded. "I guess the toast would do if I could have some freshly squeezed wheatgrass to go with it."

Robert closed his eyes. He was sure God didn't intend for him to show any brotherly love to a ninny like Laurel. Still.

"There's three feet of snow out front," Robert said mildly. Patiently, he thought. "No one's going shopping today."

"But my regime—"

"Will have to wait," Robert finished for her. "There's not a blade of fresh wheatgrass for miles around anyway. If there had been one that FBI agent's horse would have eaten it by now."

Robert thought he'd been pleasant. A monk filled with brotherly patience couldn't have done better.

The pink left Jenny's face and her chin went up. Then Jenny looked at him like he'd been deliberately rude to a kitten.

"Some people—like your fiancée—have health concerns," Jenny said. "You might be more understanding and not compare her diet to a horse's."

Laurel gave a horrified choking sound. "Horses eat that?"

Robert turned to Jenny.

"She's not my fiancée and I didn't say she eats with horses. I understand wheatgrass is healthy." He didn't even say he knew it wasn't health that was on Laurel's mind. It was social standing. "By tomorrow, who knows, maybe there's grass at some store in Miles City. We'll be able to go for supplies and check it out."

"I doubt it," Mrs. Hargrove said cheerfully as she stood up and turned to go get the coffeepot. "The snowplow won't get all the roads plowed today. They need to come over from Miles City. Usually takes a day or two. Maybe three."

"Three days!" Jenny looked horrified. "But we need to get supplies before then."

"Do you have a regime, too?" Laurel asked. It was the first time since she'd come into the barn last night that she looked genuinely interested in anyone but herself.

"No, but those kids. They'll drive me crazy if I feed them macaroni and cheese again. I'd planned on going shopping today, or tomorrow at the latest."

"What do you need?" Robert sensed an answer to prayer. He could give Jenny something she wanted. *Good work, Father.*

"Ten dozen taco shells and some hamburger would

be a good start. Some pizza dough mix and some pepperoni. And some fresh romaine lettuce with vine-ripened tomatoes."

"Romaine lettuce? That doesn't sound like the kids," Robert said. He'd taken out a check and was writing the list on the back of it. He caught Mrs. Hargrove's eyes and deliberately turned the check over and quickly wrote "VOID" so she'd know the check was only a piece of notepaper to him at the moment. She smiled her approval.

"Oh, the kids don't like romaine. The salad's for me." Jenny smiled like she was remembering a special meal. "Just for me."

Bingo, Father. "I'll get you some."

"Don't be ridiculous," Jenny said. She spooned up some oatmeal. "In case you haven't noticed, the only store around is the hardware store. Trust me, they don't have any lettuce of any kind." Jenny suddenly remembered that farm animals sometimes eat vegetables—all that talk about horses and wheatgrass. Maybe there was hope. She looked over at Mrs. Hargrove. "They don't, do they? Maybe there's some special horse stuff. Really, any kind of greens would do. Like celery or something like carrots. I know horses like carrots."

Mrs. Hargrove shook her head. "Nobody has any fresh produce of their own, either. No gardens this time of year. Old man Gossett used to have some wild celery in that area behind his house, but that's buried under a foot of snow. Besides, I'm not too sure it's not poisonous. Tried to get him to dig it up, but he's a stubborn old fool."

Robert looked at Jenny. "Anything else you want?" Like maybe a small island or a diamond ring.

"Black pepper. We're running low on black pepper."

Robert wrote it down. He had his list and he had a plan.

Chapter Eight

Steam rose from the sink in the café's kitchen, but instead of warming the cold air in the room, it only made it damp and more miserable. The drinking glasses from last night felt like they had dew on them as Jenny picked them up to put them in the hot dishwater.

"I should have done these before I left last night," Jenny half apologized to Linda, who was operating the café with her boyfriend, Duane.

"Are you kidding? It would have been freezing in here then," Linda said as she reached up to the top shelf and brought down a couple of coffee cups. Linda wore thick, black leggings under a short black leather skirt. "It's not all that warm right now—would be colder if Duane hadn't made a large order of biscuits already this morning for the sheriff. The oven doesn't work right, but it does manage to heat the place some. Any of you want coffee?"

Linda spoke casually and seemingly to the air, but Jenny could see the young woman was not that unfocused. She kept looking at Laurel, Robert's friend.

Well, it wasn't so much that Linda was looking at Laurel as it was that she was studying the other woman. Linda, herself, had unnaturally red hair swept up in spikes that were tipped with gold glitter. Her lips were lined with black and one eyebrow was pierced so that a silver ring accented her pixie face.

She looked an unlikely woman to be so taken with Laurel, but she obviously was.

Jenny couldn't really blame her. Laurel looked as if she belonged in some classic movie. All she needed was a feather boa and one of those little dogs named Fluffy. Laurel should be lounging in a late-night dinner club. Actually, she would fit in almost anywhere better than this tiny café kitchen in Dry Creek, Montana, with its worn linoleum and chipped appliances.

Laurel wore a champagne silk dress. She had gold chains draped around her neck and diamond earrings dripping from her earlobes. Her lips weren't just red, they were glossy. She looked like she'd bitten into a large berry and kept the stain on her lips and fingertips. Her cheeks were smoothly colored and her platinum blond hair was ruffled expertly. There had to be mousse involved, but it didn't show. Laurel had the kind of casual elegance that costs a fortune.

If the woman didn't look so stiff, Jenny would have cheerfully hated her.

Jenny had deliberately decided not to compete with Laurel's style. Jenny was wearing a pair of black sweatpants, a white T-shirt and a large beige sweater. Nothing draped from her neck or dripped from her ears. Her only ornament was the small pin on her sweater announcing she had donated money to a Seattle animal shelter. Her only makeup was lip balm that she'd put on to keep her lips from becoming cracked in the winter weather. Her hair was clean and combed. That was about it.

"Or I could make you some tea if you'd like," Linda offered shyly, now addressing her remarks to the glamorous Laurel. "Something with an herbal spice to it maybe?"

"No, thanks, I couldn't possibly drink anything," Laurel said as she walked over to the window in the kitchen. "Unless you have some bottled water." She shuddered delicately. "I never drink tap water when I travel. It's one of those rules."

"That's for Mexico," Robert said as he walked into the kitchen. He was carrying a tub of plates that had been left out in the main part of the café after dinner last night. "This is Montana. They both start with *M*'s, but there's a big difference. Besides, you can drink boiled water anywhere. That kills the germs."

Laurel shuddered again. "But then they'd be dead in the water floating around. I couldn't possibly drink something with anything dead in it."

Robert snorted. "If you're that fussy, you'll have to stop breathing. There's germs everywhere—dead and alive."

Laurel looked alarmed.

"Well, except for the really cold places like just outside the door," Robert continued. His mission for the morning was to get Jenny alone. So far, Jenny wouldn't even talk to him. He was hoping she would if they were alone. "Real good clear air there."

"But it's cold outside," Laurel wailed.

"That's what kills the germs," Robert responded matter-of-factly as he unloaded the plates from last night onto the counter. "Talking about germs—these old plates are a hotbed of activity."

Laurel moved back from the plastic tubs Robert was using to carry the dishes around. There was a tub for silverware, another for coffee mugs and another for punch cups. Half of the cups had lipstick stains on them and the other had spots of something or another.

"It's perfectly safe in here," Jenny said. The sudsy

water felt good on her hands, but she was still glad for the long johns she had on under her sweatpants. "Restaurants have health inspectors that come around and check out things like that."

"They do?" Linda said with a gulp. The younger woman paused in the act of pulling a platter down from the cupboard. The eyebrow with the silver ring in it rose in panic.

"You mean you haven't?"

Linda shook her head. "Jazz—that's Duane—never said anything about health inspectors. Maybe he's done something about them. He takes care of all the business details. I'd better go ask him."

Jenny could hear Duane in the dining area of the restaurant putting salt and pepper shakers on the tables and getting the place ready to open. Linda walked out there and the mumbled sound of their voices reached back into the kitchen.

"I hope they don't get a fine or anything," Jenny worried aloud. She was automatically washing glasses as she worked. She set the glasses in a large tub so that they could be rinsed with scalding water before they were set to dry. She couldn't recall ever being in a restaurant that didn't have a machine that washed dishes. "I wonder if you need things like a sterilizing dishwasher machine to pass all the rules."

"I doubt they can afford to buy any equipment yet," Robert added. He doubted they had insurance, either. He'd have to remember to ask if they needed a small business loan. They'd never have collateral on their own to get one, but from what he'd seen they had a good shot at making a sound business.

"I'm surprised no health inspector has shown up already. They can just come unannounced. Maybe they do it different when you're not in a city." Jenny moved one of the tubs so she could start on the silverware.

"Maybe." Robert shrugged as he wrapped one dish towel around his hand and offered another towel to Laurel.

"For me?" Laurel's voice came out in a surprised squeak. She backed farther away from Robert. "But I can't—I've never even—not even at home. Why, I have a housekeeper."

By the time Laurel finished talking, she was at the doorway between the café's kitchen and its main dining room.

"I need to go to the house for something." Laurel managed to smile as she stepped into the other room.

"I thought that'd scare her off," Robert said as he picked up a bowl from the rack of dishes to be dried. He rubbed the towel around its edges. "She's not used to doing dishes."

"And you are?" Jenny looked at him skeptically. She still couldn't believe how competently and willingly he was working. She couldn't have paid anyone to work harder than this rich man was doing.

Robert was standing in front of the counter where the dried dishes were setting. He had modified his tuxedo when he came over to the café. He'd taken off the black jacket and was wearing a yellow sweatshirt that had been hanging on a nail by the kitchen door. It had paint splatters on it. Jazz had said he'd used it when he painted the café and had not gotten around to throwing it away yet. Jenny noted that the shirt had a tear under the armhole and a burn spot where Jazz had leaned too close to the stove.

Robert no longer looked like a rich man. His hair was mussed where he'd wrapped one of Mrs. Hargrove's wool scarves around his head because he was walking between the barn and the café bringing over the dirty dishes. The weather outside was frigid. The cold air made his cheeks blotchy.

It was more than that, however, Jenny thought. It was the look on his face that had changed. He no longer looked like a rich man because he no longer looked stressed. He smiled like he didn't have a dime in the world.

"Me? As a matter of fact, I've done a few dishes in

my time," Robert answered, and then plunged into his story. "Not so long ago, in fact, when I was visiting a friend of mine outside of Tucson."

"I can't believe any of your friends would ask you to help with the dishes."

"The dishes were the fun part. The warm water felt good on the calluses I got on my hands from chopping wood. Took me a while to get the hang of it all. Long steady strokes worked best. You build up a rhythm that way."

Jenny stopped washing dishes and turned her full attention to Robert.

There was only one explanation that came to mind. "You can't possibly have lost all your money!" He must gamble or something. "Is that why you need to be on that list at my sister's paper?"

"Lost it? I didn't lose any money. Fact is, the Buck-walter Foundation has made money this past year. How I don't know, at the rate we're giving it away. But, no, I didn't lose my money. And—let me say this again—I don't want to be on any list. I'm doing my best to get off of it."

Jenny heard the words, but she couldn't make sense of what he was saying.

"Well, if you're trying to get off that list, why did you kiss me?" Jenny held up a frying pan that she was cleaning and frowned at it fiercely. It was a solid cast-iron pan usually used for frying bacon. "You must have known I'd tell my sister."

Jenny brought the pan down to the counter and attacked it again with a wet dishrag. Cast iron couldn't be washed with the rest of the dishes. "Kissing me like that—how was that supposed to get you off the list? I thought you did it because you wanted to get *on* that list."

Robert watched Jenny scowl at the bottom of the cast-iron pan. Her jaw was set, but a thin sheen of pink spread over her cheeks. She was flustered.

"You liked the kiss," Robert said.

Jenny looked up from her scouring and frowned at him. "I never said that."

"I'm going on faith." Robert felt like whistling. "If you hadn't liked it, you would have told your sister it was awful and you wouldn't even think that would help me get on that list."

Jenny kept the frown and added a full-blown blush. "I don't think—"

Robert put his fingers on her lips. "You don't need to think when it comes to kisses. Not then. Not now."

Robert bent his head and kissed Jenny. This time there were no cameras. No flashes. No audience. Just the two of them. And more steam than either one of them had ever seen before.

"The hot water's still running," Robert finally said as he pulled away. The frying pan was pressing against the hot water handle and a steady stream of scalding hot water was filling the air with clouds of moist steam. The steam made Jenny's cheeks pinker and her lips soft. "But hot water is good."

Robert bent to kiss Jenny again.

Jenny wondered what was wrong with her. Every time this man kissed her she got warmer and warmer. Last time it was the lights that had confused her and made her think she was near a crackling fire. This time it was the heat. How did it get so hot in this kitchen when it was ten below zero outside?

"Tropical," Jenny whispered. She was trying to grab hold of her sanity and keep it. She felt as if she were under a spell that stopped time and created puffs of white steam. "It's tropical in here."

"Perfect. It's perfect in here," Robert said as he pulled away.

The moisture in the air made Jenny's hair curve toward her face. Robert knew that somewhere in the chef apron pocket lurked a hairnet that would squash her hair even further. Jenny wore no makeup. The pink in her cheeks was from the heat and not from any brush.

"You're perfect."

Jenny started. The spell was broken. "No one's perfect."

No one except Laurel, Jenny thought to herself. She could hardly believe Robert Buckwalter III was happy to help with the dishes. But there was no way she'd ever believe he would prefer the hired help to someone like Laurel. Laurel might be overdressed and she might be a snob, but she still was his kind. They belonged to the same social set. It was clear.

"Why are you helping with the dishes?"

Robert looked up.

"It doesn't seem fair," she said. "Your mother is paying me to do the dishes and then you're helping me anyway."

Robert shrugged. "I want to."

Jenny didn't have an answer to that one. But she knew for sure something was off center. Who wanted to do dishes?

There were twenty bins of dirty dishes. Jenny thought Robert would lose interest before the second bin was emptied. The novelty of doing dishes wore off fast, even to people who hadn't done many in their life.

But Robert stayed. He washed dishes and talked about his months in the desert. He explained about Bob and how good it felt to be free of the life of a rich man. Then he talked about his childhood and how much he still missed his father. He was curious about her brothers and sisters. She told him. He wanted to know how she felt about her parents. She told him.

All the while, he washed and dried dishes. The stack of damp dish towels grew, but he didn't complain.

The phone call came when they were almost done with the dishes. It was ten-thirty and Linda and Jazz had started their famous spaghetti sauce simmering.

"Oh, hi." The phone was on the counter closest to Jenny and she clicked on it first. It was her sister.

Jenny was still standing in front of the sink, but she moved back a little and used one hand to untie the apron strings wrapped around her waist.

"I'm calling to talk to Robert Buckwalter. Is he around?" her sister asked.

"Yes." Jenny smiled over at Robert. "He's right here."

"With you?" Jenny's sister dropped to a cautious whisper. "Are you saying he's with you?"

"Mmm-hmm."

"You two aren't dancing or kissing or anything? I always seem to have this bad timing and catch you just when things are getting good."

"We're washing dishes."

"Dishes! You've got to be kidding. I thought you'd at least be sitting down and talking or something."

"We have been talking. Just standing up and doing the dishes at the same time."

Robert almost winced. He hadn't realized until just now how far from the mark his romancing was when viewed objectively. Women were independent these days, but they liked to know a man wasn't totally without manners. He looked around. He didn't even have a chair to offer her.

He'd already called his pilot friend and made an arrangement to have him fly over and make a supply drop near Robert's plane early tomorrow morning. Robert had even made plans to have his plane moved so it would be out in the open and make a good drop site.

But Robert suddenly realized he had a lot riding on that plane drop. The more he talked with Jenny, the more he cared what she thought of him. A few boxes of food—most of it for other people, and hungry teenagers at that—might not be enough of a gift to say he cared about her.

"Hey." Robert walked over and tapped Jazz on the shoulder. The younger man was standing at a side counter, chopping onions to the beat of the music coming out of the headphones he wore.

"Yeah." The younger man pushed an earphone away from his ear so he could hear. He put a hand up and brushed away some tears from his eyes. "Man, them onions'll get you. Ever chop an onion?"

"Not that I remember."

"Oh, you'd remember all right."

Robert didn't have time to talk about onions. Jenny would only talk to her sister for so long before the sister would want to talk business with him. "You don't happen to have carnations, do you?"

The younger man looked up. "Do they make the tears stop? I've heard there's ways to chop onions without the tears. Never heard of carnations. Do you eat them, or what?"

"I don't know anything about onions and you shouldn't eat carnations for any reason. I'm just asking about carnations. A lot of restaurants put cut flowers on the table. I thought you might have carnations you use."

"We have red candles."

Robert had never heard of a bouquet of red candles, but he was pretty sure it wouldn't work.

"People like them," the younger man said. "They're kind of romantic."

"I don't suppose you have any vine-ripened tomatoes, do you?"

Jazz shook his head. "We've got them in cans. Sauce or paste."

A can of tomato sauce wouldn't make it, either.

"What do you give your girlfriend when you want to get her something nice?"

"I've had Earl put aside a set of tires."

Robert wondered if he was talking to the right guy. "Tires?"

Jazz ducked and then offered hesitantly, "They're snow tires. You need them around here this time of year and hers are thin. Besides, I was also going to give her a nose ring, too. She's been wanting one."

The door to the café opened and the FBI agent and Francis Elkton, the rancher's sister, came inside. They were talking quietly to each other and Robert noticed they had snowflakes on their hair.

"Gotta go," Jazz said as he went back into the front part of the café. "Customers, you know."

Robert nodded. He wondered if that FBI agent had any ideas about how to get a romantic gift in the middle of Montana with no stores in sight. There weren't even wildflowers to gather. It was just snow and rocks outside.

Linda picked up a pot of coffee and followed Jazz out of the kitchen.

At least, Robert thought, he was now alone with Jenny. That was something. He could see the happiness in her face while she talked with her sister. He'd seen the affection on her face earlier when she spoke of her sisters and brothers.

Now Jenny was someone who knew what it meant to love other people. He wondered if she had gotten any of that knowledge from reading the Bible like he'd done last night. He wouldn't be surprised if she had.

"My sister needs to know what story you're offering," Jenny called over to Robert. "She said the senior editors have been asking her."

Jenny could hardly believe that Robert didn't want to be on that list. But her sister was adamant. She wasn't sure she could help him get off, but she was going to try.

Jenny gave the phone to Robert.

"Have they said they'd trade stories?" Robert asked in the phone.

"They said it needs to be something big—bigger than the bachelor story."

"I could tell them what I've been up to for the past five months—about being in the desert."

"Let me see." The sister covered the mouthpiece on the phone and was obviously talking to someone. Finally she came back. "They said not unless it involves you eating wild locusts and taking religious vows to be a monk—a bed of nails would help."

Robert snorted. "Help who?"

He thought further. "I did have a persecutor in the desert. A farmyard rooster. A cranky bird. Bit me once."

Robert heard the muffled sounds of talking at the other end again. "They asked if the bird has been certified by a priest as being possessed or if it's been abducted by space aliens."

"What would space aliens want with Charlie?"

"Maybe they'd want to study him."

"He's just a farm rooster." Robert was defeated. He was half tempted to say that he was in the midst of a religious makeover, but he didn't want to joke around with that. The tabloids never knew when to stop. They knew what they wanted and it had to be sensational. "I could offer a Buckwalter Grant to space aliens. Broadcast it on radio frequencies. Ask them to come pick up a million-dollar check. Get some of those groups involved who scan the airwaves for messages."

"Hmmm, not bad." He heard more muffled sounds as the sister conferred with her editors. "Not believable enough."

"Not believable! You've got to be kidding!"

"Well, we need our readers to trust us," the sister said a little louder than normal. "We don't fool around about money." Her voice dipped and she whispered. "I think they're holding out for the story of your engagement to Laurel what's-her-name. That's what they really want."

"I'm not engaged."

"Their sources tell them otherwise."

"Laurel is their source."

"I can't confirm that."

"You don't need to. I know what's going on."

"Do you?"

Robert wasn't sure when they'd stopped talking about the story and had started talking about him. The sister didn't even try to hide her resentment.

"I can't control what Laurel is saying." Robert knew he was talking to both sisters. "I never proposed to Laurel. Cross my heart and hope to die—on a bed of nails if necessary. I'm telling the truth. I haven't even seen Laurel for months. I think we went out on two dates in high school. That's it. I'm not even her type and she's certainly not mine. She's a publicity hound. She'll drop the idea of marrying me quick enough once I'm off that cursed list."

"Hmmm."

Robert thought the sister was softening.

"Still, you could use the story," the sister offered kindly. "Even a solid lead of an engagement—like 'sources close to'—that kind of a thing. And a couple of photos of you kissing Really, even the photos themselves would do. It would be enough to keep the editors happy."

"How much time do I have to come up with something else?"

"We can give you until tomorrow at noon. If we absolutely need to we could go another day, but that's pushing back our press time."

"I'll call before then."

Robert handed the phone back to Jenny. He knew he couldn't use a fake engagement story. It would ruin any chance he had with Jenny. But he had a day to think of something else.

Robert wondered if space aliens could be bribed to come down and take Charlie for a spin on a UFO. It wouldn't even need to be a big UFO as long as Robert could get a picture of it.

Chapter Nine

"Flint Harris, FBI." The man seemed to walk into the kitchen and flip his badge open in one seamless movement. He stopped in front of Robert.

"Mind telling me what your business is in Dry Creek?" The agent looked like he'd had a tough night, but his voice was one hundred percent official.

"Me?" Robert was surprised. He had walked over to the tall cupboard to put back some bowls.

"It's my fault." Duane the Jazz Man followed the agent inside. "The man asked me if anyone had been asking funny questions and I told him you had been."

"Me?"

"Yeah, the carnations that you're not supposed to eat and the cans of tomatoes—the sauce kind and the paste."

Robert winced. He set the bowls down on the

counter. "I was trying to think of a gift for someone special."

The FBI agent looked at him even more suspiciously. "Someone special? Cans of tomatoes? Carnations? Aren't you the rich guy?"

Robert nodded. "Sometimes a gift should count for more than its price tag."

The agent snorted and looked over at Jenny.

He lowered his voice so only the men could hear. "I thought a guy like you'd go more for orchids or roses or something fancy that men like me haven't even heard of—night crawlers or something."

"Night crawlers are worms."

"I mean night bloomers." The agent shook his head. "See what Francis does to me? I can't even think straight. But I can't make any headway with her. You'd think we'd never been, well, you know. Turns out we were actually married—but you'd never know it now. I was hoping someone would have flowers."

"You see any floral shops around?"

"I know." The agent looked at the woman who'd come to the kitchen door. It was Francis. His face softened to mush. "I was just hoping. Sometimes a guy could use a little help, if you know what I mean."

Robert knew exactly what he meant. He nodded toward Duane. "He's reduced to snow tires."

Duane ducked his head in acknowledgment. "And a nose ring."

"Well, I guess I should keep my mind on business anyway," the agent said. "Unless I miss my guess, this rustling thing is going to break wide open here soon, and when it does the citizens of Dry Creek are going to find some nasty surprises."

Robert lifted his eyebrow.

"I figure there has to be someone local involved. And from the amount of information that has been sent along about Dry Creek, it's either someone who knows everything really well or it's more than one person. Maybe a group of people."

"Here?"

The agent nodded.

"But all of the men I've seen are ranchers themselves. They know what the rustling means to others. And the women, well—" Robert tried to picture Mrs. Hargrove leading a band of female informants. They could knit in code and send neck scarves out with the information. "I don't think so."

"Still, keep your ears open. And let me know if you hear of anyone asking unusual questions." The agent looked over at Duane. "Unusual questions about cattle— who's got winter pasture where and who's moving their herds at what time. Those kinds of questions. Even weather questions might lead to something. A lot of the cattle movements are determined by weather."

Duane nodded. "Old man Gossett would be the one asking about the weather. But that's just because his television is broken. He comes over and asks almost every day. Then he moans about it. Snow. Rain. It doesn't matter. He complains. The amount of time he spends worrying—I guess it's just his way."

That was the old man he'd invited to dinner last night. Robert remembered him clearly. "I expect the cold weather troubles his joints."

The FBI agent grunted. "He might be someone to watch at that if he's talking to lots of people."

"Oh, he don't so much talk as listen," Duane corrected. "Sort of listens on the side if you know what I mean."

"Eavesdropping?"

Duane nodded. "Everybody knows. They don't pay him much attention anymore. They just let him be. Who's he gonna tell anyway? Never talks to nobody."

"That kind of listening is the most dangerous. People don't watch their tongues around him. Besides, he's getting money from someplace. I figured he was living on Social Security until last night. Did you see him in his new coat? He wouldn't get money to buy stuff like that on his government check."

"I gave him the coat." Robert doubted the older man had the connections to be a rustler. He seemed more like a lonely old man than a criminal.

"Nice coat. Expensive."

Robert hoped that meant the old man got off the suspects list, but he couldn't read the agent's face. "It'll keep him warm."

The agent nodded and looked more closely at Robert. "What are you doing here in that getup?" He jerked his head toward the sweatshirt.

Robert knew the sweatshirt was paint spotted and yellow. Bright yellow. But it was warm and that was enough. "I'm here doing dishes. A tuxedo seemed a little overdressed."

The agent looked over at Jenny and then back at Robert.

The agent lowered his voice. "I see. Not a bad idea. You might not need roses at that. Never knew a woman that could be mad at a man when he was doing dishes for her. Good move."

Robert looked at Jenny. She was fifteen feet away from him and she might as well be fifteen miles. She'd stopped talking to her sister and was back to scowling at that frying pan.

"I could still use some roses," Robert said. "I

don't think there's enough dirty dishes in the world to win her over."

"I'll let you know if I find a magician who can pull a few roses out of his hat."

"Same here." Robert didn't tell the agent that the last time he had given roses to a woman she'd been insulted. She had thought roses were too common a flower to come from a Buckwalter. "Any particular color you'd like?"

"Yellow. Francis loves yellow roses—or at least she did when I knew her back in high school."

Robert made a mental note to call that pilot he'd hired and see if he could put three dozen long-stem roses in the drop he was planning for tomorrow morning. A dozen deep red ones for Jenny. A dozen yellow for the agent to give to his Francis. And—he looked over at Linda and Duane assessingly—maybe a lavender bouquet for the young couple.

"What was that about?" Jenny asked when Robert came back to the sink. Without waiting for him to answer, she continued as though she'd rehearsed the words. "You can do it, you know. If you want to run that engagement story, that's fine."

Robert couldn't see Jenny's face. She was looking down at something in the sink.

"Not that it's any of my business," she added with

a quick look up at his face before she looked down again. "I just want you to know that no one who knows you would blame you. And you could always tell them the truth later. People would understand. I know you want off the list."

Robert laid down the dish towel he'd been holding. The dishwater no longer steamed up from the sink. The pink in Jenny's cheeks was natural. Lashes half hid her brown eyes. Her lips curved in a hint of a smile. Robert thought she looked absolutely adorable.

"I'll find another way to get off the list."

"My sister says there is no other way."

"We'll see." Robert comforted himself and her. Then he added impulsively, "I'm going to pray about it."

Jenny looked up in surprise. "I didn't know people like you prayed about anything."

"I've become a new man. That's what I've been telling you all morning."

"And the 'new you' prays?"

Robert nodded. "The new me has to pray. Sometimes I don't have a clue. Not that I always knew everything before—but, now, well what kind of a fool wouldn't pray? It's like having a million dollars in the bank and never writing a check."

"You've always been rich."

Robert nodded. "Money, yes. But prayers, no. I'm

beginning to think that—in the important things—
I've lived like some fool who's starving to death in a
fully stocked deli just because he doesn't know how
to stand in line."

Jenny decided Robert no longer had the heart of a
rich man. He'd become a regular kind of guy. He'd
even admitted he might need help with his life. She
liked this new guy much better than the rich guy he
used to be.

She hoped she didn't like him too much. Just
because Robert Buckwalter changed one day didn't
mean he couldn't change right back the next.

The day divided itself into meals. Jenny couldn't
think beyond that. The teenagers at the ranch were all
coming into Dry Creek for lunch and to clean up the
decorations from last night's dance.

"We have four hamburger patties left and seven hot
dogs," Linda said. The younger woman was looking
in the top compartment of the old refrigerator. "We
aren't able to keep too much on hand in the way of
supplies in this old thing. We're having trouble with
the stove, too. Plus we're out of almost everything. The
spaghetti sauce we have going is straight marinara—
not even mushrooms. There's no potatoes for French
fries or ice cream for shakes."

"That's all it seems the kids want to eat," Jenny

worried aloud. She'd finished wiping down the counter and was folding the dishrag. "I know they'll eat anything if they're hungry enough, but I hate to put them back on the macaroni-and-cheese diet they've had for the past week."

"Ah—Sylvia called from the ranch," Linda said hesitantly as she stood up and closed the refrigerator door. "That's why we started the spaghetti sauce. She said they used the last of the boxes of macaroni and cheese yesterday. A quick lunch for the boys. There's none left. And the spaghetti sauce won't be enough for everyone."

"We're doomed then."

Jenny walked over to a kitchen chair and sat down.

"I learned how to make Navajo fry bread when I was in the desert," Robert offered. He finished drying the last cup. "I've checked and we have what we need. We could make it a cultural ethnic kind of a night."

"Spaghetti's Italian—we could put an extra dose of the authentic seasoning," Linda offered. She walked to the stove and opened the lid on a pot. "No one will have a full serving, but we could stretch it so they each have a small plate of it. We have a big jar of kosher pickles, too—they'd fit for the Jewish touch."

"I could make a Mexican flan for dessert—we've got lots of eggs and milk still," Jenny added. She went to a cupboard and looked inside. The cupboard was empty except for dishes. "It's not much, but—"

"Kids love an adventure," Robert folded his dish towel. "We'll sell them on the fun of it."

"Duane can play his guitar. He knows all kinds of music. Some sounds like mariachi music from Mexico. He might be able to do some Navajo drumming for the fry bread, too."

"It just might work." Jenny closed the cupboard.

"If anyone has a sturdy box, we can make a homemade piñata. Fill it with whatever's handy." Robert walked to the pantry. "I bet there's something in here to use."

"We've got those old candy canes left over from Christmas. I think they're in there." Linda opened a side cupboard near the refrigerator. "Ah, here they are. We had Santa giving them out."

Linda pulled out a large plastic bag filled with candy canes. "Maybe we shouldn't give them to the kids—" she looked up at Jenny "—you know our Santa was a hit man, don't you? Went right after the Christmas angel with a gun! If it wasn't for the preacher, she'd be dead. 'Course now she's married to the preacher." Linda paused to look into the other room at Duane. "It was so romantic. Him risking his life for her."

"But he could have been killed," Jenny protested.

She didn't want the younger woman to be under the wrong impression. There was nothing romantic about life-and-death danger. "I heard the preacher didn't even have a gun."

Robert envied the man who had almost died. Now there was a man who had a chance to impress the woman he chose. No wonder he had been able to close the deal with a wedding band. Somehow, carving up carrots and washing dishes seemed too tame by comparison.

"I told Mrs. Hargrove I'd check with her about now," Jenny said as she walked over to the café's back door, the one that led off of the kitchen. "She's promised to give the church a quick cleaning for services tomorrow and I wanted to be sure she got over there all right."

Jenny pulled a parka off a peg by the door and slid her arms into the sleeves.

"I can get her there," Robert offered. "You can stay here. It's slippery cold out there and you don't even have snow boots."

"Neither do you." Jenny pulled a wool scarf from the large pocket of the coat and wrapped the scarf around her head.

"But I've got bigger feet." Robert pulled a man's jacket off of the peg. The jacket was denim lined with some kind of furry material. "I can keep my balance better in the icy places."

"Nonsense."

Two minutes later, Jenny was lying on the icy ground on her back, looking up at the sky. She'd gone outside anyway, not even waiting for Robert. She didn't want him to think she was incapable of walking a few steps in the snow.

Well, so much for that, she thought as she winced. After the fall she'd taken, he'd think that incompetence was the least of her worries.

"I knew you should have waited," Robert said as he stepped out of the kitchen door and knelt down beside her. "Where does it hurt?"

"My left ankle."

"Here, let me see." Robert slipped off his gloves and rolled down her thick socks.

For a second, her leg tingled from the cold air and then Robert wrapped his warm hands around it and gently probed. "No broken bones."

"I'll be all right." Jenny could almost be back in the kitchen with the steam. She was starting to feel warm again. "Just help me up. I'll be fine."

"You'll be no such thing," Robert said as he rolled her sock back up to cover her leg. "You've got a sprain. You'll need to stay off your foot for a while."

Jenny looked around her. She was sprawled in front of the café.

The main street of Dry Creek wasn't so much a street as it was the widening of the road that cut through town. The barn and the church were on one side with a few houses between them and the café was on the other side with a few more houses.

Jenny was ten feet from the café, which would place her on the shoulder of the road, she supposed. It was hard to tell where the road began and ended because of the ruts in the snow left from all the cars and trucks that had been parked here last night. The ruts were now covered with fresh snow so the whole area looked soft, white and lumpy.

"It's not so bad." Jenny looked up at Robert. The midmorning sun gave off a subdued white light but it still reflected off the sprinkling of blond hairs on his head. She'd never seen him in the full sun before. That must be why she'd never noticed before that there was any blond in the dark of his hair. She wondered how it had gotten so blond in places. "It must be the desert sun."

Robert's eyes were bluer than the sky. Jenny decided she'd have to remember to tell her sister about them. "Does the desert change the color of blue?"

The blue in Robert's eyes turned gray and his hands left her ankle.

"Did you hit your head?' Robert's hands cupped

Jenny's skull gently and started to feel their way around her forehead. "Can you count to ten?"

"Of course."

"Backward?"

"I didn't hit my head." Jenny's hair was on fire. She couldn't breathe. She was undone. Something in the universe was very unfair. She was no match for Robert Buckwalter. She'd done fine with him until she'd really looked at him. Now she needed mercy. She needed air. Her sister was right. The man was an Adonis.

"Count to ten then."

"Huh?"

"Ten. Nine—"

"You need to leave me." Jenny finally gasped the words out. She needed to get a handle on herself. Even if she hadn't hit her head, maybe she was sick or something. "I can't breathe."

"It's your ribs!"

Robert didn't leave. Nor did he take his hands away. He only moved them to gently feel along her rib cage. "They seem fine."

"They *are* fine. It's you." Jenny's cheeks flamed. She hadn't felt this awkward since she was thirteen. "You need to leave so I can breathe."

"Oh."

Robert rocked back on his heels. He took his hands off her ribs.

Jenny closed her eyes and concentrated on taking slow, deep breaths. She was just rattled, that's all. Her sister was right. She, Jenny, needed to get out more. If just looking at an attractive man sent her into a tailspin, it was only proof that she needed to date more. She'd do that, just as soon as she got back to the safety of Seattle.

"Better?"

Jenny opened her eyes and nodded.

"You're sure you don't hurt anywhere but the ankle?"

"I'm sure. I just got the wind knocked out of me."

Jenny forced a smile on her face. That was it. It was the shock of falling down that suddenly made the man look so gorgeous. Maybe it was like one of those near-death experiences. Not as serious, of course. But something that happened that made the next few minutes of life look more attractive than it really was. If she'd been looking at a cactus, she'd have thought it was diamond studded. It was just a case of misperception.

"I'll be fine. Just give me a hand up."

Robert grunted. "Even if everything else is fine, you still can't walk on that ankle for a while."

"Well, I can't just sit here in the snow," Jenny said as she sat up and lifted her arm for assistance. "Besides, I have lunch to worry about."

Robert took her arm and helped her stand.

Jenny had snow stuck to the back of her coat and the back of her sweatpants, but she didn't bend to brush it off.

"You don't need to worry about lunch. Or dinner," Robert said as he slipped his arm under one of hers and scooped her up into his arms.

"Oh." Jenny blinked.

Jenny blinked again. The sun was still behind the man. That must be why she suddenly felt so giddy.

Chapter Ten

"Another cup of cocoa?"

Jenny looked up at Robert. She was lying on the couch in Mrs. Hargrove's living room. The same couch that Robert had laid her down on over eight hours ago when she'd twisted her ankle. He'd only let her get up a few times to hobble around the house briefly. He'd spent all of that time, except for when she took a nap, being her nurse.

"I can't drink another drop." Jenny liked this Robert better—the one inside the house. The sun didn't play with his hair and confuse her. He looked more like a normal man in the shadows of the house. "You don't need to bother, you know."

"I know," Robert said the rest of the words along with her "—you're fine."

"Well, I am. The swelling has already gone down. And everyone says it's only a sprain. I could be walking on it by now."

Jenny looked at the empty cup she'd just set on the coffee table. Robert had originally pulled the coffee table close, saying she needed a place to set her cup.

That was six cups ago.

The table had served as his command center. First, he'd brought ice for her foot. And a pillow. Then a cup of tea with honey in it. Then he'd gotten a thick salve from the hardware store and rubbed it on her ankle. He wouldn't let her look at the label, but Jenny strongly suspected the salve was something ordinarily used on cattle. Before she could ask, he was off to bring back a cup of cocoa and some toast.

"I wanted marshmallows, but there weren't any," Robert apologized. He had a towel draped over his arm like a high-class waiter. "The closest I could get was buying a breath mint from one of the kids. Stirred it around and it made a mint-chocolate cocoa."

Jenny took a sip. The liquid was rich and warm. And just a little minty. "It's perfect."

"I'm still learning." Robert sat down on a straight-back chair that he'd pulled near the couch earlier so they could play a game of cards. "Mrs. Hargrove has been teaching me all about preparing food. She's on the care of pots and pans now. Never realized there was so much to this cooking business."

"I never realized Mrs. Hargrove cared so much about her pots and pans."

Robert grinned. "Not sure she does. She's using them to teach me lessons, I think."

"About?"

"Gratitude, for starters. Have you ever thought about where we'd be without a pot or a pan to our name?"

Jenny shrugged. "We'd have to cook stuff on a stick, I guess."

"We wouldn't have soups or stews." Robert began reciting the list. "No gravies. No puddings." He paused. "Tell that to your sister. Maybe next time she should impersonate a cookware salesman. It's more basic."

"She shouldn't impersonate anyone. And I've talked to her about it."

Robert grinned.

Jenny eyed him suspiciously. "What's that for?"

"I'm just practicing doing what Mrs. Hargrove recommends."

"And?"

Robert paused, then grinned wider. "I'm thinking how grateful I am for the fact that you always speak your mind."

"My sister wasn't. She thought I was bossy."

"Well, tell your sister I'd trade places with her any day in that regard. When you're rich, you never know if people mean what they say or not. No one dares to be bossy and I've kind of missed it."

Jenny looked at Robert more closely. He just wasn't what she expected when she thought of a rich man. He wasn't living up to her stereotypes at all. "Have you ever abandoned a kitten?"

"Me? Never."

"A dog?"

"Of course not."

"Any other pet that you may have owned?"

"The closest thing I've had to a pet is a rooster named Charlie. And he wasn't mine. He just lived next door."

"Well, were you good to him?"

Robert chuckled. "He was the sorriest excuse for a neighbor I've ever seen. He was loud. Demanding. Inconsiderate. Worse than a boom box playing at dawn. But I still gave him his handful of grain every single day that I was there. Even the day he pecked at me."

"Good." Jenny lay back on the pillows on the couch.

"Good he almost bit me?"

"No, good because you fed him and didn't hold a grudge. He was only being what he was—a chicken. It's his destiny."

"He could have been a chicken without pecking at

me. He's a chicken—I don't think he has a destiny. But, even if he did, just following your destiny isn't enough. Sometimes it's nothing but an excuse not to do better. That's why I want you to know I'm working on changing myself, Jenny. I know I haven't always been the most thoughtful, considerate guy in the universe, but I believe that—with God's help—I can change."

"Mrs. Hargrove tells me you're a fine young man." Jenny bent down to drink out of her cocoa cup. That's not all Mrs. Hargrove had said. She'd also told Jenny that Robert was a man in a million and she should snap him up before someone like that Laurel made good on her threat and got her hands on him. Jenny wondered how Mrs. Hargrove thought she, Jenny, was supposed to do that. She might as well have commanded her to sing an opera or float in the air.

"Mrs. Hargrove is prejudiced," Robert said.

Jenny raised an eyebrow.

"While you took your nap earlier, I went over and cleaned the church for her. I even followed her instructions."

Jenny raised her eyebrow even more.

"That's right. There are lessons to be learned in cleaning, too. Mostly they've got to do with being humble and using the right bottle of stuff when you scrub the floor on your hands and knees."

"Mrs. Hargrove shouldn't be scrubbing those floors on her knees. Not at her age."

"I know. I've already called in an order for a small commercial floor scrubber. It'll work to her specifications. She doesn't believe in hand mops. She thinks they miss the little spots."

"What are the lessons there?"

"Thinking some sins are so small they don't need God's forgiveness." Robert smiled. "I know it's a little corny, but I like what she's done with her life. She's made everything have meaning. So cleaning a dirty floor in the church isn't just about scrubbing. It's about honoring God. It's about paying attention to the small stuff. No wonder she goes about her days like a drill sergeant. Everything is important."

The day had long since drifted into early evening and the light in the living room had become even dimmer. Shadows filled the corners. The couch where Jenny lay was square in front of the fireplace that took up one wall of the room. A row of windows took up another wall and a dozen framed snapshots took up the final wall.

"I wonder what my life will be like when I'm as old as Mrs. Hargrove and I look back over it." Robert stood up and switched on the floor lamp that stood at the end of the couch. "Wonder what my picture wall will look like."

"Lots of shots of you handing out money—lots of those big checks like they show on the lottery."

Jenny kept holding on to the differences between them. Robert had money with a capital *M*. She had loose change. She was walking through quicksand and she needed a firm place to stand. The difference in their bank accounts was as good a place as any.

"We all write checks and spend money." Robert sat down on the floor near the sofa where she was lying. "When it all ends, we've either spent or given away every dime we've ever made. If we haven't, the government does it for us. I might have more dimes to give away than most, but it all ends the same. It's all gone to one place or the other. We sure aren't taking it with us."

"Those kids that are over at Garth's don't believe that." Jenny wondered if Robert could really be so blind to the difference that money made in someone's life. "They're not worried about taking it with them, but they've seen what being poor can do to a person."

"And I've seen what being rich can do to a person."

"Most people would pick rich."

"I suppose so." Robert nodded and then looked around at the room. The light of evening was dimming even further. The light gave a soft circle of warmth. Mrs. Hargrove had gone to the café to help prepare the dinner for the teenagers tonight. She had convinced

Laurel to go with her, telling her the ranch hands would be disappointed if she didn't come.

Robert was alone with Jenny and he was tired of talking about money.

"I'm going to make a fire in the fireplace. Maybe light a few candles," Robert said as he walked out into the kitchen. "I'll need to bring in some wood first."

Jenny nodded. She was grateful he was stepping outside. She pulled the cell phone off the coffee table and quickly dialed.

"Yeah, it's me." She spoke softly when her sister answered and then she listened a bit. "No, he's outside. That's why I called. Have you had a chance to talk to your source?"

"My source isn't the main source. I want you to know that. But the woman did know Robert some years ago. She gave a good recommendation. I don't think you need to worry. Your Robert sounds like a nice guy."

"He's not my Robert and I'm out of my league here."

"Well, short of hiring a private detective to dig through his trash, I think we'll just have to assume he's datable. That's what you really want to know, isn't it?"

"We can't date—I mean, look at the differences. Besides, Dad wouldn't approve."

"Dad's not lying there on a sofa with a drop-dead gorgeous Adonis cooking for him. Is he wearing a shirt?"

"Of course he's wearing a shirt! It's twenty degrees below outside."

"Oh," her sister said and then brightened. "But he is cooking for you. That's so romantic."

"He's only done tea, cocoa and dry toast. He worries about my foot. It's more medical than romantic."

"Forget the foot. You don't get cocoa in hospitals. Tea and dry toast maybe, but cocoa is definitely romantic. Did it have a marshmallow?"

"No, it had a breath mint."

"Now that's romantic. I'll bet he's kissed you again."

"No."

Her sister was silent before she said cautiously, "But you're lying on the sofa."

"With ice on my foot."

"You don't still have that hairnet on, do you?"

"No. And Mrs. Hargrove even brought me a comb-and-brush set so my hair looks all right."

"Then why isn't he kissing you?"

"I asked him about money."

"Forget about his money. Pretend he's poor. Absolutely broke."

Jenny snorted. "You don't just pretend someone like that is poor. It's condescending. You talk about the problem like a mature adult."

"You're talking about problems?" Jenny's sister

wailed. "Don't talk about problems. This is a date. It isn't supposed to have problems."

"It's not a date. He's just being kind to me because I sprained my ankle."

"You. Him. Alone. Hot cocoa. I'm counting that as a date. I've already reported to Mom. She's been worried that you're not dating enough."

"I'm dating just fine."

"Well, now you are since you've met Robert Buckwalter the—"

"I know."

"—the Third. Say what do you call him anyway?"

"Bob. He wants to be called Bob."

"Really? He never mentioned that in any of his interviews."

"That's because he's a changed man now."

"Really? He never mentioned changed in his interviews."

Jenny could hear her sister flipping through papers.

"You're sure he said changed?" her sister asked.

"Yes."

"Well, I wonder what a man like that would want to change about himself? He's rich. He's gorgeous. He's kind."

"He wants to be Bob."

"And he hasn't kissed you again?"

Jenny shook her head. "No."

"Hmmm, I wonder why—"

"He's been reading the Bible—"

"He's not becoming a priest, is he? That would really upset the editors. We couldn't name a priest as the number one bachelor."

"I thought you were going to back off on that bachelor thing."

"My editors aren't sure. I've tried to back them off, but then I stopped. I think when I tried extra hard to convince them, they called their source and asked a few questions and now it's all gotten confused."

"What's confusing? The man has perfectly sound reasons for not wanting to be on that list. I'd think they'd respect his privacy and do what he wants."

"That's just it. They're not sure why he wants what he says he wants. They think he might be creating a— what did they call it?—a smoke screen. A diversion of sorts to cover up the real story."

"And what's the real story? They're not still on that engagement thing, are they? Bob, I mean Robert, he sure doesn't act engaged."

Her sister was silent for a minute. "They've had another tip. Something their source said by mistake."

"Robert thinks their source is Laurel. So if she claims they're engaged, I suppose they would listen."

"No, they've decided he's not engaged to Laurel. She's worked for them for years and they know her pretty well."

"Well, good—at least that's settled."

"They still think he's engaged."

Jenny's heart sank. She hadn't considered that. She'd been so worried he was involved with Laurel, she didn't count the billion other women in the world who would want to marry the man.

"Is she someone nice?" Jenny asked stiffly.

The room had suddenly gotten colder. Jenny told herself she shouldn't begrudge the man a fiancée. She was, after all, the hired help. It was none of her business.

"I think she's nice."

"Oh." Jenny blinked back a tear.

"They think it's you."

Jenny heard her sister's voice at the same time as Robert came back into the living room with his arms full of logs for the fireplace.

"Me?" Jenny squeaked, and blinked again.

Robert walked over to the fireplace and put the logs down. "Let me say hi to your sister. I'm assuming that's her. She's the only one who calls on that number. I'm wondering what the editors have told her. Maybe I should talk to her."

Jenny blinked again. "She can't talk to you."

"It's okay," her sister said on the other end of the phone. "I won't tell him about the—you know what. Besides, I know it's not true. I just couldn't convince my editors. They think that because you're my sister, I'm protecting you from the media frenzy."

Jenny looked up at Robert as he walked back to the sofa. The outside cold had added white to his forehead and pink to his cheeks. His chin was strong with a faint smudge of whiskers covering it. He'd left his head bare when he went outside and a few specks of snow glistened on his black hair. The lamp near the sofa gave a soft light that left the room full of partial shadows. Jenny wished she could go hide in one of them.

"Is your sister on a deadline?"

Jenny's mouth was dry. Robert's blue eyes had deepened to midnight and they were looking down at her. "What?"

"Is that why she can't talk to me? I thought your sister might be writing something. Last time I talked to her she said they were giving her the simple assignments. Grunt work she called it. She's just waiting for her big break." Robert smiled at Jenny. "I hope she gets it. She's a nice kid."

"Yeah." Jenny swallowed.

"If it's the deadline, tell her I'll only take a minute. I know how it is when every minute counts."

"It's not that. It's just that there's nothing new." Jenny forced her voice to be bright. "The editors are still making a decision. I asked. There's nothing new at all."

"Oh, well, thanks." Robert turned to walk back to the fireplace. "That's what I wanted to know."

Jenny looked down at the phone in her hand as though it had turned into something strange and exotic.

"You still there?" her sister said on the other end.

"Barely," Jenny said into the phone quietly. Her heart had finally started to beat again. "But I have to go. We'll talk later. Call me back."

Robert looked over his shoulder as he knelt down to the fireplace. "Tell her to call in the morning. I've got plans for tonight."

Jenny heard her sister squeal on the other end of the phone. "Plans! He's got plans!"

"He's talking about dinner." Jenny kept her voice even. She didn't want to encourage any rumors. "I think the plan is vegetable soup."

"For starters," Robert said as he lit a match to the log in the fireplace. "Only for starters."

Chapter Eleven

The next morning Jenny sat in the front seat of the four-wheel-drive Jeep Robert had borrowed from Linda and Duane at the café. Robert had promised her a surprise last night and this morning, after seeing that she could hobble along fine on her ankle, he told her she might as well come and see it firsthand.

"This isn't the road to Billings." Jenny had steeled herself for the surprise. She didn't dare tell him that she could give him a surprise of her own.

How in the world had those tabloid editors put two and two together and come up with such an outlandish idea? Robert could very well be engaged. He could even be engaged to Laurel despite all his protesting. But one thing Jenny knew for sure was that he wasn't engaged to her.

She'd sorted through what her sister had told her and decided Robert could be taking her to Billings to meet some mystery woman who was flying in to the airport there. That would explain the confusion in the tabloid editors' minds. Laurel must have said something about another woman. The fact that Jenny was one of only four single women in Dry Creek right now who were under seventy and over seventeen must have been what made the editors take such a leap of faith.

"Good thing it's not the road to Billings. We'd be stuck about now. Last I heard the road to Billings is closed. Too much drifting."

The sun shone a thin gray light down on the snow-packed road they'd taken out of Dry Creek. The air inside the Jeep was steamy warm, but the outside air had been heavy and damp. It could snow again anytime.

Jenny looked at Robert more closely. She wished the editors could see the man now. He didn't look like a man on his way to meet a woman he was planning to marry. There were no little twitches of repressed excitement. He hadn't even styled his hair. He'd combed it, but that was about it. Of course, that might just be because no one really styled their hair around here. Between the wind and the wool scarves, there were too many ways to mess it up.

"You never told me who owned Charlie." Jenny

said cautiously. She wondered why she'd never considered that that old man in the desert might not have a daughter or a granddaughter or something. That would explain why Robert had spent five months there. He might have been doing more than chopping wood. Five months was plenty of time to fall in love.

"Charlie?" Robert looked over at her blankly. "I told you about Harry. He's the old man. Reminded me of Mr. Gossett who came to the lobster dinner the other night. He was hanging around the café the other day, too. Lonely, I suppose."

"The man you gave your coat to? The one the FBI is worried about—"

"Well, Mr. Gossett is more paranoid than Harry, but outside of that they're a lot alike. They live alone except for their pets. Harry has Charlie and I hear that old man Gossett has a whole bunch of cats. Feeds them real well from what I hear. Duane says it's mostly tuna—and not cat tuna, either. That's got to be quite a sacrifice on his Social Security income."

"So Harry lives alone." Jenny wondered if the sun wasn't suddenly shining a little warmer. "Just him and Charlie."

To the right of the road, Jenny could see the foothills of the Big Sheep Mountain range covered in a thick collar of snow. Snow hadn't collected on the sides of the mountains and they were a gray-brown. On each side of the narrow country road were wide ditches that caught the snow. Beside each ditch was a fence running along the road, dividing the grassland. The road rose and then dipped along with the low rolling countryside.

"At least this road looks usable," Jenny said. Things were looking up. All she had to do was screw up her courage and tell Robert about the latest engagement rumor. He knew all about the tabloids. He'd understand how a mistake like that could happen. All she had to do was tell him. Then they'd chuckle about the whole thing.

But not yet. She stalled. "Yes, the road is really all right."

Robert grunted. "If you don't count the bouncing."

Jenny felt the bumps in the road. She couldn't help it. The gravel road they were traveling over had obviously frozen solid after a muddy spell. The snow ahead filled in the ruts and made the road look smooth when it wasn't.

Thin lines of barbed-wire fence divided the various sections of land on each side of the road even though there were no cattle near the road.

"Makes me remember why I took up flying," Robert added as the Jeep bounced over another rut. "The ride's a lot smoother up in the sky."

"Speaking of flying, isn't your plane out this way?"

Robert turned to flash her a grin. "No questions. This is a surprise, remember."

"I thought you'd bring Mrs. Hargrove, too." Jenny unwrapped the wool scarf she'd wound around her head earlier.

Jenny should have told Robert about the rumors this morning at breakfast with Mrs. Hargrove and Laurel looking on. The older woman would have found a lesson in the absurd situation and afterward they wouldn't need to dwell on it. Laurel would have seen to that. She would turn the conversation back to herself as soon as possible. Yes, Jenny should have spoken up when the two of them were around.

Jenny added, "We should have brought Mrs. Hargrove. There's room in the Jeep for three people— even four. Laurel could have come, too. If it's some sort of rock formation or something, Laurel would like to see it."

"Laurel?" Robert snorted. "The only rocks she's interested in are the kind that slip on her finger. Besides, it's not a rock formation."

"Mrs. Hargrove says we're close to the Chalk Mountains. They have strange rock formations. She says the only things out this way are rocks and cattle."

The older woman had been excited that Robert was taking Jenny for a little drive with the promise of a surprise at the end of it. She'd bundled them both up and thrust a thermos of coffee into their hands early this morning before they'd started off.

"It's not a rock and it's not a cow. And Mrs. Hargrove doesn't know everything that's out here this morning."

Jenny revised her earlier opinion. Robert was beginning to look more and more like a man on his way to meet a special woman. His blue eyes were filled with anticipation. He looked boyish with his secret.

"So is it smaller than a bread box?" Jenny decided to play along.

Robert grinned. "I hope not. If it is, that means it got squashed."

"Bigger than a truck?"

"No."

"Is it a living thing?"

"Not at this moment."

Jenny considered a moment. "Would this thing interest the tabloids?"

Robert laughed. "You know, it just might at that. I'll have to ask your sister if she'd like to know the kind of gift I'm giving these days to impress a woman. That should convince them I'm not bachelor list material."

"I think they're already beginning to wonder about you being bachelor material."

"Really? You talked to your sister."

Here it goes, Jenny said to herself, as she took a deep breath. "Not this morning. It's from yesterday. She told me their latest theory—seems they still think you're engaged."

"I knew Laurel was talking to them."

"Not to Laurel."

"They know I'm not engaged to Laurel?" Robert looked even more carefree than he already had been. "That's great!"

Jenny should speak now and finish the revelation. But she didn't. The road turned and she shifted on the seat. Then she looked out the side window and saw what was ahead. "What's your plane doing there? I thought it was back at Garth Elkton's ranch."

Jenny remembered that plane well. She and Robert had flown from Seattle to Montana in it and landed it on a small road near Garth Elkton's ranch. The containers of lobster had filled up the back of the plane and she'd been strapped into the copilot's seat for the flight over. Robert had been preoccupied during the trip and she'd spent her time watching the instrument panel and wondering what all of the extra features were meant to do. She'd heard he had the instrument panel custommade so he could include some high-tech gadgets.

"I moved the plane when you were napping yesterday. I needed to get it off the road. Besides, I needed it to be in a more open area. I'm using the homing device in it to coordinate with the plane that flew over." He turned to look at her. "You know, that's just great about the tabloids. Those guys are smarter than I gave them credit for being."

"Don't give them any credit yet."

Robert looked over at her. "Why not? They figured out Laurel was lying."

Jenny took another deep breath. She'd spit it out this time. "They think it's me."

"You?" Robert put his foot on the brake and turned to look at her. "What have you got to do with Laurel lying?"

"Not the lying." Jenny squared her shoulders and looked out the front window. The window was splattered with dirt. "They think it's me you're engaged to."

She couldn't see Robert, but the silence in the vehicle could only come from astonishment.

Jenny continued to study the dirt on the windshield. "My sister is young, you know, and really very romantic. Not that she told them we were engaged. I'm sure she'd never do that. But she might have mentioned the kisses—and, well, they're just so intent on having a story now that anything will do."

"Well, the old foxes," Robert said softly. "I'll never underestimate the tabloids again."

Jenny slipped a glance at him. He had eased up on

the brake and was driving again. He looked happy. Maybe he hadn't understood.

"Hopefully they won't print their nonsense. I just thought you should know. Of course, I've told my sister to tell them once again that it's not true. You're my employer and I'm just working a job here."

"You can't be working now." Robert started to whistle. "You don't have your hairnet on."

Jenny's hands automatically went to her hair. "Well, I'm not working right now, of course, but—"

"Good," Robert interrupted her. "Because we're on a date."

Jenny gasped. "But we can't be on a date!"

"Granted, it's not a common date." Robert reached over and turned on the radio. Instrumental guitar music came from the small speakers on the front panel. "I wanted to get flowers, too, but we'll have to start with music. I had to call a station in Billings and beg them to play this stuff for us. Did you know that the guitar is one of the most romantic musical instruments ever played?"

"No." Jenny swallowed. Her hands were suddenly clammy. "No, I didn't know that."

"Some people hold out for the harp," Robert continued as he steered the Jeep to the side of the road and turned it to go down a small path that ran on the field side of a fence. "I've always found a harp to be almost too sweet for my taste. Reminds me of funerals. But maybe you like the harp. I don't think I'll find a radio station that even has it on file around here but I could patch it in from someplace else through my satellite connection on the plane. I get radio, phones and television from anywhere. Custom designed. I can get you harp if you like harp."

"No, no, the guitar is fine."

Jenny twisted the wool scarf she held in her hands. The man really must not have understood. "There's probably no need to worry. I'm sure the tabloids have to verify their facts before they print anything."

Robert stopped whistling. "These are the tabloids! They print interviews with Big Foot!"

"Well, maybe they don't always verify. But space aliens can't sue. And I'm going to call my sister and tell them you'll sue them for everything they're worth if they print a story about you being engaged to—" Jenny's throat closed, but she pushed the words out "—to me."

"You want me to sue them?" Robert's voice was quiet. "For saying we're engaged."

Jenny glanced over at him. He was starting to frown. Good, she thought, he was finally beginning to understand. "Well, there won't be any need to sue if they just back off. I'm sure they're reasonable people and will understand it is in their best interests to not print such nonsense."

"You think it's nonsense?"

"Well, it's not true."

There was another moment of silence in the Jeep. Then Robert spoke. "It might not be true today, but who knows what might be true tomorrow."

Jenny's mind blanked. He couldn't be saying he'd consider—no, that was nonsense. If he was going to marry anyone, surely he'd pick someone like Laurel. Even the tabloids had. Jenny's mind stopped. Of course.

"I forgot that it would be convenient for you to be engaged to someone." Jenny's voice was small. "Even someone like me would stop the list. And I'm not like Laurel. I wouldn't be any trouble."

"Not any trouble?" Robert's voice was incredulous. "I can't even get you to date me. How do you figure you're no trouble?"

"Well, no one would know me." Jenny had helped her younger brothers and sisters get out of scrapes. She wondered if she'd be able to help this man, as well. "I mean, in your world, no one would know me. Your friends wouldn't be asking any awkward questions."

"I wouldn't count on it. I've found people always ask the awkward questions."

"Well, at least no one knows me except your mother.

And you'll have to tell her the truth, so no one will be disappointed when the wedding doesn't come off."

"What about me? Maybe I would be disappointed."

No, Jenny thought to herself. She couldn't help this man get out of his trouble. "Fine. Be that way. If you're not going to take any of this seriously, you can just be on that list. It'll serve you right. Forget I even offered to help."

"I don't want you to pretend to be engaged to me."

Jenny blinked back a tear. "Of course not."

The Jeep stopped. Robert turned off the ignition. The radio stopped. The hum of the heater stopped.

"I just don't want to have any pretending between us," Robert said quietly.

Jenny nodded. She put her hands up again to feel her hair. The static from when she pulled the wool scarf off made her hair fly. She tried to press her hair down. She should have worn her hairnet after all.

"Especially not to just feed the tabloids some story," Robert added. He opened the driver's door. "Now, if it was your sister doing the writing, that would be one thing."

"She'd never write about an engagement that wasn't true!"

A cold wind edged around the partially open driver's door. Robert turned to look at Jenny. "Then she should stick to selling pudding. Or move to another paper."

"She's just getting experience. It's not easy starting a career when you don't have connections."

"I know."

"She just needs a break."

Now this was the Jenny he knew. Her color had returned when she defended her younger sister. She no longer reached for a hairnet that wasn't there. Her eyes flashed.

"We'll give her one."

Jenny looked up at Robert. He looked serious.

"The next big thing that happens, it's all hers," Robert declared. "And if nothing happens on its own, I'll make some news."

"Like what?"

"Maybe I could invite the Queen Mother to tea with a group of Elvis impersonators. Give your sister an exclusive press invitation."

"You know the Queen Mother?"

Robert nodded. "I even know the world's best Elvis impersonator. He's better than the King."

"And the Queen Mother would come if you invited her?" Jenny was stunned.

"Well, I'd probably need to rent a suite at some fancy London hotel—she doesn't travel much—but I could do that. Maybe invite the queen, too. Has your sister ever been to London?"

Jenny shook her head. She'd gone on a drive with a magician. What would he pull out of his hat next?

"Have you ever been to London?"

Jenny shook her head.

Robert nodded in satisfaction. "Good. Then it's settled. You and your sister will both come."

Robert liked the dazed look in Jenny's eyes. It had occurred to him last night that his surprise of boxes of food might disappoint her. He knew it would disappoint most of the other women he'd dated in his life. Now he knew he had London in his pocket just in case.

"To London? To meet the queen?"

"And the Queen Mother if you want." Robert congratulated himself. He was making progress.

Jenny looked at the dirt on the windshield again. What did one say to an invitation like that? "The guitar music was sweet. Thanks for arranging it."

Robert started to whistle. "My pleasure. And now for the other surprise—it's not much. But you need to let me come help you out of the Jeep before we go see it."

Robert fully opened the driver's door and stepped out. Jenny watched him walk around the front of the vehicle. That's when she noticed that the white outside was uneven. A wide piece of land had been scraped clean of snow. Probably yesterday. There was a dusting of white snow on it now, but the layers of snow that sat on the ground around it had all been scraped off the land and pushed to the side of an area. The scraped strip could be a runway for a plane.

The runway wasn't the only thing unusual beside Robert's small plane. There was a large white tarp— or maybe a parachute—that was draped over a lumpy pile of what looked like boxes next to the plane.

Robert opened Jenny's door with a bow. "The surprise awaits. Permit me to help you down."

Jenny had borrowed an old pair of Mrs. Hargrove's snow boots this morning. Then Jenny had pulled the bottoms of her gray sweatpants down over the tops of the snow boots and she'd wrapped a very old black wool jacket on before tying a beige scarf around her head.

Jenny knew she looked fat as a snow bunny and as uncoordinated as a church mouse. But Robert looked up at her like she was royalty.

"The surprise is in the boxes," Robert said.

Jenny gave him her mittened hand and swung around. "You didn't need to actually get me a surprise. I thought the surprise was something to look at."

"Well, the first step is to look at the boxes," Robert pointed out as he helped her down from the Jeep. "I had a pilot I know make a special drop for me."

In Robert's mind, he had planned to kiss Jenny when she stepped out of the Jeep. But he didn't. She was looking skittish and he didn't want to scare her off.

The air was damp and heavy with the promise of snow. Gray clouds hung in the sky. Jenny tightened the scarf around her neck.

Robert picked up one end of the parachute and pulled it off of the boxes. Ten industrial-size boxes stood in the middle of the tangle of cords. Two other smaller boxes were on one side of the pile.

Robert reached inside his coat for the pocket knife he'd brought. Those two smaller boxes might be the roses, he thought. He had only been able to leave a message with the pilot making the delivery. But the man must have added the roses at the last minute. Those two boxes sure didn't match the others.

"Let's start here." Robert ran his knife down the tape holding one of the smaller boxes together.

Robert had his mind on red roses and that was the only excuse he had for not looking at the box more closely. He'd opened the edge of the box, before he saw what it was. White lace started to spill out of the box. "That's not roses."

Jenny looked more closely at the box. A small tag was taped to the top of it. It was an airline baggage sticker that had been routed to the Billings airport.

Robert opened the box further. There were no roses hidden in the lace.

"That must be Laurel's dress," Jenny finally said. "The one she brought with her for the wedding."

"What the—" Robert looked into the box more closely. Jenny was right.

"The pilot must have stopped at the Billings airport."

"Well, she'll just have to take the dress back with her." Robert closed the flap on the box. "It was a fool stunt to bring one with her anyway."

"Would have been good for pictures, though." Jenny stepped closer to the boxes. The air was cold enough to make gray puffs around her when she breathed. She rubbed her hands together even in the mittens. "I've got to give her credit for thinking of that."

"Oh, Laurel can plan all right."

Robert looked over at Jenny. She was crouched down by the boxes. She was wrapped up in scarves and mittens. Her nose was red and her cheeks were white. What hair wasn't covered with a wool scarf fell every which way. She was adorable. "Wish I'd thought of pictures."

Jenny looked up at him. The sun fell on her and she smiled.

"I should have brought a camera with me. My mother probably still has one or two of those disposable ones," Robert said.

Jenny chuckled. "Not if those kids are around her. I heard two of them at the dance asking her for another camera. She said she'd given them all out. And no wonder, they way those kids were shooting pictures. Heaven only knows why they were taking so many pictures of us."

Robert didn't say anything. He and half of the Dry Creek population knew why the kids were taking pictures of him and Jenny. He was relieved that Jenny still didn't know.

"We'll just set Laurel's boxes aside." Robert pushed them to the side of the stack. "We've got some other boxes to open."

Chapter Twelve

"It's Romaine. The good kind." Jenny sat in the snow and hugged the lettuce. "You even had it packed in something so it would stay cold but wouldn't freeze. I can't wait. We'll have salad."

"With vine-ripened tomatoes," Robert couldn't help adding.

"And an avocado," Jenny added in supreme contentment. "Two avocados in fact."

Robert congratulated himself. He'd given women emeralds and rubies before and gotten less enthusiastic thanks.

"I'm sorry the roses didn't make it." The pilot had apparently not gotten the message Robert had left, but it didn't matter. Jenny was happy with her salad.

"And you have stuff for tacos. The kids will thank you."

Jenny forgave Robert any of his faults. He had thought of her and the kids, too. He'd remembered her craving for a romaine salad. Her sister was right. This man was special.

"I'm not so sure the kids are going to thank me. I've got some caviar stuck in those boxes someplace. My mother told me she wanted to expand the kids' horizons a little further. I'm not so sure about it myself. I think she might have pushed them to the limit with the lobsters. I told her she could tell the kids what she'd ordered for them." He shook his head. "I don't want to be responsible when they hear they have to eat caviar."

Jenny smiled. "The boys will love her."

Robert lifted an eyebrow. "You think?"

Jenny nodded. "They'll sneak the caviar off their plates and use it for ice fishing. After all, it's just fish eggs. I heard some of them worrying about what they could use for bait. They can't dig for worms in the frozen dirt around here."

"Fishing. Really? I think I have some fish hooks in my plane."

Robert stood up and held out a hand to Jenny as he continued. "Why don't we go see? Besides, it would be good to get out of the cold for a little bit and warm up. The plane has a heater I can turn on."

"You're sure you have enough fuel?"

"I have plenty of fuel. I could get back to Seattle and have some to spare."

The step into the plane was a high one, but once inside Jenny was glad she'd moved. The plane formed a cozy cocoon around the cockpit, partially because the sun shone in through the windows and heated the space enough so that it was very comfortable—especially if one was wrapped in wool like Jenny was.

To get to the cockpit, Jenny had needed to crawl through the small cargo space behind the pilot and copilot seats. When they left Seattle, that space had been filled with seafood boxes and boxes from Mrs. Buckwalter's house.

Jenny sat in the copilot seat. The windows were frosted around the edges, but she could see the Big Sheep Mountains straight ahead. A barbed-wire fence was to the left and open space was on the right. Everything was coated with snow.

"Is the heater on?" Jenny asked before she realized it was impossible. But there was a sound that made her think something was running.

Robert looked up. He heard the sound, too. "Someone's coming."

The two of them stood in the open space of the plane door and watched the pickup drive closer to them. Whoever was driving the pickup was doing a good job of it, but Robert felt a prickle of unease. Something was not right. There were three figures in the cab of the pickup and they were packed tight together. Which made sense. Then he saw it—

"Move back—" Robert swung his arm around to bring Jenny back into the shadow of the plane, but he was too late. He knew what had made him uneasy— that tall, skinny shadow in the window was a rifle.

A voice—Robert recognized the FBI agent's voice—called out. "Anybody home? You've got company. And trouble."

There wasn't room to maneuver and Jenny couldn't move too far. So Robert did the only thing he could. He stepped in front of her.

"Stay behind me," he whispered. *Dear Lord, don't let that gun go off.*

"What's wrong?"

"I don't know. Something with the FBI agent and that woman friend of his." Robert was looking out the plane door. The three figures got out of the pickup.

"Francis?"

"Uh-huh," Robert said as he raised his hands

slowly until they were clearly in the open. "And our friend Mr. Gossett."

The old man didn't look drunk this morning. He did look a little crazy though. He was pointing that rifle of his at anyone and everyone. The barrel of it bounced around enough to show that the old man was nervous.

Robert had training in combating terrorist activity and knew an anxious criminal was the most dangerous kind. The old man walking toward him shouldn't be underestimated. Nor should his beat-up old rifle.

"Welcome." Robert schooled his voice to be calm as though nothing out of the ordinary was happening. Robert saw that the old man had a much newer pistol in his other hand as well as the rifle. "Nice day for a drive, isn't it?"

Robert noticed that Francis Elkton was wearing a dress and Flint Harris a suit. They huddled together as they walked closer to the plane with Mr. Gossett. They must have been on their way to church.

"Especially for a Sunday drive," Robert added as he leaned farther toward the opening in the plane. "Give me a minute to come down and I'll join you. Mrs. Hargrove packed us a thermos before we left. I'm sure there's enough coffee for five."

The thermos was the old-fashioned kind. It might do as a weapon. Or the diversion might be enough. With guns in both hands, however, the old man was dangerous. Robert waited until Jenny had reached the cockpit.

"Don't talk to me about Mrs. Hargrove," the old man grumbled. He stood in front of the open door on the plane. "Her and her Christian principles and then her not even willing to give me a ride to Billings today. I've been in her car plenty of times. I told her it was important and she doesn't listen to me. The woman just never listens. Worried about the snow, she says. What does she care if she gets stuck anyway? Someone would come looking for her in a blizzard. But me? No, nobody'll come for me. I had to stop them for a ride," Mr. Gossett pointed to Francis and Flint. "Mrs. Hargrove can go stew in her own coffee. I ain't drinking any of it."

"No problem. I won't pour a cup for you," Robert said easily as he held on to the side of the plane and swung down to the ground beside Mr. Gossett. "But maybe you don't mind if the rest of us have a cup."

The old man grunted. "Don't be too sure about that. I got me some business to get taken care of and I ain't got no time to waste on folks drinking coffee."

"Maybe Mr. Buckwalter has something stronger that you'd like instead," Francis suggested as she stepped into the circle. She looked at Robert, desperation edging her eyes. "Mr. Gossett is fond of his alcohol, you know."

"I could do with a beer," the old man admitted. "Should have brought me a couple. But I packed too fast."

No one remarked on the fact that the old man hadn't packed anything at all except for his rifle and the hat on his scrawny head. He hadn't even brought along much of a jacket.

"I don't have—" Robert wished he'd thought to put in some alcohol. He'd trade a whole ship full of the French-imported water that he had brought along right now for a pop-top can of the cheapest beer around.

"I saw some vanilla in those boxes," Jenny said as she showed herself again in the plane's door.

"I thought—" Robert started to scold Jenny as he turned to look up her.

Jenny lifted her chin and climbed to the ground. "It might be very good actually. It's a big bottle and would make quite a drink. Mrs. Buckwalter only buys pure vanilla—the beans have been soaking in alcohol for some time now."

"Well, goodness, girl, there's no reason to waste good alcohol on beans soaking it up," Mr. Gossett said as he used his rifle to gesture to Jenny. "Go get it for me. Me and your man here—" the old man pointed his gun at Robert "—we've got business to discuss in the meantime."

Robert smiled in relief. There for a second he thought the rifle barrel would follow Jenny. He shifted his position so it was even farther from the others. The rifle barrel followed.

"What can I do for you?" Robert asked politely, although he was almost certain he knew. The FBI was looking for the local informant who had tipped off the rustlers and, unless Robert missed his guess, the informant stood before him now as nervous as he deserved to be for betraying all the people of Dry Creek.

"I need me a plane ride."

Robert nodded like the request was reasonable. He kept his suspicions off his face and out of his voice. Let the man ask for what Robert knew he wanted. "Lots of people like to take a spin up in the air. I'd be happy to take you up for a few minutes." Robert turned and lightly slapped his hand against the side of his plane. "Nothing like a plane ride."

"A few minutes won't do it. I need to get me to another town. Maybe even across the border into Canada. I need to get out of Dry Creek one way or another. I'm what you might call a fugitive."

Well, the old man wasn't shy about laying his cards on the table. Robert took that as a good sign.

"The border won't work then." Robert calculated how long he could stall the old man. Robert looked up at the sky as though reading the signs of weather. "Not the best day for flying, either. Gusty winds. A blizzard could blow up. You wouldn't want to be in the air then. Maybe you'd be better off going tomorrow instead. I could drive you somewhere tomorrow personally. Keep your feet on the ground that way."

The old man snorted. "By tomorrow I'll be arrested and my feet won't care where they are. I think I'll take my chances with getting to Canada."

"Canada?" Robert stalled. "I don't know."

"That's where people always run to," the old man persisted stubbornly. "They say they're going across the border and they do. That's where I'm going."

"That's the Mexican border they're talking about," Robert confirmed patiently as he shifted his feet again. He wanted to keep the old man's attention, and Robert figured the best way to do that was to fidget enough to keep the rifle focused on him. "But I don't have enough fuel to fly that far. And there's no point in flying across the Canadian border. There might be more paperwork to ship you back, but they'd do it all the same. You wouldn't be solving any problems that way."

"I don't want to go to jail," the old man said stubbornly. "I can't stand them small cells they have."

"Claustrophobic, huh?"

"Clausta' who?" Mr. Gossett squinted at Robert.

"No need to get fancy in the word department. It was only cows missing anyway. Not like anyone around here was killed or anything."

Robert bit his tongue before he could remind the old man that Glory Beckett had almost died because of the rustling business the old man had treated so lightly. The fact that no one had died yet was only because of God's grace. The old man in front of him surely couldn't take any credit for that.

"The plane's got enough fuel to fly to someplace like Fargo, North Dakota, or we could head into Billings if you'd like." Robert said the destinations clearly and turned so his voice would carry clearly to the others. If he was flying anyone anywhere he wanted it to be only one or two choices and for those choices to be heard by everyone around.

"I'll take Fargo. Let's all get inside."

"You don't mean everyone, I'm sure." Robert was sure of no such thing, but he nodded calmly and then added as an afterthought, "Taking everyone will slow us down. Plus, the fuel will last longer if the plane is lighter." Robert measured the old man with his eyes. "I'd say you're about one hundred seventy pounds?"

Mr. Gossett nodded.

"I'll go with you to fly this thing, but you don't need the others."

The old man pondered a moment. "I'll need a hostage."

"That would be me," the FBI agent stepped forward.

Robert nodded slightly. Yes, if Flint and he got Mr. Gossett up in the air, they could handle him.

The old man snorted. "I don't think so. I'll take her." He jerked his head at Jenny who was just returning with a large bottle of vanilla in her hand. "She's a skinny little thing. Can't weigh much."

"You don't need her," Robert protested. "I've got fuel enough to fly three men."

"It's not just about weight," the FBI agent added. "In case something goes wrong, I can talk to the authorities for you."

"Nothing had better go wrong."

The agent shrugged. "You never know."

"You speak fancy enough, don't you?" the old man demanded of Jenny as he held out his hand for the vanilla bottle.

Silently Jenny gave him the bottle as she shrugged.

"Well, it doesn't need to be all that fancy. She can talk for me," Mr. Gossett insisted as he slipped the bottle into the pocket of his coat. "Now, you two men see that all of the boxes are out of that plane. I don't want any unnecessary weight holding us back."

Robert's heart sank. He had hoped the old man

would tip the vanilla bottle back the minute he got it. That would give them their one good chance to get that rifle away from him.

"Jenny's heavier than she looks," Robert offered easily.

Jenny started to sputter then realized what Robert was doing. "I guess I am pretty heavy. We burned a lot of fuel flying in from Seattle."

Mr. Gossett snorted and pointed his rifle directly at Jenny. "Don't start giving me trouble now. I'm the one who says who is going and you're going 'cause I say you're going."

"Of course," Jenny said softly.

"She's not going," Robert said flatly as he turned his body so he could shield Jenny if the old man swung that rifle around again. *Please, God, help me on this one. I'll go. I'll go gladly. But not Jenny.*

"An' why not?" the old man reared up and demanded.

"The plane won't fly with her in it." Robert said the words in his most authoritative voice hoping the nonsense would pass for truth. "We almost didn't make it into Dry Creek. Had to crash-land over by the Elkton place. Something to do with the instrument panel. One of those energy things related to chemicals in the body. Makes the instruments go haywire. Something to do with energy fields or hormones, maybe both."

The old man snorted, but Robert could see that he wasn't sure.

"Well, if she doesn't go, she hits the ground with the two of them," Mr. Gossett finally said.

The ground would work, Robert thought to himself. Jenny would get a little snow on herself that she'd have to brush off when the plane left, but the ground would be safer than the air.

"You two—get down on the ground." The old man jerked his gun at Francis and Flint.

"What?" the FBI agent questioned.

Robert could see that the agent was trying to move behind the old man, but there was no way.

"It's just that the ground is frozen." Robert stepped in. "Let them at least go sit in the pickup—or even the Jeep. There's no way they can catch us in a Jeep once we're in the air."

Robert was starting to breathe again. Jenny would be even better in the Jeep. The heater would keep them warm and they could drive back into Dry Creek and get help. The sheriff would call over to the airports at Billings and Fargo and let them know what was happening.

"The ground. Now," the old man insisted. "I don't have all day. I gotta get out of here."

Francis lowered herself to the ground. The snow was not yet packed down and she sank into the few inches that covered the place where the snow had been scraped off earlier.

"You, too," the old man ordered Flint. "I want you with your back to her—" the old man shifted his gaze to Jenny "—and you get some rope from those boxes to tie them up."

"You're not going to leave them like that?" Robert protested. He hadn't counted on the people on the ground being tied up. That changed everything. If they were tied, they needed to be someplace warmer. "Why not just tie them up in one of the vehicles?"

Robert hadn't lived in Montana. He didn't know about the winters here. But it didn't take much knowledge of weather to realize that the two people before him could freeze to death if they were tied up out here in the open.

"What does it matter to me if they get cold?" the old man snarled. "That'll teach them to come snooping around, asking questions. Butting into a man's private life. Looking through his trash cans."

The old man kept the rifle pointed at Jenny the whole time he ordered her to tie up Francis and Flint and then he walked with her over to the two vehicles and ordered her to pull out some wires and give them to him.

Robert didn't remind the old man that there had been any suggestion that Jenny wait with the other two on the ground instead of joining them in the air. He could tell by the expression on the FBI agent's face that the ground could be a death sentence. At least if Robert had Jenny with him in the plane, he could call some of the shots. The old man wouldn't know how to fly a plane. He would need Robert's cooperation.

Robert kept reminding the old man that a plane did not fly itself the whole time the three of them were preparing to take off from the makeshift runway on that cow pasture just north of Dry Creek.

"You can put the gun away," Robert repeated. He had started the engines and was checking out the instrument panel. "No one's going to sneak up on you when you're inside here."

The old man was crouched in the baggage compartment of the plane. Jenny was strapped into the copilot's seat and Robert was in his own place. The man had kept the rifle pointed at Jenny.

The sound of the engine was a constant background noise as Robert maneuvered the small plane for takeoff.

Robert was almost ready to turn around to begin the take off when they all heard it.

The cell phone was ringing.

Robert looked at Jenny. The cell phone was in the pocket of her parka. "Let it ring."

The old man shifted the rifle in his hands. "Give it to me. I'll decide who answers what."

Jenny nodded as she reached into her pocket and pulled out the small black phone. "It's probably just a wrong number."

The old man grunted as he took the phone and looked at it. The phone rang again in his hand and he studied the phone for a moment before he pressed the button to receive the call. "Hello?"

Chapter Thirteen

Jenny held her breath as though she could will her sister to hang up when she heard a strange man's voice. *Lord, let her know it's trouble.*

"Yes," Mr. Gossett answered hesitantly. "He's here, but he's busy."

Jenny looked over at Robert. He was glancing back at Mr. Gossett by looking at the old man's reflection in the instrument panel. It was close to freezing inside the cockpit of the small plane and yet Robert had a thin sheen of sweat on his forehead.

Jenny felt the coldness in her bones one minute and she flashed hot the next. The shoulder strap of the seat belt dug into her arm when she turned to look at Mr. Gossett.

The old man was concentrating on the phone, but

he still had the rifle angled at Jenny. He frowned like he was arguing with someone. "Can't it wait? He's busy right now."

Robert moved his hand slightly to turn one of the knobs on the instrument panel. He looked over at Jenny. "I'm sorry I got you into this."

"You?" Jenny looked at him in astonishment. "What did you do?"

"If I wasn't so intent on impressing you with the fact that I could give you anything, we wouldn't have been out at the plane this morning. We would have been in church like Mrs. Hargrove would want."

"Mrs. Hargrove thought it was great that you were giving me a surprise."

"She thought I was going to show you a rock."

"Well, still—you couldn't have known what would happen."

The old man interrupted their conversation by thrusting the black cell phone up front. "This woman says she needs to talk to you—claims she's a sales-woman for some big pudding company. I've been trying to tell her you're busy."

Robert looked over at Jenny as he took the phone from the old man.

"Hello, Robert Buckwalter speaking." Robert put the phone to his ear.

Jenny hoped her sister would take the hint from the formality in Robert's voice that they were in a serious situation.

Jenny twisted her neck so she could look back at the old man. She'd hoped he'd relaxed some. He hadn't. He had the rifle angled toward her and his eyes were suspicious.

"Sorry about the phone call," Jenny said. She kept her voice calm and low. She thought that if she talked to the old man it would mask any conversation Robert was having with her sister. Maybe he could slip her a hint about their situation.

"Fool things—them portable phones."

"Yes, I suppose they are." Jenny agreed.

Jenny heard Robert talking about an order for chocolate pudding. Apparently the old man did as well because he relaxed somewhat.

"Those salesmen—they'll find you anyplace you go," the old man grumbled. "There's no peace anywhere."

"It does seem that way." Jenny wondered what salesmen had had the nerve to call at Mr. Gossett's home.

"That's what's wrong with the world—all this buy, buy, buy…" The old man's voice trailed off.

"No, I can't place an order now. I'm getting ready to fly my plane—delicate cargo." Robert's conversation filled in the gap in the old man's complaining.

"Did you need more money?" Jenny frantically tried to keep her conversation with the old man alive so that he would not be listening to Robert just in case Robert was fool enough to mention anything concrete about the danger they were in.

"Me?" Mr. Gossett seemed startled. "Why would I need more money?"

The old man was starting to look at Robert suspiciously. At the moment, Robert was talking about the number of calories in a cup of pudding.

"But then why did you do it?" Jenny knew it was a gamble, but the question pulled the old man's attention back to her. She hoped her sister could decode whatever message Robert was giving her. "The rustling. Why did you tip them off about the cattle?"

"Dry Creek owed it to me," Mr. Gossett said. "They owed it to my family. My father founded Dry Creek, you know. Wouldn't be no town without him."

"You must have been very proud."

"I wasn't proud. I wasn't nothing," the old man grumbled, and then turned to Robert. "You're done talking to that saleswoman. It's time for us to get out of here."

"Yes, the delivery is important," Robert said into the phone. "I expect the pudding to be there when I arrive at two o'clock."

"An' I expect you to hang up when I say hang up," the old man said nastily.

Robert put the phone into a cradle in the instrument panel. Jenny was surprised. She hadn't realized it was the plane's cell phone they had been using since their arrival in Dry Creek.

"The pudding will be ready when we get there," Robert said to Jenny quietly as he adjusted a few knobs on the instrument panel.

"Ah—" Jenny gave a small barely audible gasp when she saw that the cell phone's light was still lit. The phone was still on. Her sister could still hear everything. Jenny quickly coughed to cover her slip.

Now that Jenny thought about it, Robert had received a phone call when they were flying in from Seattle. He had explained that he had some kind of satellite reception capability in the plane's system. No wonder that cell phone worked in Dry Creek when her own personal one didn't.

"You sure do set an unnatural store by that pudding of yours," the old man grumbled. "In my day, we used to make our own pudding Real milk and cream. Butter. Flour. None of this prepackaged stuff they feed you today."

"We're ready for takeoff," Robert said and then looked toward the back of the plane. "You might want to lay your rifle down, Mr. Gossett, for the ascent portion of the takeoff. Change in cabin pressure and everything. Jenny here's going to start feeling like she's your hostage."

"She is my hostage—thought I said that before," the old man insisted.

"Well, it's a long ride to Fargo," Robert continued easily. "No point in having your rifle out all that time. Nobody here's going anywhere until we land this plane at the airport there anyway."

"Thanks, but I'll keep the rifle ready if you don't mind. I don't aim to be no fool."

"Of course not," Robert agreed easily as he started to move the levers and buttons on his panel. Several clicks followed each other.

"Not that I'm not thankful that you haven't shot your rifle at anyone," Jenny clarified for her sister. She wanted her sister to alert the authorities, but not worry their mother.

Robert grunted a warning. Jenny knew the warning was for her although she suspected Mr. Gossett might think it was for him. She was right.

"I aim to be comfortable on this trip," the old man said defiantly. "That means keeping my rifle pointed where I want it pointed."

"Of course," Robert said smoothly.

Jenny felt the small plane start to rise.

The plane rose in the air gracefully. They were up a hundred feet when Robert banked slightly as though waving to the two people on the ground. Jenny looked down and watched the figures of Flint and Francis grow smaller.

Be with them, Father. Jenny prayed. *Send them someone. And in the meantime, keep them warm.*

If it had been another morning, Jenny would revel in the plane flight. Robert rose high enough that they were flying just under the gray clouds. It was like flying through the underside of a cotton ball. Strings of gray swirled around the plane, but visibility was never gone.

"At least we have heat up here," Robert said as he pushed a lever and the flow of warm air increased. Robert turned his neck slightly so he could see the old man in the cargo area. "Warm enough for you back there?"

The old man snorted. "You can't fool me."

Jenny's heart froze. The old man must suspect the telephone was still working.

"You've got plenty of heat," the old man continued talking. "I see it on the gauge here. No need to be skimpy with the heat. Don't let it hang down there at sixty degrees. Crank it up. Remember us old folks feel the cold more than you young ones. And don't be thinking you can pull anything over on me. I'm watching."

"Of course," Robert said once again. "Just sit back and pretend you don't have anything to worry about."

The old man snorted. "Got me plenty to worry about. I've figured that one out."

"If any of your troubles are related to money, I've got plenty that you're welcome to have if we get landed safe and sound." Robert had seldom laid down such an obvious bribe.

"Don't tell him you're rich," Jenny whispered softly. "He'll keep us for ransom."

Robert laughed. "I think he already knows by now I'm rich. Not many poor people have their own planes."

"Yeah, that ransom bit though, that's not a bad idea," the old man said gleefully from the back of the plane. "I had to leave all the money I got from those rustlers back home. Didn't have time to dig it up now that the ground's frozen."

"You had it buried!" Jenny turned around to look at the old man. He was huddled against the wall of the plane, hugging the barrel of his rifle. "Why?"

"You never know who's watching," he said indignantly. "I didn't want one of my neighbors to rob me!"

"Robbed in Dry Creek? By who?"

"I've got my enemies there. You can be sure. But you youngsters wouldn't know about things like that. How everything gets tangled up when you live with the same folks for seventy-some years," the old man said stubbornly.

"But surely they wouldn't rob you."

"They would if they could. But I'm too smart for them. I know how to take care of my money." The old man took a deep breath. "And I'll be thinking of what money I'll need for a ransom for our friend here." Mr. Gossett jerked his head toward Robert. "Being a rich man, he'll be worth a penny or two."

"And Jenny, too." Robert looked into the rearview mirror, which showed him the back of the plane. "I'll pay a good amount for her, too."

Robert could see the protest grow on Jenny's face, but he continued. "My only condition is the obvious one."

"What?" the old man demanded.

"We need to both be safe and free. She and I— we're together in this. You hurt her, you've hurt me. If you're going to hurt anyone, it's me. If you harm a single hair on her head, the only thing you get from me is a lifetime of trouble."

The old man grunted. "You lovebirds. If I'd have known it was like that, I'd have brought the FBI agent instead."

The air inside the small plane was overly warm now. Jenny felt sweat in her palms. "We're not lovebirds."

The old man grunted. "Don't make me no never

mind if you are. I was young once. I know what it's like to love someone." He focused on the back of Robert's neck. "How much money you figure your lady friend here is worth?"

"You're welcome to every penny I have if you keep her safe."

"Don't suppose you know what time it is?" the old man said suddenly, and leaned forward to look at the instrument panel. "Hey, what are all those gadgets?"

Jenny scrambled for something to say. She didn't know if Mr. Gossett would realize the significance of that little red light on the cell phone or not.

"I thought you said you didn't help the rustlers because of the money," Jenny reminded the man boldly.

Her distraction worked. He reared back from his squatting position indignantly. "I always believe in getting my due from people—and Dry Creek owed me and my family. It was time they paid and paid up good."

Robert made some adjustments to the altitude. Not much, but it would be enough to make the old man sit back down.

"Sorry," Robert said smoothly as the plane dipped a little. "Must be some turbulence. It'd be a good idea to slip one of those seat belts on back there. Keep you from bouncing around."

"There wasn't much wind earlier," Mr. Gossett said suspiciously.

"From the looks of it, there's a blizzard coming in," Robert cautioned the man. He didn't add that the blizzard appeared to be twenty hours away. They'd be safely landed somewhere by then. He only had fuel left for four hours.

"But where will I go in a blizzard?" Mr. Gossett asked quietly from the back seat. He had belted himself into one of the side seats. "I can't go back home."

"I'm sure there's a hotel," Jenny comforted the man. "Just ask the desk at the airport. They'll tell you how to get a cab to a hotel."

"I've never been to a big city before."

"Fargo's not that big," Robert stated clearly. "You'll see when we fly within range of it in an hour and—" Robert looked down at his watch "—thirty-five minutes. And, oh, by the way, my watch reads one-fifteen."

"Mrs. Hargrove would have brought my Sunday plate over by now," the old man mumbled wearily. "Probably that meat loaf of hers. I love that meat loaf. And maybe some mashed potatoes."

"She's been a good neighbor to you."

The old man grunted. "That's all you know about it."

"Well, I don't know what else she could have done." Jenny wanted to keep Mr. Gossett a little upset so he didn't pay too much attention to the red light on the cell phone as it jutted out of the instrument panel.

"That's just it," Mr. Gossett said emphatically. "You don't know. Nobody knows, not even Helen herself."

"Helen?"

"Mrs. Hargrove to you. Used to be Helen Boone." The old man's voice softened. "She used to be the prettiest thing when she was Helen Boone. I used to leave flowers on her desk at school some mornings."

"Isn't that nice." Jenny was hoping for some common ground. "I didn't know you used to be sweet on her."

"Me?" The old man sounded startled. "I never said that. I never said that to anyone. Not ever."

"But you left her flowers." Jenny turned around so she could see the man clearly even though he was no longer looking ahead at her.

Mr. Gossett grunted. "For all the good it done me. She thought it was Frank Hargrove leaving them."

"And you never told her."

The old man shrugged. "Thought she should have known it was me leaving the flowers. So I was stubborn. Next thing I knew Frank Hargrove up and asked her to marry him and she said yes. It was too late then. They were beholden and I knew Helen wouldn't go back on her word."

"So you've loved her in silence all those years?"

The old man didn't move for a moment and then he finally said, "Didn't seem to be much I could do about it."

"But to not even tell her."

The wrinkles on the old man's face seemed to fold into him, but he didn't answer the question. Of course, Jenny thought to herself, what could he say? He'd not even had the courage to tell the woman he loved how he felt. Instead, he'd let his love sour him until he became a bitter old recluse.

"I don't suppose you've been to Fargo?" Robert cut into the silence with a question for Jenny.

Jenny looked over at him. He obviously wanted the talk to continue so that her sister, or by now probably the police, could monitor them.

"There was a movie by that name," Jenny offered. "But I missed it."

"It'll be small-town America at its best," Robert added as he shifted in his seat to look in the mirror that allowed him to see where Mr. Gossett sat. He called back to the man. "Feel free to take a nap if you'd like."

The old man grunted and sat up straighter. "Don't take me for no fool."

"Of course not," Robert replied smoothly. "Just want you to be comfortable."

"I can be comfortable when I'm back home in my bed."

"Back in Dry Creek?" Robert asked in surprise.

Jenny looked at Mr. Gossett and said softly, "We're headed to Fargo."

"Yeah." The old man nodded wearily. "I'm gonna miss that old bed at home."

Jenny did her best to bring up conversation topics. She went through stories of her growing-up years. She talked about her favorite recipes. She recited a favorite poem. Robert would answer here and there, but mostly he just sent her thankful glances. By now the plane was encountering some real turbulence and he had to watch the instrument panel closely.

Jenny periodically glanced over her shoulder to see if Mr. Gossett had nodded off yet. She didn't quite know how they would manage, but she knew that she or Robert would need to try and take the rifle from the old man if he fell asleep.

The air inside the plane was warm and Jenny had been talking for over an hour. She had almost forgotten the reason why she was talking.

And then it happened—from the other end of the cell phone came the distinct sound of a sneeze.

The old man sat up straight. "What was that?"

Jenny's heart stopped. She looked at Robert.

"I sneezed," Robert said easily. "Must be coming down with something."

There was silence for a moment and Jenny started to relax.

"No, you didn't," the old man finally said. "That sneeze was too far away—besides, it was a woman's sneeze."

Jenny resisted the urge to say that the sneeze was hers. She knew the old man had been able to see her clearly all along and he would know she was lying.

The old man leaned forward so he could put his head between Jenny and Robert and look at the instrument panel clearly.

"That phone's still on," the old man announced. "That pudding person's still listening."

Jenny shivered. The old man who had talked about his young love was gone. The man who sat behind them now was a hard man. And he had a rifle in his hands.

Jenny felt the round cold circle of the rifle barrel pressed against the side of her head.

"I don't like being double-crossed," Mr. Gossett said. "I don't like it at all."

Robert positioned the plane so it would fly as smooth as possible without him.

"I'm the one who left the phone on," Robert said. "Threaten me if you're going to threaten anyone."

The old man laughed. Robert felt his heart constrict. There was no amusement in the laughter. The old man no longer sounded pathetic. He sounded dangerous.

"I'm not going to threaten," the old man announced wearily as he slowly cocked the rifle. "I'm tired of people not treating me right."

"You can't blame Jenny for Dry Creek," Robert said as he unhooked his seat belt so he could move. "What happened there happened many years ago."

Lord, keep him talking, Robert begged.

"And Robert—he gave you his coat," Jenny added.

The old man grunted. "It's all too late."

"Put that rifle down." Robert tried again. "If you don't, I won't fly you to Fargo. I'll set us down right here. Look down—it's nothing but white. We'll all freeze to death."

"I don't much care where I die. But I do figure that I may as well get even before I go."

"Hurting Jenny won't make you even." Robert moved everything so he could twist and tackle the man in one smooth movement. Robert knew he'd have to be quick about it.

"I suppose you'll be lonesome without her," the old man turned to Robert and snarled. "Just like I was—all those years alone."

"As a matter of fact, I would be lonesome without

her," Robert said softly. "I can't imagine living the rest of my life without her."

Jenny had watched Robert move around so that he was free of all the belts and the levers keeping him in the pilot seat.

"Now I lay me down to sleep." Jenny started to pray the old prayer she and her sister had prayed as little girls. Then thinking of the sneeze that might have come from her sister, she added, "No matter what happens here today, I want everyone to know it's no one's fault."

The old man grunted in protest. "It's the fault of someone."

"Who?" Jenny asked. The barrel of the rifle no longer pressed so hard against her head. She wasn't sure if that was a sign of hope or a sign of doom.

The old man was silent for a moment before he whispered, "Helen. It's her fault She should have known."

Mr. Gossett might have had a tear in his eye. Robert believed that he did and that was why, when Robert swung back and tackled him, the old man just seemed to crumble. Taking the rifle away was not even difficult.

Robert reached for a length of rope that had been tied around some boxes on the trip out from Seattle and handed it to Jenny. "Can you tie him up?"

Jenny nodded as she slid past Robert on his way back to the pilot's seat.

The old man sat in silence for the ten minutes it took them to reach the Fargo airport. Jenny spent the first five minutes of the ten speaking into the cell phone and reassuring her sister that everything was fine. The final five minutes Jenny spent wondering why Robert was so quiet.

"What's that?" Jenny said as she looked out the window.

It was the middle of the afternoon and the land all around the runway was blanketed with white snow and ice. But a crowd lined the runway anyway. There must have been a dozen vans with block letters on their doors and shiny reflectors on their top.

"What's happening—a parade?" Jenny asked.

"Not quite," Robert said. "Those are television crews getting their lights set up for interviews."

"Interviews? With who?"

Robert grimaced. "Us."

Chapter Fourteen

Jenny's throat was sore and her face was tired. She had never before smiled until the muscles in her face hurt. And her eyes! Her eyes burned from being in the flash of a hundred camera shots.

She was a wreck.

"No, it was Mr. Gossett who said that—the gunman," Jenny repeated for the tenth time. Or was it the twentieth? "Robert Buckwalter and I are not love-birds. He is my employer's son. I'm the chef."

"Then why was he willing to ransom you even if it took every penny he had?" a reporter called from the back line. "You must be some cook."

"Miss Black is refusing to answer any questions about ransom and so am I." Robert came out of the room where he had been talking with the police. "And if you have a shred of decency, you won't print that remark in any of your papers." Robert stopped to eye the reporters sternly. "A remark like that would set Miss Black up as a kidnapping target and you know it."

"Kidnapping? Me?" Jenny blinked. She'd never given much thought to the problems of a rich family, but she was beginning to see that there were many. Even though the arrest of Mr. Gossett would have stirred up some news by itself, the number of reporters at the Fargo airport would have been reduced by almost ninety percent if the Buckwalter family hadn't been involved in the story. Only a few of the reporters had even bothered to take a picture of the old man being arrested by the police when he walked off the plane.

"So it was just the old man talking," a woman reporter called out. "There really is no secret engagement?"

Robert looked at Jenny. She looked scared and a little bewildered. She'd had enough pressure for one day. He turned and formally addressed the group. "No, there's no secret engagement. Now, excuse us, we've had a long day."

The reporters gave a unified sigh of disappointment.

"But won't you give one of us an exclusive on the story?" one reporter called out as he waved his arm. "I volunteer."

All of the other arms started to wave.

"Sorry, but the exclusive is already spoken for," Robert said as he guided Jenny out of the spotlight from the cameras.

Two airport security staff flanked Robert and Jenny as they walked away from the reporters.

"Sorry about that," Robert said to Jenny as he steered her quickly into the office of some airport official. "I thought they were going to put you in a locked office, too."

"I had to leave to use the rest room."

Robert nodded. "Oh, well. They might have found you anyway. But don't worry. It'll be over soon. The plane I've ordered will be here in fifteen minutes or so. It'll take you home."

"Oh, we're going back to Dry Creek?"

Robert looked at her strangely. "I thought you might want to visit your mother in Seattle for a few days, so I arranged for a pilot friend to fly you there. You can get your ankle checked out better, too."

Jenny looked down at her foot. "It's fine. It hasn't hurt all day."

"Still, it should be X-rayed. And you'll want to rest."

"Rest?"

Jenny was speechless. She was being sent home like she was some pet that had suddenly become inconvenient. She had come to believe that Robert was not like that kind of rich person. She had come to believe he was different. She had come to believe he was— Jenny stopped herself and then silently admitted the truth—she had come to believe he was the one and only one for her.

No wonder he was sending her home.

"I'll ask someone to pack the suitcase I have in Dry Creek and send it back, as well." Jenny walked stiffly to the door.

Robert almost lost his courage. He'd hoped she would refuse to go away for even a minute. He knew she'd be a target for every tabloid reporter in the country if she stayed in Fargo tonight or went back to Dry Creek with him tomorrow, and yet he could hardly bear for her to go.

"I don't think the press will find you in Seattle." Robert handed her a folded piece of paper, "But if they do call, tell your mother to have them call this number. I'll come to see you in a few days and we'll talk."

Sure, Jenny thought, and all those owners who dumped off their pets in the abandoned lot were really only going for a little drive to the store before they came back to pick up their beloved kittens.

But what had she expected? He was richer than King Midas. And she was the cook. He had more millions in the bank than she had spoons in the kitchen.

Suddenly Jenny wanted very much to see her own family for a few days.

"There's the plane now," Robert said softly as he bent down and kissed the top of her head. "I'll see you soon. Very soon."

"Sure." Jenny didn't look back as she walked out the door.

The weather in Seattle was cold and damp. Gray clouds seemed to be all there was to the sky. Jenny's mother had welcomed her home with a tight hug. Her mother had already heard a news report of what had happened.

The first day Jenny was home she slept for twelve hours. The next day she slept for ten. On the third day her mother's fussing started to turn to alarm and so Jenny got up.

"You've been working too hard," her mother said when Jenny padded out into the living room in stretched-out sweatpants that had been left behind by one of her sisters. "Those dinners you give—there's a lot of hard work in doing them. And, if that's not bad enough, you have to go up in an airplane with some gunman."

"Mr. Gossett wasn't your usual gunman," Jenny protested. As the days passed, she'd felt more and more sorry for the old man. He'd looked so defeated when he was arrested. "I'm not sure if he'd have ever actually pulled that trigger."

The latest report said Mr. Gossett had turned state's evidence and worked with the FBI to arrest the major criminals in the rustling ring.

Jenny's mother snorted. "Well, I'm glad your Robert didn't wait around to find out if the old man was going to shoot you or not. At least he showed some sense."

"He's not my Robert." Jenny had made the protest already a dozen times since her mother had first heard the story.

"That's not what it said on television yesterday."

"Television? What was on television?"

"It was yesterday afternoon—I can't remember the name of the show—it has that cute man as a host. Anyway, he interviewed someone who had heard the telephone tape of what had happened in the plane—and the witness said that you were Robert's new girlfriend."

"It's not true," Jenny said patiently. She wanted to wrap herself in hairnets and shapeless sweatpants. "It was only the old man talking. And he was half-crazy."

Jenny wanted nothing more than to go back to sleep. She figured this media frenzy was like a virus. If you just went to bed, it would all go away in a few days.

"You need to get dressed." Jenny's mother eyed her

critically. "Put on something cheerful. What if someone comes?"

"No one is going to come—" Jenny stopped and eyed her mother suspiciously. "You haven't gotten any phone calls, have you? You know that if a reporter calls, you're to ask them to call that number I gave you."

Jenny's mother drew herself up. "The man assured me he's not one of those reporters. He just has a question."

The phone in the kitchen rang.

"I'll get that," Jenny's mother said. "You go get changed."

Jenny went into her old room and stared into the nearly empty closet. She had only a few clothes left from the days when she lived here with her mother. The best of the lot was an emerald-green linen dress. But that would require nylons, she supposed, and she didn't want a reporter to think that she had dressed up just to tell him to leave.

Jenny knew there was only one logical question for the reporter to ask. It was the question everyone else was asking—was she Robert Buckwalter's new girlfriend?

Jenny grimaced at herself in the mirror. The best way to answer that question was to stay in these old sweats. No one would even think to ask if she was some rich man's girlfriend then.

"Are you dressed?" Jenny's mother called from the kitchen. "Your sister wants to talk to you."

"I'll be there in a minute." Jenny slipped the sweatshirt off and the linen dress on. She'd forgo the nylons.

Jenny brushed her hair on the way to the kitchen.

Jenny's mother gave her the phone.

"I can't get any pictures," her sister wailed the minute Jenny put the phone to her ear. "I got some really good quotes from Robert about you and he cooking that lobster dinner, but the editor wants pictures."

"Well, surely someone has pictures," Jenny said. So Robert had kept his word and fed the story to her sister. "I wish I had some, but I don't. I'm sure someone does, though. There were more of those little disposable cameras at that dinner than there were salt shakers."

"I know. But no one's selling."

"Why not? Oh, of course. The kids think they are being loyal by not dealing with the press."

"I don't know about that. They're sure dealing with someone," her sister said. "I've offered a couple of them five hundred dollars for a shot of you and Robert dancing, but they won't sell—they tell me they have an offer for a thousand dollars minimum."

"What? Who would pay that for those pictures? Besides, those kids took dozens of pictures. Surely someone will sell one of theirs."

"I asked around," Jenny's sister said quietly. "Apparently all of the pictures are spoken for."

"And someone's paying a thousand dollars for each one! That's amazing! Are you sure the kids aren't just trying to jack the price up?"

"They did jack the price up," her sister protested. "I finally just asked one of them to name their price— and they said that it wasn't for sale. They said someone would pay a hundred dollars more than any offer I made."

"What kind of a fool would do that?"

There was a long pause. "I think it's Robert."

"But why would he do that?" Jenny protested. "Surely he doesn't really want all those pictures."

Then it hit Jenny. Robert may not want the pictures, but he wanted even less for the media to have them.

"I was wondering if you could talk to him for me," Jenny's sister asked hesitantly. "I mean you still work for him—"

"—for his mother." Mrs. Buckwalter had called and left a message that Jenny was to consider herself on a paid vacation for the week she was spending with her mother.

"Well, could you ask? I've tried to reach him on the phone, but he's not answering. I think he'd throw a picture my way if he remembered I need one to feature my story. He was so nice. He called me and actually suggested we do this interview. My editor was so impressed. The only thing Robert wouldn't talk about was that lovebird remark the old man made."

"He's worried people will believe it."

"Well, of course they'll believe it if they read about it," Jenny's sister said cheerfully. "How do you think progress gets made?"

"Progress!"

"Just kidding."

"Besides, you should call Robert if you need to talk to him." Jenny didn't feel up to explaining that she had no influence with Robert.

"I haven't been able to reach him."

"I suppose he's not answering his phone." Jenny knew how Robert felt about interviews. Apparently he also felt that way about having his picture in the paper with her. "But I don't know how to reach him, either."

"You don't?" Jenny's sister sounded surprised. "He made it sound like you two were friends."

"Yeah, well—"

"He kissed you," her sister said emphatically. "With your hairnet on. Even Mom thinks the man is serious about you."

"That's just because she watched some program on television yesterday."

Jenny heard the doorbell ring and the sound of her mother's footsteps as she started to walk toward the front door.

"Look, I've got to go," Jenny said into the phone. She didn't dare leave her mother alone with some reporter. "Someone's at the door. I'll call back in a few minutes."

"No problem."

Jenny clicked the phone off as she set it on the kitchen counter. She smoothed back her hair as she walked toward the door separating the kitchen from the living room. Knowing her mother, she would offer the reporter refreshments if Jenny didn't act fast.

Jenny called out to the reporter as she started to swing the door open. "I'm so sorry, but we can't—"

The day had started out gray and it was still gray. There wasn't much light coming into the living room and Jenny's mother had the lamp by the sofa lit. It created a warm, yellow glow in one corner of the room.

The reporter had already been invited into the living room and he stood with his back to the kitchen door Jenny was swinging open. For some reason, her mother was showing him the family pictures on the wall.

Even in the gray half-light of the room, Jenny still had to blink. The reporter's back showed off the plaidest plaid suit she had ever seen. Blue stripes met with shades of red and green. And the tip of the shirt that showed above the suit collar promised even more plaid.

"We aren't doing interv—" Jenny continued her speech until the reporter turned around.

She stopped midsentence. She stopped midstride.

She was losing her mind.

"Robert?" She managed to croak out the name as she stood and stared.

"I told you I was coming," he said softly. "And you can call me Bob."

"Bob?"

Yes, she was definitely losing her mind.

"You told me Bobs wore plaid. I know it's a bit extreme. I thought you could use a laugh."

What she could use was a straitjacket.

"It's very clever." Jenny tried to pull herself together and smiled. "Really, very clever. Really."

Someday she'd laugh about it…maybe. Her sister would laugh soon enough, that's for sure.

"Bob's going to stay for some tea," Jenny's mother announced as though it was the most normal thing in the world. "I was just showing him the family pictures on our wall."

Jenny groaned inside. She knew what was coming.

"He thought your kindergarten picture was so cute," her mother boasted.

"That picture should be burned," Jenny said. Her hair had stood straight up. Big clumps of dark hair that no brush or curler could tame.

"Definitely cute." Robert smiled. His blue eyes crinkled just like Santa Claus's. Jenny swore to it. He looked harmless and congenial one minute and the next minute he turned into the playboy that he was. "You're still cute, for that matter."

"Thank you." Jenny smoothed down the linen dress she wore. "My hair does much better now."

"I don't know. I kind of like it when it's doing its own thing. It has a sense of freedom about it."

Jenny couldn't believe Robert—or Bob or whoever the man was—had come to her mother's door so they could discuss Jenny's hair. Of course not, she thought. He was a busy man. He must have another purpose. Ahhh, yes.

"You don't need to worry about any of my pictures appearing next to yours in any paper in the world," Jenny said as she walked over to the picture wall. "My mother would never let a reporter take one of these pictures off the wall. Would you, Mother?"

"Of course not." Jenny's mother sounded offended that the question was even asked.

Robert looked bewildered.

"I know you bought up all the pictures of us dancing

in Dry Creek," Jenny explained. "I understand why you did it. I really do. But I don't think anyone will come here looking for another picture of me."

"You know about the pictures?" Robert sounded cautious.

Jenny nodded. "I know you were afraid a tabloid would pick one up and print it after Mr. Gossett...well, after he said those things—and so you bought the pictures from the kids."

"I bought the pictures the night they were taken."

Sometimes the earth turns slowly. Sometimes it spins like a top.

Jenny blinked. That couldn't be right. "But there weren't any reporters around that night."

"No," Robert quietly agreed.

"No one had said anything about us."

"No."

"Then why would you want the pictures?"

Robert glanced at her a little shyly. "Someday I thought we'd have a picture wall of our own."

Jenny's mother cleared her throat as she started toward the kitchen. "I think I'll go see about that tea now."

"But picture walls are for—" Jenny began.

"Families, I know. But I'm not pressuring you. I know we haven't known each other very long. I'm willing to wait."

Jenny tried to make sense of what she was hearing. "Wait for what?"

Robert smiled. "I'm just willing to wait, that's all. To let you adjust to the idea of me. I'm not the easiest person in the world to know."

Jenny didn't know what to say.

That didn't bother Robert. He continued. "I thought we'd start with a date. Maybe you'd go to a movie with me?"

Jenny could only nod.

Jenny couldn't understand it all. "Are you still working to get off that list? Is that what you're doing?"

"Oh, it's too late for that. All I could do was to get them to knock me down to second place."

"So you're going to be one of the bachelors no matter what?" Jenny was trying to make sense of what she was hearing.

Robert nodded. "I could marry twins right now and it wouldn't bounce me off the list. I'm stuck with it."

If it wasn't the list, what was it? Jenny wondered. "So you're just trying out being Bob again—is that it?"

Robert shrugged. "Bob does sound friendly. But I can answer to either name. It's not a big deal."

"Of course it's a big deal," Jenny protested. "It's your name. I need to know what to call you."

"I was hoping you might call me dear—when

you're comfortable with it, of course. But only when you're ready. The first step is a date."

Robert took a step closer. "And a kiss. That'd be a good place to start, too."

Jenny looked up as Robert bent down. They met and the world tilted just a little bit. The air grew warmer. The room grew darker.

"I hear bells," Robert murmured.

Jenny listened to the hissing and whispered, "Teakettle."

"No." Robert smiled softly. "I think it's bells. It'll always be bells with you and me."

Epilogue

Bob was right, Jenny thought six months later. The first step was the date. She'd fallen a little in love with him over buttered popcorn in the movie house. She'd fallen hopelessly in love the next day when he showed her the album he'd used to mount their kissing pictures.

Except for the one picture they sent to Jenny's sister, the other pictures from Dry Creek were all proudly mounted in the plastic sheets of Bob's family album— even the ones that were missing a head or two.

Jenny and Bob both went back to Dry Creek to continue cooking for the teenagers and to begin regular meetings with the pastor. They laughed together, they talked, and they built a pyramid of empty pudding cups for her sister's first assignment in her new job writing for a health magazine.

No one was surprised when Bob and Jenny set a wedding date of September 1.

The Dry Creek church polished the pews for the day even though no outside reporters were allowed. The Billings paper was allowed to run a small paragraph in their Newly Married section written by their local reporter. It primarily talked about the bride's gown.

Even though no outside reporters were allowed at the ceremony in the Dry Creek church, there was no lack of people taking pictures.

When the minister gave the signal for Bob to kiss his bride, fifty disposable cameras flashed almost in unison.

"Now I know why love is blind," Bob whispered to Jenny as he nuzzled her lip. "It's all the flashes."

"Kiss her again," one of the teenagers with a camera yelled. "I've got plenty—"

"What does he mean by that?" Jenny leaned into her husband.

"I got them special cameras—fifty shots apiece."

"That means—"

"That's right—they're set for fifty kisses tonight."

"Hmmm," Jenny said as her husband's lips met hers again. "Fifty's a nice number."

* * * * *

Dear Reader,

Thank you for coming with me once again to Dry Creek, Montana. I have enjoyed writing this book and hope you have enjoyed spending more time with the people who live in this fictional town.

In this book of the DRY CREEK series, I'd ask you to especially think about the old man, Mr. Gossett. His bitterness toward others has been evident in all the books in the series, but in this book you discover that his bitterness goes back many years to a grudge against the town of Dry Creek and a disappointment with a woman who did not love him. The combination of all this pent-up unvoiced resentment soured the old man until he was willing to steal from his neighbors and even contemplate the murders of Jenny and Robert.

We all have disappointments. We have all been wronged by someone sometime. These experiences can sour us unless we talk about them, pray about them and practice forgiveness toward others. I like to meditate on these words in the Lord's Prayer—"forgive us our debts as we forgive the debts of others." It puts forgiveness in perspective for me.

Again, thank you for making the trip to Dry Creek with me.

Sincerely yours,

Janet Tronstad

A HERO FOR DRY CREEK

It is a good thing to give thanks unto the Lord.
—*Psalms* 92:1a

Dedicated to the princess in our family,
Aurora Borealis MacDonald,
currently four years old.
May all her dreams come true.

Chapter One

Nicki Redfern didn't believe in fairy tales. Instead of glass slippers she wore cowboy boots—and not the highly polished ones rodeo riders wore. No, her boots were sturdy, working boots meant for riding horses and chasing cattle.

Her feet sweat in those boots.

Still, recently, in the early-morning hours while she was lying in her twin-size bed—as the pink sun rose over the Big Sheep Mountains and shone through her small second-story window—her dreams turned to fanciful things such as waltzing with princes and blushing with love.

In the full light of day, of course, Nicki stopped those kind of daydreams. No good would come of them.

A woman like her had no time for Prince Charming

or ballroom dancing. She was a farm woman with calluses on her hands and responsibilities on her shoulders. Unless Prince Charming knew how to pitch hay bales, she had no use for him.

When her father died last year, Nicki and her brother, Reno, had inherited equal shares of the Redfern Ranch. The ranch was four thousand acres of prime grassland, starting at the bottom of the Big Sheep Mountains and spreading south to the gully that each year guided the spring run-off into the Yellowstone River just east of the small town of Dry Creek, Montana.

The ranch had been in the Redfern family since 1890 and Nicki was fiercely proud of its history. But it took every ounce of energy from both her and Reno just to keep it going. The price of cattle dropped each year and the dry spell hitting Montana didn't seem like it would end anytime soon.

Nicki needed a hired hand, not some fairy-tale prince.

Besides, Nicki had a weary suspicion that those fluffy dreams were meant for her mother—they had just arrived over twenty years too late. When her mother had left, she'd taken the family honor and eight hundred dollars from the church building fund with her.

Nicki shook her head. There was no point in remembering the woman who had deserted them. No one got everything they wanted in life, and Nicki had learned to be content with what she had—a father, a brother and some of the best ranch land in Montana.

When her father tried to show her some newspaper clippings her mother had sent once, Nicki refused to read them. One look at the accompanying picture of her mother dressed as a Vegas dancer was all Nicki needed to see.

Nicki was half-asleep as she limped down the stairway in her old chenille bathrobe to start the coffee. She was alone in the house this morning. Reno had left yesterday with a truckload of steers. The final cattle sale in Billings fell the day before Thanksgiving each year, and the Redferns always saved their best stock for this sale because the cattle were at their heaviest by then and the buyers more inclined to pay higher prices.

Her brother hadn't wanted to leave her alone. Reno never liked going to Billings and the tumble Nicki had taken yesterday only gave him another reason to fret about leaving the ranch. Nicki had to assure him repeatedly that she was all right. Her horse, Misty, had stumbled into a gopher hole, tossing Nicki to the ground. Nicki was so relieved that Misty hadn't broken any legs that she didn't pay much attention to the bruise coloring her own thigh. Nicki's leg was sore and she couldn't walk far if the old cattle truck Reno was driving had trouble. She'd only slow Reno down if there were problems, and they both knew it.

Nicki yawned as she limped into the kitchen. She headed for the chipped enamel sink and put the nearby coffeepot under the cold water faucet. The sink in the kitchen was right under the window that looked out of the front of the old ranch house. She'd looked out that window thousands of times in her twenty-nine years of life. She always saw the same thing—the old oak tree that had the rope swing dangling from its branches and the mountains in the distance.

It was still more night than day outside. Nicki looked out the window wondering if it would be light enough to see the rope on the tree. The swirl of snowflakes made it especially dark outside. She could only see outlines and pinpricks of white snowflakes. Actually, it was the snowflakes that made her look twice.

She blinked and then closed her eyes before blinking again.

Whoa—the man didn't disappear like she'd thought he would.

He was right there, standing like a figure in a darkened snow globe. The man was looking at the house and leaning against the side of a long, white limousine—a limousine so unexpected and shiny, it could as well be a pumpkin carriage sprinkled in fairy dust.

And the man! She only saw the outline of the man, but he looked…well, wonderful. Magical. A white scarf was wrapped around his neck and dangled down over a black jacket that looked suspiciously like a tuxedo. Nicki's eyes followed the man's long legs all the way to the ground and then back up again because there was Hunter, Reno's half-wild dog, standing politely at the man's side.

Nicki had to blink. Oh, my word! Nicki woke completely.

Prince Charming! She was looking at Prince Charming. And he was apparently there with a limousine to take her away to the royal ball.

The cold water ran over the sides of the pot and chilled Nicki's hand. She slowly set the pot down in the sink and turned the water off.

She kept staring. The man didn't fade.

She told herself it was time to sit down before she lost it all together. Limousines didn't appear in the driveway of the ranch. Neither did Prince Charming. As for Hunter, the dog would never calmly stand beside a stranger.

Nicki was hallucinating. Her mind had somehow reached into her dream and pulled out the image that had been filling her nights. That much was obvious. She couldn't remember hitting her head when she'd catapulted off Misty yesterday, but she must have done so. What else could explain this?

Nicki stumbled over to a chair.

She needed to stay calm. She'd close her eyes for a bit and wait for it to grow lighter outside. She didn't want to wake Dr. Norris this early. She'd be fine. She'd sit a minute before she tried making coffee again.

And, in the meantime, she'd try to pray. Her father had stopped going to church when Nicki's mother left, but he had still insisted on driving Nicki to services in Dry Creek. So every Sunday Nicki sat in the same pew her family had occupied before her mother left. She sang all the hymns and joined in all the congregational prayers.

But, in private, Nicki never prayed. If she thought about talking to God, no words came. Even now, instead of talking to God, she stared at the bare lightbulb hanging from the kitchen ceiling and started to talk to it. *Oh, my, I think I could use some help here… It's not possible—I know it's not. But I'm seeing Prince Charming standing outside my window! Do you think I'm crazy?*

Garrett Hamilton liked the cold of the morning as the snow settled in damp patches on his face. The weather was bracing. And at least when he was standing outside the limousine he didn't feel so much as if he were in the middle of a bad prom date. Nobody but an aging Vegas dancer would insist he wear a tuxedo uniform to fill in for her sick chauffeur, especially when he was doing her a favor.

Well, technically he was doing the favor for his cousin, Chrissy. Or was it his aunt Rose who was responsible for him being here?

"Yeah, it had to be Aunt Rose," Garrett said to the dog who stood silently and watched him. He'd been talking to the dog for a good hour now, and he'd swear the animal understood. "Aunt Rose got me into this one."

Garrett had resisted Aunt Rose's worries about her daughter, Chrissy, for weeks now. But that last conversation had gotten to him. She'd said Chrissy had asked him to come.

Garrett snorted. The dog whimpered in agreement and Garrett nodded. "Yeah—I should have known better."

Chrissy hadn't asked him to come, especially since she knew Aunt Rose wanted him to find out more about what was going on with Chrissy and her boyfriend. "Can't say I blame her. Don't know what Aunt Rose was thinking. Shoot, I don't know what I was thinking."

Garrett looked down at the dog.

When Garrett had cut the engine on the limousine and let it coast into the driveway of the ranch late last night, the dog had been there. When Garrett opened the window, the dog moved out of the black shadow under the tree and growled low and deep in his throat. Garrett knew the dog wouldn't give much further warning if Garrett were foolish enough to just open the door and step out of the limousine.

It was too dark for the dog to see whether or not Garrett was looking at him directly, but Garrett knew the dog could sense any fear and would use that as a trigger to attack. Even as the dog growled, Garrett admired the animal. The dog had a torn ear and a scar along its left flank. "You've had a hard time, haven't you, Old Boy?"

Garrett knew that the way to settle a wild animal's nerves was to give him time to get used to you. So he took his old leather coat, the one that he sometimes wore for sixteen hours at a stretch when he was on a long haul, and gently threw it out the window for the dog to sniff. After the dog scratched at the coat and rolled it around in the snow, the dog seemed resigned to Garrett's scent. Not happy, but at least not growling anymore.

"That's a good dog." Garrett knew how the dog felt. Sometimes, even if you got used to something, you still might not like it much.

That's how Garrett felt about this mission his aunt had sent him on. Aunt Rose meant well, but if she hadn't been able to convince Chrissy not to marry her high school sweetheart, Garrett wasn't likely to, either. Besides, Garrett would rather have a tooth pulled than see Chrissy cry. This gave Chrissy a tactical advantage that she used shamelessly.

Garrett was the last person who should give marriage advice anyway. He knew he wasn't a family man.

Garrett was even more of a mutt than the dog beside him. Garrett's mother had died when he was five. After that, alcohol had been all the family his father needed. Garrett had raised himself and, while he had no complaints, he knew less about being a family man than the dog beside him did.

Which was all right.

"I've got my life and it's a good one." Garrett was a legend among truckers. He'd set a record from New York to San Diego that hadn't been broken yet. "A man can't ask for more than that." Garrett loved all that asphalt rolling under his wheels. There were plenty of strangers along the highways and not one of them gave Garrett any grief.

Giving him grief had become Aunt Rose's job. The odd thing was Garrett hadn't even known his aunt Rose until his father died and she showed up at the hospital. She'd told him then that she wanted to adopt him and have him come to live with her and Chrissy, but the thought of being part of any real family had scared Garrett spitless. He told Aunt Rose he'd do fine on his own, and he had.

Garrett wouldn't admit it, but he had grown fond of Aunt Rose over the years. They had made their compromises. She no longer expected him to spend any holidays with her and Chrissy. But they had their own tradition. Every September after Labor Day Garrett came to spend a few days with Aunt Rose and Chrissy. He'd clean out the rain gutters and do any heavy chores they needed. Plus, no matter where he was, he made it a point to pull off the road on Saturday at three in the afternoon and make sure his cell phone was on. That's when Aunt Rose would call.

Aunt Rose didn't ask much more of him than that and so, when she'd asked him to talk to Chrissy, he'd known she was desperate. What could he say but yes?

He should have had his head examined.

Chrissy had flatly refused to talk to Garrett when he pulled into Las Vegas. All she needed, she said, was a favor. Garrett had agreed to help her before he even knew what she was going to ask.

"Bad habit of mine," Garrett mentioned to the dog before glancing back at the limousine just to be sure the woman his cousin had asked him to drive to Montana was still sleeping on the long back seat. Chrissy had met

Lillian at the casino where they both worked—Chrissy as a waitress and Lillian as an entertainer. "I thought she was going to ask me to move some furniture in the back of my truck or something I could move a whole city block in the back of Big Blue."

Garrett had already told the dog about Big Blue. Garrett's fourteen-wheel big rig was now parked near the casino where Chrissy worked. The dark blue cab had Hamilton Trucking stenciled in white lettering on the door. It wasn't the fanciest rig on the highways and it certainly wasn't the newest, but Garrett knew Big Blue and he had confidence in her.

Garrett looked back at the ranch house. Surely someone would be up soon. He thought he'd seen some movement at that window, but then he'd looked closer and decided he'd imagined it.

He felt a stirring of sympathy for the poor man who lived inside. The man had no idea what a surprise this morning would bring. Garrett's passenger had asked him to go to the door and prepare the man for her arrival.

From the few remarks the older woman had made and the engagement ring she'd asked him to return, Garrett figured Mr. Redfern had wanted to marry the woman at one point in time and didn't know she was coming to visit.

A visit like this could give an old man a heart attack.

Failing that, it could give Garrett one.

"Ah, here we go." Garrett relaxed.

Someone had turned a light on in the kitchen.

The morning sun still had not made its way completely over the mountains so Nicki didn't risk looking out the window this time. She focused on filling the pot with water. Once that was done, she'd start the coffeemaker and sit down again. It was a good thing she didn't have many chores to do today.

The knock on the kitchen door came just as the pot was filled with water. Nicki calmed herself. No need to panic. She told herself that the still falling snow had muffled the sound of someone driving up. It must be Lester.

Lester Wilkerson was her neighbor—and friend, Nicki added to herself somewhat guiltily. The fact that he made her nervous wasn't his fault. So far she'd managed to derail most of his hints about getting married, but he didn't seem discouraged.

Nicki figured she would eventually marry Lester, but she just needed more time to get used to the idea. She had no illusions about why Lester was interested in marrying her. His land ran along the east side of the Redfern Ranch, and he had his eye on more grazing area for his cattle.

Nicki knew some people wouldn't see that as a good reason to get married. But Nicki preferred it to some nonsense about love. Land stayed with a person. Love, on the other hand, could fly away at any time.

Lester didn't expect love and neither did Nicki. They would suit each other well. And things between them would be better once they actually got married. Nicki hadn't been able to bring herself to meet Lester's lips yet when he attempted his clumsy kisses, but she supposed she'd come to accept him before long.

In the meantime, Nicki expected Lester would continue his plodding courtship. He had started going into Dry Creek early every morning to pick up the mail for both ranches and then coming over to have coffee with her and Reno.

Yesterday morning Lester had bought her a lavender orchid in a plastic box. The petals were waxy and the flower felt artificial even though it was real. Still, it was a sensible flower for snowy weather in Montana and Nicki appreciated that. The brief yearning she'd had in her heart for roses was easily stamped down. She was a practical woman and should be pleased with a practical flower. Roses wouldn't last long here.

Nicki flipped the switch on the coffeemaker before she wiped her wet hands on her chenille robe. She limped over to the door and looked out the small window. All she could make out through the frosted glass was the general shape of a man.

It had to be Lester on the other side of that door, but Nicki wasn't fool enough to just open it for anyone unless she was ready.

She looked over by the ancient refrigerator. There it was. Reno had bought a thick-handled broom at a farm auction last year. Then he had taught her how to hit with it. They were both thinking of that stubborn cow's head when she practiced her swing, but it'd stop a man as quick as a cow. She brought it over.

Nicki unlocked the door and opened it.

Her jaw dropped and she stared.

If it had been the Boston Strangler on the other side of the door, she wouldn't have been able to raise the broom in defense of herself.

It was him. Prince Charming. Flakes of snow sparkled in his hair. He sparkled everywhere. His teeth sparkled. His eyes sparkled. Even the shine on his shoes sparkled. But, as much of a fairy-tale prince as he appeared to be, one thing was clear. "You're real."

Chapter Two

Garrett waited for the woman to finish her sentence. He thought she was going for "real cold" or maybe "real lost." Even "real strange" would do, but the sentence just hung in the air.

Garrett looked past the woman into the kitchen of the house, but he didn't see anyone else there. Having a woman answer the door certainly complicated things. He'd assumed Mr. Redfern was an old bachelor or maybe an old widower. The woman he'd brought up here wouldn't welcome the presence of another woman, especially not someone twenty years younger than her.

"Good morning." Garrett cleared his throat.

The woman still stared at him.

Garrett looked at her. She seemed dazed. Maybe she

was a little slow. He softened his voice. "Sorry to bother you, but I'm looking for your husband."

The woman's eyes widened and her voice squeaked. "My husband?"

Nicki began to realize something very important. Prince Charming was standing on her porch talking about husbands and she hadn't combed her hair. Or washed her face. Or put on any clothes except her ratty old robe. Oh, my, she was a mess.

"I can wait for him outside. I'm sure you'll be more comfortable with him around."

"He's not—" Nicki breathed. "I mean, I'm not married."

This is where the music starts, Nicki thought to herself. Her heart literally tingled. She'd been wrong all those years. Fairy tales did come true. Forget about her boots. Forget about that waxy orchid in her refrigerator. They didn't matter. Her world had shifted on its axis because Prince Charming was here. Any second now he was going to hold out his arms to her and she was going to float away into some beautiful fairy-tale land where totally impractical rose petals would softly fall on them as they waltzed together. Just like in her dreams.

The prince frowned. "I must have the wrong place," he said, and then turned to walk away.

Nicki gasped. This wasn't how the story was

supposed to end. The prince didn't just leave before one rose petal even had time to fall. "It's cold. It'll only take a minute for you to warm up inside."

Nicki stepped back so the man could come into the kitchen.

Prince Charming didn't go into the kitchen, but he came close enough to the door to feel the heat. Nicki forgot to breathe. Outside, the shadows and half-light of the morning had hidden all but the outline of the man's face. But up close in the light she'd turned on in the kitchen—well, his nose and chin were classical; his eyes were a smoldering pewter; his raven hair was thick and wavy. And there—when he smiled—was a deep dimple in his chin.

Nicki was staring. She knew it. But all she was able to do was stand there leaning on the open door as the man stood on the porch. Even the cold wind blowing into the house didn't make her move.

Nothing could make her move—and then she heard the slam of a car door.

"Garrett," a woman's voice called out in exasperation. "Garrett—where are you?"

Nicki's heart sank when "Garrett" turned in response to the woman's call.

Nicki looked out the open door and saw…*her*.

The woman was wearing one of those glamorous

wide-brimmed hats so Nicki couldn't see her face but, even without seeing the woman's face, there was no mistaking the fact that she was beautiful. Blond and svelte—with enough gold draped around her neck to bankroll a small kingdom.

Why was it, Nicki thought, that when Prince Charming finally showed up on her doorstep, he had Cinderella in the car with him?

Nicki's eyes looked down at the woman's feet. Yes, the woman was Cinderella right down to her tiny little feet perched on some ridiculously high-heeled shoes that did little to protect against the snow.

Nicki expected the man to go to the woman, but he didn't. She heard Hunter's low vibrating growl as the woman walked closer, but the dog didn't leave the man's side. Garrett put his hand down and rested it on Hunter's head. The dog stopped growling. "Maybe you could tell me how to get to the Redfern Ranch. I'm looking for Mr. Redfern."

"Reno?" Having a stranger ask for her brother was almost as shocking as seeing some unknown man silence Hunter with a touch. The dog never let anyone touch him except Reno.

"No, it's Charles Redfern I'm looking for."

"My father is dead."

"Oh. Are you sure? Mr. Charles Redfern?"

"Of course I'm sure."

"Garrett," the woman from the car called out to the man.

"Your friend—" Nicki had to look around the man to see the woman from the limousine "—she sounds angry."

"I'll get to her in a minute." Garrett reached into his pocket and pulled out the diamond ring that the woman insisted belonged to Charles Redfern. The ring had found one of the holes in the pocket of Garrett's uniform and it kept falling out at the most awkward times like last night when he was talking to that kid in the café, getting directions to the ranch. Garrett wanted to be rid of it. The woman before him was the man's daughter. That was enough for him. "This ring belongs to you now, I guess."

Nicki stared at the ring. It was a delicate ring with one small center diamond and a circle of fiery opals around it. She heard the sound of the woman muttering angrily, but Nicki didn't turn to look again. She couldn't be bothered with Cinderella.

Nicki wondered how a hallucination could be this real. But it must be a hallucination. The man was wearing a tuxedo and holding out an engagement ring that he said belonged to her. And something about the memory of it made it seem as if he was right.

"It's real," Garrett said, as if sensing her disbelief.

"I—I don't think—" Nicki heard her voice squeak. Oh, my. "Could you—could you—pinch me?"

Garrett froze. Surely the woman didn't want him to pinch her, but she looked as if she was going to faint.

"Please."

As the woman's face went whiter, the green of her eyes grew deeper. Like emeralds, Garrett finally decided. They were like muted emeralds. Deep pools of muted emeralds. A man could be pulled into those eyes and drown before he knew it. She really was quite…unusual. But still. "I can't pinch—"

He thought she was going to faint.

He slipped the ring back in his pocket and reached out to pinch her, but found himself holding her arms instead. He couldn't pinch her if he wanted to. Not through the thick robe she wore. But he had to do something.

So he kissed her. On the lips.

He meant it to be a pinch of a kiss. Just a peck to say he hoped she didn't faint. But she gasped, and he—well, he forgot why he was kissing her. He just knew that he was experiencing the sweetest kiss he'd ever shared with anyone. He didn't want it to end.

Nicki couldn't breathe. She'd never been kissed by a hallucination, but she figured it couldn't be like this. She really thought she'd have to faint after all.

"Oh, for Pete's sake, I'll pinch her!" The woman's

annoyed voice penetrated Nicki's fog just before she felt the sleeve of her robe being raised.

Cinderella used her nails to deliver a solid pinch.

"Ouch!" The fog left Nicki instantly. She was definitely not hallucinating.

Nicki looked up at the man. He looked dazed. But the petite woman standing beside him had lifted the brim of her hat and didn't look the least bit vague.

Oh, my. Nicki suddenly wished desperately that she was dreaming after all. The woman's hair was bleached so blond, it shimmered in the faint morning light. Her lips pouted a well-penciled pink. Diamonds dangled from her ears and hung from her graceful neck. The woman looked like she was forty, but Nicki knew that she would turn fifty-five this coming May 13.

"What are you doing here?" Nicki said the words. They sounded defensive to her own ears. But then, she decided, she was entitled to be defensive. The woman hadn't even written in twenty-two years. If it wasn't for the photos in the news clippings that came in the mail periodically, Nicki wouldn't even recognize her now.

The woman's jaw lifted slightly. "You must be the housekeeper. I came to see Mr. Redfern. Would you tell him I'm here?"

Nicki wished with all her heart that she had gone with Reno into Billings. She could have crawled home if the truck had broken down. The woman standing before her didn't recognize her, but Nicki would know the woman's face anywhere. It appeared life really wasn't a fairy tale, after all.

Nicki opened the kitchen door farther. "Maybe you should come inside."

Nicki let the woman walk in front of her and enter the kitchen, but she didn't follow her. She needed to wait.

Nicki forgot she was still holding the end of the broom handle until she felt it pressing against the length of her thigh. That meant it was not only pressing into Garrett's leg, it was also resting on his foot. "I'm sorry, I— my brother makes me use this when he's not here."

Nicki and Garrett were standing facing each other in the middle of the doorway to the kitchen. The main door swung out over the porch, letting cold air come in. The screen door swung back into the kitchen, letting warm air seep out. Neither one seemed able to move.

Garrett's ears were ringing. He decided it must be the altitude. His ears felt as if they were stuffed with cotton, as well. "Huh?"

"The broom. He wants me to carry it." Nicki told herself she was barely making sense. She was feeling a little dizzy. But it was only natural. She needed more than a minute to think before she faced her mother.

"Whatever for—?"

"So I can hit heads." Nicki knew she should step aside so they could close the kitchen door, but she was afraid her legs wouldn't work. She'd just stand where she was for a bit more. She needed to focus on the man's face instead of the woman in the kitchen. No, his face wasn't a good thing to look at, either. How could a man be so sexy that even his Adam's apple made her wobbly?

"You want to hit me? On the head? You'll need a stepladder."

Nicki looked up and saw in surprise that it was true. The man was a good six inches taller than herself. It wasn't often that a man was that tall. "You're supposed to be a cow."

"I beg your pardon?"

"I'm supposed to hit the cows' heads with the broom handle. Just on the forehead. To show them which way to go."

"I see," Garrett said. He seemed bewildered as he put his hands around the broom handle so she didn't drop it.

"It doesn't hurt them," Nicki added. She let the broom fall into his hands. Now, why did she have to tell the man something like that? He'd think she was a barbarian. Not that his opinion mattered. He was only her mother's— Nicki stopped herself. Just who was the man in her mother's life anyway?

"Have you known her long?" Nicki jerked her head in the direction of her mother. She could hear her mother inside the kitchen as she walked across the floor to the counter where the coffee was.

The hostility in this woman's voice cut through Garrett's haze and reminded him the other woman was Chrissy's friend. "Long enough. And you?"

Nicki gave an abrupt laugh. "Me? I barely knew her."

The wind had blown snow across the wooden porch. Nicki could see white puffs coming out of her mouth when she talked. She could feel the goose bumps on her arms, and the frozen boards of the porch chilled her feet even though she had her winter slippers on. She was used to the weather in Montana and she was still cold. "She won't want to stay for long so you might as well go inside and get warmed up. It's freezing out here."

Garrett nodded. The cold would explain the tingling he still felt all over his body. Yes, that would be it. And his breathing. That would explain why his breath was coming hard. But as the woman backed up farther against the doorjamb, all he could think about was that she had to be even colder than he was. "You go ahead—you must be freezing. You're in your pajamas."

The sun was rising and the day was taking on a faint pink glow. Garrett couldn't help but notice how delightful the woman's face was when she blushed.

"It's a robe."

Nicki had never wished for silk in her life until now. Her chenille robe must be twelve years old. It had been faithful and warm, but it was not what a woman dreamed about wearing at a moment like this.

Not that, Nicki assured herself, it would matter for very long. The man in front of her would be leaving with her mother and, if Nicki had anything to say about it, that would be happening soon. Nicki pulled on the ties of her robe to knot it more securely. She was a sensible ranch woman. She didn't need silk. She didn't need her mother. She didn't need some fantasy prince. She had her land, her boots and her pride. That had to be enough.

Garrett looked at the woman. The cold had turned her nose red and the wind had blown strands of her hair this way and that way until they finally just gave up and tangled around her head. Her hair was neither permed nor colored nor highlighted. She kept it brown—not honey-brown, not mahogany-brown. Just plain brown. And she didn't have a dab of lipstick anywhere.

Added to that, she was wearing an old bathrobe that kept her shape so well hidden, a man couldn't tell if she was a woman or a fence post.

Still, she appealed to him in a crazy sort of way. Garrett wondered if the snow could have frozen his brain or something. The woman sure wasn't the usual kind who caught his eye. He liked a woman who strutted her stuff and wore her clothes tight enough so a man didn't have to strain himself wondering what was underneath.

And that robe wasn't his style. He liked the black see-through kind that was worn more for invitation than for warmth. The bulky old robe this woman wore wouldn't get her noticed in a monastery.

Besides, the robe said loud and clear that the woman who wore it was a nice woman who wasn't inviting anybody to look at her twice.

Garrett made it a policy to stay away from nice women because they always thought a man like him had promise. It wasn't true, of course, but try convincing a woman who was intent on reforming him. If he knew one thing about himself, it was that he was a short-term kind of a guy. He liked the freedom of the road. Given that, he felt it was only right to keep his dating to women who weren't interested in a long-term arrangement, either.

Granted, Garrett had grown a little tired of dating strangers lately. He told himself he was just off his game. He hadn't been out on a date in six months.

But that was bound to change soon. Somewhere, someplace, a woman in black spandex was waiting for him.

Still, if he had been the sticking-around kind of guy, there was something about this woman that interested him even more than the black-spandex ones. Maybe it was the freckles on her neck. She'd tied the belt of the robe tight around her waist and that made the collar bulge just enough so he could see the light sprinkling of freckles that scattered out from her collar bone. The bone itself was fragile and made him feel protective. But it was the freckles that were his undoing.

For the first time in his life, Garrett wished he knew a thing or two about marriage.

"I'm sorry, I—" Garrett began. He didn't know what he was going to apologize for exactly. Maybe the fact that cold air had gone into her warm kitchen. Or that he had snow on his shoes. Or that he hadn't been born into an Ozzie-and-Harriet kind of a family.

Nicki shifted in the doorway. A faint pink made her face glow in embarrassment. The man didn't need to apologize. She wasn't such a ninny that she thought he was serious. Of course, she was acting like one. The man had been making her agitated and that wasn't like her. She was usually very calm and sensible.

"I know it wasn't a real kiss." Nicki waved her hand vaguely, as though she'd experienced a million kisses that were real and so could tell the difference instantly. "You don't need to apologize."

Garrett frowned. "What do you mean it wasn't a real kiss?"

"That's what I'm saying—it wasn't like the kiss was supposed to be real, so you don't need to apologize."

"I wasn't apologizing for kissing you."

The pink on Nicki's face deepened. "Oh, well, I just wanted you to know I know it didn't mean anything. It was just because of the ring, and me asking to be pinched and you in that tuxedo and all."

"It's not a tuxedo, it's a uniform. Besides, every kiss means something."

Nicki could hear her mother's high-heeled footsteps as she continued walking from the counter that held the coffeepot to the counter that held the dishes. "Where do you keep the cups?" her mother called out.

Nicki forced herself to turn and look. Everything in the house looked shabbier than it had when her mother left. Because of her fall yesterday she hadn't even done the dishes from yesterday. Three mugs stood around the sink. "There are more mugs in the cupboard."

Every Christmas the hardware store in Dry Creek gave away a mug to its customers with the store's name on one side of it and the year on the other. In addition to the three by the sink, another dozen of those mugs sat in the cupboard.

Nicki's mother took one look at the dirty cups.

"I'm not talking about mugs. I'm talking about real cups. I always drink my coffee from a real cup. Something pretty and tasteful. Surely, Charles still does the same."

"I'm afraid the mugs are all that we have." Nicki tried to hold back the defensiveness in her voice, but she didn't succeed. Nicki wasn't sure she wanted the woman in front of her to realize that she was her daughter. The fuss the woman was making over cups that were functional instead of pretty only reminded Nicki of how critical her mother had been of her. Nicki had never been the pretty little girl her mother wanted. Nicki remembered that her hair never curled enough and the lace on her dresses always made her itch so she couldn't wait to change into her jeans.

"But these mugs don't even match."

"They don't need to match to hold coffee."

All of a sudden, Nicki realized what her mother was looking for. Nicki's mother had had a set of English bone china that served sixteen, but Nicki and Reno kept it packed away in the old bunkhouse where their father had put it. The dishes were the one thing Nicki hadn't even dreamed of replacing over the years. Her mother loved that china with its clusters of pink roses and the gold rim around each plate.

Nicki decided she needed to get the mugs so that her

mother could drink her coffee and leave. She forgot about her leg, however, and her first step made her wince.

"You're hurt!" Garrett said, and stepped toward her. Unfortunately, he let go of the broom handle so that he could steady Nicki just as she moved again. Instead of falling to the floor harmlessly like it should have, the broom landed on Nicki's foot.

"Oooh." Nicki felt the pain shoot up through her leg. The broom hit her toes and her slippers weren't enough of a cushion. To make matters worse, it was her good foot that had been hit. The bruise was on her other leg and so now she didn't have one good walking foot between the two legs.

The dismay on the man's face made Nicki wonder if her face had turned white with pain. "Don't worry. I'll be fine. It's just that yesterday my horse fell and now this—"

"You need to stay off your feet," he said.

"I'm fine. Really." Nicki gathered the collar of her robe around her more closely. To prove she was all right, Nicki carefully put one foot in front of the other and started walking toward the cupboard that held what dishes they did have. She smiled to show it didn't hurt.

Her smile turned to gritted teeth as she bit back the moan. Oh, my, that hurt.

"It's my fault the broom fell," Garrett said as he stepped forward and scooped Nicki up in his arms.

Nicki gasped in surprise. Maybe she was still dreaming. Her cheek was pressed against the tuxedo's satin lapel. The suit even smelled of class. Nicki wished she were wearing perfume. Forget perfume— she wished she were at least wearing deodorant.

"You need to put me down. I can walk," Nicki said. But maybe she couldn't walk. Everything seemed dizzy. Her whole world was shifting. Her heart was building up to a pounding close to thunder. Being swept up by Prince Charming was a fantasy come true.

Nicki's mother walked closer to the two of them and frowned. "Are you Mrs. Hargrove's daughter? You look familiar."

Nicki kept her cheek pressed against the man's shoulder.

"Doris June? No, I'm not her," Nicki answered when she knew her mother couldn't see her eyes. Doris June Hargrove had gone to school with Nicki. She lived in Anchorage now and was working for a television station there.

"Oh, I was just wondering." Her mother didn't sound convinced. "I'm sure Charles needs someone to look after the house for him since both of the kids took off like they did on him."

"Who told you anyone took off?" Nicki asked quietly when she was finally sitting on the kitchen counter. She reknotted the tie on her robe just so she had somewhere for her eyes to focus that didn't involve looking at her mother.

"Why, Charles, of course. He wrote me a letter. Years ago. I'd written to ask about the kids, and he said they'd just up and left. I was surprised about that, but I suppose they had their reasons. He promised he'd let me know if he found out where they were. Have you worked for Charles long?" Nicki's mother smiled thinly. "I know I'm going on, but I would like a cup of coffee before I have to see Charles. Do you think he'll be up soon?"

"No, no, he won't be up soon," Nicki said. Everything seemed fuzzy. Her whole world was shifting. Her heart was pounding. She didn't know whether it was because of seeing her long-lost mother or because she'd woken up to see Prince Charming.

Nicki immediately rejected the idea that her mother could affect her like this. She'd gotten used to living without a mother and she was doing fine. The woman standing by the sink could be any woman. Nicki didn't feel anything for her.

Not that, she remembered with a start of guilt, she should be so willing to think the dizziness was from the man, either. She shouldn't be swooning over any man. She was going to marry Lester. That thought alone was enough to bring her back to earth with a thud. At least it settled her stomach.

"Oh," Nicki's mother said as she turned to leave the kitchen. "If he's not going to be up soon, I'm going to visit the ladies' room while you finish making the coffee. It was a long drive."

"The bathroom's upstairs," Nicki offered. "The first door on your left."

"I remember where it is."

Nicki didn't say anything as she listened to the staccato tapping of her mother's heels as she climbed up the stairs.

Garrett wished he could offer to clean out the rain gutters on this woman's house or something. She looked drawn and pale, and he'd always had a soft touch for any wounded being. Of course, it hadn't helped anything that he had dropped the broom that hit her foot. And the broom wasn't half-plastic like the ones they made today; it was pure oak and could do some serious damage. "Let me look at your toes."

"What?" Nicki looked up in time to see Prince Charming reaching for her slippers.

"I'm hoping no toes are broken."

Nicki was just hoping she'd survive.

Garrett had never seen more elegant feet. The toes themselves were worthy of a poem. "I like the pink."

Nicki blushed. She had never meant for anyone to see the nail polish on her toes. She didn't want to wear polish on her fingers, because someone was sure to comment on that. But she figured her toes were safe from the eyes of others and a good way to practice using nail polish just in case she ever wanted to do her fingernails. "There's nothing wrong with having good toe hygiene."

Nicki almost groaned. She was sounding like a schoolteacher. No wonder there had never been a line of men waiting at her door to date her. "I'll be fine in a minute. My foot will be better."

"I'm sorry I dropped the broom."

The man didn't need to apologize, Nicki thought. A man that good-looking—women probably flocked to him to have their toes bruised. It must be the tuxedo, she decided. That, and the way he had of lifting her into his arms, as though she didn't weigh any more than a feather.

Nicki wondered why Lester had never swept her off her feet like Prince Charming here had done. She might mention it to Lester. That's right, she told herself. It was the action that had made her heart all jumpy. It had nothing to do with the man. If Lester put on a tuxedo and swung her up into his arms, she'd feel the same breathlessness as she felt now. She might even want to kiss Lester after something like that.

Nicki heard a motor in the driveway. "I'd better get down four mugs."

Seeing Garrett's bemused expression, Nicki said, "Lester's here." She reached for the mugs and put them down on the counter beside her.

"And who's Lester?"

Nicki hesitated. "Our neighbor. To the east of here."

Nicki told herself she didn't owe this man any explanations. "He's just here for his coffee. Oh, and some coffee cake."

Nicki started to brace herself to slide off the counter.

"No, you don't." Garrett stepped over and held out his arms to scoop her up again.

"You shouldn't."

"The floor's cold."

Nicki nodded. She supposed once more wouldn't hurt. It might actually be a good thing. She probably wouldn't be dizzy this time, and she'd know it had only been a momentary thing before. It was really for scientific research that she was going to let Garrett carry her again.

Nicki slid into his arms.

Garrett was a happy man. The fuzzy material of Nicki's bathrobe brushed against his cheek and the pure soap smell of her surrounded him.

"You didn't need to carry me. I can walk if I have to."

Garrett knew that. But he wasn't fool enough to pass up the opportunity to carry her again. He'd even walk slow. The refrigerator was way across the kitchen. If he worked it right, he could almost make a waltz out of the whole thing.

Nicki heard Lester's footsteps on the porch. Fortunately, the door was already unlocked. "Come on in."

Garrett felt the cold air rush into the kitchen, but that's not what made the back of his neck tingle. Something was wrong. He heard the door slam. It was followed by the quick hissing indrawn breath of an angry man.

"What the—?" The bellow coming from the doorway made Garrett turn as the man charged toward him. The man was small, but wiry—and red enough to explode.

Garrett had been in enough street fights as a kid to know what was coming, but he'd never had someone in his arms before. If he had even a second longer, he could have slid Nicki down to the floor. But the man was coming too fast. All Garrett could do was protect her as best he could. He pivoted so that Nicki was not between him and this madman.

"Lester," the woman squealed.

Garrett only had time to bend his shoulder so he could hide Nicki in the hunching of his shoulder. The man's fist caught him high on the right cheek.

"Lester!" Nicki tried to twist out of Garrett's grasp so she could slide down to the floor and get her broom. What had gotten into him? She'd always assumed Lester was shy and that was why he was so patient with her about kissing and things like that. But the man in front of her wasn't shy. He was acting like a deranged man. "Stop that! What do you think you're doing?"

Garrett's hands held her to him like steel.

"What do I think I'm doing?" Lester exploded. Garrett wondered how the vein in the man's head could throb that hard. "Just what do you think you're doing here with some man and you in your nightgown?"

Ah, so that's the way the story went, Garrett thought to himself. Well, he supposed the woman had to have a boyfriend. Even in a remote area like this, the men would be foolish not to notice the—Garrett stopped himself. It wasn't beauty he noticed. It certainly wasn't stylish clothes. What was it about the woman?

"I've got a robe on—not just my nightgown," Nicki corrected him. "And if you'd bothered to notice, you would see everything is perfectly innocent and—" she could hear her voice rising "—just what do you think is going on anyway?"

Nicki had lived by the rules all her life. Lester should know that.

Lester flushed. He was so red already that he

actually grew less red when he flushed. Now he looked mottled as he mumbled. "Duane at the café told me some guy stopped last night at midnight and asked how to find the Redfern place. Some guy in a tux. Everyone knows Reno took those steers down to Billings and that you're here alone."

"What's Reno got to do with—?" Nicki stopped and then realized what he was implying. "Lester Wilkerson, you have your nerve!"

Garrett felt the swelling start on his cheekbone. He hadn't had a bruiser like this since he'd stepped between two fighting truckers once. He supposed it was safe for Nicki to slide down to the floor now, but Garrett didn't want her to leave his arms. Some primitive part of him figured he was entitled to carry her now that he'd taken a fist to his face on her behalf.

Nicki heard her mother's footsteps as she came back down the stairs.

"Did I hear something about Reno?" Nicki's mother stood in the doorway and asked. "Reno still lives here?"

Everyone in the kitchen forgot Nicki's nightgown and the bruise on Garrett's cheek.

"Let me get you your coffee." Nicki slid to the floor and tested her foot. Garrett let her rest against him until she was steady and then she stepped away. "I put the clean cups on the counter."

"Why would Reno be here? Charles said the kids had both left." Nicki's mother walked over to the counter. "He said he would let me know if he heard from them."

By now the older woman had picked up one of the clean mugs Nicki had put on the counter and was rubbing the side of it almost unconsciously. She had stopped smiling and her face seemed to age ten years as she stood there. "I know Charles was angry with me. But if Reno's here and he didn't tell me, that's not fair. When Charles wakes up, I'm going to have to tell him that's not right."

Nicki felt her face was so tight, it would rip. She refused to cry in front of this woman. "There's nothing you can tell him. He's dead."

The woman dropped the cup and no one noticed. "Oh, dear."

For the first time since she'd recognized her mother, Nicki had a glimpse of the woman her mother used to be. "I'm sorry. I shouldn't have blurted it out like that."

"No, no—" Nicki's mother waved the apology away. "I just wasn't expecting this is all. Does Nicki know? Did anyone find her to tell her? She'd want to know."

"She knows." Nicki swallowed. She'd never thought herself to be a coward, but she found that the words to tell her mother who she was wouldn't come without forcing.

"But—" Lester started to speak until Garrett put his hand on the man's arm to silence him.

Nicki looked at both men. There was nothing to do but say it. "I'm Nicki."

Nicki wished her mother had another cup to drop. Anything would be better than the silence that greeted her announcement. The other woman just stared at Nicki.

Nicki reminded herself that she didn't need fairy tales, not even ones that involved mothers coming home again to their daughters.

"Well—" Nicki finally found her voice. The silence was unnerving. "Let me pour you some coffee before you go."

Nicki was proud of the fact that her face didn't crumble. No tears came to her eyes. Even the anger was gone. She would give her mother a cup of coffee and that would be that.

Nicki didn't even limp as she walked toward the coffeepot.

Chapter Three

Garrett was losing his touch. He would have bet Big Blue that Lilly would melt into a puddle of sentimentality at the fact that her daughter was standing before her. Aunt Rose would have been crying into her tissue by now.

But the woman stayed dry-eyed. He thought her hands trembled and her face did grow paler, but she certainly wasn't smiling with joy. She looked over at Garrett. "We're going to have to leave. I didn't know she was here."

Garrett felt a clutch in his stomach at her words. Something was going on here and he had a feeling it was something worse than anybody's sore toes. He took a step closer to Nicki just in case she needed him.

"I'm in the room. You can talk to me," Nicki said

as she gripped the handle on the cup she had pulled from the dish drainer.

"Oh, dear— It's just that I'm surprised. Your father's letter said— Well, I just didn't expect you to be here," Lillian said as she walked over to the sink.

Garrett knew people didn't always say what they meant the first time around. He turned to Lillian. "Maybe if you told her why you're here. Surely there's a reason."

The older woman hesitated. "I just came to see Charles, that's all."

The man's question brought Nicki back into focus. Why was her mother here? Nicki turned to face the woman. If you took away the powder and the makeup, you could see traces of the woman she had once been. "You could have come to see him years ago."

The clock ticked and the old refrigerator gurgled.

"And what's he doing here?" Lester finally spoke and jerked his thumb at Garrett.

"I'm Garrett Hamilton. I'm a trucker. I drove Lilly Fern up here."

"And why did you come again?" Nicki turned from the man and addressed her mother.

"I came to talk to your father," Nicki's mother said defiantly. "There's no harm in that."

"You can't possibly think he would want to see you now even if he were alive. You left him years ago."

"He was my husband. I never did divorce him."

"That's it? You came to ask him for a divorce after all these years?"

"Of course not. I don't need a divorce."

"Then what is it—is it money?"

Lillian laughed. "Charles never had any money. All he ever had was this ranch of his."

"He loved this ranch—" *And he loved you.* Nicki almost said the words and then choked them off. What did it matter now?

Lillian wasn't even looking at her any longer. "I know we can't always go back, but I have unfinished business in Dry Creek and I needed a place to stay for a little bit—"

"You're in trouble?"

Lillian shrugged. "In a way, I guess."

"And you need a place to hide?" Strangely enough, Nicki was relieved. Her mother really hadn't come looking for her father because she missed her father or had any fondness for him. She'd just come looking for a safe harbor in some storm she was facing.

"Your father would want me to be here now. He'd feel he owes me that much."

Nicki felt her world click back into place. Everything was as it had been. It felt good to know her way around once again. The fact that her mother had come to her father hoping for comfort in some crisis didn't surprise her. Her father never turned away anyone in need. He might not talk to them much, but he'd let them stay.

"Nobody here owes you anything." Nicki wasn't her father.

"Don't worry. I couldn't possibly stay here now anyway." Lillian Redfern reached out her hand for a cup of coffee. "Once I've had a cup of coffee, Garrett will drive me back to Dry Creek and we'll stay there for a few days."

"Dry Creek?" Nicki didn't like the sound of that.

Garrett wasn't sure he liked the sounds of it, either. He frowned. "No one said anything about days. I thought we were planning to leave tonight." Garrett planned to be in Las Vegas tomorrow night so he could pick up Big Blue and hit the highway.

Lillian looked up at Garrett. "I'm sure you won't mind. It's just going to take longer than I thought."

Garrett did mind, but he didn't have time to speak up before Nicki was talking.

"You can't just stay. Not around Dry Creek," Nicki said.

"No one would deny a widow the right to stand by her husband's grave."

"You're going to tell them you're going to the cemetery?"

"Of course. And I will be. It's the respectable thing to do. I have a black dress with me. I always travel with at least one black dress. And I'm sure someone in Dry Creek will let me stay with them."

"After what you did when you left?" Nicki's hand shook ever so slightly as she poured another cup of coffee into a hardware store mug. "I wouldn't think you'd be very welcome."

Lillian sat down at the kitchen table and took a sip of coffee. "Oh, yes. The money. I suppose they still remember that."

Nicki looked at her mother incredulously. "Of course they remember the money. You stole over eight hundred dollars from the church building fund. I don't know how many bake sales the women of the church had. How could you possibly think they might have forgotten?"

Lillian smiled slightly. "I thought they might have had other things on their mind at the time." Lillian took another sip of coffee and then looked at Nicki. "My leaving was hard on you, wasn't it?"

"No. I did fine."

Nicki could feel Lester looking at her. She glanced up at him. Even now that he was calm, he looked odd. She'd never seen him look like this. His face looked blotched. But he was her Lester. She could count on him. "Haven't I done fine?"

Lester grunted and jerked his thumb at Garrett. "You're sure you don't know him? Jazz at the café said he had a ring and everything ready to propose."

Garrett felt his heart stop. He'd thought the teenager had looked at him strangely when the ring fell out.

Garrett cleared his throat and looked Nicki in the eye. "You did just fine. I can tell."

Nicki was annoyed. Lester should have been the one to say that. "Thank you, but you don't know me well enough to judge."

Garrett grinned. He rather liked the vinegar look on Nicki's face. "It's early. I've got time."

"What's he talking about?" Lester mumbled.

"Oh, for Pete's sake, he's not proposing," Nicki said firmly as she smiled at Lester and glared at Garrett. This was all Garrett's fault. Everything had been fine—until he came up here. Who went around carrying an engagement ring and wearing a tuxedo in the middle of Montana farmland? No wonder poor Lester was confused. "Look at him. He's not even from around here."

Garrett frowned at that. "Good people come from other places, too."

Nicki took a deep breath. "What I meant is that you don't know me and I don't know you so there's no reason to think you'd be proposing. We're strangers."

"I've seen your toes."

"What's he talking about? And what's he doing here anyway?"

Nicki wondered why she'd never seen Lester like this before. What had happened to his hair? She hadn't noticed how his light brown hair was starting to thin and the pink of his scalp showed through, making him look old. And when he squinted like that, his eyes made him look like a ferret. Maybe it was only the cold weather that had scrunched up his face like this. She'd need to get him a warm cap for Christmas. That's what she'd do, she thought. A warm cap would make him look better.

"He brought me here," Lillian said graciously to Lester. "I don't believe we've met. Were you here when I was around? I'm Nicki's mother."

Lillian held her hand out to the man.

Lester had his hand halfway out to meet hers and he stopped in midair. "That's what Nicki's talking about—I remember hearing about you—you're the one who stole the church's money?"

Nicki saw her mother's polite smile tighten. "Is that what they say about me?"

"Yes, ma'am," Lester agreed doubtfully.

"Well, then, I'm getting off easy, I guess."

"Well, I don't know about that—taking money is pretty serious."

"Well, they'll just have to forgive me," Lillian said

firmly. She lifted her chin up slightly. "Once an apology is given, it is their Christian duty to forgive."

Lester looked at Lillian, frowning slightly. "I must have missed hearing about the apology."

Nicki could have gone to Lester and hugged him. Now this was the Lester she knew. Unswayed by flattery. Polite and logical, with his feet firmly planted on the earth and no hint of sentiment about him. Not at all like Prince Charming who stood looking at her like she needed some kind of rescuing.

"Well, I haven't given an apology yet," Lillian admitted with a hint of reproach in her voice. "I haven't even finished my coffee." Lillian took a slow sip from her cup. "What do you suppose they'll say?"

"What do you mean?" Nicki felt a small ball of dread starting to roll around in her stomach.

"Why, when I go into Dry Creek and apologize, of course."

"You don't really need to apologize," Nicki said. The last thing she wanted was for her mother's name to again be the primary topic of conversation for Dry Creek. "That's all over and done with."

"I can't do that. You two convinced me of that." Lillian nodded at Lester. She took another sip of coffee. "I can't have people saying I didn't apologize."

"You could write a note," Nicki offered in desperation. People never got as worked up over a letter as they did when someone talked in person. Besides, who knew what her mother would say when she opened her mouth. Nicki could correct a letter.

"What kind of a lady would write a note about something like that?" her mother asked.

The same kind of lady who would steal from the church on the way out of her children's lives, Nicki thought, but she held her tongue.

"No, I'm right," Lillian said firmly. "I'm going to apologize and put an end to all of this. All I need to do is find the minister of that little church. We'll all drive into Dry Creek and find him."

"All of us?" Lester shuffled his feet and looked at Nicki before glancing at Garrett. "You're sure that guy's not proposing?"

"Absolutely."

"Then I'm going to get back to my place. I still have some cattle to feed."

"I could come help you," Nicki offered.

Lester brightened. "You could?"

"She's coming with me." Garrett interrupted them. It was one thing for Nicki to reassure the man that no one was proposing to her, it was another to run off for a cozy drive with her boyfriend while she left her mother with Garrett.

"Nicki and Garrett will take me to Dry Creek," Lillian said airily, as if she was in charge. "They won't need anyone else."

Lester looked at Nicki and shrugged before heading toward the door.

Nicki tried again. "It's early morning. The minister won't be up yet."

"Then we'll wake him up," Lillian said as she stood. "It's his duty to hear confessions."

"You're thinking of priests." Nicki groaned. "Priests hear confessions."

"Priest, minister, it's all the same," Lillian said as she adjusted her skirt and turned to Garrett. "Would you mind bringing the car closer to the door this time? The snow is so slippery and in these shoes—"

Garrett could tell from Nicki's face that her Lester had disappointed her when he made his exit without her. Garrett shouldn't be happy about that fact, but he was. To make up for it, he turned to Nicki and asked, "How about it? Would you like me to bring the car closer so you don't have to walk in the snow?"

"Me?" Nicki breathed lightly. Her Prince Charming was worried about her feet. That's when she remembered she was in her slippers. "Oh, I can't go. I'm not dressed."

Nicki had been searching for a reason not to go,

and when she found one she realized she was oddly disappointed.

"Well, I can't leave you here." Garrett didn't want to drive Lillian back into Dry Creek all alone.

"And put on a dress, darling," Nicki's mother called out as she walked toward the kitchen door. "We have time for you to look nice."

Nicki couldn't believe she was hearing those words again. The only time Nicki had worn a dress since her mother left was to her father's funeral. And she certainly wasn't going to wear that dress for her mother's return, Nicki told herself as she limped up the stairs again.

Nicki did have some nice pants outfits that she wore to church. She pulled one of them off its hanger before she reconsidered and hung it back up. No, she wasn't going to fall into the trap of trying to please her mother.

Instead, Nicki put on the jeans she generally used to muck out the barn. They were clean, but they didn't look it. She topped them off with an old sweater of her father's. Her mother might not like it, but Nicki didn't care.

She didn't want to hear what her mother said about dresses and looking good, anyway. Nicki knew she was hopeless. She only had to look in the mirror to know she wasn't princess material. Her mother had been as delicate as the lily that gave her its name. But there was nothing delicate about Nicki's face. She had her father's square jaw and determined forehead. Her hair was plentiful and shiny, but it never took on the styled look that some women's hair had. She just kept it cut and tied back out of her face.

There was never any reason to fuss with her hair. The cows didn't care. Reno wouldn't notice. Even Lester wouldn't care.

Nicki decided her mother would have to accept her as she was.

Nicki felt foolish the minute Garrett opened the passenger door of the limousine for her. She felt like a rebellious Cinderella who had declined her fairy godmother's offer of new clothes but had gone to the ball anyway. The interior of the car was sleek—if it was proper to call the limousine a car. It looked more like an ocean liner to her eyes. Nicki had never seen such a long length of leather that wasn't attached to a cow. And there was a small refrigerator. And her mother.

"Maybe I should drive the pickup in to Dry Creek and just meet you there," Nicki suggested softly as she looked up at Garrett. "I don't really know that I should ride in here dressed in jeans—"

Garrett shrugged. "You can ride up front with me if you'd like. It's not so fancy up there."

Garrett told himself that Nicki was just like any other woman he'd taken for a drive. Any kind of breathing problem he'd had after that kiss had only been because of the freezing temperature.

"I do have a dress," Nicki said when Garrett turned the heater on inside the limousine. The defroster slowly blew a clear space on the front window. "I should have worn it. I imagine all of the women in Las Vegas wear dresses."

Of course they wore dresses, Nicki told herself. Sexy black dresses that pleased men more than mothers.

Garrett grunted. "I'm not from Vegas."

"Oh. I just thought that since Lillian was from there—" Nicki turned her head and noticed the glass window that separated the driver's area from the rear of the limousine was firmly closed. At least her mother and Garrett hadn't been chatting away cozily.

"I don't know your mother. I'm just doing a favor for Chrissy."

"Oh." Of course there was a Chrissy in his life. Or a Suzy or a Patti. Some petite blonde with style. A man that good-looking wouldn't be alone. "I see. Well, good for you."

"I don't know about that."

"Well, of course it's good. And I'm sure she appreciates it."

"She'd better. If she doesn't I'm going to tell her mother about it."

"You're good friends with her mother, too?" Nicki smiled stiffly. The man was practically married whether he knew it or not. "That's nice."

"Well, it's my aunt Rose. Chrissy Hamilton is my cousin."

"Oh."

Nicki decided she should look for something else to wear when she was in Dry Creek. Really, the only store in town was the hardware store, but the stock had changed so much since the minister's new wife, Glory, was doing the ordering that maybe, by some magical coincidence, there were dresses hanging on a rack by the farmer's overalls.

The window separating the front of the limo from the back opened and Nicki smelled a trace of her mother's lily perfume.

"She's getting married, you know. Chrissy is," Lillian announced. "It'll make her mother proud."

"It'll make her mother mad if Chrissy doesn't invite her," Garrett said.

"You can hear back there what we're saying?" Nicki wondered what the point of having a window like that was if it offered no privacy.

Her mother didn't even bother to answer her. "Chrissy said there was no need for anyone to come to her wedding."

Nicki thought about her own mother. "I expect Chrissy has her reasons for not inviting her mother."

Garrett snorted. "Well, if she does, she'd better get them spelled out in a letter or something. And mighty quick. Aunt Rose is a force to be reckoned with when it concerns her family. I should know."

Garrett still remembered the determined look on Aunt Rose's face when she met him at the hospital the day his father's liver finally gave out and he died. Garrett was quickly learning something about the forms that needed to be filled out when someone died.

Garrett hadn't even finished half of the forms before Aunt Rose came to the hospital and took over. She'd told him he wasn't alone in this world as long as she was around and she was going to take him home to live with her and Chrissy. Garrett had already made arrangements to stay in the house where he and his father had lived, but he was touched. Not many single mothers would take on a belligerent sixteen-year-old nephew who knew more about hospital forms than college applications.

"Oh, I'm sure Chrissy will have some pictures taken." Lillian shrugged. "And maybe a video. Some of the chapels include a video with the service. Chrissy's mother can watch that. It'll almost be the same thing."

"Aunt Rose won't think so. She's still hoping

Chrissy will go home for Christmas and get married in the living room where she grew up."

Nicki wondered what it would be like for someone to want to be at your wedding that bad. She supposed Reno might be upset if he wasn't invited to her wedding. Of course, he would also be relieved since he hated any public gathering. "Do you think Chrissy will do that?"

"Not likely."

"Well, I think Christmas would be a lovely time to get married. Or even Thanksgiving," Lillian said as she leaned closer to the partition that separated the back from the front. "Too bad she won't be up here tomorrow. Thanksgiving was always my favorite time on the ranch. All those pies we used to make."

"We don't do Thanksgiving at the ranch anymore," Nicki said curtly. Who was her mother trying to fool? It almost sounded as if there was some nostalgia in her voice.

"Really? For the first years I was gone I used to picture you and your father and Reno sitting down to these big Thanksgiving dinners. You know how your father used to like to have the table bulging with food and half the families in Dry Creek coming over to eat with us. There'd be the Hargroves. And the Jenkins. And, of course, Jacob and Betty Holmes—"

"We don't have company at the ranch anymore."

"Well, you should—the Redfern Ranch is important to this community. Besides, I was sort of hoping to relive one of those Thanksgivings while I'm here," Lillian said as she leaned back into her seat and her face was no longer in the window. "I can almost smell the turkey now."

"Sounds like you have some good family memories," Garrett said after a minute or two had passed.

Nicki looked up at him in surprise. How could they be good memories when they only reminded her of what she had lost? "All that ended."

"I see."

Clearly the man didn't see at all, Nicki thought to herself miserably. "You wouldn't know what it was like. Reno, Dad and I made peace about celebrating Christmas, but Thanksgiving was just never the same. Last year I made meat loaf."

"Nothing wrong with that. The fanciest we ever got in my family was a can of turkey noodle soup."

"Well, at least you had your family with you."

Garrett grunted. The only reason his father had been with him on Thanksgiving was because the bars were closed in the morning and he was too drunk to walk anywhere else by the afternoon. He liked to start his holiday celebrations early. It was Garrett who heated up the soup.

But Garrett didn't believe in telling people about his past. What was done was done. He was doing fine in life now. Of course, he had spent more Thanksgivings in truck stop cafés than he could count, but there was more to living than eating a plate of turkey on some cold Thursday in November.

Besides, he reminded himself, he liked not having the kind of family ties that meant he had to sit himself down to a Thanksgiving table every year. He was a free man.

Chapter Four

Meanwhile in Las Vegas

Chrissy sat up on the edge of her king-size bed in the Baughman Hotel. Today was going to be her wedding day and it would be a good day if she could only stomp down the nausea that threatened her. Now that she had Garrett hundreds of miles north of here and her mother hundreds of miles south, Chrissy was ready to take her vows.

She'd made the appointment with the wedding chaplain for nine o'clock in the morning so that no one would be hanging around the Rose Chapel in the Baughman Casino.

She knew it was bad luck for the groom to see the bride before the ceremony, but she figured her luck couldn't get much worse. Besides, she was too tired to put on her work clothes just to give a loud wake-up knock on Jared's door. Instead, she slipped on the wedding dress Jared had bought for her.

Chrissy hadn't planned to buy a special wedding dress. She had a gray suit that would have worked fine. Besides, a wedding dress seemed a little expensive under the circumstances. They were saving their money to buy a house, and Chrissy didn't mind scrimping on a wedding if they could find a house sooner.

But Jared had showed up with this dress anyway so she slipped it over her head. She turned to look at the hotel mirror. She looked even worse in it than she feared. The dress was short, strappy and it had some kind of iridescent, glittering sequins sewn on every inch of the fabric.

If she had feathers in her hair, Chrissy would look like a showgirl in it. Which was probably why Jared had chosen the dress. Chrissy looked at the material a little more closely. She hoped he hadn't just lifted the dress off one of the costume racks at the back of the casino.

Chrissy had always dreamed of an elegant ivory wedding gown that would sweep the floor and make her look like one of those brides she'd seen on the covers of magazine racks in the drugstores in Glendale.

All of which just went to show that weddings weren't

always what a girl imagined they would be. Sometimes there were more important things to consider.

Jared's room was just down the hall from Chrissy's, and she was surprised to find his door was slightly open. She hadn't expected him to be still up. He'd had his bachelor party last night with a couple of friends, and that was why he was staying in a separate room. He said he didn't want to disturb her when he came in late.

Chrissy wasn't happy about the party, but she had smiled gamely. She didn't like the two guys he hung out with, but she never said anything. When they were married, Jared would be all hers. Jared had promised they could leave Las Vegas then and buy a house in some little town somewhere. Chrissy couldn't wait for that day. She hated the crush of people in Las Vegas. She wouldn't even mind waiting tables so much if she knew some of the customers.

"Jar—" Chrissy pushed the door open and stopped. At first she thought she must have the wrong room because all she saw was the back of a woman kissing a man. But then she noticed that whoever had his arm around the woman was wearing one of Jared's favorite shirts.

Chrissy told herself there could be hundreds of shirts in Las Vegas with black spades embroidered on their cuffs. She looked down at the man's shoes.

Then she looked back up at the woman. The woman was wearing Jared's bathrobe.

Shirt. Shoes. Bathrobe.

Chrissy took a step back and stumbled over a high heel that had been left on the floor. Her soft cry made both people turn and look at her.

The woman was one of the casino chorus girls.

"Chrissy!" Jared smoothed back his hair. "You're early."

Chrissy wondered if she should have known Jared had been involved with a woman. She believed in trusting the man she loved. Maybe she'd been too trusting. Had there been signs?

"Just let me get dressed and we'll go downstairs and get married right now." Jared was regaining his voice.

Chrissy held her hand up. "Don't—don't bother. You might as well stay here."

"Don't be silly. You're not going to let a little bit of fun stop us from getting married."

"Yeah, you're all dressed and everything. That's a great dress, by the way. It looks even better on you than me," the blonde said.

Chrissy wondered if the woman was as insensitive as she sounded. She turned to Jared. "You got the dress from her—no, don't answer. Just give me the keys to my car."

Chrissy had brought her car with her to Vegas. It was her car even though Jared borrowed it most of the time.

"Ah, Chrissy, don't be that way."

Chrissy took a step back as Jared walked toward her.

"Don't touch me." Chrissy hoped the burning in her eyes didn't turn into tears. She wanted to leave with dignity. "Just give me the keys."

Jared smiled. "Ah, don't be mad. Remember, the car's in the shop. They have the keys. It won't be ready until tomorrow."

"Maybe they'll finish early."

Chrissy backed out of the hotel room. She'd talk to the mechanic. She needed to leave Vegas and she needed to leave soon. But where would she go? She couldn't go to her mother's. Maybe she could connect with Garrett and Lilly. Lilly had talked about the people in Dry Creek, Montana. That's where she'd go.

Chapter Five

"The café's open," Garrett announced as he slowly drove down the gravel road that was Dry Creek's main street. It was nine o'clock in the morning and just about time for some bacon and eggs in Garrett's opinion. He hoped the café served a hearty breakfast.

Garrett stopped the limousine in front of the café. He had to park parallel to the road because the limo was so long. The café had been lit up last night, and here it was all lit up again this morning. "Somebody puts in long hours."

"That's Linda Evans and Jazz, well, really Duane Edison. He just goes by Jazz—they're trying to raise enough money to buy the old Jenkins' farm. They're very responsible youngsters."

Nicki didn't know why she kept spouting off like

an old schoolteacher. It must be because, even with the bruise around his eye starting to swell, she'd never met a man so gorgeous as Garrett. He might have stopped sparkling, but he still made all of her frustrations rise to the surface and scream their heads off. Not that she had any intention of letting him see how he affected her.

No, she'd keep her emotions in tight rein. She could do that. After all, her reaction had nothing to do with him personally. She would be rattled by any man who looked as if he'd been sprinkled with gold dust. Not that a man like that would ever be hers in real life. She was destined for a solid plodding man like Lester, who would be useful on the ranch. That was her future. She needed to be practical and stop dreaming about sparkling princes and men like Garrett.

"Is everybody around here so set on staying?" Garrett opened his door.

Nicki looked up at Garrett like he was speaking a foreign language. "Dry Creek is our home."

Garrett grunted. When he was talking to the dog this morning, he'd wondered if all the people in Dry Creek already had their burial plots picked out. He was beginning to think he'd guessed right when he said yes. That kind of certainty made him itch under the collar.

How could a man breathe if he knew every step he'd be taking for the rest of his life?

If Garrett was ever fool enough to marry, it would have to be some poor restless soul like himself. He delayed swinging his legs out of the cab of the limousine. "Don't you ever feel the urge to go other places?"

"I go to Billings."

Garrett grunted again. "Why stop there?"

"That's as far as we need to go for cattle sales." Nicki wasn't sure about going into the café with Garrett. He was dressed in his tuxedo and she had on her barn clothes. "You go ahead. I'm really not very hungry."

"Well, I am." Garrett stepped out into the snow-covered road.

Garrett looked down the long gravel road leading into Dry Creek. For the first time since he could remember, looking at a road made him feel a little depressed. There was something lonely about the thought of one man traveling it all by himself. Garrett decided it must be because he was missing Big Blue. Or maybe he needed to get a dog to travel the road with him so he'd have someone to talk to during the long nights.

Garrett walked around the limousine. Breakfast would make him feel better.

A light sprinkling of snow settled on the front window. Nicki was comfortable in the car watching

Garrett until she heard the small window click open behind her.

"I'm glad to see you remember some of what I taught you. A lady never eats breakfast like some ranch hand," Nicki's mother said. "Speaking of which—I hope you're taking care of your hands, too."

Nicki turned to stare at the woman behind her. The woman might be her mother, but Nicki saw nothing of herself in the face that looked through the small window. Her mother's face was like a porcelain doll's. It was flawless, but not real.

"Mother, look at me. I never was the pretty little girl you wanted me to be. I don't have time for lotions and fancy manicures. We need summer help on the ranch, but we don't have money to pay anyone. So, Reno and I do everything. I bale hay and brand cattle. I'm not a lady, I'm a working ranch hand." Nicki opened the door and stepped out. She stood tall and took a deep breath. Nicki knew she was going to order the full stack of pancakes. The morning was beginning to look better.

Garrett already had a foot on the step that led up to the porch that surrounded the café door when Nicki caught up to him. She felt she should caution Garrett about the steps leading up to the café, but she knew Jazz had fixed them all. Maybe it was the door that she should warn him about.

Nicki's heart sank when she heard the woman's voice. Now *that's* what she should have warned Garrett about.

"Oh my, oh my—" Linda shrieked the moment Garrett stepped inside the café. Nicki and Garrett were both just inside the doorway now and Linda saw them. "Jazz said—but, oh, my!"

Nicki knew it was a mistake bringing Garrett to town without a hat on his head to hide his handsome face, but what could she do now?

"This is Garrett Hamilton." Nicki introduced the man beside her. "He's just in town to—to—"

"I know, I know—" Linda squealed. The teenager had a red streak in her hair and a row of silver earrings circling her left ear. She wore a long black dress with a white chef's apron over it. She had a tattoo of a butterfly over her left eye. She was the last person in Dry Creek who should be making a fuss over how someone looked and, if Nicki got her ear privately for a moment, she would suggest that to Linda. "Jazz said—but I never…I mean, I thought he was mistaken or—well, I just never thought." The teenager stopped to take a breath and reached her hand out to Garrett. "Pleased to meet you."

Garrett was beginning to wonder if Dry Creek might be a little too far off the beaten path. Jazz, the young man he'd talked to last night, looked at him oddly and then this young woman acted as if she'd never seen a stranger. "The pleasure's all mine."

Four empty square tables, each with four wooden chairs, stood in the middle of the café. Garrett liked the casual fifties look of the place. The floor was black-and-white linoleum and there were red-checked vinyl cloths on the tables. Each table had a squeeze bottle of maple syrup. That was a good sign. He liked pancakes. "This is a very nice place you have here."

"Oh." Linda turned to Nicki. "And he has such nice manners. That's a good thing in a…well, a—" Linda put her head close to Nicki's ear and whispered "—in a husband."

"In a what?" Nicki was glad her teeth were attached. Otherwise, they would have fallen out of her mouth. She had completely forgotten that Lester had gone on about Jazz seeing the ring the man had.

"Oh, I hope I didn't spoil the surprise." Linda put her hands over her lips. "I shouldn't have said anything. I just thought that by now he would have asked."

"Garrett isn't—" Nicki closed her mouth. Garrett was looking at her puzzled. He hadn't heard what Linda had whispered and Nicki wasn't about to tell him. She came as close as she dared. "That was my mother's old engagement ring. Garrett's just passing through Dry Creek and he returned it. Besides, you know I'm not dating anyone."

Linda lowered her voice so only Nicki could hear. "But you want to, don't you? He's the best-looking man I've ever seen around here. You've got to want to date him."

Nicki blushed and shook her head. "No, I—"

Linda winked at Nicki and turned to Garrett. "Sorry about that. Nicki was just telling me about her latest date with Lester. You probably don't know him—"

"Oh, I know him." Garrett turned so the young lady could see the bruise on the right side of his face. "He gave me this."

"You were fighting." Linda stopped and frowned. "Nicki doesn't like fighting."

"Tell that to Lester."

"Lester started the fight? That doesn't sound like Lester."

Linda moved over so she could whisper in Nicki's ear. "You don't want to marry him if he's always picking fights with people. I don't care if he begs you. Say no."

"I don't need to say no," Nicki whispered back. "He's not asking."

Linda nodded and continued brightly, "Yes, Nicki is almost married to Lester. He's got a big ranch north of here."

"He doesn't care about Lester." Nicki felt her blush deepen. Why didn't Linda just put an Available sign on Nicki's forehead and set her out on the street so every man who drove through Dry Creek could stop and refuse to ask her out?

Linda barely stopped to listen to Nicki. She continued speaking to Garrett. "Lester took her to the Christmas pageant last year. I remember they had the spaghetti dinner here that night, too. Jazz's band was playing romantic music and Lester was very attentive." She shrugged. "It's only a matter of time."

Nicki shook her head. Why did everyone think she needed to be dating? Lots of perfectly fine women didn't date. Of course they were mostly nuns. "Lester doesn't need to ask me on a date. He's a friend of the family. He invited Reno that night, too."

"She's got you there," Garrett agreed cheerfully. "Sounds like a friend-of-the-family dinner instead of a date to me."

"Family's important to Lester," Linda continued. "That's why he invited Reno."

Nicki frowned. She'd never really thought about why Lester had invited Reno. Now that she thought about it, she realized Lester had talked mostly with Reno. Nicki wondered for the first time if she was as boring to Lester as he was to her. They always did seem to run out of conversation after they covered the weather and the crops. Sometimes cattle prices kept them going longer.

It was depressing to realize that the man you were going to marry had nothing to talk to you about and you were halfway through the dating phase. This was supposed to be the fun time.

"What do you think about the weather?" Nicki looked at Garrett and demanded. "You're a trucker. Weather is important. Do you talk about it?"

"I guess so." Garrett shrugged.

"I mean on a date. Do you talk about it on a date?"

Garrett turned to Nicki. The light was coming in the window of the café and it hit Nicki on the cheek. It gave her a golden Mona Lisa kind of a glow. Something was bothering her and, for the first time in his life, Garrett truly wished he understood women.

"No." Garrett hoped this was the right answer. "Unless you do, that is."

"I was afraid of that." Nicki shoved her hands into the pocket of her coat. She'd forgotten all about her hands until her mother reminded her. They weren't the hands of a dating woman. She didn't wear polish. She kept her nails clipped short. And the skin on her hands was rough and sometimes chapped. She was a fool to think for a moment that Garrett would date someone like her. At least a man like Lester wouldn't worry about her hands or her lack of conversation. "I need to get back and help Lester feed the cows."

Garrett didn't know how one man could be so annoying. "I'm surprised Lester doesn't feed them by himself. Or is it some kind of a date in disguise where you sit and talk about the weather and look at the cows?"

"I don't date," Nicki said.

Linda turned to frown at Nicki. "What Nicki means is that she's been too busy to date very much lately."

"What I mean is that I have to get back and get to work," Nicki repeated.

Garrett grunted. So she didn't date. That meant she'd never go out with him, but it cheered him up anyway. "That's too bad. I don't date much, either, these days."

Nicki stiffened. Who was he trying to fool?

The scent of baking biscuits came from what must be the café's kitchen. Garrett breathed in. "That smells good. Can I put in an order for some of those biscuits with some eggs and bacon?"

Linda thought a moment. "The early rush wiped us out. You're welcome to wait but it will be a few minutes. Will that be a table for two?"

"No, we'll need a table for three."

Lillian was still in the limousine, no doubt writing her apology speech. But Garrett was pretty sure breakfast would lure the woman out of the car. They hadn't had a decent meal since Salt Lake City.

"Three?" Linda frowned.

Garrett nodded.

Linda shrugged and headed back toward the kitchen. "I'll bring out more silverware then."

"How long will it be before you're ready?" Garrett called after her.

"Give us ten minutes." Linda swung open a door to the kitchen and walked into the other room.

Nicki decided disaster had been averted. She didn't know where Linda got such strange ideas, but hopefully Nicki had set the record straight. "Since we have to wait, I think I'll go over to the hardware store and see if the pastor is there."

"I'll go with you."

Nicki hesitated and then decided it was just as well that Garrett didn't stay at the café within reach of Linda's voice. "Good."

Garrett cleared his throat when he opened the door for Nicki to step out into the street. "So you don't date?"

Nicki stopped walking.

Garrett grinned.

"Yeah, I don't much, either," Garrett said as he continued walking.

Nicki hurried to catch up with him.

The morning's light gave a crispness to Dry Creek. A thin layer of white snow coated the road and all of the buildings. Smoke came out of the large building across the street from the café. A dozen or so houses were scattered around the small business buildings. A church with a white steeple was set back off the main road to the east and a barn was set off the main road to the west.

It only took a few minutes to walk over to the hardware store.

Nicki could smell the burning wood as she stomped the snow off her boots on the porch outside the store. Pastor Matthew Curtis was clerking here, and he and his new wife, Glory, kept the potbellied stove in the middle of the large room going all day long when it was snowing. Several straight-backed wooden chairs were usually gathered around the stove and as often as not, a game of checkers was being played beside the stove. Glory kept her art easel set up by the window and painted portraits.

"I don't suppose they sell any jeans here?" Garrett asked as he put his hand around the stone-cold doorknob. He might as well be comfortable for the flight back to Vegas. If Lillian was staying, her chauffeur could come drive her back. That meant Garrett would need to fly back and he sure wasn't getting on any airplane dressed like a butler.

The hardware store door had a half-dozen small panes of glass in it, but Garrett could not see inside the store because of the frost on the glass. He could already smell the flavored coffee brewing inside, though.

"They have overalls." Nicki couldn't picture Garrett wearing them. "Farmer overalls."

Garrett opened the door wide and then waited for Nicki to enter first.

Nicki had known the two old men sitting beside the stove all her life. In fact, Jacob Holmes's wife, Betty, had been her mother's best friend. After Betty died, Jacob spent his mornings at the hardware store.

They both looked up at her with smiles that turned to surprise when they saw Garrett come in behind her.

"Hi. Is Pastor Matthew around?" Nicki asked.

"The pastor?" Jacob was the first of the two men to recover his voice and his manners. He stood up and nodded to Garrett. "Pleased to meet you, young man. Any friend of Nicki's here is a friend of mine." Then Jacob turned to Nicki and beamed. "Of course, I can see he's more than a friend. We heard you had a fella heading out your way. And here I see he's already in his wedding suit and asking for the pastor. Are you eloping or something?"

Nicki froze. Here was where the thunderbolt reached down from the sky and struck her. Please, let it strike her. "Garrett's not—"

"We don't need the pastor." Garrett frowned and then realized what all the whispering had been about.

"I know it looks like I'm in a tuxedo, but it's really just a chauffeur's uniform."

"Looks like a tuxedo to me," Jacob said suspiciously. "You're not just trying to pull the wool over our eyes are you, young man, so you can marry our Nicki with no one knowing?"

The sudden vision of what it would be like to be married to Nicki made his knees shake as if he were heading downhill in Big Blue with no brakes. But his throat didn't close up like he'd have expected. At least he could still breathe. He wondered why that was.

"Garrett is a stranger. He's just passing through. We don't know each other. And we are not dating."

Garrett frowned. She could have been a little less emphatic—just to be polite. She swatted the whole idea away as if it was annoying. Maybe that's why his allergic reaction didn't kick in. Nicki was making it clear she had no interest in even dating him, let alone marrying him. Which should make him feel good. "We're not strangers. You know my name."

Jacob nodded and turned to Garrett. "You wouldn't be the first man to be smitten with a Redfern woman before he knew more than her name. Nicki here is a prize. I knew her father—shoot, I knew her grandfather before that. I used to work on the Redfern Ranch back in the good old days when it was the biggest ranch between Canada and Texas. I wouldn't take kindly to some man doing wrong by her."

"He's not—" Nicki wondered how many ways a person could die from embarrassment. "He's not doing me wrong. He's not doing anything. He's not smitten with me."

Did Jacob ever look at her? Nicki wondered. She wasn't exactly a femme fatale in her barn-cleaning clothes.

Jacob kept his eyes narrowed on Garrett. "It's a funny thing about the Redfern women and love. Why, I remember hearing that your great-great-grand-mother—"

Nicki knew she needed to stop this one. "She wasn't a Redfern. She was an Enger. And she didn't agree to marry Matthew Redfern because she was in love with him, she just needed that gold nugget he was offering up in the saloon so she could take care of those little kids of hers."

"Maybe so," Jacob agreed. "But that doesn't explain what happened with your great-grand-mother. Why she—"

"My great-grandfather didn't fall in love with her at first sight, either. He just told that to the ranch hands so they'd stop trying to win her in those poker games and get back to herding the cattle."

"Well, still." Jacob didn't back down. "You've got the same blood running in your veins. The Redfern women always were a passionate lot." Jacob scowled at Garrett. "Not that you need to be knowing about that, young man."

Garrett grinned. "Yes, sir."

Nicki groaned. The thunderbolt was sounding better all the time.

No thunderbolt roared, but the phone did ring.

"Dang it, that phone's been ringing all morning," Jacob complained as he went to sit back down on his chair by the stove. "A man can't get any peace anymore."

"Well, why don't you answer it?" Nicki said as she walked over to the counter.

"It's not my phone," Jacob said righteously. He pulled his chair closer to the stove. "It's not polite to answer someone else's phone. Gotta be for the pastor. But he's been gone. Should be back soon but—"

"Hello," Nicki said into the phone.

"Is this Dry Creek?" a woman's voice asked. She sounded breathless, as if the woman was rushing and worried.

"Yes, can I help you?"

"This is the only Dry Creek number the operator had. I'm trying to locate a Mr. Redfern."

Reno? "I'm Mr. Redfern's sister."

"Oh. Is Lillian Fern there?"

"I can get her for you."

The woman gasped, as if she had seen something she didn't like. "There's no time for that. Just tell her I'm getting gas outside of Vegas and she's to stay where she is until I get there. This is Chrissy."

"Garrett's cousin?" Nicki asked, but the line was dead. The woman had hung up.

"That's Chrissy?" Garrett walked over to the counter. Why would Chrissy be calling the hardware store?

"She said my mot—I mean, Lillian is to stay here until she gets here. Chrissy's left Vegas."

"Chrissy's coming?" Garrett wondered if his cousin had had a change of heart and had decided not to get married after all. "Did she mention any fiancée?"

"No."

"So she's coming alone?"

Nicki shrugged. "Sounds like it."

Well, that's good news, Garrett thought. If Chrissy was just leaving Vegas, she'd be here sometime tomorrow morning. Maybe she'd be willing to stay with Lillian a few days and drive the older woman's limousine back to Vegas so he could fly back. "So she's coming here."

Jacob held his hands out to the heat that was coming from the potbellied stove. "Won't that be nice. We could use some more young women in this town—especially if we're going to be having another wedding. Someone to help throw all that rice."

"They use birdseed these days," the other old man, Elmer, said as he looked up from the wooden stove. He had his shoes off and his legs stretched out toward the stove. "It's the modern way."

"But Nicki's an old-fashioned girl. She'll want rice." Jacob had a satisfied look on his face.

Nicki groaned. "No one's getting married."

"Well, you never know, now, do you?" Jacob drawled as he tipped back his chair. "We've had us a whole lot of weddings ever since last Christmas when the angel came to town."

"She wasn't a real angel," Nicki hastened to add. She didn't want Garrett to think they were completely nuts. "She just played the angel in the Christmas pageant."

"You should have heard her sing," Jacob reminisced. "Almost made me cry. It's a wonder Santa Claus had the heart to shoot at her afterward."

Nicki groaned. "It was a hit man that had dressed up as Santa Claus who tried to kill her."

"I see," Garrett said, appearing bewildered.

"Of course, the reverend risked a bullet to save the angel," Jacob continued.

"That's because he was in love with her," Nicki

finished the story for the old man. Everyone knew how the story ended. "Well…and the twins—that would be his young sons—would have been brokenhearted if something had happened to their angel."

No wonder she was having those fairy-tale dreams, Nicki thought to herself. After all of the excitement and romance in Dry Creek lately, it was a miracle she wasn't flying off to enter some dating show in Hollywood. "But all of that romance is behind us now. Matthew and Glory are just another married couple. Dry Creek really is a very quiet little town."

"I see."

Nicki groaned. There was no way a stranger would see that Dry Creek really was a nice sensible place. At least no one had mentioned the rustlers that had kidnapped a local rancher and his girlfriend—well, she wasn't his girlfriend at the time, but she soon came to be. There seemed to be something about danger that made people fall in love around here.

"You know the pastor is going to insist on doing marriage counseling with the two of you," Elmer said thoughtfully as he leaned forward from his chair and cupped his hands around the warmth coming from the woodstove.

"We don't have any need for—" Nicki groaned at the disapproving look on Elmer's face.

"Now, I know you try to hide it, but you've had bad feelings about church ever since your mother left. And I can't fault you for that, but that don't mean you can just wave God goodbye on the most important day of your life."

"I'm not waving God goodbye. I'm not having an important day."

Elmer grunted in disapproval and turned his eyes to Garrett. "And you, young man—are you planning to ditch marriage counseling, too?"

Garrett had forgotten that pastors knew more about marriages than anyone else. They certainly attended more weddings than the average person. Maybe that's where he could get some advice on what to say to Chrissy just in case she hadn't jilted her boyfriend. "Not on your life. If someone claims to have the answers to getting married, I'll sit down and listen."

Elmer beamed. "That's the attitude. The pastor will be glad to know you're open to talking. Now that he's married again, he sure does like to see people walk down the aisle."

Nicki knew her face was getting red. She didn't want to open her mouth because she knew she would sputter. Elmer was the kind of man whose mind ran on a single track. He wasn't going to let go of his marriage idea unless something came along and knocked that idea off his track.

"Lester's been stopping by the ranch, you know."

"Lester Wilkerson?" Elmer frowned. "I know he picks up your mail and has been asking around about what kind of feed you buy for your cattle, but I wouldn't think he'd be the one for you."

"Well, he's asked me out."

"Didn't he bring you and your brother to the Christmas pageant?" Jacob asked with a matching frown.

"He likes to include the family. Family is important to him."

Elmer shook his head. "If he ain't out-and-out asked, you've got no obligation to wait for him. But it does make me think you'd do good to hear what the pastor has to say about getting married."

"I am not getting married," Nicki said through clenched teeth. "What I am going to do is go back over to the café and have breakfast."

Jacob nodded sagely as he leaned back in his chair. "I read in *Woman's World* that people in love eat more. Of course, it's mostly chocolate."

That stopped Nicki. Jacob had ridden the range with her father. "What are you doing reading *Woman's World*?"

Jacob tilted his head toward the small table that

stood behind the stove. "Glory says we need to keep informed so she brings in her magazines. That's where Elmer read about the birdseed at weddings."

Elmer frowned. "I didn't know there was so much to know about getting married. It'd make a man think twice about it all if he knew what was involved in guest lists and place cards."

"Well, fortunately, we're not getting married," Garrett said as he started to make his move for the door. Of course, he couldn't go without taking Nicki with him and she was looking shell-shocked.

"We just met," Nicki added for emphasis. "We're just both hungry. We're not even dating."

Garrett stopped. He was forgetting something. "You say those magazines tell you how to do a wedding? With all the trimmings?"

Elmer nodded. "Step by step."

"Save them for me, will you?" Just in case Chrissy didn't stop her wedding, maybe she'd at least do it right and invite Aunt Rose.

Jacob beamed. "You can pick them up when you get back from your breakfast date."

"Date?" Nicki asked.

Elmer nodded. "*Woman's World* would say it was. Eight out of ten readers said a meal alone together counts as a date."

"Then it's not a date," Nicki stated firmly. "My mother's going to be there."

Nicki regretted mentioning her mother the minute she saw the shocked look on the faces of the two older men.

"Lillian's back?" Jacob whispered. His face had turned white.

Nicki nodded miserably as she turned to go. "But she isn't staying."

"She's back?" Jacob said again to no one in particular.

"Yes," Nicki said softly as she started walking toward the door. How could she have forgotten? Jacob used to be her father's best friend just as Betty had been her mother's best friend. Jacob and Betty had been as upset with Lillian as her father had been.

Nicki remembered how withdrawn her father had been after Lillian left. For months, Nicki's father didn't want to see anyone, not even Jacob. Jacob would drive out to the ranch and Nicki's father would send him away. Finally, Jacob stopped coming. The only time the two men had seen each other since then was for Betty's funeral.

Jacob must blame Lillian for the loss of his best friend. He might even blame her for the sadness that Betty had until the day she died.

It seemed that Nicki wasn't the only one who would be upset by seeing Lillian Redfern again.

Nicki and Garrett stopped at the limousine before they walked back to the café, but Lillian waved them on. She had more to worry about than breakfast.

Lillian sat in the back of her limo with the envelope in front of her. No matter how many times she read the papers inside, the diagnosis remained the same. Cancer.

Oh, how she wished Charles were still here so she could talk to him. He'd always been the brave one when it came to facing problems. Her style was to run away. Even coming back to Dry Creek she needed to be sure no one pitied her. The limo was to prove she was somebody now.

Of course the cancer didn't care who she was.

And, before she went in for treatment, she had wanted to make things right with Charles.

Since Charles wasn't here, she'd just have to make things right with the whole town of Dry Creek instead.

Lillian just wished she didn't have to tell Nicki. She couldn't bear to hurt her little girl any more than she'd already been hurt by life. That's why she wouldn't have come back if she had known Nicki was here.

Chapter Six

Nicki swore she was going to walk home and sit in her kitchen where there was no prince, no limo and no mother. This day was so mixed-up, she was beginning to think she needed to start it over. After hearing Elmer and Jacob talk about reading *Woman's World,* nothing should have surprised her.

Nicki only had to open the door to the café to know the day had one more surprise for her. Everything was turned upside down inside the café too. Someone had strewn shiny red paper hearts all over the tables and floors. It looked as if there was something tacked to the walls, but she couldn't see what it was because the lights had been turned off and the window shades drawn down.

Without the morning light, the café was dim. It would be deep dark except for the individual candles burning at each of the tables and on the high shelves that lined the room. The yellow light coming from the candles made the black-and-white floor of the café gleam.

Nicki sniffed. Gone was the smell of baking biscuits. In its place was the scent of raspberries and vanilla from the candles.

"Linda?" Nicki called out.

There was a love song coming from the radio in the kitchen that was so upbeat it would make a man on crutches want to start dancing.

Nicki looked up at Garrett. The candlelight touched his face and made him look like someone in a Renaissance painting. "I'm sorry, people aren't usually this—" Nicki looked around again "—strange."

Garrett smiled. "I have a feeling they're just campaigning for you to date someone other than this Lester fellow." Garrett decided he rather liked the people of Dry Creek. He'd always heard that people in small towns minded each other's business, and it looked as if Dry Creek was no exception. Maybe it wouldn't be so bad to have a whole town filled with dozens of Aunt Roses. Of course, they had *Woman's World* in addition to Aunt Rose. "I'll bet they have something all planned out from one of those magazines. Besides, they're having fun."

Garrett pulled out a chair for Nicki and she sank down into it as though she would really prefer to slide all of the way under the table. "The people in this town need to get a hobby."

"Sounds to me like they have one." Garrett decided the cold air had finally numbed his brain. He didn't even mind that half of the town's population was trying to set him up with the woman in front of him. If he couldn't outromance Lester, he'd have to retire from dating.

Garrett had to stop and remind himself he had stopped dating, at least for a while. He hoped that wasn't a bad omen.

"So what do people do around here for fun?" Garrett asked Nicki as he sat down in a chair opposite her. He wasn't going to give this one up without a fight.

"Besides torturing me?"

Garrett looked over at Nicki. Her cheekbones were high and there wasn't a trace of blush on them. But she sparkled in the candlelight from the melting snowflakes that had fallen on her as she'd walked back to the café.

"Well, there really is only one way to stop them," Garrett said. He waited until Nicki looked at him hopefully. She had the most amazing green eyes. Even in the candlelight, they changed color constantly. A man could get lost just looking into them.

"Yes?" Nicki finally prodded.

"Oh." Garrett cleared his throat. "We have to go on a date, that's all."

"A date?" Nicki squeaked.

Garrett nodded. "And not just any date. A date that would be better than anything *Woman's World* could offer."

Nicki was speechless. "You think they got this from the magazine?"

Garrett nodded and then suddenly remembered something. "And before you ask, your brother can't come."

"I wasn't—"

"And neither can this Lester fellow. Actually, especially not this Lester fellow. Let him get his own date."

Nicki was speechless, which was just as well because she heard Linda walking out from the kitchen.

"All set to order?" Linda held a small pad of paper in one hand and a pen in the other. Linda had changed her clothes so that she was wearing a chef's hat with a red ribbon tied around it and a long white formal dress with shiny red heart pockets. "The special of the day is heart pancakes with strawberries on top. It comes with scrambled eggs, bacon and hazelnut coffee."

"I've had breakfast here before—" Nicki said bewildered. "You never—" She waved her hand to indicate everything. "Even the dress."

"Left over from Halloween," Linda explained cheerfully. "I was the Queen of Hearts and Jazz was the Joker. We were reading one of Glory's *Woman's World* magazines, and it said people were more likely to eat out if it was a fun experience. So we thought costumes are fun. I wanted something that said good health—you know with the heart and all."

"So it's for health," Nicki said. "And *Woman's World*."

She looked over at Garrett. He winked at her.

Linda continued. "Well, eight out of ten women rank dining out as their favorite date. Jazz and I have maxed out the lunch crowd. If we want to expand, we need to have another angle. So we thought we'd turn to romance eating—you know, people eat more when they are in love."

"We heard."

"I'd eat here," Garrett offered. "It's a good idea to expand your menu."

"But they used to have regular pancakes." Nicki mourned. The whole world was going crazy around her.

"Nothing wrong with making them into hearts." Garrett defended the café.

Linda looked at Garrett and smiled. "I'm glad you feel that way. I talked to Jazz, and we decided you're the one we are looking for. I didn't think so at first, but you're a good choice. You could teach the men of Dry Creek a thing or two about romance. You've got the tuxedo and the look."

"Me? This isn't a tuxedo. It's a chauffeur's uniform. And it's not even mine. I'm a trucker. I don't have a look. I'm not a romantic kind of guy. I hate poetry. Can't stand the opera."

Linda walked over to a shelf and pulled down a magazine, flipping it open "Would you buy a woman roses in the middle of winter?"

"Well, yes."

Linda eyed him as she looked over the magazine. "Not just something planted in a pot, but the real thing—those long-stemmed ones."

"Yeah."

Nicki remembered the orchid blossom that Lester had gotten for her. "Roses don't last long in winter." She almost sighed, but she felt she owed it to Lester to defend him. "They're not a practical choice."

Linda waved Nicki's objection aside and kept questioning Garrett. "Question number five. If you were out on a date and a robber threatened to shoot your date unless she gave him her purse, what would you do?"

"Tell her to give it to him."

Linda kept reading in the magazine. "What if she refused and the man held up his gun?"

"Can I knock the gun out of his hand?"

Linda looked up from the magazine. "No."

"Well, where are the police?"

"Not close by. And the robber is counting to three. He's already said two. What do you do?"

"I step in front of her—"

"Excellent choice."

"—and rip the purse out of her hands and give it to the man."

"Oh." Linda looked down the column. "You would be a hero for stepping in front of her, but it doesn't say anything about taking her purse away from her. I think you lose points for that."

"I'm not going to die for some woman's lipstick."

"Not all women want some man to be their hero, either," Nicki said firmly. Where did Linda get this nonsense? "It's better to let the authorities deal with things."

"I asked about the police," Garrett protested.

"That's good. That's the right thing to do." Nicki was getting a headache. "It doesn't matter what the magazine says, people need to use common sense."

"Common sense never made anyone fall in love," Linda said softly as she pulled her order pad out of her hand again. "So, what will it be, folks?"

Nicki hadn't meant to hurt Linda's feelings. A woman Linda's age was supposed to be giddy about love. Nicki gave up. "I believe I'll have the heart special."

"Really?" Linda brightened. "With the strawberries?"

"With extra strawberries if you have them."

"Make that two specials," Garrett added with a grin. "And I swear I'll take a bullet if someone tries to steal it away from me."

"You're only supposed to take the bullet if they try to steal Nicki's," Linda said softly. "It doesn't count if you're protecting your own breakfast."

"In that case, I'll have a side of bacon with that." Nicki smiled. "Now that I know it's safe."

Nicki should give a man some warning when she was going to smile like that, Garrett thought. His mouth went dry from the beauty of seeing it. Her green eyes lit up like jewels and sparkled with fun.

"You're beautiful." Garrett wasn't aware that he had spoken aloud until he saw the surprised look on Nicki's face. "I mean, it's beautiful—the café and all."

"Oh, yes." Nicki seemed relieved.

"We need some publicity on this one though," Linda said as she tapped her pen to her order pad. "You know, something that will get the romantic idea across—we can't just advertise heart-shaped pancakes. It needs to be more to make the married folks come out on a cold winter morning and have breakfast together. We've thought of making a poster.'

"You don't need a poster. Just take a picture of your breakfast and tack it up on the bulletin board over at the hardware store. All of the men around here go into the hardware store at least once a week. They'd see it."

"Great idea—Jazz has a camera in back, we could take some pictures right now if it's all right with the two of you."

Why did Garrett have the feeling he and Nicki had been led down this path a little too smoothly? Oh, well, let the kids have their fun.

Garrett looked at Nicki. "I don't mind if they snap a picture or two of our plates before they bring them out of the kitchen, do you?"

"Oh, the plates won't be enough," Linda reached over and moved the candle on the table so that it reflected off Garrett's face even more. "To sell romance. We need romance. We need you two in the pictures."

"Us?" Nicki said, then she blurted out what she really meant. "Garrett's great. He's dressed for it. Can't you just use his picture?"

"One man sitting alone and eating heart-shaped pancakes? That's not romantic. In fact, it's kind of creepy." Linda looked more closely at what Nicki was wearing. "Oh."

"I should have worn a dress."

"Don't worry. I have just the thing." Linda started walking toward the back of the kitchen. "The Queen of Hearts costume came with a whole bunch of other costumes. They're made out of paper, but that won't show in the picture. One or two will even go with the tuxedo."

"Uniform," Garrett corrected automatically.

Nicki looked over at Garrett. She had to give the man credit. He seemed to be enjoying himself. She couldn't help but think that Lester would have stormed out of the café by now. Maybe that's why he never talked about anything but the weather. Maybe he didn't allow himself to do enough things in life.

"I've never been in a commercial before—" Garrett wondered how he could get the conversation back to where they'd left off. A photo of romance was fine, but he wanted a date with Nicki before people forgot about *Woman's World* and he lost his excuse. "I wonder what else people do around here to date."

"People in Dry Creek don't date." Nicki frowned slightly. "I know it sounds like they do because of the way everyone's been trying to get you to take me out on a date. But don't worry. There's no place to go on a date anyway. You're safe."

Garrett was beginning to suspect Nicki didn't want to go out on a date with him. "There must be someplace people go."

"Well, there is the café, but we're already here." Nicki wondered if she should suggest that Garrett frown while the picture was being taken. In his tuxedo, the frown made him look fierce. Which was pretty much how most of the men in town would feel about taking their wives out to a romantic breakfast. He might pull in some viewer empathy that way. "The kids go over to the mountains in the summer evenings and party some."

Garrett caught his breath in his throat. "You'd go there with me?"

"It's winter. Nobody goes there in the winter. It's cold."

"Well, where do people go in the evenings around here?"

Nicki shrugged. "Tonight they're having a Thanksgiving Eve service at church."

Garrett heard the sound of boots on the porch outside the café. He didn't want to get interrupted again. "Let's go there, then."

Church certainly wasn't equal to a moonlight evening in the summer, but Garrett wasn't going to quibble at this point in time. He'd told himself he'd have a date with Nicki, and he wasn't going to shy away just because he'd never even heard of a church date before—in fact, he couldn't remember the last time he'd been inside a church. "What's a Thanksgiving Eve service?"

"Everyone brings a candle and they light it and tell something they are thankful for—"

The door to the café opened.

"What happened to the lights?" Elmer asked as he stepped inside. "Something wrong with the electricity?"

"Nothing's wrong with the electricity at the church. And we're on the same line." Another man stepped into the café.

"Pastor Matthew?" Nicki asked as she looked up.

The door from the kitchen opened again, and Linda came back out with several long dresses draped over her arm. "I've got the costumes. Take your pick. Jazz is looking for the camera."

"We're making an advertisement," Nicki explained to the three men who were now inside the café. Jacob had been the last to enter. "Something to make men bring their wives in for a romantic breakfast."

Elmer grunted suspiciously. "Isn't bacon and eggs enough to bring in the customers?"

"Not according to *Woman's World*," Garrett explained.

"Oh." Elmer nodded.

Linda stopped at the table where Nicki and Garrett sat. She held up the first of the paper dresses. It had a red cross on it in several places and a paper stethoscope in the pocket. "No, that won't do. Jazz wouldn't like to have a nurse in the picture. It'd give people a bad feeling about the café."

The next costume was of a judge. Linda tossed it aside. "Not very romantic."

"But orderly." Nicki wasn't so fast to give up on the judge costume. "And it matches Garrett's tuxedo—I mean the uniform—and it's dignified."

"Dignified's not romantic."

"But it's nice."

"No, this is what we need." Linda held up the last costume.

"Oh," Nicki breathed out.

Nicki heard four men echo her.

It was a princess costume.

"That pink reminds me of the inside of a seashell I saw once when I was a boy," Elmer said. "I've never forgotten it."

The skirt on the dress flared out and had dozens of tiny tucks drawn onto it. The bodice plunged low and the cleavage that was drawn on the paper would have made any prince drool. "I can't wear that. It's—"

"It's winter out, that's why." Garrett hoped they didn't choose the princess outfit. It made his breath stop just to look at the dress and then to think of

Nicki wearing it. He certainly didn't want to be sitting in church with those thoughts in his head. He'd be excommunicated for sure, and he hadn't even joined anything.

"Well, we'll take the pictures inside, of course," Linda told him.

"Of course."

"Just as soon as Nicki puts the dress on, in fact."

A bell rang in the kitchen and Linda turned. "Your specials are ready. I'll be right back with them. Nicki, you can just pull that dress over what you're wearing."

"I smell bacon," Elmer said as he pulled a chair over to the table beside Garrett and Nicki. "Mind if I join you?"

"Me, too," Jacob said as he found another chair. "That smells mighty fine."

"Well, I only came over because they said you were looking for me," Pastor Matthew said, but he pulled over a chair all the same.

Garrett was beginning to see why no one dated in Dry Creek. They were never alone long enough.

"It was my mother who wanted to see you," Nicki told the pastor as she stood up. "Maybe she'd like to talk to you in the limousine. There's more privacy there."

Nicki hoped her mother would talk to Pastor

Matthew in the limousine. That way her mother could ease her conscience and not be so public about it all. "I'm going to go in the kitchen and put on my dress."

"But it's paper. Stay away from the grill." Garrett saw another reason why people didn't date in Dry Creek. You felt responsible for a person before you even had the opportunity to date them. It wasn't quite fair. It made it hard for a man to concentrate on his moves. "I'd better come with you."

"To put on her dress?" Elmer said as he started to rise.

"It's just a costume," Garrett protested. "It'll go over all her other clothes."

"Oh." Elmer sat down.

Garrett felt all three men watch him as he followed Nicki into the kitchen. Then again, this might be the main reason nobody dated in Dry Creek. There were too many chaperones.

Garrett couldn't remember ever dating anyone who was so protected. He'd have thought it would bother him, but it didn't. He liked knowing there were men who would take care of Nicki and protect her from someone like him. It was depressing to know that he was the kind of man that a town wouldn't want their favorite daughter to date. But he couldn't fault the men for their judgment. They knew he wasn't the kind of man who stayed around for long.

Still, he wished he was sitting back out there with those three men and scowling at the back of some other stranger passing through instead of being the stranger himself.

Chapter Seven

Garrett changed his mind. He didn't wish he was anywhere else in the world right now except inside the kitchen of Dry Creek's café.

The men outside in the dining area didn't know it, but they should have followed him into the kitchen. Garrett was standing so close to Nicki he could feel every curve along her back. He blessed the makers of those paper dresses, whoever they were.

The paper dress didn't just slip on easily. It had to be coaxed over the sweater Nicki was wearing, inch by blessed inch.

Garrett had not noticed the back of Nicki's neck until now. She had reached up and clipped her hair behind her so it didn't get in the way of pulling the dress on. Garrett had already brushed his hand across her hair several times and, if he was lucky, he'd feel its wispy softness several more times before they left the kitchen.

"It's stuck," Nicki said.

Garrett could feel her nervousness and frustration in the way she held her back. "It's just got a twist here."

Garrett reached up and smoothed the hair off of Nicki's neck before he let his hand smooth the paper dress over her shoulder. "We're almost done."

Nicki grunted. "We'd better be."

No one was in the kitchen but the two of them. Linda and Jazz were outside in the other part of the café arranging their breakfast plates.

Garrett gave the dress one last tug. "There."

The dress covered Nicki from her neck to her toes. Even her arms were covered. Still, the whole thing made her feel naked.

"A princess wouldn't really wear something like this, would she?" Nicki looked down at the dress. The drawing showed as much paper skin as it did paper dress. Nicki had tucked the collar and sleeves of her sweater inside the costume so it was just her head sticking out. "It would shock the palace."

While Nicki talked, she had slowly turned around until she was facing Garrett. The morning light filled the kitchen and the air smelled like biscuits and bacon.

Garrett was speechless. No wonder all the princesses he'd ever heard about had become queens. If women dressed like that today, they'd get all the political votes, at least the ones from the men.

"I can't walk in this," Nicki said as she started to move toward the door leading to the rest of the café. The paper dress trailed along with her. "You'll have to carry the train to this thing."

Nicki opened the door to the main room of the café.

Garrett was glad that Linda had covered the windows. Not that it looked as if there was anyone left to peek in the windows from the street outside. All of the people of Dry Creek must have come inside while he and Nicki were in the kitchen.

"Oh, there you are." Nicki's mother was standing at the front of the crowd. Jacob and Elmer were on one side and the young couple who ran the café stood on the other side. "I'm getting ready to say my few words."

"Now?" Nicki squeaked. There wasn't any place to hide. Maybe if she had Garrett lift the train on her dress a little higher she could crawl under it. She might look like a garden slug, but she'd be hidden.

Lillian Redfern looked around and frowned. "No, I can't speak yet. Mabel Hargrove isn't here. She'd never forgive me if she wasn't here when I said what I have to say."

"Good," Linda said as she motioned for Nicki and Garrett to come forward. "We have time to get the pictures taken first then. We don't want the food to be cold for the pictures."

"No one can tell if the food is cold," Nicki reassured her as she sat down.

The table was set for romance. A red napkin was laid carefully across the middle of the table, as if it was an afterthought. Three candles of different lengths stood beside the salt and pepper shakers. A plate of strawberries sat to the right of a small pitcher of cream. Water glistened on the just-washed strawberries.

Jazz, tall and thin, was standing and frowning at the table. "I don't want any shadows hanging over the table." He looked up at the people crowded around the table and lifted an eyebrow.

"I'll go out on the porch and wait," Pastor Matthew offered as he nudged one of the older men.

"And I'll go ask Mabel Hargrove to come over here," Elmer said as he reluctantly backed away from the table. "Just don't start anything without me."

"And, Lillian and I—" Jacob looked around for an excuse. "We'll go sit over in the corner. You won't even know we're here."

Jazz had the camera to his eye before anyone even stepped away from the table. "Let's try this angle first."

He brought the camera away from his eye and frowned. "No, that's not right. Maybe if we try it from some height."

It took Jazz ten minutes to decide the angle of his first shot. Garrett was sitting at the table and his jaw was beginning to ache from smiling so much.

"I can't hold this much longer," Nicki said through clenched teeth. She sat at the table across from Garrett. Her hand was falling asleep as she held her spoon in midair. "No one eats eggs with a spoon anyway."

"Creative license." Linda was in charge of the staging. She shifted the spoon slightly so it got more candlelight. "Have you ever noticed the way a spoon reflects the light? It's so much more elegant than a fork. Once we start shooting it won't take long."

Linda pulled away from the table and Jazz snapped the picture.

"Look dreamy now," Linda said as Jazz repositioned himself.

"Dreamy?" Nicki wondered if cross-eyed would do.

Linda nodded. "Like you're in love. Remember, romance sells pancakes here."

Nicki had avoided looking at Garrett for that very reason. She didn't want her heart to be out there for anyone who was interested in buying a pancake to see.

Jazz took four more shots before he mentioned the strawberries. "For the last one, let's do a strawberry shot."

"I'm starving." Nicki thought it might be worth mentioning.

"And she almost fainted once this morning," Garrett added helpfully.

"The food's getting cold." Nicki nodded.

"We'll heat it up for you." Linda sprinkled some pepper on the eggs. "Besides, you'll like the next shot. It involves food."

"We get to eat the eggs?"

Linda shook her head until her earrings swayed. She picked up a whole strawberry from the plate. "You get to split this."

Half of a strawberry didn't look like enough to halt her hunger pangs, but Nicki lifted her knife anyway. She'd be fair.

"No, you don't split it with your knife. You kiss it apart."

"What?"

Garrett was starting to grin. He had a feeling he was going to see more of those green sparks fly out of Nicki's eyes.

"With our lips?" Nicki looked skeptical. "Can't we just each take a bite? That's a lot more sterile."

Linda shook her head and held the strawberry out to Nicki. "Just hold it in your teeth. Garrett will do the rest."

"I—" Nicki was silenced with a strawberry.

Garrett had barely begun to kiss Nicki when Jazz took the first picture.

Nicki wondered why she'd never really tasted a strawberry before. The fruit was warm and soft and sweet with just a hint of something stronger. Maybe the strong part was Garrett's lips. No, they were the soft part.

Jacob had to clear his throat three times before Nicki realized the flashing had stopped.

"Oh." Nicki pulled away from Garrett. She wondered if she had the same bewildered look on her face that he had on his. "Something was wrong with that strawberry. You must have soaked it in something."

Linda grinned. "You liked it, huh?"

Nicki didn't have to answer because the door to the café opened and Mrs. Hargrove walked in.

"Where is she?" Mrs. Hargrove hadn't bothered to put on her coat or take the metal curlers out of her hair. She was wearing a green-checked gingham dress with a white apron over it and clutching a coin purse in her hand. She entered the café and looked in all directions until her gaze settled on Lillian. "There you are."

Nicki felt the blood start to flow in her veins again. It was time someone gave her mother a good scolding and Mrs. Hargrove was just the person to do it. Mrs. Hargrove had taught the first grade Sunday school class for the past thirty years in Dry Creek and she didn't hesitate to speak her mind.

"Hello, Mabel," Nicki's mother said as she stood. "You're looking well."

"I've got baking powder on my face and curlers in my hair. I know I look a fright." Mrs. Hargrove studied Lillian where she stood. "You dyed your hair blond."

Lillian nodded. "I've worn it that way for years now."

"You could have written, you know. I worried about you."

"I didn't think you'd want to hear from me—not after I took the money."

Mrs. Hargrove shrugged. "Charles and Jacob paid it back."

"Oh." Lillian frowned. "I didn't mean for anyone to do that. I meant to sneak into some Sunday service and slip it into the offering plate. At first, anyway. Then I was worried someone would recognize me and I didn't know what I would say."

Mrs. Hargrove nodded. "I see how that could be."

"I want to pay it back now though." Lillian had a purse strap on her shoulder and she swung the purse around to open it. "I could write a check."

"You can't just write a check," Nicki protested. If Mrs. Hargrove wasn't going to scold her mother, someone else would have to do it. "Money can't make up for the hurt you caused the people around here."

"You're right. I did mean to apologize first and ask everyone to forgive me." Lillian looked at the people in the café. "Do you forgive me for doing something so foolish?"

Lillian smiled and blinked as if she were on the verge of tears.

Elmer caved first. "Don't mention it."

Mrs. Hargrove wasn't far behind. "We just worried about you, not the money."

Jacob looked at Lillian, but he didn't say anything.

"Nicki's right, though," Pastor Matthew said, and everyone looked to him. "Money isn't enough."

Lillian smiled. "I meant to include a little extra for the minister of the church, as well."

"I don't take bribes," Pastor Matthew said mildly. "I was just thinking that if you spent some time praying about it, you might think of a better way to make peace with the people of Dry Creek."

"Pray about it?" Lillian covered her surprise quickly. "Why, yes, of course, I can do that."

Nicki felt that someone was finally taking her mother's actions seriously. Good for the pastor.

"Maybe Nicki can pray with you about it," Pastor Matthew continued.

"Me?" Nicki decided the pastor was going too far.

"It'll do the two of you good to pray together," Elmer said.

"We'll all pray about it," Mrs. Hargrove said decisively. "That's what friends and family are for."

Garrett was liking the people of Dry Creek better the longer he was around them. They were an odd group of people, but he could see they were loyal to each other. Kind of like Aunt Rose would be if she was here.

"And, of course there's the Thanksgiving service tonight," Elmer suggested. "We'll all be there, won't we?"

Elmer looked around for nods.

"I'll be there. Nicki and I have a date," Garrett volunteered.

"Really." Pastor Matthew brightened. "You're coming to the Thanksgiving service on a date?"

Garrett nodded cautiously. He wondered if anyone else had ever used church as a dating plan in Dry Creek—he supposed not even Lester had sunk that low.

"I'll have to throw in a few of the love verses in my meditation," the pastor said. "You know the 'love is' ones."

Garrett nodded. He had no idea what the man was talking about.

"I always liked those." Mrs. Hargrove smiled. "'Love is patient. Love is kind.' They are true, true words."

"If you're going to be talking about love, maybe you could mention our pancake heart special," Jazz suggested. "You know just at some break or something."

"I could mention it in the announcements," the pastor said. "Sort of a community service thing."

"Good." Jazz put the cap back on his camera lens. "And tell people to look for the pictures in the hardware store of the guy in the tuxedo."

Garrett felt as if his smile was frozen on his face. He turned to Nicki. "You said the store sells some kind of overalls?"

"We'll go back after breakfast." She was just as anxious as he was to get him into other clothes. No man sparkled in farmer overalls. Once Garrett didn't have the tuxedo anymore, she was sure he'd settle down into looking really quite ordinary.

Nicki sure hoped so. Ever since the strawberry kiss she'd felt her appetite slowly leaving her. She'd never had even the smallest dent in her appetite around Lester. Maybe she was catching a cold or something.

"Do you have more of those strawberries?" Garrett asked Linda as he poured some syrup on his heart-shaped pancake. "They're some of the sweetest ones I've ever eaten."

Linda gave him a strange look. "They're frozen without sugar. Jazz said they were bitter. He wanted to return them to the supplier."

"I thought maybe they had something on them— maybe that's what Jazz thought was bitter." Nicki decided her eggs weren't too cold to eat and looked around for her fork. All she had was a spoon.

"What's in the eggs?" Nicki frowned. She guessed it tasted good, it just didn't taste like eggs.

"Jazz added some grated Parmesan cheese and a sprinkling of dill."

"Humm." Nicki took her second spoonful. They weren't bad. "They kind of set off the pancakes."

Nicki was beginning to see that married people in Dry Creek might like to have a special breakfast at the café. The breakfast would give them something to talk about at home. It might even change the way everyone cooked eggs. A change might be a good thing. How long had everyone in Dry Creek been cooking their eggs the same way anyway?

Chapter Eight

Nicki knew she was wrong about the eggs by the time she finished eating them. They sat in her stomach and protested. Maybe there was a reason everyone made their eggs the same way they always had.

She knew she was also wrong about Garrett's tuxedo the minute she saw him wearing the overalls he was planning to buy over at the hardware store. It hadn't been the tuxedo that sparkled. No, the tuxedo was draped over a chair in the stockroom where she couldn't even see it, and her mouth was going dry just looking at Garrett in the overalls. It was him that sparkled, not his clothes.

Of course, he wasn't making it easy for her.

"You'll freeze to death," Nicki informed him. "Nobody wears those overalls without a shirt."

Where did the man think he was anyway? Venice Beach?

Garrett could pose for the sexy farmer calendar if they had one that went with the sexy firemen and sexy policemen ones. She looked at him closer. What was a truck driver doing with a tan in November? And muscles?

Nicki had seen her share of haying crews, and the sight of working men with muscles was not new to her. She'd even seen those same men shirtless and her only thought had been that someone was saving on the laundry. She wondered if she had been missing something before. Maybe she just hadn't been paying attention or she was too worried about whatever crop was being harvested. Maybe that was it.

"Just give me a minute," Garrett said as he frowned and moved his shoulders. "I don't think this shirt is the right size, either."

Glory had stepped from behind the counter in the hardware store to get Garrett the clothes he wanted. She was walking up to him now with a black shirt in her hand. "Maybe this will fit."

Glory took the shirt and measured it against Garrett's back.

Nicki frowned. She supposed Garrett liked to have Glory smooth the shirt across his back like that. What man wouldn't? Glory was beautiful. She had copper-red hair and skin that was all white and pink. The people of Dry Creek would always think of her as their angel because of the part she played in the Christmas pageant. Nicki thought she looked the part. Yes, any man would like to have someone like Glory fuss over him.

"Glory's married, you know," Nicki offered, just in case their was any question on the matter.

Garrett looked over at Nicki, puzzled. "I know. To the pastor, isn't it?"

Garrett smiled at Glory. "I really appreciate all the time you're taking with me. I would be lost without it."

Nicki frowned.

Glory smiled back. "It's not easy to find things in the store yet. We're working on organization, but we haven't gotten past the bolts. The twins were helping us with them and we got sidetracked."

"Glory's a mother now, too," Nicki added just in case Garrett didn't understand what the mention of the twins actually meant.

"And loving every minute of it," Glory agreed. "They keep me busy."

"I think this one'll fit," Garrett said as he took the black shirt from Glory's hands. "I'll just go in the back and put it on."

Glory watched Garrett step into the back room

before she turned to Nicki. "He's a nice man. I'm so happy for you. Jacob and Elmer—" she nodded her head toward the potbellied stove even though the chairs around it were now empty "—they told me how it is."

"I told them a dozen times Garrett doesn't know me. He just drove my mother up here and he's hanging around until she's ready to leave. He'll be back in Vegas before the tuxedo is due back at the rental place."

Glory smiled. "If he's hanging around, that's something. I was only hanging around when I met Matthew, and look what happened."

"Yes, but Matthew—he wanted to get married."

Glory arched her eyebrow. "Not when we first met. He thought I was some kind of a freak because his little boys thought I was a real angel and he thought I told them I was."

"Yes, but it didn't take him long to change his mind when he saw how pretty you are."

Glory straightened a shovel as she walked back to the counter. "Well, you're pretty, too, so maybe Garrett will change his mind."

Nicki wondered if anyone in Dry Creek ever really looked at her or if they were just all being overly polite. "Well, I'm healthy. And I suppose my teeth are all right."

Glory stepped behind the counter and laughed. "Don't sell yourself short. It's not just your teeth. You could be a striking woman if you wanted to be."

"What do you mean?"

"You've got the bone structure and your eyes are dramatic with all those greens. A little touch of makeup here and there and you could have any man you wanted eating out of your hands."

Nicki sighed. "I've been thinking I should marry Lester. It's the practical thing to do."

"Not if you don't want to marry him." Glory stepped out from behind the counter again. "Let me show you what I mean about that makeup. I've got all my stuff over at the house, but if you watch the store here for a minute or two I'll go get it. It won't take but a few minutes. Everybody's still over at the café anyway so no one will probably even come by."

Glory was right. Nicki could see out the window of the hardware store and into the open door of the café. The café windows were all fogged up from the breathing of the dozen or so people inside. And the people weren't just breathing. Nicki could see them shaking with laughter. "Wonder what they're talking about."

"Matthew said your mother was telling them stories about her Vegas dance days. I'm surprised you're not there listening, too."

Nicki smiled tightly. "I don't think I'd find those days as funny as everyone else does."

Glory nodded and walked over to where Nicki was standing by the window. "You missed her."

"I did fine."

Glory looked out the window toward the café. "I wonder why she left."

"Things here just weren't pretty enough for her." Nicki swore she could hear her mother from across the street. Or maybe Nicki was just remembering her mother's soft pleasing laugh. Her mother had always liked fine things. "I suppose that's what she liked about Vegas. All those dancers in those pretty costumes." Nicki turned to Glory. "Have you ever been to Vegas?"

Glory nodded. "It's not all that pretty. I like Dry Creek a lot better."

Nicki shrugged. "I've never been there. I thought about it a time or two, but it always seemed too complicated. What if I saw her on the street someplace?"

"Well, I'm glad she came back to Dry Creek." Glory gave Nicki a hug. "She should get to know you."

"Oh, there won't be time enough for that." Nicki backed away a little. She didn't want all of Dry Creek to go sentimental on her. "I don't think she's staying long."

"Who's not staying long?" Garrett walked out of the back room with the black shirt all buttoned up.

"My mother."

Glory waved goodbye from the doorway before she left the store.

"I had thought we were just going to be here for a few hours. But now with Chrissy coming—" Garrett realized he wasn't in as much of a rush to get back on the road as he had been. "I know it's an imposition since tomorrow is Thanksgiving, but I'd like to stay another day if that's all right with you? Chrissy should be pulling in sometime tomorrow. Your mother will probably want to stay in the house, but I can stay in the limo tonight."

"It's too cold for that. Reno won't mind if you stay in his room."

Nicki hadn't thought about the sleeping arrangements. Reno truly wouldn't mind if someone slept in his room while he was away, but that meant her mother would have to sleep in her father's old room. Neither Nicki nor Reno had seen any reason to change the room after their father died and her father hadn't given it much thought when he was alive. The last person to hang a picture or pick out a rug had been her mother. It would be like stepping back in a time warp for her.

"If you're planning to have anyone over for Thanksgiving or anything we can be gone for a few hours."

"We're not celebrating Thanksgiving at the ranch this year."

Garrett smiled. "In that case, the turkey soup is on me—if there's a store around here to buy a few cans."

"There's no point in driving into Miles City for that—"

"Well, I'd buy a pumpkin pie, too." Garrett walked over to the window and looked across the street. "Maybe two pies if Chrissy is here and your brother."

"Reno should be back early morning. I guess he'd want to sit down to eat with—our mother." Nicki wasn't sure Reno was any more ready to see their mother than she was, but he deserved the chance to find out for himself how he felt about it. Nicki hoped he stopped at a pay phone on his way back and called, though, so she could warn him about their guest.

"I should go home and dust." She knew it was hopeless to expect her mother to have any good feelings about the home she left, but Nicki wanted the old place to be at its best.

Garrett turned back from the window. "I think it's breaking up over there. I was hoping the pastor would come back so I could pay him for the clothes." He already felt more like himself. The overalls were a little stiff, but they would do.

Garrett heard the sound of footsteps on the porch before the door to the hardware store burst open and a half-dozen people stomped inside. He was glad to see that the pastor was one of them. "I need to pay you for these."

The pastor walked toward the counter. "Before I work up a bill, let's figure out a good time to talk. I understand Jacob and Elmer tried to sign you up for marriage counseling a little prematurely."

"We're not getting married." Nicki wanted to be sure there was no lingering misunderstanding on that point. "I'm not sure I'll ever get married."

"I thought you were interested in Lester," Elmer said as he walked over to the potbellied stove and sat down in one of the chairs. "I was almost going to start looking through *Woman's World* for wedding gift ideas."

Garrett wondered where on the long highway he'd be when Nicki settled down and tied the knot with her Lester.

"She's not marrying Lester." Garrett glared at Nicki for emphasis. He sure hoped she wasn't fool enough to marry that man. Not that it was any of his business. But it did seem a waste if she was. Besides, he just remembered—"He hasn't even asked."

"Well, not in so many words. But when he does I just might say yes." Nicki glared right back at Garrett.

"Good," the pastor said before either one of them could carry the argument further. "Then you're both interested in getting married—just not to each other."

"You can't do marriage counseling with two people who are going to marry other people." Nicki looked over at the stove where Elmer now sat, looking innocent. "Did he put you up to this?"

"Me?"

"Well, I don't see why it wouldn't work." Garrett decided the pastor was on to something. This way he could prove to Nicki that she should not marry Lester. "I'm sure there are times when people go in for counseling and then decide not to marry each other."

Garrett looked to the pastor for confirmation and the man nodded.

"So what's different with us? If we're not going to marry each other, then we just know that up front instead of later. But we still get to think about all the questions."

"Besides," Elmer said from his chair, "your mother is over talking to Mrs. Hargrove and then Jacob wants to talk to her. She won't be ready to go home for another hour. You might as well give the pastor some practice on his counseling technique."

"Oh." Nicki hadn't thought of it that way. She supposed Matthew did need to practice once in a while. "Well, sure. I don't see why not."

"The two of you can sit over here," Elmer said as he got up from his chair. "I need to be getting home to do some chores anyway."

"I didn't think you did chores anymore since you retired." Nicki eyed the chair warily. "Don't leave because of us."

"People should have some privacy when they have marriage counseling." Elmer started to walk toward the door.

"That's only when the counseling is real," Nicki said, but she was too late. Elmer had already opened the door.

"It's a good thing Lester isn't here." Garrett went over and sat in one of the chairs. He liked the way they were grouped around the open stove that had the fire smoldering inside. "He might think it's a little insulting that his bride doesn't care if she talks about their marriage in front of the whole town."

Nicki's eyes started to spark just like Garrett had intended. He held back his smile. He didn't know which warmed him more—the fire to his left or Nicki's eyes to his right.

"I'm only going to be talking about marriage in general."

"Good. That's where we start with the counseling anyway," the pastor said as he pulled one of the chairs close to the fire and motioned for Nicki to take the one empty chair. "We need to talk about what you want out of marriage."

Garrett was surprised. "Isn't that kind of obvious?"

The pastor smiled. "Not always. That's why I have a series of questions that I start the session with."

"Okay. Let's go." Garrett decided he was going to enjoy this. He'd sure like to know what reason Nicki had for even considering marriage to a man like Lester.

"Well, first I'm going to ask which of the following you think is the most important to you in marriage." The pastor looked up at Garrett and then Nicki. "Common activity interests, common financial values, common family values, or a common faith?"

Garrett was lost already unless you counted sex as an activity interest. He did have a six-figure savings account and he owned Big Blue outright, but he didn't know that that was fancy enough to be called a financial value. He just hadn't had a lot to spend his money on once he had paid off Big Blue.

"Well, what do you think?" the pastor asked.

"For me, it's the land," Nicki said in a rush. "I don't know if that is family or financial or what—but I need to marry someone who understands I always want to be part of the Redfern Ranch."

The pastor nodded. "And that's important to you because…?"

"The land will always be there," Nicki answered without thinking. "It can never leave me."

"Ahh, like your mother did?" The pastor nodded

again as he marked something down on the tablet he held in his hand. "Commitment to stay. I'll put that as a family/faith value. I can see that would be especially important for you because of your mother."

Nicki looked around the hardware store to make sure no one else was in the place but the three of them. These questions were a little too revealing for her taste. "I got along fine without my mother."

Garrett had always thought that it was the sight of a crying woman that made him most want to ride in and save a woman from whatever was paining her. But he was wrong. The sight of Nicki fiercely holding back any sign of tears was even worse.

"You've done great," Garrett agreed loyally. "Just great."

"And you? What's important to you?" Nicki turned to him.

"I just want to be able to make her tears go away," Garrett answered without thinking, and knew he had spoken the truth. Maybe that was half of the reason he'd stopped dating. He wanted to be more than a date to a woman.

"So, you want to be your wife's hero." The pastor nodded and wrote something on the tablet just like it was the most ordinary thing in the world. "Again, I'd say that's family values."

"Some women can take care of themselves," Nicki offered. She sure hoped Garrett wasn't going to end up with some whiny woman who didn't even know how to tie her own shoelaces. "Some women don't need a hero."

"Well, I don't need to be a hero every day. It's just that—when the time comes, I want my wife to look to me for help."

Nicki scowled. She supposed she couldn't argue with that. It's just she had never been the kind of woman Garrett wanted to marry. She relied on herself in life and that was about it. She didn't even tell her problems to Reno. "Isn't that called codependency?"

The pastor chuckled. "It's natural for a man to want to protect and help his wife. I'm sure Lester will want to help you with your problems when you're married."

"Lester?" Nicki couldn't imagine telling her problems to Lester. Maybe that's why they never had any conversation beyond farming concerns. Still, she didn't like the smug look she saw on Garrett's face. "Yeah, sure. He does even now."

Garrett grunted.

"So we have two family value answers," the pastor said as he consulted his notebook. "Not bad."

Garrett snorted. "They couldn't be further apart as answers."

"Oh." The pastor looked up from his notebook. "I

didn't know we were trying to match the answers. I thought you were both marrying other people."

Garrett groaned. "That's right. Lester and—Bonnie."

"Bonnie? I've never heard you talk about any Bonnie." Nicki knew she was right to not trust that man. He waited until now to tell her there was a Bonnie.

"Well, I haven't met her yet. But if you've got a Lester in your future, I can have a Bonnie."

"So you do plan to marry someday?" the pastor asked quietly. He didn't even mark anything in his notebook. "I got the impression you weren't really considering it."

"Well, I'm not." Garrett crossed his arms. He'd made that decision years ago. He should stick with it.

"So what does this Bonnie look like?" Nicki decided it was only fair that she know more about Bonnie since Garrett knew all there was to know about Lester.

"How would I know?"

"Well, you must have some picture in your head."

"She wears black spandex." Garrett knew it wasn't much to go on, but a picture was starting to form in his mind. "And her eyes are green—yeah, a real feisty kind of green that flash when she's upset."

"That could be anybody." Nicki crossed her arms.

Garrett didn't even need to look at her to know her eyes were flashing just like his mind was remember-

ing. That would never do. Nicki clearly wasn't de-
scribing him as her ideal mate so he shouldn't
describe her. "And she likes to ride with me in Big
Blue—my truck."

"Where would you go?" Nicki was beginning to
wish Garrett was the kind of guy who could put down
roots. Not that she had a future with him anyway on
account of the black spandex stuff. Black spandex was
what men said when they wanted a woman who was
exciting in all of the ways that Nicki wasn't. Garrett
would probably even meet his Bonnie when he went
back to Las Vegas. The city had lots of spandex women
who'd like to meet a hero and drive off in Big Blue.

"I just go where my deliveries take me. No place
special." Garrett frowned. He hadn't realized until now
that he didn't have a special place to go to. One city
was pretty much the same as the next one. A man ought
to have a place that he longed to reach for more reasons
than that he could deliver whatever he was carrying.

"I see." The pastor was thoughtfully looking at
Garrett. "I'd say you don't like to be tied down. I
hope—ah, Bonnie, is it?—feels the same way. Most
women like to have a home."

"I have a home. In the back of Big Blue's cab—
there's a bed and a battery-operated television. I even
have a small refrigerator." Garrett wondered when his

life had gotten so depressingly single. "The bed sleeps two if they're cozy."

Nicki didn't like thinking of Bonnie in Garrett's bed. She turned her attention back to the pastor. "Do you have any questions about how much conversation a married couple need to have for a good marriage?"

"Well, there's no set amount. But don't worry. You two seem to be talking pretty good."

"I mean with Lester."

"Oh." The pastor didn't even look down at his questions this time. "I'd say if you're bothered by the amount of conversation, then there's a problem."

"But if I'm not bothered, then it's okay?" This was the first good news Nicki had heard in this whole time. She was fine with not talking to Lester.

"Well, I wouldn't exactly say that—"

The door opened and a gust of cold air blew into the store followed quickly by Glory. "Sorry it took me so long."

The pastor stood. "That's all right. We were just doing a practice marriage counseling session."

"Oh." Glory raised her eyebrow. "What makes it a practice one?"

"We're marrying different people." Nicki wondered how a woman ever got the kind of polish that Glory had. Her copper-colored hair waved and curled and just generally shone. "So it's a practice for when we do it for real."

"I find it helps people relax for the Big One," the pastor said as he walked over to his wife and gave her a quick kiss. "It'll only take us a minute to wrap up."

"Take your time."

Garrett frowned. Watching the pastor kiss his wife made him realize what he was missing. Those kind of affectionate kisses weren't part of his moves. When he kissed a woman, it was just a rest stop on the road to someplace else. That used to be enough for him.

"Actually, your husband has already given us lots to think about." Nicki shifted in her chair. "We could save the rest for later."

"Yeah," Garrett agreed quickly. He didn't like the feelings those questions stirred up. He'd been a perfectly happy single male a week ago. "I should go check the limo anyway."

Garrett got up from the chair and smiled a goodbye. He would have gone to check the *Titanic* if it would have gotten him out of the store, but no one needed to know that. They didn't even ask what he needed to check on the limo. It was a good thing, he told himself as he stepped out of the store, because he didn't need to check anything.

"I should go check on the twins, too," the pastor said

to Nicki. "They're at Mrs. Hargrove's place. Her niece is taking care of them, and they can be a handful."

Nicki waited for the pastor to leave before she turned to Glory. "You don't happen to sell black spandex stuff in the store, do you?"

Glory shook her head. "We have black duct tape that stretches, but that's about all."

Nicki doubted Bonnie would wear duct tape.

"I do have the makeup, though," Glory said as she held up a paper bag. "You're welcome to pick out what you'd like to borrow. I hear you've got a big date coming up tonight."

Nicki nodded. "The Thanksgiving Eve service at church."

"Why, that's a good idea—I've been looking forward to the service ever since Matthew told me about it. I hear it's been a tradition in Dry Creek since the turn of the century."

"That's why people bring their own candles. Back in the early days, the church couldn't afford to buy any candles, and since the service was at night they needed light. The church didn't have electricity back then—actually, the church didn't even have a building. Everyone just met in the back room of Webster's store for services. I don't know who came up with the idea of people taking their candle to the front of the church and leaving it on the alter when they said what made them thankful."

Glory nodded. "Matthew told me the altar back then was made of a stack of cans set on top of some boxes. I can almost see those first candles in my mind. I've been thinking I might paint a scene of them—Elmer and Jacob told me there were all kinds of candles and candleholders. The cowboys sometimes just brought their candles in their tin drinking cup. That was all they had."

"And Mrs. Hargrove has a silver candelabra that belonged to her mother—she says her mother bought it specially for the Thanksgiving service so she'd have enough candles to represent every member of her family."

"Candlelight can be very romantic," Glory said as she opened the paper bag and rummaged around. "I even put some perfume in here."

"It's only a little bit of a date. He'll be gone after Thanksgiving."

Nicki wondered if going out on a date with a handsome man who was leaving town was the smartest move a woman could make. She'd be forever comparing her dates with Lester to her one date with Garrett.

"Then you'll need a touch of lipstick, too," Glory said as she examined Nicki. "I think with your coloring we need to go with the rose."

"I'm not very good with the lines," Nicki confessed

as she peered into the bag of cosmetics Glory had brought over. There were lipsticks and lip liners. Mascara and eye shadow. "What's that?"

"A pot of smudge for your cheeks—it adds some glitter."

"Won't I look kind of funny?"

"Not if you ask your mother to help you with it all."

"Oh." Nicki had almost managed to forget that her mother was here. "She and I don't have that kind of a relationship."

"Who knows what kind of a relationship you can have? Give it some time."

Nicki was going to point out that twenty-two years was a lot of time to give someone when they made no move to contact you, but she didn't get her mouth opened before she heard footsteps on the porch and the door of the store opened.

"There you are," Nicki's mother said as she entered the store and saw Nicki standing at the counter. "Garrett said you were here. I asked him to go into Miles City to buy groceries and wondered if you would go with him."

"We have enough groceries at the ranch."

"Do you have a hundred and ten pounds of turkey and forty pounds of potatoes?"

"No, but we don't need those kind of groceries," Nicki said even as her unease grew.

"We do now," Nicki's mother announced with a flourish. "Garrett said you didn't have plans for Thanksgiving dinner so I took the liberty of inviting guests."

"You mean Mrs. Hargrove?" Nicki hoped that was all her mother meant. That would be fine. She would have invited Mrs. Hargrove herself if they were having more than soup anyway.

"I mean the whole town of Dry Creek."

"The whole town? That must be fifty, sixty people."

"Seventy including me and Garrett. Eighty if we can reach everyone at the Elkton Ranch. Garth and his new wife, I think it is Sylvia, might have gone to Seattle—Jacob is going to call them and see. Even if they are not there, their ranch hands will probably like to come. I've never known a cowboy to turn down a turkey dinner."

"We can't possibly—" Nicki tried to calculate just how many turkeys that would be.

"Don't worry—everyone's helping. The kids at the café agreed to bake the turkeys for us early tomorrow morning. And Jacob will help them bring them out to the ranch."

"But we'd need pies and sweet potatoes and rolls—"

"We've got it organized. All you need to do is ride along with Garrett into Miles City to buy the food."

"I haven't even dusted yet." Nicki wondered if there

might not be something to say for living out of a truck like Garrett did. No one ever expected him to entertain.

"Everything will be fine," Nicki's mother said. "We're not fussy."

"You—not fussy? You made Dad use a coaster when he drank water at the kitchen table. And it was Formica. It was made for water spills."

"That was a long time ago. And it wasn't water he was drinking. I thought if I insisted on a coaster he would think twice before he drank in front of you kids."

"Oh."

"A child's eyes see everything," Nicki's mother continued. "I knew Charles would hate himself if you and Reno didn't grow up to respect him. Next to the land, you were all he had."

"He had you."

Nicki's mother winced. "There's more to the story than you know."

"Then tell me."

Nicki could feel her mother measuring her.

"It's not just about me. But if I can, I'll tell you. I have to ask someone's permission first."

"Is that why you're going to visit Dad's grave? To ask him if you can tell us it was all his fault?"

Nicki wondered if she was too old to run away from home. She had already lost her mother. She didn't want to have the memory of her father tarnished as well by hearing that he had displeased her mother because he drank too much. Even if her father had done that, her mother was probably the cause.

Another pair of footsteps sounded as someone stamped the snow off their shoes before opening the door to the hardware store.

"Everybody ready to go into Miles City," Garrett said as he rubbed his hands together. He'd heard Mrs. Hargrove give the food calculations and he'd joked that he shouldn't have left his truck in Las Vegas. He'd surprised himself when he'd joked. Usually a holiday meal like Thanksgiving gave him a headache. But sitting down with the bunch of people he'd met in this little town didn't seem so bad.

Garrett wondered if something was wrong with him. He'd lived his life by one rule—keep moving in life because then everyone stays a stranger. It was a good rule. That way he didn't disappoint anyone, not even himself. Odd, how that rule no longer sounded very appealing to him.

Chapter Nine

Nicki glittered. She could see it out of the corner of her eyes. She hadn't put on any of the "pot of smudge" Glory had loaned her so she must have gotten sugar on her cheek when Mrs. Hargrove, who had been making pies all afternoon, hugged her. The fortunate thing was that in the darkened church no one cared if Nicki glittered or glowed or downright sparkled like Garrett did.

The day had quieted down and the church looked elegant in the candlelight. The work for the day was done, and all was peaceful except the rustling of little feet in the back pews of the old church. The church walls were white but the flickering of the candles turned the walls golden. Long shadows stretched along the walls as people filed into the church.

Nicki was wearing a plain navy pantsuit with a very ordinary silver pin. She'd looked at the makeup Glory had lent her and quietly set it aside. She could dress up like she was a princess but that wouldn't make her one. She needed to keep her feet firmly planted and, for her, that meant looking the way she always had. She knew there were no fairy-tale endings, and she needed to remember that Garrett was going to leave soon.

The fact that she had dressed plainly didn't mean that Garrett had. He was wearing the tuxedo again and he looked every bit as handsome as he had early this morning.

Even without the limousine, he took Nicki's breath away. But it wasn't just the tuxedo or the limo. She would have found him handsome if he was wearing an old jogging suit and standing beside a bicycle. All of which was why Nicki needed to keep her feet planted in reality. It would be all too easy to let herself become too attached to him. She needed to keep her heart safe.

Nicki and Garrett were on their date. The people of Dry Creek had given them their own pew in honor of the occasion. At least Nicki assumed that was why everyone said hello to them but no one stayed to sit beside them.

The evening had transformed Dry Creek.

All afternoon, everywhere Nicki looked, someone was chopping vegetables or peeling apples or grinding cranberries. She and Garrett had driven to Miles City and returned with enough bags of groceries to fill up the limousine. Nicki's mother had given them a wad of fifty-dollar bills, insisting the Thanksgiving dinner was on her.

By the time they got back to Dry Creek, the work teams were aproned and ready to go. Mrs. Hargrove took the ingredients for the pies and her helpers went with her to her house to bake. Jazz and Linda took the turkeys and the bread for the stuffing. Glory and Matthew were in charge of vegetables and took the bags of green beans, muttering something about hoping the twins liked to snap things.

Even Elmer had been put in charge of the butter when Lillian remembered he liked to carve. He was commissioned to shape the butter into five large turkeys with lines fine enough to show the feathers.

Nicki had volunteered to bake pies, but her mother said she and Garrett were needed back at the ranch to clean the main room in the bunkhouse and put up enough sawhorse tables to seat eighty people.

"We used to get over a hundred people in there when we had guests before," Lillian had said when Nicki had started to protest. "The room can't have shrunk. We get ten to a table and you can fit eight tables in there easy if you put them sideways where the beds used to go."

The bunkhouse had had cowboys sleeping in it for over a hundred years, and the metal legs of the beds left scars that still could be seen in the hardwood floors. Nicki supposed if you matched the bed markings you could get eight tables. There used to be sixteen beds, eight on each half of the bunkhouse.

Garrett drove Nicki back to the ranch in the limousine while her mother stayed in Dry Creek to help with the food.

If everyone hadn't been so intent on their tasks, Nicki would have suspected they had conspired to leave her and Garrett alone. But they didn't give the two of them a second glance when she and Garrett pulled out of town so Nicki decided they'd just paired Garrett with her because he looked strong enough to swing a sawhorse around. She would need that kind of help to set up the tables.

Once Nicki decided she and Garrett were just a work team, she didn't have any trouble talking to him. She'd started out where she'd usually start with a new ranch hand. She'd told him stories about the early days of the ranch. She even told him about the time the cowboys on the ranch had sent back East for a bride and then played poker all winter trying to decide who would get to woo the young woman first.

In turn, Garrett told her about some of the places

where he'd driven with Big Blue—how the trees of Tennessee were thick and green and the ocean off the Florida coast was pale blue in the morning.

It wasn't until they opened the closet and found the old pair of children's ballet shoes, however, that they started talking about themselves. Nicki had forgotten about the shoes. Her mother hadn't always been disappointed in her. When Nicki was small, she and her mother had loved to dance together in the kitchen, twirling on the old linoleum until they collapsed in a tangle of giggles. Somehow, after her mother left, Nicki had forgotten there were any good times. When Garrett responded by telling her about his dad dying of liver failure and all of the lonely days he had spent waiting for his father to be a father to him, they both knew they were friends.

Now that they were on their date, sitting in the church that was lit by candlelight, however, the ease of the friendship wasn't the same. Nicki couldn't think of a thing to say. Garrett in overalls was a lot easier to talk to than Garrett in a tuxedo.

"The flowers are lovely," Nicki repeated for the tenth time. She still didn't know when Garrett had slipped away in the grocery store to buy the two red roses. It must have been when she was asking the produce clerk how many yams eighty people might eat if they also had mashed potatoes. "And they're perfect in this vase."

Garrett hadn't stopped with the roses. He'd bought a tiny glass vase that had room for the roses and for a single white taper candle.

His first thought had been to get the biggest vase and the biggest bouquet of flowers that the store had. But then he'd seen the vase that also doubled as a candle holder and he knew he'd found what Nicki would like the best.

"I've never had a prettier candle for the service." Nicki usually followed the old cowboy tradition of melting enough wax in the bottom of a cup to make a candle stick to it. She'd usually just used one of the half-melted, broken candles she kept in a kitchen drawer for when the electricity failed. It might be a white candle or a red candle left from a previous Christmas. But the candle had never been special, and she seldom had anything new to say when she stood up and listed what she was thankful for that year. Over the years she had usually mentioned the ranch or her 4-H calf or something. "I should have gotten a better holder for you."

Garrett grinned. "I'm happy with my cup candle."

Garrett hadn't been to church more than twice in his life and this was nothing like those two other experiences. There were no women in hats and no rustle of important people. People here came in old knit scarves that had been washed until they were all the same colorless gray. Some wore jeans with shiny knees and jackets that were frayed. But they all seemed humbly glad to be together. They smiled and shook hands with each other as though they were longtime friends. Garrett supposed they were.

He wondered why that thought depressed him. He might not have a roomful of friends, but he'd probably seen more different cities than anyone in the church here. That had to count for something. Besides, he could feel Nicki's arm as she sat beside him. He wasn't quite without friends.

Garrett inched a little closer to Nicki. When Nicki had showed him those ballet shoes this afternoon, he had realized that someone else had had a lonely childhood beside himself. Sharing with Nicki had made him feel less of a loner. He supposed it didn't change anything, but he'd realized he wanted Nicki to remember him when he was gone. Usually, he wanted the women he met to forget him as soon as he pulled out of town. But not Nicki.

Nicki wondered if anyone could see her blush in the candlelight. She didn't know if she had moved closer to Garrett or if he had moved closer to her, but she suspected it was she who had done the moving. There was something about the darkness that made her want to be closer to him.

Garrett looked around the small church. "I don't see Lester."

"He'll be a little late." Nicki wondered for the first time why Lester always came to church just as it was almost over. It was as though he wanted points for attending, but didn't really want to be there.

"Oh." Garrett wondered if he could get Nicki to leave the service before Lester arrived. No, he supposed not. Especially not now that it looked like it was going to start.

Mrs. Hargrove stood and walked to the piano beside the altar. The piano playing signaled the beginning of the service and everyone was looking forward as the pastor rose and went to stand behind the altar.

"Each year in Dry Creek, we come together as a community and give thanks for what we have." The pastor looked out over the group of people assembled and smiled.

"We started doing this in the late 1890s when the Redfern Ranch had a harvest dinner that brought everyone from miles around together. Before this town began, we moved the tradition to the back of Webster's store and called it our Thanksgiving Eve service.

Today we celebrate here. No matter where it has been held, we have kept the same spirit of thankfulness. Together this community has survived droughts and depressions. Together we've seen good years and bad years. We've seen children born and grow up and move away. We've welcomed strangers and said goodbye to friends. Let's again be thankful for what this year has brought to us. Bring your candle in your own time and share with us what God has done for you."

Garth Elkton and his new bride, were the first to come to the altar. They carried a candleholder made of dozens of old keys. One fat white candle rose from the key base.

"The kids in Seattle made this for us for tonight so we came back early," Garth said proudly. He'd met Sylvia while she was director of a youth center that helped troubled teenagers. "We're thankful that they are doing well and are coming back this summer for a full six weeks. They told us that the old keys stand for old habits they are throwing aside."

A murmur of approval went through the congregation as Garth lit their candle. The Seattle kids had been popular with the people of Dry Creek.

"And what about your new bride?" someone yelled from the back of the church. "What's she thankful for?"

"She's thankful for him," Nicki whispered to Garrett. Marriage had transformed Garth into a man who couldn't stop smiling, but Sylvia still told everyone she was the luckiest one. "She found someone who shared her dream."

"The camp for the kids." Garrett nodded. He had heard about the Seattle youngsters who were putting down roots in Dry Creek even though they had only been here for one month last winter. Many of the kids still wrote letters to the town of Dry Creek and the townspeople took turns writing back.

The next ones to bring their candles to the front of the church were the Curtis twins, the two six-year-old boys that belonged to the minister and his new wife. Their blond heads were bent as they carried two tin can holders to the altar. When they set the holders on the altar, their father reached out to light their candles from the main candle on the altar.

Nicki could see that the twins had made their candleholders from two identical aluminum cans. They had each cut out a figure in the can so the light from the candle would show through. One figure had wings and had to be an angel. The figure in the other can looked more like a mortal woman.

"We're thankful because we have two mommies now," the first twin boy said.

"And one of them's still an angel," the other boy added eagerly. "Mrs. Hargrove says. Our first mommy is our guardian angel and she flies over us with her supersonic wings that go zoom-zoom."

"All I said was that I'm sure she's watching out for you boys if there's any way she can," Mrs. Hargrove added from where she sat at the piano. "She knows that we need all the help we can get with that particular task."

The adults in the church smiled.

"And angels don't zoom around," Mrs. Hargrove added indulgently.

"They don't need to," one of the twins agreed. "They have those wings that fly like this." The twins demonstrated how angels fly as they flew back to the pew where they were sitting with their new mother, Glory.

"Those are the cutest little boys," Nicki whispered to Garrett.

He nodded in agreement.

Mrs. Hargrove left the piano and was the next one to bring her candles to the altar.

"Mrs. Hargrove brings candles for all of the Hargroves," Nicki whispered to Garrett as they watched the older woman bring two heavy silver candelabrum to the front. "I think she's up to twenty-two candles that she lights and for each one she mentions a relative by name."

"The Hargroves are grateful," Mrs. Hargrove began. "Two new babies in the family this year and Doris June is coming home next summer to stay for a spell with me."

A ripple of surprise went through the congregation.

"She might even open a business here," Mrs. Hargrove added proudly. "She's got quite a business head on her."

Mrs. Hargrove went on to announce the name of each Hargrove family member as she lit the corresponding candle for them. By the time she had finished, the church glowed brighter inside.

Linda went to the altar next and lit a small green candle standing in a cup from the café. The candle was scented with pine and it started to give off its scent as soon as she lit it.

"I'm grateful for the café," she said quickly as she turned to walk back to her seat. "Business is good."

"And it will be even better with their new Romance Special," the pastor added from where he stood. "See me later for details."

Linda turned around and smiled at the pastor. "Thanks."

"We're determined to get that Jenkins' place bought." The pastor looked over the congregation. "Besides, a little bit of romance will be good for this town."

Everyone laughed and then grew silent.

Garrett watched the candles burn as others in the church brought up their candles. Before long there were candles of every color and size. And the holders were as individual as the people in this town. But almost all of the candle holders looked as if they'd been brought to the altar for many years and had followed the lives of their owners during the good and the bad of that time.

"I'm going to go up now," Garrett whispered to Nicki. "Do you want to come with me?"

Nicki nodded and Garrett didn't know when he'd been as proud. Nicki was willing to walk with him in front of the whole town.

Nicki felt her hand tremble slightly as she steadied her candleholder and took a quick look at the man beside her. The soft light of the candles played on Garrett's face and Nicki decided her first impression of him had been right. He was kind and handsome and—"She's got flowers," a young girl said in awe when Nicki walked past. "And they're beautiful."

Nicki smiled down at the girl, Amy Jenkins. The six-year-old was clearly writing a story in her head about the flowers and the romance they implied. Nicki almost corrected her and then decided to let it be. Maybe there wasn't as much harm in fairy tales as she'd come to believe.

"You first," Garrett whispered when they reached the altar.

Nicki put her candle on the altar and lit it. Then she

turned to face her friends. "This year I'm thankful for—" Nicki stopped. She always said the ranch. But the flowers seemed to promise more than land. She looked out at the candlelit faces around the church. So many of them looked back at her with hope and love on their faces. Why hadn't she seen it before? She might not have had her mother around to help her grow up, but she'd had dozens of mothers and fathers in this church. "I'm thankful for all of you."

"And him," Amy Jenkins whispered from her pew. "You have to be thankful for him."

Nicki knew who the little girl meant. "I'm thankful for everyone tonight."

"I hope she doesn't mean Lester," Garrett said out of the side of his mouth as they stood in front of the altar. "That man isn't good enough for you."

Nicki didn't think he needed to know who made the little girl's eyes sparkle. "It's your turn to light your candle."

Garrett hadn't noticed until he set the cup down next to Nicki's that he was using one of the mugs that advertised the hardware store. He turned around to face the people. "I'm thankful that I get to meet new people and travel to new places like Dry Creek."

A ripple of appreciation went around the pews.

"We're glad you're with us, as well," the pastor said

as Garrett reached to light his candle. The pastor also turned to Lillian. "We have two special guests this Thanksgiving."

The warmth of the people in the church made Garrett bold and, when he and Nicki sat back down, he took her hand to hold. It wasn't much of a move. He'd made bigger one's before and never given it a thought. But holding Nicki's hand seemed momentous.

He felt complete.

Everyone stood and, with Mrs. Hargrove playing the piano, sang "Amazing Grace." When the last chord of the song faded, everyone remained standing for a minute as though savoring the evening together.

"Now let's give your neighbors a hug and wish them a happy Thanksgiving," the pastor said. "Then go home and get some sleep. I understand we have ten turkeys waiting for us tomorrow—not to mention Mrs. Hargrove's apple pie."

Garrett was grateful that none of the townspeople had sat in the pew with Nicki and him. Nicki wouldn't have a question about who she should hug since he was the only one sitting next to her.

Nicki's hair smelled of lemon and strands of it gently tickled Garrett's chin while he hugged her. Garrett thought he heard Nicki give a soft sigh of contentment, but he couldn't be sure. Maybe it was just his heart giving the sigh. For the first time in his life, he felt at home.

Garrett kept Nicki in his arms. The townsfolk silently filed out of the church and soon they were the only two left inside. Still, he didn't want to let her go.

Nicki stirred. She was sinking and she couldn't afford to. She was the one who would need to get on with her life when the fairy tale ended. She looked around the empty church. "Did you see Lester leave?"

Garrett frowned. "I didn't even see him come in."

"Oh, I'm sure he's here. I wanted to be sure he got an invitation for tomorrow."

Nicki stepped back farther so she could breathe easier. "I'll catch up with him before he leaves. People generally hang out for a few minutes outside and talk. He'll be there."

Garrett felt the cold as Nicki walked away from him. Did Lester even know what a lucky man he was? He followed her down the aisle of the little church and out into the cold dark night. There was no snow falling, but small drifts of snow stood at the edges of the spaces where the cars had parked.

"Brrr—" Garrett rubbed his hands together. Sharp tingles of cold ran up and down his fingers and, when he breathed, a white puff of air circled his head.

Clusters of people stood and talked together in the

area where the cars were parked. The night sky was clear and as black as velvet. Garrett looked up and saw a million stars twinkling down at him.

"That's something, isn't it?" the pastor said as he came over to Garrett. "I never get tired of looking at all those stars."

Garrett grunted. "Makes the sky kind of crowded."

The pastor laughed. "I understand that when you get close to them, there's lots of room between the stars. Some might even think an individual star might be lonely. I imagine even a star wants company sometimes."

"Yeah, well." Garrett saw that Nicki had found Lester. He was standing over there talking to Elmer. The cold didn't seem to bother Lester and he had his coat open in the front as he talked. The man wore a plaid Western shirt.

Garrett frowned as he thought of the overalls he had waiting for him back at the ranch. All he had was either workclothes or the tuxedo. Neither one showed him off to his best advantage. He needed a sweater. Women always liked a man in a sweater.

"So, how's it going?" the pastor asked a little tentatively.

Garrett turned to look at the pastor square and forced himself to stop the frown. "She's gone to give Lester a personal invitation to Thanksgiving dinner. She didn't give anyone else a personal invite."

A couple of cars had turned on their headlights and the stars were no longer visible. But the people were a lot clearer and Garrett could even see Lester smile.

"Ahh."

"Not that it matters, I suppose. I'm heading out as soon as my cousin gets here anyway." Garrett pulled his eyes back away from Lester and looked at the pastor again.

"I see." The pastor nodded. "Well, then, I guess it's just as well she's inviting Lester. He's a solid man and he'll still be around."

Garrett snorted. "He's too old for her. Besides, she deserves somebody better."

Garrett could see that Nicki had turned and was walking back toward him. She was smiling so he assumed Lester was coming to dinner.

"Nicki deserves to be happy," the pastor agreed.

"He's coming," Nicki said when she came close to Garrett again. "I wanted to be sure he was coming because Reno should be back. Reno likes to have someone he can play cards with once the dishes are done."

"Oh, well." Garrett felt immediately better. "That's good he can come then."

If Lester kept Reno busy playing cards, Garrett would have even more time to talk to Nicki. He might even convince her to sneak out under the stars with him and dance a waltz or two. If they didn't freeze to death, it would be quite romantic.

"Maybe Chrissy will be here, too, by then," Nicki continued. "Maybe she and my mother can play bridge with Reno and Lester."

Garrett was beginning to like the sounds of Thanksgiving better and better all the time. It was all a matter of planning things.

"Well, I'd better get home and get the twins into bed so we can enjoy tomorrow." The pastor smiled as he turned to join Glory and his sons. He had only walked a couple of steps when he turned and looked at Garrett. "You know, you deserve to be happy, too. Don't sell yourself short. Think about it—we'll talk more later if you'd like."

Garrett almost automatically disagreed with the pastor. He wasn't selling himself short by knowing his limitations. He'd always believed happiness was too much to ask for and he was right. He was no good at things like marriage and forever after. His highest hope had only been to have short-term fun.

"What was that about?" Nicki asked.

"We'd been talking about the stars," Garrett answered with a small smile. He doubted the pastor knew about short-term fun. "I think he's trying to get them to move a little closer together."

"Oh. That doesn't sound very easy." Nicki frowned.

"He didn't say it would be easy." Garrett wondered if the star who stood beside him could be any prettier. The cold had turned Nicki's cheeks red and her eyes sparkled. "Come on, let's go home."

Nicki rode in the front of the limo with Garrett and Nicki's mother rode in the back.

"I never knew this road could ride so smooth," Nicki said as Garrett made the turn onto the Redfern Ranch property. "I wonder if Reno will let us trade the baler in and get a limo." But in spite of her words, she wondered if a limo would be the same without Garrett at the wheel.

"I wish I had Big Blue here so you could take a ride in her, too. She'll show you some smooth riding. Too bad she's back in Vegas at Chrissy's."

"I don't suppose you ever drive by Dry Creek when you're delivering your loads?" Nicki held her breath. She'd wondered about that more than once this evening. "You could stop in."

"There's not much trucking that goes by here."

"Oh." It was probably just as well, Nicki thought. It would be hard to settle down with someone like Lester if she kept remembering Garrett.

"You could meet me someplace when I'm in Vegas or Salt Lake City."

"Sure." Nicki doubted she would ever hear from Garrett after he left. She certainly wasn't going to hang out in either place hoping to catch him when he drove through. It sounded too depressingly like what her mother must have done years ago. Nicki wasn't like her mother, and she wasn't going to make the same mistake of leaving her land for the empty promise of excitement somewhere else.

Oh, well, Nicki thought to herself as she saw the house come into view. She might not have more than a memory, but it would be something to remember that she'd once had a date with Prince Charming. How many ranch women could say the same?

Somehow the thought of it didn't cheer Nicki like she thought it would. Regardless of what moment she had in her past, living a practical life day in and day out was sounding duller with each passing hour. At least things would return to normal when Garrett and her mother finally left.

"We're here," Garrett announced as he pulled the limo under the tree that had become its parking space. The dog, Hunter, seemed happy to share the area once he'd smelled the tires a few times this afternoon.

The kitchen was chilly when they came inside.

"Well, I'm tired," Nicki's mother announced. "If no one minds, I'm going to head up to bed."

No one minded. In fact, no one even noticed the smile Nicki's mother had on her face as she started up the stairs.

"I should be going to bed, too," Nicki said as Garrett helped her off with her coat. "Unless you'd like some tea?"

"I love tea." Garrett hoped no one ever got struck down for lying. His fellow truckers would laugh themselves silly if they saw him drinking a cup of tea. He bet it was even herbal.

"Peppermint okay?" Nicki asked as she walked over to the counter.

"It's my favorite." Garrett figured as long as he was lying he might as well go all the way. And he could convince himself that peppermint tea was nothing but a liquid breath mint and a breath mint was a good dating move. Even a trucker would understand the need for a breath mint.

"Reno doesn't like it, but tea always warms me up on a cold night," Nicki said as she put the kettle on the stove and almost fanned herself without thinking. The night might be cold, but she didn't need warming up. What she needed was something to relax her and keep her sensible. In case the tea wasn't enough, Nicki also turned on the radio and started to move the knob. "How about some news?"

Garrett knew he didn't have much time to store up his memories of Nicki and there were many things they hadn't done together. Listening to the news wasn't top on his list of memories to make. In fact, it didn't even make it to the bottom of the list. "Here, let me find a station."

Garrett stepped over to the radio and turned the knob until he found what he wanted. The sounds of a slow-moving song softly filled the kitchen. "Care to dance?"

"In the kitchen?" Nicki stood with the kettle in her hand. She was ready to pour the hot water into the teapot.

Garrett shrugged. "We're on a date. We can dance anywhere."

Nicki set the kettle back on the stove. "I used to dance in the kitchen with my mother."

Garrett smiled. "I know. You told me."

Nicki knew she shouldn't dance in the kitchen. It was opposed to everything she had done with her life since her mother had left. It spoke of foolishness and dreams of impossible fantasies. It was definitely not sensible. "My dance shoes don't fit me anymore."

"It doesn't matter if you dance barefoot." Garrett held out his arms to her. "You can even dance in your boots if you want."

"I really shouldn't," Nicki said, but her feet betrayed

her and she moved toward Garrett anyway. "I haven't danced in years."

Try twenty-two years, Nicki thought to herself as she melted into Garrett's arms. She'd avoided dances in high school for more reasons than because she'd never had a serious boyfriend. Dancing was for women like Nicki's mother, not for women like Nicki.

"I don't know how to dance," Nicki murmured even as she felt her feet giving lie to what she was saying. Her feet were moving in rhythm with Garrett. She hadn't forgotten a thing about dancing over the years. Except— "My mother used to let me lead."

Garrett smiled into her hair. "I'm not your mother."

Oh, my, Nicki thought. She really should have that cup of tea. It would settle her stomach and make the butterflies leave. But Garrett pulled her even closer and she forgot about the tea.

By the end of the second song, Nicki had also forgotten about the ranch and the dinner tomorrow. She'd even forgotten that Reno was out on the road coaxing the old cattle truck home tonight. All she knew was that she was dancing with Prince Charming, and he was holding her like she was a princess to him.

Chapter Ten

Meanwhile, on the open road about ten miles from Dry Creek, Montana

Reno Redfern cursed turkeys everywhere. Or was it pilgrims he needed to curse?

He was lying on his back on the road embankment somewhere between Miles City and Dry Creek while looking up at the underside of his old truck. The ground was frozen solid beneath his back and oil was dripping on his forehead. And it was all because he was trying to get his truck running so he would be home for Thanksgiving.

Not that Nicki or he would be cooking any turkey. But he knew that it was important that he be home for his sister so that they could ignore the day together.

Before Reno had slid under his truck he had looked at his watch and it showed it was almost midnight. His first hope had been that someone would stop by and give him a ride into Dry Creek. From there he could call Nicki and she could come get him. But there wasn't much traffic on this road at noon during a busy day; he doubted there'd be any passing through at this hour the night before a holiday.

That leaking oil made him think there was engine trouble in the old truck. He wondered if they could find a used truck anywhere for a thousand dollars or so that would have enough power to get their cattle to market. He figured a thousand was as high as they could go unless they went into debt, and Redferns never went into debt.

Reno sighed. It wasn't always easy to have one's ancestors looking over your shoulder, but that's the way it had been for him and Nicki If they even thought of doing something different, several kind souls in Dry Creek would remind them that the Redferns never did it that way.

The only thing the town had ever let them change was the Thanksgiving dinners the ranch used to hold for the whole community. Reno knew that was because they felt sorry for Nicki and him ever since their mother had abandoned them.

Reno felt the rumble of a vehicle coming down the road before he turned and saw the lights.

Hallelujah! Those lights were too high for a car so they must belong to a truck or at least a pickup. It was probably some farmer coming back from somewhere and that suited Reno just fine. A farmer wouldn't mind the smell of the oil that would hang around Reno even after he wiped the actual oil itself off of his forehead. Besides, Reno always had something to talk about with another man.

Reno heard the truck start to slow and so he figured he might as well try to plug that oil leak as best as he could. No sense leaving an oil spill like that on the ground. He'd already have to dig up the dirt around the oil or nothing would grow there for the next decade. Reno wadded up his handkerchief and jammed it up into the underbelly of the truck.

If Reno hadn't been concentrating on his handker-chief, he would have noticed earlier that the man had an awfully light footstep. And that he made a tinkling sound when he walked.

Not that Reno was in a position to be fussy about his company.

"Nice of you to stop—" Reno began as he slid himself out from under the old truck.

What the—? Reno was looking up into the night's darkness and there standing in front of the headlights was a woman who shone and glittered from the top of her low-cut dress to the bottom of its too-short hem. "What are you, an angel?"

Reno was prepared to die right then and there if she was. My, she was a sight to behold, all curvy and golden in the light.

"No," the woman said, and her voice started to tremble. "I'm a bride."

That's when Reno saw the tear that trailed down the woman's cheek. If there was anything that made him more nervous than a woman, it was a woman who was crying. "Ah, ma'am—"

Reno reached for his handkerchief—which was a futile thing to do considering he'd already used it to plug another leak. "Look, ma'am, don't cry. It's going to be okay."

"No, it's not." The woman started crying in earnest now. "He never did love me."

Reno figured he didn't know anything about angels and even less about crying women, but he did know one thing for sure. He pulled himself to his feet so he could say it square. "The man's a fool then if he can't see who you are."

"That's right," the woman said, and she took a shaky

breath. Then she started to cry again. "But he's not the one who got be-betrayed."

Reno usually didn't feel comfortable when he met a new woman. He always worried that he had salad stuck in his teeth or that his conversation was boring or his hair was doing something funny. But this woman was so wound-up, she wouldn't notice if he had a tree growing out of his skull.

"That bad, huh?" Reno asked. He nodded sympathetically. "Then we'll just have to go get him."

The woman nodded a little uncertainly. "Get him?"

"Yeah, we could do a pie in the face. That's always good. Or maybe a kick in the seat of the pants. Or—"

The woman had stopped crying and was smiling just a little. "We could sell his name to a hundred telemarketers."

"That's the spirit."

"Or tell his new girlfriend what a creep he is."

Reno nodded. "Or we could drive into the next town of Dry Creek and get us a cup of coffee if the café is still open."

"Oh—" The woman smiled even wider. "Are we close to Dry Creek? I thought I'd never get there."

"You're going to Dry Creek? Not just through Dry Creek?"

The woman nodded. "Actually, I'm going to the Redfern Ranch near there to visit a friend."

Reno knew every friend Nicki had made since she was ten years old and none of them could be this vision in front of him. And he'd certainly know if she was a friend of his. That meant the woman was either truly an angel or she was thoroughly confused. Reno's bet was on confused. She probably had the Redfern Ranch mixed up with the Russell Dude Ranch that was located two counties away.

But stopping by the Redfern Ranch wouldn't make her late for seeing her friend whoever the friend was. Not even the cowboys would be up at the Russell Ranch at this time of night.

"What a coincidence! I'm going to the Redfern Ranch, too. Do you mind if I ride along?"

"Would you? I can't figure out where I'm going at night like this. There's not even any signs anyplace."

"I'd be happy to show you the way."

Chapter Eleven

Garrett hadn't slept at all during the night. Instead he had lain on the sofa in the living room of the Redfern Ranch until a faint light started to seep into the windows. He just kept asking himself if what he felt was happiness. He'd never expected to be happy in life and he didn't quite know what to make of it.

The feeling had started last night when he and Nicki waltzed around the kitchen floor. They hadn't talked much; they'd just snuggled together and moved to the music.

It was the feeling of belonging that made him first suspect it was happiness. Garrett had never belonged anywhere, not even when he was growing up with his father. They hadn't had a home; they had only had an address. Garrett wandered the streets and his father drank.

His father never acted as if Garrett belonged at home. In fact, he always seemed surprised to see him there.

When Aunt Rose had mentioned taking him into her home when he was sixteen, Garrett had been terrified. A real home with a real family was foreign to him. He'd felt awkward, as though he would be all elbows in a place like that. And he hadn't gotten any better. But here he was. Longing for something that scared him spitless.

It was all Nicki's fault.

He hadn't been happy, but he'd at least been content before he met her.

The one dependable thing about going from place to place as a trucker was that he was safe. There was no one to disappoint him and no one he could disappoint. He didn't have to say any goodbyes because no one ever expected him to stay anyway. It wasn't the best way to live, but it didn't involve any risk to his heart, either.

And now there was Nicki. She had become home to him and he'd never be safe from heartache again.

Well, Garrett told himself, there was no sense in brooding about it. A man didn't break trucking records because he believed in taking the slow route. There was no going back to the way things were. Nicki had danced her way into his heart, and the only way he knew to remove her was to prove to himself that she wouldn't marry him if he were the last man on the earth.

He figured that's pretty much how it would stack up if she chose Lester over him.

Garrett shifted the pillow under his head and eased farther into the sofa. There was no point in getting up yet. He'd lie here and try to figure out how to ask Nicki to marry him so that he could make a quick getaway when she said no.

Knowing he couldn't stay once she'd rejected him meant he'd have to wait until after the dinner to ask Nicki anything. He couldn't leave her with all of those people to feed and it would be uncomfortable for both of them to work together after she'd said no. Lester sure wasn't the kind of guy to stay around and help with the dishes so Garrett had already decided he'd be the one with his hands in the hot water.

Given the number of people coming for dinner and the amount of pots and pans that would be used, Garrett figured he had a good ten hours left of this happy feeling. Maybe he should get out a piece of paper and write down how it felt so he could read it to himself when he was old and gray.

Now that was a depressing thought.

Upstairs, Nicki stared at the ceiling. She'd been afraid to sleep. She knew if she started to dream she would see the real face of Prince Charming in her dreams. Hadn't she read somewhere that if a person died in their dream, they died in real life? Well, it probably wasn't true. But why chance it? The very least that would happen is that her dream would dissolve into tears, and she didn't want that to happen.

Her dreams might have been annoying to her before last night, but at least they weren't self-tormenting nightmares that involved a lot of tears and gnashing of teeth.

The dark in her room got a very little bit lighter. In a few minutes, the darkness would be tinged with pink and Thanksgiving Day would begin. At least the kitchen would be crowded with all kinds of people before too long. There would be no time for quiet dancing with Garrett so she wouldn't have to worry about stopping herself from asking him to dance with her again.

Nicki sat up when she could see the pink of the sun outside her window. Maybe if she got up and fixed some coffee she would feel better. There was no mail today so Lester wouldn't be coming by, but the coffee would settle her stomach anyway.

Nicki tightened the belt on her chenille robe as she tiptoed down the stairs. She didn't want to wake either Garrett or her mother. The day would be long enough even if it started an hour later.

The staircase in the old house went from the second floor hallway to the kitchen and Nicki was grateful for the fact. Garrett was asleep on the sofa and she didn't want him to know that she hadn't been able to sleep. She supposed he was used to nights like last night, but she wasn't.

Nicki almost expected the kitchen to be changed when she got down the stairs and looked up. But there was no golden web covering the room and no sprinkling of fairy dust on the counter. The refrigerator was still old and gurgling. The sink by the window was chipped and the faucet still needed replacing. There was no sign whatsoever that a fairy tale had been born here last night.

At least the coffeepot still sat on the counter by the sink and Nicki walked over to fill the unit with water. Her feet were bare and the linoleum was icy cold so she hurried to reach the rug in front of the sink.

Nicki turned the faucet and the water line hiccuped once before water started to pour out. She put the pot under the faucet before she looked out the window. The night was still dark and no snowflakes were falling like they had been yesterday morning. But—Nicki peered out the window more closely—what was that?

The limousine was parked under the old tree, but there to the side of the limo was a big shadow of something that was as high as the lower branches on the tree.

The pot wasn't full of water yet, but Nicki pulled it

away from the stream of water and set it on the counter. She wasn't going to question her sanity again over something strange appearing in the night. She'd just get her broom handle and go investigate.

"Good morning," Garrett said from the doorway that opened into the living room. He had heard Nicki's footsteps and then the sound of running water. "How are you this morning?"

"Well, I'm not crazy," Nicki said firmly as she walked toward the coat rack beside the refrigerator. "I'm going to do what I should have done when you were out there and take the broom to it—whatever it is."

"Okay." Garrett wasn't so sure about her not being crazy. Not that it mattered when she was so cute in that robe of hers. "Chickens get out or something?"

Nicki had wrapped a knit scarf around her neck by the time Garrett walked over to the door. He'd at least had the sense to put a shirt and his overalls on as well as his shoes.

"That broom'll flatten a chicken." Nicki had picked up the broom handle she'd greeted Garrett with yesterday morning. "Maybe you need to take something smaller."

"There's some funny thing out there." Nicki waved toward the window. "Looks like a truck with only its nose."

Garrett took four big steps to the window. "That's Big Blue."

"Your truck? I thought it was still in Vegas."

"It was." Garrett wondered if Nicki would let him borrow her broom. "And the reason it's only the nose is because she's not hooked up to a load. She shouldn't be here."

"Well, do you think someone stole it?"

Garrett nodded. "And she'd better have a good reason."

"I'll let you know," Nicki said as she finished wrapping the scarf around her neck.

"You're not going anywhere." Garrett put his hand out for the broom handle. "You shouldn't be out investigating strange things anyway. What if there was something dangerous?"

"Well, it's no better for you to be out there if there's trouble."

Garrett kept his hand outstretched. "Yes, it is."

Nicki's chin went up. "Just because you're a man—"

"It's not because I'm a man," Garrett said as he looked down at Nicki's feet. "It's because I've got shoes on my feet."

"Oh." Nicki handed him the broom handle. "I forgot you wanted to be every woman's hero anyway."

Garrett grinned as he took the broom handle and

grabbed a jacket off the coat rack. Nicki's eyes were sparking again. "Not every woman's hero. Just yours, sweetheart."

Garrett was out the door before Nicki had her breath back. Sweetheart. She'd never thought she liked any of those "darling" names that men called women. Lester had called her Pumpkin once and she'd snapped his head off. But "sweetheart" was kind of nice. At least it didn't call to mind something that was fat and orange.

Nicki decided she'd take some of the coffee cake out of the freezer so she, Garrett and Lillian could have a nice breakfast before they started getting ready for the dinner. It was something she would have done for any other guests.

The fact that she could already hear herself humming while she made the eggs, well, that was just a holiday thing.

Outside, the temperature had to be close to zero degrees. Garrett had put the jacket on the second he walked out the door and he had still felt his breath catch in his throat. The ground cracked beneath his shoes because of all the frost.

Big Blue was darker than the just-dawning sky, but Garrett could easily make out the white letters of Hamilton Trucking on the driver's door. Chrissy had done a good job of parking the truck beside the limo.

There wasn't that much room between the car and the fence and Big Blue fit in snugly.

Maybe Chrissy had learned a thing or two about driving since he'd given her those quick two lessons in Vegas in case she needed to move Big Blue while he was gone. Of course, she didn't have a trucker's license. It was a fool thing to just take off in Big Blue.

Garrett put his hand on the door of Big Blue. It was cold enough to give a man frostbite. The windows were all frosted over. He hoped Chrissy had had the sense to turn on the small heater he had in back by the bed. If she had, she'd have been comfortable enough for the night.

Garrett knew Nicki's broom handle wouldn't do him any good in a fight, but he felt better keeping it with him anyway. At least if he had the broom, Nicki wasn't going out chasing something else. So he pulled the broom up with him as he opened the door to Big Blue and stepped up.

The night was still dark and Garrett couldn't see much inside of the truck's cab. There was nothing wrong with his hearing, however, and he definitely heard two grunts of surprise. One of them was Chrissy. The other was from a man.

She's gone and brought Jared with her, Garrett thought to himself as he plastered a smile on his face. He was going to have to be cordial to that man if it killed him.

"Garrett," the wail came from Chrissy, and Garrett saw movement in the bed area.

"Come in and shut the door." Chrissy said as she hugged a jacket to her and moved closer to the front seats in the truck. She was dragging half of the blankets with her. "It's freezing out there."

Garrett sat in the driver's seat and closed the door. He set the broom handle in the passenger's seat and turned around.

"I hope you and Jared had a good night's sleep." Garrett put his smile back on. He could be pleasant.

"I slept like a baby," Chrissy said sweetly. "I doubt Jared slept at all if he heard the things we were plotting to do to him last night."

"We?" Garrett made the connection as he looked at the other form in the bed. Jared didn't have a muscle to spare on his body and the arm that was reaching up to pull the rest of the blankets back had muscles to spare.

"What do you mean 'we'?" Garrett whispered as he took back the broom handle. "Who's here with you?"

"Well," Chrissy said as she yawned, "I couldn't find the place, you know. Dry Creek isn't on any of the maps I got in Salt Lake. I thought there would be signs, but no. I was lucky that his truck had broken down and he needed a ride."

"That's a hitchhiker back there?" Garrett wondered

what decade he was in. Any sensible woman knew not to pick up a hitchhiker in this day. Especially on a back road in Montana. Especially at night. "What were you thinking?"

Didn't his cousin watch the news?

"Well, he's not really a hitchhiker. I mean, I know I gave him a ride and all, but—"

Garrett was no longer listening to Chrissy. "Why don't you go in the house and wait for me?"

"But he belongs here. It's not like I just picked up someone," Chrissy protested as she crossed her arms and refused to move.

The man in the bed swung his legs around and put his hand on Chrissy's arm. "That's okay. I want to ask him what he's doing with Nicki's broom anyway."

"You know Nicki?" Garrett frowned. This man looked as if he would be a whole lot more trouble than that Lester fellow. He had a faint smear of oil on his forehead and the air of a man used to taking charge.

The man nodded. "I'm her brother."

"Reno?" Garrett's frown turned to a smile. "Well, why didn't you say so? She's been waiting for you."

The man grunted. "I'm surprised Hunter let you get this close to the truck."

"Hunter's a good dog, but I think he's given up on biting me."

The man grunted again but he didn't smile. "Well, tell Nicki we'll be inside in a minute."

Garrett noticed that Chrissy wasn't making any move to leave with him. He wasn't sure he liked the possessive air that Reno had with Chrissy, but his cousin didn't seem to mind it.

"Well, I'll see you inside then." Garrett opened the door again.

The air wasn't any colder than when he had walked across the ranch yard a few minutes ago, but Garrett noticed it more. Hunter didn't even bother to follow him to the door.

Nicki met him at the door. "Was it Chrissy?"

Garrett nodded as he stepped into the kitchen. "And Reno."

"My brother?" Nicki asked in surprise. "What are they doing together?"

"I don't know, but I intend to find out." Garrett stomped the snow off his shoes as he stood on the mat just inside the door. "It's not like Chrissy to just pick up with some man."

"Reno's not just some man," Nicki protested as she ran her fingers through her hair. She had managed to comb her hair before she came down to the kitchen this morning. "And you don't need to take that tone. Reno's shy with women."

Garrett snorted. "He didn't look shy to me."

"You're sure it's Reno out there?"

"Hunter seems to like him."

"Well, that's Reno then," Nicki said as she moved and stood in front of the sink and looked out the window. The morning had grown lighter and she could see clearly as the door to Garrett's truck opened and Reno stepped out. "Maybe you just missed that he's shy."

Nicki saw Reno turn and offer his arm to the woman who stood behind him. Garrett was right. Reno didn't look the least bit hesitant as he helped the woman out of the truck cab. And she was wearing Reno's jacket.

Nicki didn't know her mother was up until she heard the sound of footsteps on the stairs. She turned.

Lillian Redfern stood in the stairway and she was fully clothed. She was wearing a red pants suit with matching lipstick and had her blond hair perfectly combed. "Did I hear you say Reno's shy with girls? I can't believe Charles Redfern's son would turn out shy."

"He's not just Dad's son. He's your son, too."

"What are you saying? That Reno's shy because of me?" Lillian Redfern laughed. "I don't have a shy bone in my body."

"Maybe Reno would have gotten to know that if you'd stayed around long enough for him to know you."

"Oh."

Nicki turned away from her mother and opened the door for Reno and Chrissy.

"It's cold out there," Chrissy said as she stepped inside the doorway, rubbing her hands. "Is it going to ever warm up?"

"It'll be warmer by the time everyone comes for dinner," Nicki said as Reno followed Chrissy in.

"People are coming for dinner?" Reno asked as he turned to close the kitchen door. "You invited people?"

"I'm the one who invited them," Lillian Redfern said as she stepped into the center of the room.

"Mom?" Reno asked quietly.

"Lillian is just staying for a few days," Nicki rushed to reassure everyone. "And she wanted to do one of the Thanksgiving dinners like we used to do—you know, where everyone in town comes over."

"Everyone in town?" Chrissy looked shocked. "You invited a whole town for Thanksgiving dinner?"

"Well, a few people are away at this time of year." Lillian kept smiling brightly. "It'll be fun. The only thing we have to do this morning is grind the cranberries and then set up the tables."

"The whole town?" Chrissy still looked shocked. "That's ten times worse than a wedding reception."

"We used to do it all the time," Lillian said. "Charles insisted. He loved to have people around."

"No, he didn't," Nicki said as she turned to get some plates out of the cupboard. "After you left, he stopped seeing everyone, even Jacob." She turned to her mother. "He even stopped going to church. You ruined his life."

"I didn't tell your father to stop going to church." Lillian walked to the sink. "That was his decision. Now, I'm going to have some coffee. Would anyone else like some?"

"You're not even sorry you left," Nicki said tightly.

"I wish you could understand how it was. I couldn't stay here. Not after—" Lillian broke off. "I still need to ask—"

"I know," Nicki said. "You need to ask someone if you can tell us."

"It's the truth." Lillian took a deep breath. "In the meantime, is there anything I can do to help with breakfast? I'm assuming everyone is hungry."

Nicki turned to the coffeepot. The day would be spent feeding hungry people. For the first time, she was glad her mother had invited the whole town to dinner. With all the people around, Nicki had a chance of forgetting her mother was here.

"I'll do the eggs," Garrett offered as he walked to the stove. "Just give me a pan and I'm set."

Nicki wondered how many people would need to be coming to dinner for her to forget Garrett was here.

Chapter Twelve

The inside of the bunkhouse was still musty so Nicki opened both of the doors. ' It smells like old boots in here. Let's hope the air's better by the time people are ready to eat dinner."

The wood floor in the bunkhouse had been scrubbed clean yesterday and the windows had been washed.

Garrett had a sawhorse slung over his shoulder and he was walking to the end of the bunkhouse. He was wearing his farmer overalls and one of Reno's plaid flannel shirts. His hair was messy and straw dust had fallen on his neck when he took the sawhorse out of the barn. He looked more like a beggar than a prince.

And yet Nicki had to keep recounting the black scars on the floor where the bedposts had stood. They needed the information to place the sawhorses correctly for the tables. One moment Nicki would have all of the numbers straight and then Garrett would bring in another sawhorse and she'd lose track of her numbers because she was watching him.

It was, Nicki decided, only because everyone in Dry Creek had made such a fuss about them dating that she was distracted like this. It would pass. She just needed some cold air.

"I still say your mother is worried about something," Garrett said as he set down the sawhorse on scars number three and five. "Give her a little bit of time."

"I'm not telling her to leave," Nicki said as she braced herself to push open one of the windows that years of rain had warped shut.

Garrett snorted. "You're not asking her to stay, either."

Nicki tried to force the window open. It stayed shut. "She doesn't want to stay. She just wants some kind of cheap forgiveness and then she'll be on her way."

"She spent six hundred and ten dollars on Thanksgiving dinner. That's not cheap. She could have just sent a card or something."

"I wish she would have."

Garrett walked over and opened the window for Nicki. Cold air blew in. "Well, I can't say as I've done any better with my parents. Sitting in church last night, I wondered if I didn't need to do some forgiving of my own."

Nicki looked out the window. The yard outside the bunkhouse was rough. Reno had driven the truck through this area during the last muddy spell and the tire tracks had frozen in place and were now covered with a light layer of snow. A few stalks of dried wildgrass poked through the snow here and there. There was nothing pretty about the ranch or her family. "It's God's fault, you know."

"Huh?"

Nicki turned to look at Garrett. "Our whole family went to church. My father, my mother, me and Reno. It was supposed to keep everything safe. God shouldn't have let this happen to our family."

"I know," Garrett said and opened his arms to Nicki. He didn't know, of course. He'd never given God much thought until last night. He'd never prayed in his life. But now. "Maybe we should talk to the pastor about this."

Nicki had her nose buried in flannel. Garrett's arms were around her. She didn't know why those two facts only added to her misery. "I don't need any sympathy."

"Who said the pastor will give you sympathy?"

"I mean from you." Nicki blinked back her tears and pulled herself away from Garrett's arms. She would do much better with a man who wasn't so kind. "I don't need all this—" Nicki waved her hands "—understanding."

Garrett frowned.

"I really can do fine by myself," Nicki said as she stepped back to the bedpost scars. "I think the next sawhorse goes on scars eleven and thirteen."

Nicki didn't even look up as Garrett walked out of the bunkhouse. She didn't want him to see the tears that were shining in her eyes.

Garrett rubbed his hands together as he opened the door to the barn. The day was warming, but it was still cold enough outside that he should have gloves. He kept a pair in Big Blue so he walked over to the truck.

Once he'd backed Big Blue up a few times earlier this morning, he'd forgiven Chrissy for driving her up here. The truth was he was glad to have the truck here so he could drive her away after his proposal. He figured that if Nicki wouldn't even let him comfort her, she surely wasn't going to agree to be his wife.

Garrett opened the door to Big Blue's cab and climbed up into her. He'd always liked sitting up high when he was driving down the road. He supposed that someday the fact that he was a trucker would once again be enough for him.

Ah, there were the gloves. Garrett reached into the

rear of the cab. As he picked the gloves up off the ledge by the bed, something small and hard fell to the floor.

"What the—?" Garrett twisted in his seat so he could lean over and see what had fallen.

He picked up the engagement ring. He recognized it. The last time he'd seen it had been when it was on Chrissy's finger back in Las Vegas.

Garrett knew the engagement ring Lillian had wanted to return to Charles was sitting on top of the refrigerator in the Redfern kitchen, but he would not have confused the two rings anyway. Even with the opals that surrounded it, the diamond in Lillian's ring was modest. Chrissy's diamond, on the other hand, was so large Garrett figured it had to be fake. Chrissy's fiancé, Jared, had lots of flash, but wouldn't have much money until that trust fund he'd talked about kicked in.

Holding the ring in his hand, Garrett realized something. A man didn't just walk up to a woman and ask her to marry him. He had to have a plan. He needed words. And maybe a flower or a strolling guitar player. A man didn't just wring out the dishrag after doing the Thanksgiving dishes and ask a woman to spend the rest of her life with him.

Even if a man expected the answer to be no, his dignity required that he give the matter some planning.

Garrett climbed down from Big Blue. Chrissy and

Reno were in the house now sorting through trays of silverware with Lillian. At least Garrett had some time alone to think about a proposal.

The air inside the barn was warmer than the outside air and Garrett flexed his hands for a minute before he picked up another sawhorse. Nicki's horse, Misty, was in her stall and looked over at Garrett hopefully.

"Sorry, I don't have anything for you," Garrett said as he put the sawhorse down and walked over to rub Misty's forehead lightly. The mare whinnied softly and leaned her head closer to his hand. "That'a girl. I don't suppose you have any idea how to propose to someone?"

Misty lowered her head and blew air out her nose.

"Yeah, I don't, either." Garrett ran his hand over Misty's neck and gave her a pat. "It shouldn't be all that hard—I should just walk up and say, 'Will you marry me?'"

Misty nudged at his hand.

"Yeah, you're right—that's too direct. A woman probably wants something more."

Misty nudged his hand again.

"Yeah, you want something sweet, don't you? I suppose that's what a woman wants, too. Something sentimental." Garrett thought a moment. "I was never very good at that kind of thing."

Garrett heard someone open the barn door.

Chrissy stepped into the barn and slammed the door shut. "Men."

Garrett perked up. Chrissy would know more than a horse did about marriage proposals. "Troubles?"

Chrissy folded her arms and grunted.

"Well, I guess no one has proposed today yet, huh?"

Chrissy looked at him as if he'd lost his mind.

"I mean, I was thinking about when Jared proposed to you. Did he do something special? Something that you remember?" Garrett noticed his cousin was wearing a plaid shirt that looked like it belonged to Reno, too. How many flannel shirts did the man have?

Chrissy scowled at him. "Look, you don't have to find out anything more about me and Jared for Mom. I'm not getting married to Jared. She can relax."

"Well, good. I mean, not good that you're upset, but good that you're— Well, anyway, I'm not asking the question about how he gave you the engagement ring for your mom. I'm asking for, you know, general reference."

Garrett knew now why he didn't lie. He wasn't any good at it.

"He put it in a box and gave it to me."

"But did he say anything? Did he get down on his knees or anything?" Garrett would have to remember the knee thing. He might be able to do that.

"He said, 'Here it is,' and turned the television on."

"Oh." Garrett didn't think that would work so well. "But he'd probably said something romantic earlier?"

"He asked if I wanted to order in pizza."

"Well, I see. Thanks." Garrett supposed there was no point in studying the technique of a man who had obviously lost his fiancée anyway.

"The man's a jerk who deserves to be buried up to his neck in an anthill. Nonpoisonous, of course. Reno says the revenge thing can only be something nonlethal."

Chrissy turned as the barn door opened again. Reno stepped inside.

Reno and Chrissy just looked at each other. Garrett cleared his throat then he gave a final pat to Misty's forehead. "I'll be taking another sawhorse to the bunkhouse."

No one seemed to care.

Nicki had opened all of the windows by the time Garrett brought in the sawhorse, and she was dusting the shelves along the side of the bunkhouse.

"Got anything sweet for Misty?" Garrett set the sawhorse down.

"I thought we'd save her sugar for this afternoon. The Curtis twins like to ride her and she always expects a treat for that. Can't say that I blame her—they want her to be a dragon. Besides, if the twins ride her, all the other kids will want a turn, too."

"Sounds like she's going to be busy."

"We're all going to be busy." Nicki stopped dusting for a moment. "I saw you check out your truck. I hope it's okay. I mean, the gears and all."

"It's fine."

"It's just that if there was a problem with anything we'd be happy to help you get it fixed. Between the two of us, Reno and I have fixed almost every kind of engine there is."

Nicki knew it was a long shot that there was trouble with Garrett's truck, but she was hoping he'd have a reason to stay for a few more days, and any kind of mechanical trouble would be enough reason for that.

"No, Big Blue's fine." Garrett leaned against the sawhorse. "But what about your truck—do you need any help with it?"

Garrett didn't suppose help with a truck qualified as a romantic gesture, but it was a start.

Nicki shook her head. "We can't even order parts for the truck anymore. We'll have to buy something else when we can."

"Oh. Well, if you need anything hauled in the meantime, let me know. I could even haul cattle for you if I got the right trailer to attach to Big Blue."

"There's no more cattle sales this year."

Garrett started to walk back to the door. "Well, I'll

go get the rest of those sawhorses. And then I'll start on the plywood tops."

The plywood boards had been cut to serve as table-tops to go with the sawhorse bases twenty-some years ago but they were still sturdy. Nicki's father had wrapped a tarp around them when he stored them in the barn so they weren't even that dusty.

"But we must have had tablecloths when we used those tables before," Nicki said to her mother. Nicki and Garrett had gone into the kitchen to talk to Lillian. "Even I remember white tablecloths."

Lillian shook her head. "Those were sheets. I'd gotten ten extra flat sheets to use."

Nicki groaned. "I wondered why there were so many flat sheets—I gave them away to the church rummage sale years ago. You should have said something when you left."

"About the sheets?"

Nicki nodded stubbornly. "You should have told me things like that that I would need to know. I wasn't prepared."

"I know," Lillian said softly as she reached out to put her hand on Nicki's shoulder. "And I'm sorry."

Nicki turned away without looking at her mother. "Well, we can't just eat off the plywood. We'll just have to think of something else. I think we have four or five sheets. Of course, they're all different colors and sizes."

Lillian withdrew her hand.

"Well, it doesn't have to be sheets," Garrett offered cautiously after a moment of silence. "I have lots of maps in Big Blue. We could use them for table covers."

"But they're your maps. You'll need them."

"I have too many maps," Garrett said and realized it was true. "Besides, most of the places I go these days are clearly marked on the freeways."

When had his life become so predictable? Garrett wondered. There was no more adventure in driving from Las Vegas to Chicago than there was in driving from Atlanta to St. Louis. It was all just following a path of freeways. If a robot could reach the gas pedal, he could drive Big Blue.

The maps were the perfect table covering, Nicki concluded in satisfaction when she stood up and admired the ten tables. She'd just finished taping the last of the maps to the plywood tabletops and they looked good. All of the lines and the tiny blocks of color here and there in the maps made the bunkhouse look happy.

Nicki looked more closely at the map on the table closest to her.

"What's this?" Someone had drawn lines with a red pen.

Garrett came over to look and started to chuckle. "Oh, that was a hurricane from a couple of years ago. I had to reroute myself all over the place."

"And this?" Nicki pointed to something written in green.

"Oh, that was my sunshine route. I was determined to work my way down to Florida for Christmas that year. I decided I wanted to see an alligator. Had to take loads to five states to do it, but I made it. Pulled into Florida Christmas Eve and met an alligator on Christmas Day."

Nicki looked at the other maps on the tables. The maps were taped together and wrapped around the edges of the table. She walked from table to table. All of the maps had lines drawn on them. "We can't use your maps. They'll get all dirty."

"That's fine." Garrett looked up from the folding chair he was fixing.

"You don't understand—I don't mean just a little dirty, I mean gravy-and-cranberry-sauce-spilled-on-them dirty. They'll be ruined."

Garrett shrugged. "Then we'll throw them away."

"But you can't—these maps tell all about your trips."

"I can get new maps and add new trips." Garrett

snapped the chair into place and stood. "You know how it is—new horizons and all."

"I wish I did know how that is," Nicki said. Her voice was glum. She had such a tight hold on the past, she couldn't even see the future. She'd even been a little superstitious about going too far outside of Dry Creek. It was as though she thought that if she went someplace else, she couldn't come back. "The furthest I've been is Billings."

"Well, you could—" Garrett stopped himself. Was he going to say, *come with me?* He cleared his throat. "If you're interested in traveling, I could give you a list of good places to see."

"I've never seen an alligator." Nicki thought a moment. She hadn't realized how much she had missed. "Or a crocodile. Or a whale."

"You'll want to start on one of the coasts then."

Nicki nodded. Maybe she needed to buy an encyclopedia of sea animals. Just in case she ever got a chance to see one.

Someone stomped his boots lightly on the porch outside the bunkhouse door. Then Reno opened the door.

"She—" Reno jerked his head toward the house "—wants to know if you're all set out here. They called from the café and asked if it was time for the turkeys to be brought out."

Garrett snapped the last chair into place. "We're set for eighty people."

Nicki looked around. She'd lit a couple of pine candles and the air in the bunkhouse now had a light holiday scent. The windows sparkled. The wood floor shone. The chairs were neatly lined up around each of the ten tables. "We're ready."

"And we're using paper plates?" Reno stepped over to Nicki and asked quietly. "She's okay with that?"

Reno didn't need to say who "she" was.

"I don't think she knows we have her china packed away," Nicki said. She had shoved the boxes even farther back into the walk-in closet that hung off the side of the bunkhouse. "I thought she'd ask, but she hasn't. She always used to say a lady needed her china."

Garrett was of the opinion that all a lady needed was a pair of emerald eyes, but he doubted Nicki wanted to hear that so he shuffled two of the chairs. "We got the extra-thick paper plates."

Reno nodded. "Works for me. I was just wondering."

"I'm surprised she never came back for the china." Nicki avoided looking in the direction of the closet. "Dad said she bought that china with the egg money, one piece at a time. It took her five years to get all of the pieces."

"Well, people's taste changes, I guess." Reno shrugged.

"I guess," Nicki agreed, but she wasn't really sure. Her mother's taste had been for pretty things back then and, as far as Nicki could tell, it was pretty things that her mother still wanted. Even this Thanksgiving dinner. It was some sort of pretty fairy tale all wrapped up in neighborhood cheer. Her mother couldn't just make a quiet apology and drive away like a normal person. No, she had to make a production of the whole thing with tears and hugs and cranberry sauce.

"She's not giving any speeches, is she?" The thought suddenly struck Nicki. "I mean the food is the whole thing, isn't it? She's not planning to apologize for stealing the money and leaving and everything again, is she?"

"She apologized for leaving?" Reno frowned.

"Well…" Nicki thought for a moment. "She sort of implied an apology. Then she made it sound all mysterious and said it involved someone else—she as good as said she did it because Dad was a heavy drinker back then. Dad wasn't a drinker."

"He was around the time when Mom left."

"How do you know that? You were only four years old."

Reno shrugged. "He drank some here and there for years. But it used to be worse. After Mom left, he cut back."

"Well, see—then it was because of her. When she left, he cut back."

"He cut back because of us. Without Mom, there was no one but him to take care of us."

She nodded. She wondered what their life would have been like if her mother had been willing to stick with her father in spite of his drinking. She supposed a drinking husband did not fit in with her mother's picture of a perfect life and so she just left.

Nicki looked down. She had a film of gray dust over her jeans. "Now that the room is ready, I guess we should all get ready, too."

Nicki wondered if she and Reno could ever be ready for this dinner their mother wanted.

Chapter Thirteen

"**M**ore yams?" Mrs. Hargrove leaned across the table and offered the dish to Nicki. "They're good for you."

Mrs. Hargrove had pronounced every item on the table as good for a person, even the butter in the turkey molds that Jacob had carved and the rolls that had been left too long in the oven and gotten hard and crusty.

"I'm stuffed," Nicki said.

"How about you?" Mrs. Hargrove offered the yams to Garrett who sat at Nicki's right.

"I've already had two helpings of yams." Garrett wondered why he'd avoided holiday dinners for so long. He kind of liked the friendly chaos of passing dishes and dodging elbows. He even tolerated Lester who sat to the left of Nicki, but who had the good sense to keep his mind on the food. "But thanks. I believe they were the best I've ever eaten."

Mrs. Hargrove beamed. "I put a little pineapple in them this year. It was a new recipe in *Woman's World*."

"I don't suppose you have the magazine with you?" Garrett had wondered how he could get his hands on a couple of issues. They were the experts at this male/female stuff and they should have an idea or two about how a man could propose after dinner with eighty other people around. At the very least, they should have a strategy for making sure Lester wasn't around when Garrett asked the big question.

Mrs. Hargrove looked over her shoulder. "I think Elmer took it to show to someone. But I don't see him. Unless he's over at table five."

The people at table number five all had their heads down studying something.

"There it is!" a boy whom Garrett didn't recognize said as he pointed. "That's got to be Boston." The boy looked up from the table and called over to Garrett. "Mister, have you been to Boston in that truck of yours?"

Garrett nodded. "I left the truck as close in as I could get at some delivery station and took a bus down to the Commons. I saw a boy skateboarding there about your size."

"The maps were a brilliant idea," Mrs. Hargrove

said. "Everybody's been looking up cities and talking about traveling. Seems like everybody has a special place they want to see."

Nicki was proud of Garrett. He'd answered everyone's questions about places he'd been and not made anyone feel foolish for asking anything, not even when Elmer had confused Rhode Island with Washington, D.C., on the map and asked if Garrett had shaken hands with the president there.

"Where would you go, Nicki?" Mrs. Hargrove set the half-eaten dish of yams down. "You haven't said yet."

"She wants to see a whale," Garrett answered for her. "I figure we should just drive over to Seattle and down the coast until we find one."

"Why would she want to see a whale?" Lester asked from Nicki's right. "There are plenty of animals to see on the ranch."

"I'm thinking of buying a book," Nicki added. "That way I can see pictures of all kinds of animals."

Garrett was wearing his tuxedo and Nicki had decided to wear a green pants suit that she kept for special occasions. She'd even put on some of the makeup Glory had lent her.

"A picture of a whale doesn t begin to do it justice," Garrett argued. He was glad he'd dropped the hint about taking Nicki down the coast. He figured he'd given everyone notice that way. But neither of the women even batted an eye over his statement and Lester just kept on eating. "I could drive you to see a whale in a day or two."

Lester did put down his fork at that.

"How nice." Mrs. Hargrove smiled politely.

Nicki didn't even bother to smile. "You're right. Maybe a video would be better than a picture."

"Are we going to have pie pretty soon?" Lester asked.

Garrett realized no one, not even Lester, thought he was serious about taking Nicki to see a whale. Either that or, he thought with dismay, they knew Nicki so well they were confident she would never go. If that was the case, his proposal was doomed.

Nicki wished Lester would forget about food for just one meal. How was her heart supposed to be happy at the prospect of a future with him when he seemed to care more about a piece of pie than he did about her? It wasn't that she was expecting love from Lester, she assured herself. Her feelings on that hadn't changed. She wanted a sound business relationship with him if he ever did propose. But she'd never expected to be less interesting to him than a piece of pie.

"I think there's going to be a little bit of a program before we have the pie," Mrs. Hargrove said. "It'll give everyone's meal time to settle."

"Oh," Lester said. "Then I think I'll have some more of the yams."

"I didn't know about a program." Nicki tried to keep the panic out of her voice.

"Well, 'program' is probably too formal of a word for it. The pastor was just going to say a few words—"

"Oh." Nicki relaxed.

"And then I think your mother was going to say something," Mrs. Hargrove continued.

"Oh." Nicki looked around to see how she could leave the bunkhouse. While all of the tables fit just fine when all of the chairs were pushed under the tables, when the chairs were pulled out and people were sitting in them, it was a different story. But she thought she could squeeze through to an outside aisle if she asked Mr. Jenkins to pull his chair over closer to Jacob's and lifted one of the Curtis twins up while she passed behind his chair.

Nicki stood up at the same moment that the pastor did. He had had the good sense to sit at the end of his table, however, so he wasn't caught in a sea of chairs like she was.

"Since this is truly a community Thanksgiving table," the pastor said, "our long-lost neighbor, Lillian Redfern, has asked me to invite people to share what this community has meant to them."

"Oh." Nicki sat back down.

Mrs. Hargrove was first. Then Mr. Lucas. Then Mr. Jenkins.

Nicki had decided her mother wasn't going to speak after all when her mother calmly stood up.

Lillian Redfern looked over the people in the room before she began to speak. As she looked, the room grew more and more silent. Finally, not even a fork was heard scraping against a plate.

"I came back to Dry Creek to say I am sorry I left twenty years ago. Charles and I were having problems and—well, it's not important what happened. He was angry with me. I was angry with him and swore it was all his fault. In the end, it didn't matter whose fault it was, I was the one who left. I didn't think about how many people my leaving hurt."

Lillian looked directly at Nicki and Nicki lowered her eyes.

"Especially my children. I am very thankful to the people of Dry Creek for taking care of my children in my absence." Lillian swallowed and then continued. "The one thing I regret most in my life is that I lost my children. The one thing I am most grateful for is that I have been able to see them one more time."

There was silence after Lillian sat down.

Nicki refused to look up from her plate. Her mother

tied everything up in such a pretty little bow. Lillian might be able to fool the people of Dry Creek, but Nicki wasn't so easily fooled. She knew what her mother most regretted leaving behind.

Nicki looked up and over at her mother. "We have your china, you know."

"The china!" Lillian exclaimed excitedly as she stood up again and walked closer to Nicki's table. "Why didn't you say something? I thought something had happened to it."

"It's in the back closet," Nicki said. It was the only piece of her mother that still remained on the Redfern Ranch. Maybe it was time to let it all go. "I'm sure you'll want to take it back with you."

"Me?"

The surprise in her mother's voice made Nicki look up.

"Why, the china wasn't for me," Lillian said softly. "The china was always meant for you."

"What?"

Lillian nodded. "You were so taken with fairy tales as a child—remember how you used to always make a castle out of hay bales and play princess?"

"I outgrew fairy tales."

"I was sure you'd like those dishes in your own home someday. The rose pattern was so close to the border in your book on fairy tales. I was going to give the china to you when you got married."

"Oh." Nicki remembered the roses. She still had the book on her bedroom bookcase. "I thought it was all for you."

Lillian shook her head and took a step closer to Nicki.

Chairs scraped and people moved until there was a path between Lillian and Nicki.

Nicki blinked her eyes, but she didn't move away. When her mother opened her arms, Nicki let herself be pulled into a hug.

"I'm so very sorry," her mother whispered into Nicki's hair. "Can you forgive me?"

"I can try," Nicki replied. Maybe Garrett had been right and she should talk to the pastor. Maybe, if she asked for God's help, she could forgive her mother.

"That's all I ask." Nicki's mother held her.

"I didn't open the box," Nicki said as she pulled back a little from her mother's hug. "But Dad packed them away carefully so they're probably still all right."

"We'll wash them up for you and you can start using them." Lillian blinked a couple of times, as well.

Garrett sat at the table next to Nicki's empty chair and blinked his eyes, too. These holiday meals were nothing like he'd expected. He felt warm enough inside to hug someone himself. Garrett looked across Nicki's empty chair. There sat Lester eating his yams. Garrett drew the line at hugging Lester so, instead, he reached across the table and patted Mrs. Hargrove's hand. She took his hand in hers and squeezed it.

"Is it time for pie?" Lester looked up.

"I don't see why not," Mrs. Hargrove said as she stood. "They're on the table in the back, all cut and everything. If someone will help me pass them out, we'll get started."

Garrett helped Mrs. Hargrove pass out the pie slices. In the spirit of goodwill, he even brought Lester a second piece of pie after everyone else had been served.

"They got you trained," Lester sneered as he took the extra pie. "What are you going to do next—dishes?"

Garrett nodded. He figured he could take Lester in a fair fight. Maybe after he did the dishes would be a good time. "You going to stay around for a while?"

Lester nodded.

"Good."

Garrett looked up and saw Nicki leave the room with the Curtis twins. He supposed it was time for the promised ride on Misty.

Aunt Rose would love all this, Garrett thought to himself as he looked around in satisfaction. People had taken some of the tables down and sat around in small groups talking. A fire was going in the black cast-iron stove at one end of the bunkhouse and an electric heater was plugged in at the opposite end. The day outside was cold, but the sun was shining and someone had opened one of the windows.

"Hey, mister."

Garrett looked down to see the small boy who had asked him about Boston. Three other boys were with him.

"You want to play with us?" the boy asked. "We're going to play trucker."

Garrett smiled. "Maybe you'd like to see the inside of Big Blue."

"Can we?"

Garrett looked over to Mrs. Hargrove. "Don't start the dishes without me. I'll be back in ten minutes."

It was fifteen minutes before Garrett started walking back through the yard toward the house. The boys had been excited about all of the knobs and levers on Big Blue and Garrett had been distracted by the sight of Nicki outside leading Misty around the yard in a circle for the Curtis twins.

Nicki had put a parka over her pants suit and had taken off her shoes and put on her boots. The twins looked as though they were chattering and waving their arms trying to convince Misty to be a dragon. The mare just patiently kept walking. She did, however, obligingly lift her head periodically and blow out a gust of air that turned to fog in the cold afternoon air and could almost be mistaken for smoke. The twins giggled every time Misty did it.

"Hi," Garrett said as he walked up to them all.

"Do you think something's wrong with me?" Nicki looked up from the ground and demanded of Garrett. When Nicki stopped walking, Misty stopped, too.

"No," Garrett answered firmly. Here was his chance. He could say he thought she was so wonderful that he wanted to drive away with her. Or that she was so perfect he wanted to marry her. Or that—he didn't get a chance to say any of it.

"How can I promise to forgive someone when I don't know how I'll do it?" Nicki asked.

"You'll have lots of help with that. The whole town will help, especially the pastor. He's already offered to help you sort it out. And, of course—" Garrett took a deep breath "—there's me. I'm happy to help."

Garrett didn't know anything about forgiving someone, but he figured he could learn right along with Nicki. Maybe he could even learn about being committed to someone at the same time.

"How can you help?"

The horse nudged Nicki on the back. The twins

were waving their arms around and shouting something about swords and fire.

"I could go to counseling with you." Garrett smiled. "I figure we've already aced marriage counseling. We make a good team in counseling."

The horse nudged Nicki again and she started leading the procession away. They'd gone a few yards when Nicki turned. "We flunked marriage counseling, you know."

"We were doing just fine. We only got through the first question." Garrett decided only a fool would propose to a women who was leading around a dragon being ridden by two little boys. But propose he would. He was working his way up to it. He just needed the right time and some romantic gesture.

Chapter Fourteen

Garrett stomped his shoes on the kitchen porch to make most of the snow drop off of them. He'd scrape them inside, too, after he took his jacket off. The air was much warmer inside the kitchen and Garrett stood in the entryway for a moment after he shut the door.

Garrett saw with satisfaction that a huge stack of dirty pots and pans sat on the counter by the sink. The soft sound of women's voices came from the living room.

He walked toward the voices. "Thanks for not—"

"Oh." Lillian Redfern looked up and quickly snatched her blond wig back from Mrs. Hargrove. She put the wig on her head and looked up at Garrett. "I was just—"

Garrett could see she wasn't finding the words to tell him what was wrong. "You don't have to explain. I just wanted to let you know I was going to go tackle those pots and pans." Garrett smiled. "That was a great meal you ladies put together," he said and turned to go.

"Wait." Mrs. Hargrove called him back. "Lillian, it's nothing to be ashamed of—you're going to have to tell people sooner or later." Mrs. Hargrove put her hand on Lillian's arm.

"You're right." Lillian nodded her head at Garrett. "Besides, you might be able to help Nicki understand when I tell her and Reno about it." Lillian took a deep breath. "The reason I lost my hair is because of the chemotherapy. I have breast cancer."

"And there's no reason to panic," Mrs. Hargrove said firmly. "My niece had breast cancer and she's made a nice recovery." She smiled at Lillian. "Her hair even grew back."

"I plan to tell Nicki and Reno this coming Sunday. I wanted them to get to know me a little more first," Lillian told Garrett. "So if you could keep it quiet for the time being."

"No problem. I wish you'd told me on the way up here though. I could have taken it easier and stopped in a hotel at night or something instead of just driving through like I did."

Lillian shook her head firmly. "Then we wouldn't have made it in time for Thanksgiving. No, the reason I wanted you to drive me is because Chrissy said you'd be able to drive straight through. I wasn't up to flying, but I did want to get to Dry Creek for Thanksgiving."

"I'm glad we made it for Thanksgiving, too," Garrett added softly.

Mrs. Hargrove looked at him. "I'm sure Nicki is happy you are here, too. You two seem to have hit it off."

Garrett nodded. "I'll always remember Nicki."

"Oh. You're leaving?" Mrs. Hargrove looked confused. "I thought you two were—well, maybe my old eyes aren't as sharp as they used to be."

Garrett shook his head. "There's nothing wrong with your eyes. I plan to ask Nicki to marry me later today. I just don't think she'll say yes."

"Oh." Mrs. Hargrove brightened. "Well, you don't know that until you ask, now do you?"

"I just wish I had some flowers."

"There's an orchid in the refrigerator," Lillian suggested. "In some plastic box."

"No, I think Nicki is more a roses kind of a woman. Even wild roses maybe." Garrett wondered if he could call a florist anywhere in the world and have roses delivered in the next few hours. "I don't suppose anyone grows roses around here and has one left in their garden."

"It's freezing out there. The roses are all cut back." Mrs. Hargrove thought a moment. "You could make her a cowboy's rose though."

"What's that?"

"In the early days of the Redfern Ranch, a cowboy often gave his lady a rose made out of a folded bandanna. They actually found a way to fold them that made them look just like a rose."

"Nicki would like that." Garrett was encouraged. Anything to do with her ranch would please Nicki. "Where can I get a bandanna?"

"I'm sure her father had some," Lillian said as she stood up and adjusted her wig. "Let me run upstairs and check in the drawers. He always kept a package of brand-new ones in the top left drawer."

"Here, let me get them for you," Garrett offered as he motioned Lillian back to her seat.

"See." Lillian turned to Mrs. Hargrove. "That's why I don't like to tell people. Everyone treats me like an invalid." She turned to Garrett. "I'm perfectly able to climb a flight of stairs."

"I'm sure you are, ma'am."

Garrett watched Lillian walk toward the stairs. Why hadn't he noticed earlier that she was frail? That's probably why she'd been so quiet on the ride up here. "Do you think she'll be all right with Chrissy driving her back?"

Mrs. Hargrove nodded. "I'm sure they'll be fine."

"Well, I may as well get some of those pots in the

dishwater so they can at least soak a few minutes." Garrett turned to leave for the kitchen.

"Good idea. Clear a place on the table so we can fold those bandannas."

The rose bandannas were easy to make and did look surprisingly like roses. Big, sturdy summer roses. "Now, you're sure Nicki will know what these are?"

Lillian nodded as she tied the roses together in a bouquet. "We used to make them when she was little. She'll remember."

Garrett hoped Nicki's mother was right. He was counting on the cloth roses to give his proposal respectability.

"You're welcome to use the ring, too." Lillian nodded her head toward the refrigerator. "I'd love for Nicki to wear it."

Garrett hesitated. "You know she's given me no reason to think she'll say yes?"

Lillian shrugged. "She seems to like you."

"But she's convinced that Lester is the man for her. And, to give the man his due, he does know about ranching and cattle. I only know about trucking. I don't see how I could make a living for Nicki and me here."

"Nicki would have to love you a lot to be willing to leave this ranch," Mrs. Hargrove agreed.

"That's why I'm saying I should leave the ring on the top of the refrigerator." Garrett felt the collar of his shirt grow tighter. He'd taken his tuxedo jacket off and rolled his sleeves up to do dishes. "What I'm doing is making a statement to Nicki. I don't think we can expect an engagement. I have Big Blue all packed and I intend to take off after she refuses me. To save everyone the awkwardness, you know."

"I see." Lillian smiled slightly. "Off into the sunset."

"The two of us can see to the last of these dishes," Mrs. Hargrove said. There was one last sinkful of pans still soaking. "But if you don't send me a Christmas card from wherever you are, I can tell you I'm going to be very disappointed."

Garrett looked at the two women. Aunt Rose would have approved. "I can do that."

"I saw Nicki go into the bunkhouse a little bit ago," Lillian added. "Reno is leading the horse around now."

"I don't think anyone else is in the bunkhouse," Mrs. Hargrove added. "We've been watching out the window. Last time I looked, I saw Lester talking with Mr. Jenkins over by the barn."

"Well—" Garrett rolled down the sleeves on his shirt and reached for his tuxedo jacket "—I guess there's no time like the present."

* * *

After Nicki had given the horse reins to Reno, she had gone into the bunkhouse.

The heat was fast leaving the bunkhouse, but the smell of turkey was still in the air everywhere except in the walk-in closet. The closet had obviously been added after the bunkhouse had been built and inferior lumber had been used. The slats didn't match properly and wind blew into the small room.

Nicki rubbed her arms. She'd taken her heavy coat off and laid it on the floor so she'd have something to sit on. Before that she had stopped to tie a full apron around her waist. She was grateful for the apron because no one had cleaned the closet for years and a film of dust had settled over everything. She'd also noticed water spots on the boxes so the roof in the closet must leak.

Nicki quietly sat cross-legged for a minute after she opened the flaps on the first box of china. Her father had wrapped each piece of china in newspaper, and Nicki slowly unwrapped a cup. It felt like her whole childhood came back to her. Her mother was right. Nicki did think of Cinderella fairy tales when she looked at the roses on those cups.

Last week Nicki would have sworn fairy tales were worthless and that it was best to live as though romance and flowers didn't exist. But now, she wondered if she'd just been afraid love would always disappoint her.

The door to the bunkhouse opened as Nicki took out another cup and unwrapped it. The older men sitting in the barn had come earlier to take a few folding chairs and they must want another one.

Garrett stood in the open doorway of the closet for a few moments just looking at Nicki. The white apron she wore was knee-length and it billowed out around her, as she sat with her legs folded under it. The wind had whipped her hair into disarray and it looked as if it was sprinkled with dust. He'd never seen a more beautiful woman.

"So this is the china?" Garrett walked over to where Nicki sat and got down on the floor himself. He had the rose bouquet in a brown paper bag that Mrs. Hargrove had given him.

Nicki looked over, smiled and nodded. "Silly, isn't it? What grown woman likes a china pattern because it reminds her of fairy tales?"

Garrett shrugged. "I can't think of a better reason."

"You know that pink dress we saw before—the one I thought my mother used to make me wear. I think I had it all wrong. I loved the dress. I used to pretend I was Cinderella."

"I rather like thinking of you as a princess."

"Oh, I stopped being a princess. All that feminine stuff—it's not me anymore. I gave up being pretty to be useful. I don't wear dresses anymore. It's all jeans. And boots."

"Being feminine isn't about what you wear."

Nicki smiled. "I'm independent, too. I can milk a cow, change a tire, fix a tractor engine, do my taxes."

"I get the picture," Garrett agreed. "And none of that makes you any less of a princess. It's good that you can take care of yourself. I just think you should be cherished like a princess."

Nicki blushed. "You don't have to say that. I'm feeling a little better about my mother."

"This isn't about your mother." Garrett didn't think his proposal was going very well. If he'd learned anything about women from his aunt Rose and Chrissy, it was that he shouldn't get involved in a mother/daughter problem. He needed to turn a corner here quickly.

"Well, I appreciate you trying to make me feel better anyway." Nicki smiled.

"I'm not trying to make you feel better." Garrett felt his voice rise in frustration. "I'm trying to propose."

"Oh." Nicki looked stunned. She jerked her head up so fast, some of the dust even fell out of her hair. "To me?"

Garrett figured a proposal couldn't go much worse. "Of course, to you."

"Oh."

"I didn't mean for it to be so abrupt. I tried to give you a hint earlier with the whales."

"Oh."

Garrett thought Nicki looked a little white. "You're not going to faint on me, are you? If you hang your head down between your knees and take deep breaths, it will be all right."

Nicki closed her eyes. "That only works if you're sitting in a chair. I'll be fine. Just give me a minute."

"I've got all kinds of time."

Nicki took two deep breaths. "You mean marriage. You and me?"

"That was the general idea."

Nicki wondered when her world had gone crazy on her. She'd never expected to meet a man like Garrett. He could be in a fairy tale with all his talk of wanting to be a hero for his bride. A hero was a notch above a prince any day.

Garrett had to talk. "I made you something—I know they're not real and you deserve ones that are real." He opened the bag and offered Nicki the bouquet of roses. "Your mother assured me you'd remember what these are."

"Cowboy roses," Nicki said softly as she accepted them. "They're perfect."

Nicki put the cloth roses up to her nose just as though she could smell them. "I used to dream about cowboy roses."

"That's good then." Garrett decided things were going a little better. "Well, I just wanted you to know how I feel. I've never met anyone like you."

Nicki smiled. "I'm glad."

"And I want you to remember me," Garrett continued. "Even if you get married to Lester, I want you to remember me."

"I will."

Garrett looked at Nicki. He'd keep the picture of her eyes looking up at him in his heart forever. Quiet glowing emeralds. "I'll remember you, too."

"I'm going to kiss you now, so I don't want you to faint on me." Garrett leaned toward Nicki and she didn't move away.

A kiss can be about a million things, Nicki thought. But not every kiss made a woman feel as if she was a princess. It was too bad that every fairy tale didn't have a happy ending.

"I can't go with you," Nicki whispered finally.

"I know." Garrett drew her into his arms anyway.

"I need to be sensible."

"I know."

Garrett kissed her again. He was beginning to

understand why the prince had been willing to search the whole kingdom for his princess. There would be no one else like Nicki in his life.

Mrs. Hargrove looked at Nicki's tearstained face. "Explain it to us again, dear."

Nicki had come running into the kitchen with tears streaming down her face. Lillian and Mrs. Hargrove had finished washing the last Thanksgiving pot and were having a cup of tea at the kitchen table.

"Life isn't like some fairy tale," Nicki said, and started to cry in earnest. "I have responsibilities. I can't just run off with any man who comes along who thinks I'm a princess."

"He thinks you're a princess?" Mrs. Hargrove said brightly. "That's a good sign."

"But I have chores to do," Nicki wailed. "I can't fall in love."

"Well, someone else can do the chores," Lillian said as she leaned in to hold her daughter. "That's no reason to stay."

Nicki stopped crying and hiccuped. She pulled away from her mother's reach. "I'm not like you. I keep my commitments."

Lillian sat back in her chair. "I see."

"Dear, I hope you're not talking about a commitment to Lester," Mrs. Hargrove said. "I'm not sure he's the right man for you."

"I'm not talking about Lester. Well, not much. I mean the land. I'm committed to the Redfern Ranch. Dad gave it to me and Reno. He meant for me to stay." Nicki dried her eyes and looked at her mother. "I'm not going to leave everything like you did."

Nicki sat up straighter in her chair. She was a strong woman. She had her land. She had her boots. She could do what needed to be done in life.

"Oh, dear, is that what you think?" Lillian finally spoke. "That you need to stay because I left?"

"Dad was never the same after you left. He loved you and you left him. I've learned a person can't count on love, but the land stays with you."

There was silence in the kitchen.

"Lillian, you have to tell her what happened," Mrs. Hargrove finally said as she rose from the table. "I'll go wait in the living room so you have some privacy."

"You don't need to leave." Nicki smiled at Mrs. Hargrove. "She doesn't need to tell me anything. I know what happened."

"No," Mrs. Hargrove said as she stood up. "You don't."

Lillian waited for Mrs. Hargrove to walk into the living room. "Do you want some tea?"

Nicki shook her head. "What does Mrs. Hargrove mean? You left Dad—that's all there is to it."

Lillian shook her head. "What Mrs. Hargrove wants me to tell you is why I left. I'm still not sure it is a good idea. And I'm not saying that it excuses my leaving. If I'd had as much character as you have, I would have stayed and worked the situation out. But I just didn't know what to do but leave."

"Dad said you left to pursue your dancing career."

Lillian smiled wryly. "That's what I did, but that's not why I left." Lillian looked down at her hands. "Do you remember Betty, Jacob's wife?"

"Of course. The two of them used to be over here all the time."

Lillian nodded. "Betty and your father were having an affair."

"What?"

"I didn't believe it when Jacob first told me, but then I asked your father and he admitted it."

"Jacob knew?"

"He knew. Mrs. Hargrove knew. And Elmer. Except for Betty and your father, that was all. I left the day after he admitted it to me. Jacob asked us all to keep it quiet because he was fighting to save his marriage."

"I never knew. I thought you left because you didn't like me anymore," Nicki said.

"Never," Lillian said as she leaned toward Nicki to give her a hug.

This time Nicki didn't move away.

"Don't give up on love if he's the one you want," Lillian whispered into Nicki's hair. "Don't make my mistake. If you love him, you can work it out."

"But he moves all over and I stay in one place."

Lillian smiled. "You've never heard of compromise? Maybe you could move a little and he could stay a little."

Nicki frowned a minute then smiled. "That doesn't sound so hard."

Lillian kissed her daughter on the forehead. "It won't be. Now go. I heard the truck start up ten minutes ago."

"He's leaving?"

Nicki stood and started walking toward the kitchen door. She grabbed a coat off the rack before she opened the door and went outside. Even when she shaded her eyes with her hand, Nicki could barely see the truck down the road. It was a dot disappearing on the white horizon.

She slipped the coat on over her pants suit and started running toward the barn. The keys were in the pickup. Nicki opened the side door to the barn and stopped. The pickup stood where it always did, right in front of the double doors that led outside. But it wasn't going to be easy to move it. Several of the older men from dinner had set their folding chairs around the truck. Someone—Nicki thought it might be Jacob— was even taking a nap in the back of the pickup.

Nicki turned around and walked out of the barn. It would be easier to take Misty.

"Sorry," Nicki said as she helped the last of the twins down from the saddle. "I'll bring her back in a few minutes."

"She blows smoke in the air," one of the twins announced. "I think she can fly."

The other twin nodded. "She just doesn't want to fly because she's afraid she'll scare the chickens. That's what Reno says."

"You can get the kids to the house all right?" Nicki asked Reno and Chrissy who had been leading Misty around in circles until Nicki came.

"Of course." Reno looked offended. "They're my pals."

Nicki swung herself up into the saddle. Some days it paid to wear boots. She turned Misty around and nudged the mare with her knees.

Misty gave a happy snort and galloped for the gate.

Nicki kept her head down and her collar pulled up. The wind had a bite to it, but it also smelled fresh. A few sprinkles of snow were falling. Nicki watched as the gray and white clumps of ground sped past Misty's feet. Nicki looked up once to see Garrett's truck. She wondered what he was thinking.

Garrett was beginning to wish he'd taken his swing at Lester when the man had stepped out of the barn as Garrett was walking back to his truck. Instead, Garrett had shaken the man's hand and confused him by congratulating him. Not that hitting Lester would change anything, Garrett told himself, but he was itching to do something.

Garrett decided he should have had real flowers. Maybe when he got into Miles City he could stop at a florist and ask them to deliver a bouquet of roses to Nicki. Just so she'd know he wanted her to have them.

From Miles City, he would head out to—Garrett realized he didn't care where he headed out to. He'd already been most of the places he'd ever hoped to see—some of them four or five times.

Still, he had the freedom to go anywhere he wanted.

Yeah, he thought as he turned on his truck's radio, he might be unlucky in love, but he was a lucky man because he could drive Big Blue anywhere his heart desired.

What was wrong with him? Garrett thought to himself. He didn't have the freedom to go where he wanted. The only place his heart wanted to go was five miles behind him and he was headed away from it with every turn of Big Blue's tires. What kind of luck was that?

The road Garrett was driving down was a country dirt road with shallow ditches between it and lines of barbed-wire fence. Cows watched him as he drove by, and the road was narrow. There was no place to turn around until he came to the main road a couple of miles ahead of him.

Garrett pressed a little harder on the gas pedal.

Nicki thought she'd never catch Garrett. Just when she thought she'd make it, he sped up as if he was in some kind of a race. She wondered if he saw her in the rearview mirror. She probably looked a sight, like a madwoman, with her coat flapping about her as she and her horse charged after him. She'd been trying to tell him she wasn't a princess—at least now he might believe her.

Garrett blinked. He **saw** a flash of green in his mirror and then he hit a bump and the vision vanished. He craned his neck to get a better look. He was catching glimpses of a cape or a jacket flapping in the wind. His best guess was that something was following directly behind him and a piece of cloth was flapping about. He strained his neck even farther. He should be able to see if it was a car. But it was something thinner than a car. A bicycle couldn't go that fast so it must be some kid on a motorcycle.

Garrett slowed down. He had no desire to race a kid on a motorcycle on Thanksgiving Day in the cold and snow. He'd let the kid pass him.

Garrett pulled the truck over to the edge of the road and stopped. He checked the mirror to see how far back the motorcycle was and saw it wasn't a motorcycle at all. It was Misty. And Nicki.

Garrett rolled down his window. The wind was gusty and more snow flurries were beginning to fall.

Nicki reined Misty in. Finally. She and Misty were both breathing hard and their breath was making clouds around their faces. But they were here.

Oh, no, Nicki thought. They were here. She'd concentrated so hard on catching up with Garrett that she hadn't thought of what to say to him when she actually caught up with him.

"You left," she accused him. The wind carried Nicki's words away and she leaned closer to yell inside Garrett's truck. "I didn't know you were going to leave."

"I said goodbye." Garrett wondered if the sun had come out from behind a cloud. Even with the wind and the snow, the day seemed warmer and brighter than before.

"Well, you should have told me you were leaving. And you didn't get any leftover pie," Nicki yelled into the truck, her hands cupped around her mouth.

"Oh." Had he heard right? The day dimmed again. He rolled his window completely down. "You came to bring me pie?"

"Well." Even in the cold, Nicki felt her face flush. She took a deep breath. "No, I forgot the pie."

"That's okay. Tell Lester he can have my piece."

Nicki forced herself to take another breath and then she spoke loudly. "I came about the whale. You said you'd take me to see a whale."

Garrett knew now why a deaf man would sing. He leaned out the door window and felt the bite of snow on his skin. It could have been a caress. "You don't need to go anywhere you don't want to go. I was going to turn around when I got up to the country road."

Nicki wasn't sure she had heard all of that. "You were coming back?" Nicki straightened herself on her horse. "Did you forget something?"

Garrett leaned out the window so he could see Nicki's face. The wind had whipped her hair around her head and put red blotches on her face. "I forgot you. You're my princess."

Nicki started to grin. The man was completely blind. "A princess would have waited at the castle for her hero to come back."

"Not in my fairy tale," Garrett said as he leaned far enough out of his window to kiss Nicki.

Epilogue

Nicki hated to admit it, but her mother was right. Compromise did make everything possible.

When Nicki admitted to Garrett that she had always wanted rose petals to line her bridal path, he swore that's what she'd have even though she had added that she didn't need them. She knew there wouldn't be enough roses in Dry Creek until Mrs. Hargrove's flowers started to bloom in June.

"June!" Garrett had sounded stunned when she told him that. Then he swallowed. "I didn't know it would be that long, but if that's what you want, that's what we'll do."

Nicki smiled. "There's nothing so special about roses. Maybe I could have carnations or something. Then we could get married in February."

"Carnations don't have any smell, but I like the sounds of February. We'll ask Matthew if the church is available."

"Matthew said any time we picked, he'd make sure it was available."

Nicki was surprised how much her feelings about the Dry Creek church had changed. She'd grown up in that church, but it wasn't until she forgave her mother that she was able to feel God's love wrap around her. Now she felt that love every time she walked into the church. She wouldn't want to be married in any other place.

Garrett seemed to feel the same way.

"If I'm going to be the kind of husband to you that I want to be, I'm going to need God's help," Garrett had told her one Sunday after dinner. They were sitting together on the sofa in the living room at the Redfern Ranch.

He was silent for a moment.

"I had no idea God cared about me the way He does," Garrett finally added.

"I know what you mean," Nicki said. She used to think God didn't care about the Redfern family, but now she saw His blessings everywhere.

Earlier that day, they had walked around the site of the home they were building on the other side of the bunkhouse. Garrett had pulled enough money out of his savings account to pay for the complete three-bedroom house.

Nicki had never thought she could have her own home and stay on the ranch, as well. But then, Nicki was looking forward to many things she'd never thought she could have.

For their honeymoon trip, Nicki wanted to take a trip with Garrett in Big Blue.

"We've got the bed right in back," Garrett reminded her and winked. "In case we want a nap."

"We won't make it out of Dry Creek if all we do is sleep."

Garrett leaned over to hug Nicki. Garrett never thought he'd know the kind of contentment he had these days. Maybe half of his desire to see new places was just a way of looking for a community. Now that he'd found that community, he didn't need to keep looking.

"But I still want to see the ocean." Nicki sighed as she felt Garrett's arms wrap around her.

Garrett wondered if the compromise he and Nicki had made had flipped them both around. They had agreed that Garrett would make short hauls during the winter months to make money and then help around the ranch during the rest of the year. Nicki had done the financial calculations and figured they'd double the income of the ranch that way. Garrett was happy with the arrangement and was discovering he liked the time best when he was on the ranch.

Nicki, on the other hand, was sending away for travel brochures and making her list of places she wanted to see.

"You promised me the ocean," Nicki whispered with her head snuggled on Garrett's chest.

"That's just the beginning," Garrett agreed as he hugged her even closer.

Their wedding took place on Sunday, February 1, at two o'clock in the afternoon. But the people of Dry Creek swore they would remember the day before even more than the wedding day itself.

"I'll think of that big truck every time I smell a rose," Mrs. Hargrove said. "Why, the whole town smelled like roses."

Garrett had driven Big Blue down to Los Angeles to pick up his aunt for the wedding. While he was there, he'd gone to the flower mart and bought a hundred dozen red roses.

"That's twelve hundred roses," Mrs. Hargrove told the men at the hardware store when she went inside to get out of the cold. "You should have seen Nicki's face when he opened up the back of the truck and those flowers fell out. She's still out there—just standing with Garrett in the middle of the roses."

For once the men were speechless, except for Lester who gave a low whistle of admiration before saying, "He's some guy, that Garrett."

Mrs. Hargrove glanced out the window. "She's going to get cold."

Mrs. Hargrove saw Garrett open his arms and enclose Nicki in them. "Well, maybe not so cold, after all."

Nicki knew it was cold. It was, after all, February in Montana. "You didn't need to do that."

"I know." Garrett smiled as he looked down at Nicki. The cold had turned her cheeks pink and her lips white. She was beautiful.

Nicki swore she could feel rose petals through the soles of her boots. Their perfume drifted up to her as she gazed at her very own prince She wondered why she'd ever been so set against fairy tales. "You're sparkling."

"It must be snowing."

* * * * *

Dear Reader,

I started this book with the image of a snow globe in my mind. As the characters in the book grew, I realized the image of looking through thick snow was the feeling that Nicki must have had in her life. Because she had not forgiven her mother, she had not been able to fully see the hope for love that she had as a woman. It was as though falling snow hid this hope from her sight, and she only caught glimpses of it in her dreams.

I believe the same is true for each of us. When we do not forgive others, we limit ourselves. Forgiveness is not always easy. In fact, it can sometimes seem impossible. The miraculous thing is that God is able to change our hearts and help us forgive. And by doing so, we gain freedom ourselves.

God bless us all as we seek to forgive each other.

Yours always,

Janet Tronstad

In the exciting new FITZGERALD BAY *series
from Love Inspired Suspense, law enforcement siblings
fight for justice and family when one of their own
is accused of murder.*

Read on for a sneak preview of the first book,
THE LAWMAN'S LEGACY *by Shirlee McCoy.*

Police captain Douglas Fitzgerald stepped into his father's house. The entire Fitzgerald clan had gathered, and he was the last to arrive. Not a problem. He had a foolproof excuse. Duty first. That's the way his father had raised him. It was the only way he knew how to be.

Voices carried from the dining room. With his boisterous family around, his life could never be empty.

But there *were* moments when he felt that something was missing.

Some*one* was missing.

Before he could dwell on his thoughts, his radio crackled and the dispatcher came on.

"Captain? We have a situation on our hands. A body has been found near the lighthouse."

"Where?"

"At the base of the cliffs. The caller believes the deceased may be Olivia Henry."

"It can't be Olivia." Douglas's brother Charles spoke. The custodial parent to his twin toddlers, he employed Olivia as their nanny.

"I'll be there in ten minutes." He jogged back outside and jumped into his vehicle.

Douglas flew down Main Street and out onto the rural road that led to the bluff. Two police cars followed. His brothers and his father. Douglas was sure of it. Together, they'd piece together what had happened.

The lighthouse loomed in the distance, growing closer with every passing mile. A beat-up station wagon sat in the driveway.

Douglas got out and made his way along the path to the cliff.

Up ahead, a woman stood near the edge.

Meredith O'Leary.

There was no mistaking her strawberry-blond hair, her feminine curves, or the way his stomach clenched, his senses springing to life when he saw her.

"Merry!"

"Captain Fitzgerald! Olivia is…"

"Stay here. I'll take a look."

He approached the cliff's edge. Even from a distance, Douglas recognized the small frame.

His father stepped up beside him. "It's her."

"I'm afraid so."

"We need to be the first to examine the body. If she fell, fine. If she didn't, we need to know what happened."

If she fell.

The words seemed to hang in the air, the other possibilities hovering with them.

Can Merry work together with Douglas to find justice for Olivia…without giving up her own deadly secrets?
To find out, pick up
THE LAWMAN'S LEGACY by Shirlee McCoy,
on sale January 10, 2012.

Love Inspired SUSPENSE

RIVETING INSPIRATIONAL ROMANCE

FITZGERALD BAY

Law-enforcement siblings fight for justice and family.

Follow the men and women of Fitzgerald Bay as they unravel the mystery of their small town and find love in the process, with:

THE LAWMAN'S LEGACY by Shirlee McCoy
January 2012

THE ROOKIE'S ASSIGNMENT by Valerie Hansen
February 2012

THE DETECTIVE'S SECRET DAUGHTER
by Rachelle McCalla
March 2012

THE WIDOW'S PROTECTOR by Stephanie Newton
April 2012

THE BLACK SHEEP'S REDEMPTION by Lynette Eason
May 2012

THE DEPUTY'S DUTY by Terri Reed
June 2012

*Available wherever
books are sold.*

www.LoveInspiredBooks.com

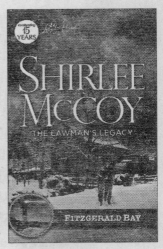

Love Inspired

After surviving a devastating tragedy, combat reporter Nate Garrison returns home to Starfish Bay. But his reunion with lovely Lindsey Collier is nothing like he's dreamed. Lindsey is now a sad-eyed widow who avoids loss and love. Knowing he's been given a second chance, Nate sets out to show her faith's true healing power.

Seaside Reunion
by Irene Hannon